The Vacant Throne

Tor Books by Ed Greenwood

The Kingless Land
The Vacant Throne

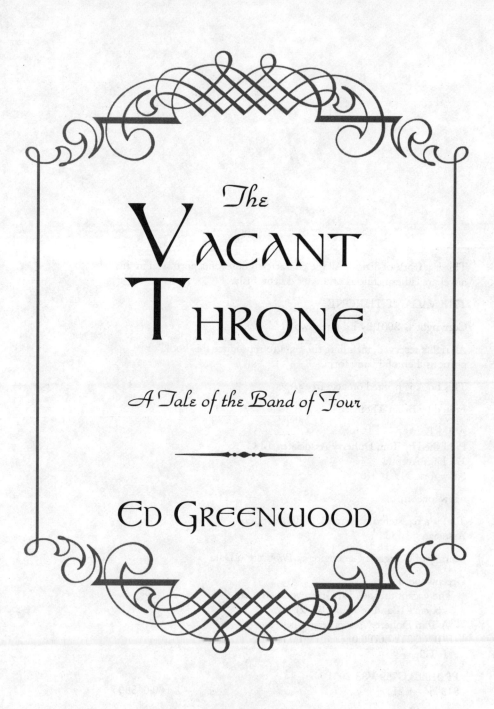

The
Vacant
Throne

A Tale of the Band of Four

Ed Greenwood

TOR®

A Tom Doherty Associates Book

New York

THE VACANT THRONE

Copyright © 2001 by Ed Greenwood

Edited by Brian Thomsen

A Tor Book
Published by Tom Doherty Associates, LLC
175 Fifth Avenue
New York, NY 10010

www.tor.com

Tor® is a registered trademark of Tom Doherty
Associates, LLC.

Library of Congress Cataloging-in-Publication Data

Greenwood, Ed.
    The vacant throne / Ed Greenwood.—1st ed.
        p. cm.–(Band of Four ; bk. 2)
    "A Tom Doherty Associates book."
    ISBN 0-312-86722-0
     I. Title.

PR9199.3.G759 V33 2001
813'.54–dc21   00-048895

First Edition: April 2001

Printed in the United States of America

0   9   8   7   6   5   4   3   2   1

To Sal, fellow dreamer

For whom the journey shineth always
as brightly as the destination

What is a king?

A grand figure on a throne

To be cursed at, and revered

The butt of muttered blame

And the whispered intrigues

Of those who reach ever for more.

Cheered and gossiped over

Loved most in hindsight

Obeyed when near and girt in power

The one who leads

The one who sends forth

The one whose gentlest word can slay.

Throw down kings who displease or despoil,

For the gods send an endless supply of new ones.

Had I the room and riches, I'd take home a few

And train them properly.

'Twould save much wear and tear on the kingdom.

FROM *Crowns for Sale*

by the Bard Castlan of Ilthrie

penned in the days of King Mortrymm

(ever so long ago)

ONDBLAS

NGS

LIRTA

AMARCH

(former)
BARONY
OF
TARLAGAR

TSELGARA

River Silverflow

LOAURIMM
FOREST

BARONY
OF

(former)
BARONY
OF
BLACKGULT

 XITHRYM

BRIVYONGARD

CASTLE
SILVERTREE

(former)
BARONY
OF
PHELINNDAR

LAKE
LASSABRA

INDRAE
(Rui

SILVERTREE

TELBONTER

NWATER

NY

CLN

BARONY
OF
MAERLIN

DARPANNEN

ALAGLATLAD

River Sheiryn

Map of
a part of

ASMARAND

. Continent of Darsar .

FELSHEIRYN

The Vacant Throne

Prologue

The old minstrel shook his head. " 'Tis hard to believe, lad," he said to the depths of his empty tankard, "even for such as us. Legends come to life—four vagabond adventurers, one of them the Lady of Jewels with her spells swirling around her like fire, rousing the Lost King back to us."

Flaeros Delcamper nodded, eyes shining. "I know," he almost babbled, "but it *did* befall, just as I've said! I was there! I stood in the throne room on Flowfoam Isle and saw the barons kneel to the Risen King!"

His voice was rising, he knew, but Flaeros cared not. So what if the remembered thrill made him babble? He was home in Ragalar, in the tankard-hung back room of the Old Lion, and the man across the table from him had been house minstrel to the Delcampers for near a century, and tutor to Flaeros since he'd been a muddy-faced boy.

Old Baergin smiled and shook his head again in disbelief, even though all Darsar had heard by now that the king had returned to Aglirta, and a shining future of peace and prosperity could well be opening up before every last jack and lady who saw the sun rise and the moon fall.

The hands that had guided the fumbling fingers of Flaeros on their first tentative pluckings at harp-strings and travels up and down pipes set down their tankard, and their owner asked softly, "So what of these famous Four now, lad? What was the last you saw of them?"

Flaeros took a generous swig from his own tankard and replied happily, "The Risen King summoned them for a private audience, just before I left the Isle, and then sent them forth on a mysterious errand!"

Baergin nodded again, glanced once over his shoulder at the folk in the

Lion who'd drifted closer to stand listening while trying not to be doing so, and asked with the wry beginnings of a smile, "And have you begun your ballad about it all?"

"Not yet," Flaeros told him, a little embarrassed. "Soon, but not yet."

Baergin lifted his shoulders in a shrug, and said in a voice that was barely more than a grim whisper, "That's a pity. I'd have liked to hear it."

He rose in a smooth, unhurried surge to lean forward across the table—and in the arm that was drawn back at his side, ready to thrust forward, gleamed the long, wicked length of a drawn dagger.

It flashed down, and almost by accident the astonished Flaeros struck it aside with his tankard.

His longtime mentor stabbed again, viciously, and Flaeros flung himself desperately sideways in his seat, kicking out at Baergin's knees and cursing in surprised dismay.

The bright steel fang bit into the paneled wall a few fingerwidths away from the young bard's ear, and Flaeros dashed the dregs of his tankard into Baergin's face as the old minstrel tugged his blade free.

Baergin spat out beer and slashed blindly, but the young bard was whirling away around the end of their table, headed for the nearest door.

And waiting trouble.

Even before Baergin shouted, "To me!" from behind him, Flaeros was twisting aside from the greasy leather stormshields that hung in front of the door—as a grim-faced armaragor burst through them, sword drawn.

There was another battle-knight behind the first, and both of them wore full armor, without any sigil on their breastplates. Some of the patrons of the Lion had their swords out now, too, and were advancing on Flaeros with warily intent faces. From the far end of the many-pillared taproom came the glint of more armor, and the bobbing helms of more armaragors.

Gods, he was going to die.

Something flashed past the young bard's eyes, caressing his shoulder with the lightest of touches as it hurtled past, to ring and clang to the floor past the nose of a farmer cowering low over his tankard. Flaeros turned with a snarl in time to see Baergin drawing another dagger, and then whirled again to the only way still open to him: the stairs.

He pounded up the creaking treads into the darkness of the Lion's rental rooms, heedless of who he might bowl over or shoulder aside, and shouts arose in the room below as the armaragors charged after him.

Panting now, Flaeros leaped up the next flight of stairs, heard with momentary satisfaction the crash of the foremost armaragor running straight into the edge of a door flung open by a bewildered renter, and raced like the wind along the low-ceilinged top floor of the Lion. There was a back stair down the outside wall, and if he could only just . . .

The door was barred. The young bard whimpered in fear as he frantically tore aside the bar and its holding-chain, flung up the latchpeg, and—

Found himself staring into the wolfish grins of three—no, five—armaragors who were mounting the last flight of the stairs, their well-used swords drawn.

Flaeros gaped at them in despair, and then in desperation swung himself around the top step, onto the little balcony where Kessra was wont to hang the washing from. Her line was far too old, gray, and fur-flimsy to hold him, and it stretched out a very long way across a deep gulf of cobbled stableyard, but the next house over had a balcony of its own, and its rail was much closer. A dozen feet away, perhaps.

Or more. Flaeros stared at the gap between the two balconies as feet pounded up behind him, and wondered if it would hurt more to smash down onto the dung-slick cobbles, or take a few swords through his guts. . . .

An armaragor shouted in exultation right behind him, and Flaeros snarled a desperate curse and sprang up onto the rail, gathering himself—

As the young bard's despairing cry echoed around the stableyard of the Lion, a cowled figure strode out onto a balcony high above the swarming armaragors and their ready blades, looked down, and hissed in anticipation.

The hand that closed on a balcony rail for support as the observer leaned out to see the fate of Flaeros Delcamper was gray and covered with scales.

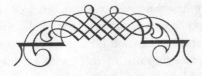

1

No Shield Like Loyalty

irds whirred, called, and shed droppings copiously in the ruined, riven place that had until recently been a high-domed library (though it had been a very long time since its shelves had known books, and its aisles the tread of folk intending to read them).

The deep wood had closed its green grip again around the ruins of abandoned Indraevyn almost uneasily, as if expecting more warriors and wizards to boil up out of the overgrown stones at any moment and split the soft forest sounds with the ringing of blade on blade and the ear-shattering cracks of striking battle spells.

But days and nights had passed, and no more such combatants had come. The carrion-eaters had plucked and crawled and gnawed at the sprawled bodies of the fallen, cracking and scattering bones, and no new alarum arose.

The creepers had advanced their patient tendrils, and things that squeaked and slithered had done so, and the Loaurimm had closed its hand over Indraevyn again. The forest had stood unbroken before men had come to Silverflow Vale to hew and burn and plough—and if the day came that all the men were gone, it would as slowly and surely reclaim the cleared banks of the Silverflow, and in the end swallow every last road and tower.

Soon after bloody battle and the hewing and burning that had preceded it, laying bare so many walls and doors, Indraevyn looked more like a forest-cloaked rockpile than something men had built. The casual eye would have seen raw nature, not the failing hand of man.

Except for six eerie shafts of glowing light that hung in a silent, vertical row in the heart of the riven library, a book floating immobile in each.

Something moved among those pillars of glowing nothingness. It shuffled often into the nether reaches of the shafts, to stand looking up vainly for silent hours before lurching over cracked and scorched flagstones to the next shaft, and the next. It was something that might once have been a man, though it looked more like the mottled brown reassembled remnants of a bad and once-shattered sculpture of one, with spindly arms of differing lengths, lopsided shoulders, and a head that was too long, thin, and jagged.

None of which kept it from lurching and shuffling its slow, eerie way around the ruins, returning always to the library, and those six silent shafts of light—just as it was shuffling into the northernmost column of glowing air now.

To stand as always, head turned up to the books floating beyond reach, the books impervious to its small magics . . . just as they were "not there" to every rock and branch it had contrived to throw up, at—and through—them.

Yet it had nowhere else to go, no other magic to sustain it but the endless glow at the heart of Indraevyn, and little magic at its command when it moved out of the library—so here it stood again, waiting with a patience that owed less to sanity than to burning hunger.

The rags of robes not its own hung from its shoulders, as tattered as the flesh beneath. Withered flesh and sinew as brown and as dry as old fallen leaves clung to its shattered bones, though someone who'd known the wizard in life would have had to stare long and hard at the withered brown skeletal thing to recognize Phalagh of Ornentar—though he was closer to his old vigor now than when he'd died, torn to glistening gobbets pattering bloodily down into the pit that had held the Stone of Life for so long. Time enough to leave behind weird weavings that had reshaped a man with agonizing slowness, building bone and rotting flesh together in a rising heap that had one day stood, and lifted arms, and climbed.

Up into the shattered hall above the pit where Phalagh had died the silent thing came, to endlessly, almost mindlessly, stumble around its gloomy rubble, exploring. Examining every crack and corner, every fallen stone and collapsed shelf, for days upon days it shuffled, until it knew them.

Basking betimes in uncovered magics as if they were warming pools of sunlight, it stretched forth sudden hands to work faltering magics, raising a wall here and the fallen rubble, like a shower of rock in reverse, springing upward in an eerie flow, to restore an arc of the dome there.

It was rebuilding the place where it had met its death, as if raising its own mausoleum. And all without a word uttered, and no sound but the lurchings and shufflings of its lopsided journeying.

That silent something now turned its head suddenly, stiffening like a dog that has scented something.

Two cold and tiny points of light kindled in empty eyesockets. Something was coming—something had disturbed its warding spells. The deathless skeleton that had been Phalagh shuffled forward a few paces, and then drew back into the nearest shadows like a thief disturbed by returning owners.

Two men stepped into the roofless library, their cautious strides almost as soundless as those of the skeletal thing whose eyes now glittered watchfully in the gloom. One was a short, slender, graceful man, the other a hulking warrior as tall and wide as many a door, the sword in his hand almost as long as his companion stood tall. Two others followed these forefarers, and all four moved warily, looking around at ruined walls and tumbled shelves as they came.

All of the Band of Four remembered well their last visit to this place. As they came to where they could at last see the shafts of light clearly, Craer even murmured, "Almost getting ourselves slain last time wasn't enough, Lady? You've brought us back to try again, until we do it properly?"

Even as the lone woman in the group twisted wry lips to frame a reply, the deathless wizard in the shadows raised clawlike hands, the radiance of a building spell flickering around them. Dark red and black were those glows, hues that betokened nothing good. As their angry leapings flared, the glittering eyes behind them flickered red and black too. The undying thing that had been Phalagh seemed to grow, standing taller as destroying magics raged up and down its arms, and skeletal fingers spread to point at the four intruders. . . .

"Your Majesty," the Tersept of Helvand said, almost snapping his words, "I cannot speak for the continued loyalty of the merchants of Helvand if royal assent is not given to our—their—plans to launch new trading barges. With every day Helvand waits, coins slip away!"

"Yet," the Tersept of Yarsimbra snarled, from the other side of the River Throne, "Your Majesty can hardly fail to have noticed that fires struck the barges of Yarsimbra at their docks on three successive nights. Lightning strikes, Helvand claims—yet no storms rode the sky on those nights. Lightnings out of a clear sky? When Helvand *just happens* to have opened a new shipyard? Me, I doubt the Risen King is quite so stupid as Helvand seems to think he is!"

"Majesty," the Tersept of Helvand hissed, "must we listen to the unbridled lies this man speaks? Does his title give him leave to impugn and sneer and slander freely?"

King Snowsar kept his face as blank and calmly patient as stone, moving only his eyes to fix a dark and level gaze on each of the two wrangling tersepts in turn. Anger and the desire to yawn rose together behind his face, but he let that inward roiling touch only his eyes.

Helvand took no notice of such subtle warnings. Like the men he served, Ul—Ulgund, that was the man's name!—strode straight forward through life, trampling or thrusting aside anyone who stood in the way. Helvand was the north shore of the Silverflow just upriver of Sirlptar, a succession of wooded estates owned by merchants rich enough to rise out of the crowding of the Glittering City and build secure castles of their own. Not that such pursuits meant they were retiring from the slap-and-dagger ways of Sirlptar . . . or bending their knees overmuch to a king who stepped out of legend to sit on a dusty throne far upriver. "What Helvand wants, Helvand gets," this strutting tersept had warned the king a few breaths ago, his tone adding the unspoken threat *or else* loudly enough for some of the surrounding courtiers to wince visibly.

Yarsimbra was hardly better. The long-independent point of land that jutted north from Sart to force the Silverflow into one last pair of bends ere it reached the sea had years ago attained the wealth and sophistication the merchants of Helvand were now so eagerly seizing—and it seemed Yarsimbra would do just about anything to keep not only its abundant coins, but its dominance over lower river trade. Poisonings and the summoning of hireswords had already befallen—and the king could well believe no one had paused for an instant to consider the danger such things brought to Aglirta.

Not caring about consequences: a problem for a king when almost all of his appointed rulers, as well as every last swaggering one of the nobility, suffered from this disease. These two tersepts had probably forgotten that he could dismiss them at will—or were prepared to ignore any dismissal he might order, according him all the authority granted to the flapping mouth of a dowager aunt shut up somewhere alone to rail at servants where once she'd lectured a baron daily.

Abruptly he was very tired of it all. King Kelgrael Snowsar rose like a rearing lion, in a single graceful bound, and spread his hands, flat and palms down, in a vicious chopping motion that brought sudden silence to the room.

This, at least, he was able to do: dominate his court by sheer presence and the heavy threat of his displeasure. A hundred eyes were locked on him now, seeking to read meaning into his smallest movement, gesture, utterance, or shift in expression.

He left them little room for sly interpretations. "Both of you have raised valid points, lords—points a wise ruler needs time to ponder, so as to dispense justice as fair and farsighted as it is royal. Blustering will not bring me to decisions any the faster, my Lord of Yarsimbra—"

He bent a colder gaze than before on the older, shorter tersept, who met it with an impassive stare that held far too little fear . . . or respect.

"Nor, my Lord of Helvand, is *threatening* your king likely to force his tongue into wagging the way you want it to."

The younger tersept was seething with boiling rage, and looked it; the king had expected no shame or deference in those glittering eyes, and found none.

He continued on, his voice calmer than he felt. "You may protest that you intended neither to bluster nor threaten, and that I misjudge you. Be reminded that misjudging is a royal prerogative—and more: that both of you are *my* Lords, to appoint or dismiss at my pleasure. Barons may claim to have some blood right to watch over, and fight for, that part of Aglirta that knew the rule of their fathers, and forefathers; you, Lords, do not. Be my agent in your demesne, not its advocate before me. Be that—or be nothing."

"But—" The Tersept of Yarsimbra saw his straying into overboldness the instant he'd launched himself, and fell firmly silent, bowing his head in apology or genuflection. His rival tersept was not so prudent.

"My father was Lord in Helvand before me," the younger tersept snarled, his face white with anger and his voice trembling, "and his father was Lord before that—while Aglirta had no king, and barons and brigands alike did as they pleased. We did what we had to do, for our people, and asked no one for 'royal permission' about anything. So now, before you demand that I plead and crawl before your throne, King of Aglirta, tell me this: just what do I, and the good people of Helvand who stand behind me, gain from having someone sitting on the River Throne again? What good is a king to me?"

Those last words echoed around a room that had otherwise fallen utterly silent. The tense silence of warriors waiting, with hands near sword hilts, for battle soon to come. A young boy among them—a boy with jet-black eyes, now grown large and awed—seemed to be trembling on the edge of tears.

All eyes were on the king, watching and waiting. Kelgrael Snowsar slowly raised himself to his full height, towering over the tersept a step below him—the Lord of Helvand who'd drawn back one wary pace, but who now stood with his hand at his own belt . . . on the pommel of the long knife scabbarded there. Ready for a fight.

The king smiled into the heavy, deepening silence, and said, "You ask a very good question, Ulgund of Helvand: what good is a king to the folk of Aglirta now? This is a question the entire realm deserves an answer to—but you ask it of the wrong man. I am king, as I was king before the grandsire you speak of was tersept over Helvand—"

The Risen King gave the young tersept a look that had quiet steel in it before he lifted his eyes to gaze around the throne room.

"—and my answer can't be seen, by most of you, as anything better than self-serving. *You* are the proper folk to answer this . . . for who better than the people of Aglirta to say what good a king is to them now?"

He set the Scepter of Aglirta in the crook of his arm and strode to the edge of the throne dais, arms crossed, to stand looking down on them all, as tall and menacing as a drawn sword. "Wherefore you shall have your time to think on this, from now until the turning of the year. At that time a recoronation shall be held in this chamber. I hope that all Aglirtans who've thought about it, and decided they do need a king, will attend. On that day I shall expect all barons and tersepts of the realm to swear fresh oaths of fealty to me. Those who choose not to, or choose not to attend, may well be replaced."

King Snowsar let his calm, level gaze travel slowly from face to face among the throngs of dumbfounded courtiers, and added, "Of course, if sufficient Aglirtans of rank choose to stand against me rather than to reaffirm their loyalties to the rightful king, it shall be my duty, for the good of the realm, to both stand aside from the River Throne—and to name my successor. To do anything else would be to plunge fair Aglirta into war. Those who would have no king, or no king of my choosing, would do well to think on this last point, and decide how well they could defend the realm if they cast it forth into the hazard of lawlessness. Or rather, the wild 'law' of barons, brigands, and wizards that arose during my long slumber."

What might have been the beginnings of a smile tugged at one corner of the king's mouth as he looked around his royal court. The same busily whispering men whose soft tongues and heartless schemings had so beset him with intrigues were—for just a few moments more, he was sure—united in their stunned silence. He had surprised—shocked—everyone.

One of the two tersepts who stood closest to the throne stirred, opened his mouth as if to say something, and then fell silent again, a puzzled frown large upon his features.

"Yes, Pelard of Yarsimbra?" King Snowsar asked gently, letting a real smile onto his face for the first time.

As the courtier shook his head, not able to frame the words that would be politic amid his racing thoughts, the smile on the face of the Risen King grew and grew, until it shone as brightly as any of the many clusters of gems worn by the splendidly garbed courtiers of Flowfoam Isle.

"An eerie place, to be sure," Hawkril murmured, taking a step back and waving at his companions to do the same.

Something tiny but black-spined scuttled from behind one fallen rock, ahead, and darted in behind another.

Craer nodded. "Perhaps so, but I'd rather be here—even with monsters or brigands waiting behind every third archway—than in that pit of vipers around the king."

Embra lifted an eyebrow. "You speak of the royal court of Aglirta, I presume?"

"The same. I wonder how many barons' wizards simply melted into other faces and names, and rushed to be courtiers so as to stand as close to power as they'd been before."

Sarasper frowned. "Now, that's a thought. Where *did* all those dandies and snaketongues come from, anyway? They couldn't just have risen in full finery up out of caves and cottages on Flowfoam Isle—not when the Bloody Baron himself—sorry, lass—"

"No apology needed," Embra murmured, waving at him to speak on.

"—had a guarded and vigilant fortress on top of the whole thing!"

"The Koglaur?" Hawkril asked.

"There're *that* many of them? And why would they step so boldly into the heart of things, when their way is to hide and work unseen?"

"Boldly into roles of greed and stupidity and self-serving scheming, too," Craer added. He caught a knowing look from the armaragor, and smilingly added, "A god's joy-bower for some of us, aye, but not the way of Koglaur, I'm thinking."

"So where did they all come from?" Embra Silvertree asked softly.

Sarasper nodded. "I'll grant we may be very wrong in thinking them all an army of allies rather than foes and rivals locked in endless dispute, but, lass, you really mean three deeper queries: who are they, who do they really serve, and what are their plans for Aglirta?"

Embra nodded. "Indeed. I'm thinking that finding those answers may be the task the king really needs us to do, rather than the Dwaer-hunting mission he sent us on."

"And I'm thinking," Hawkril rumbled, resuming his wary advance with his war sword raised and ready, "that our king is no fool—and that the task you name is one and the same thing as our royal mission."

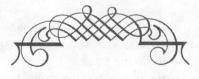

2

No Wizards Without Secrets

T all candles were flickering low in their rows of gleaming, man-high wooden holders as a man whose face was as beautiful as many a maid's threaded his way between them, for the hour was late, later than Baron Audeman Glarond was wont to be still dressed and striding about; the Lord of Glarond wasn't known as a man of stamina or firm purpose. Yet his large, dark eyes seemed hard and purposeful enough now, as he adjusted a lamp above a lectern and set down the book he was carrying in its glow, opening it to a marked place.

" 'Forsooth the flimflam jabber rose spearescent against the sun, marking its bright flight with clangour o'erwhelming the very orbs of those who so wretchedly beheld its bold career,' " he muttered aloud, before slamming the book shut and adding almost fiercely, "Great bard or no, I can't understand a word of it! Drivel—all around me, drivel!"

The light behind him changed, and the Baron of Glarond whirled around with an abruptness more suited to a man of war than a lover of poetry. This tense alertness was not lost on the man whose approach had blocked the light of the candles along the passage, and his soft-voiced murmur was swift. "Me, Lord. Only Margurpin."

"And what, good Mar, brings you hence at this hour?" the baron asked calmly, sounding very much as if he already knew.

His steward carefully did not raise an eyebrow at his master's tone, but they'd known each other for long years. His careful lack of expression, as their eyes met, meant very much the same thing.

Margurpin was swiftly growing gaunt and old beyond his years in the service of Glarond, plagued by constant small troubles—like the matter that was troubling him now. "Lord," he said without pause, "you have visitors. Two men, cowled, by their voices strangers to me. They stand now at your garden gate, saying they are expected and would have words with you, and will say no more. Three guardposts they must have passed or forced passage through, to get so far—without a horn-cry or even a shout."

The steward's weary gray eyes were almost accusatory as he lifted a habit-driven hand to stroke his thin moustache.

The baron merely nodded, and said, "Show them in, to this room, and then withdraw for the night, good steward. All is well, and shall be."

Those last words were empty, a phrase that fell from the baron's lips twoscore times a day or more, but Margurpin seemed to take comfort from his master's confidence, and bowed gracefully as he echoed, "Well, and shall be." The three flying swans of Glarond embroidered tastefully on the foreshoulder of his tabard caught the candlelight as he turned to go.

The baron plucked up the offending book of poetry with one hand, and made a certain signal with the fingers of the other; in answer, a curtain far across the room twitched aside, to reveal an old, pinch-faced man with a long, sharp nose and magnificent high-collared robes. As he stepped forth, for all his splendor, there was something furtive in his gait and manner. Not for nothing was Rustal Faulkron, Court Wizard of Glarond, called by some (behind his back and in dark streets) "Old Man Rat."

"Mar seems perturbed," the baron said, mild amusement in his tones.

"He always is," Faulkron replied, doing something deft in the air with his fingers that caused sparks to wink into brief life around his hands, "and yet the sun always rises the next morn, unmoved by his worryings."

The wizard was shrinking as he spoke, dwindling down into something gray and hairy. Something low and sinuous, that stretched, catlike, while the baron watched with a kind of fascination. It was only a matter of moments before a gray cat paused to regard Audeman Glarond thoughtfully before slinking under the baron's chair. The wand the wizard had placed ready there was winking with tiny witchlights of aroused power, but the cat curled up on top of it as if it had been the softest of sleeping-furs, hiding it from view, and settled down in feigned slumber, its eyes mere slits.

By then the baron had made his own preparations for the receiving of important guests. The book of poetry had been set flat on the wide, bare lip of a high bookshelf—and from behind the books crowding that shelf their owner had drawn forth something small and spiked that nestled easily into the baron's palm. He put that hand behind his back as he turned to face the candlelit passage.

The flames there were already aflicker, Mar's careful face seeming almost to float among them as he came. The cowled heads behind him seemed to glide along with sinister grace, like too many self-important priests the Lord of Glarond had seen, as the steward stepped into the room and stood aside.

"My lords," he announced, "behold the Lord Audeman Glarond, sun of all our days in this fair barony."

Two heads tilted in brief acknowledgment, but spoke no words. The steward turned from them to his master, and added blandly, "My Lord, two guests for you," before pivoting smoothly and setting off back down the passage. One of the cowled heads turned to watch him go; the other measured Baron Glarond, seeing a tall and muscled man wearing a magnificent green silk evening robe with the easy grace of the lion who knows his looks are splendid. Flawless skin, a mane of long, flowing, curly auburn hair bedewed with much perfume, framing a face dominated by large, nearly feminine dark eyes—orbs that almost distracted the eye from a knowing, faintly mocking smile beneath.

The rearmost guest turned his head from watching the passage, and he and his fellow doffed their cowls together.

"Maerlin," Baron Glarond greeted the foremost man politely. They shared faint smiles that their eyes did not echo, and the Baron Urwythe Maerlin lifted a many-ringed hand in an almost idle wave. "My Court Mage," he said, "Corloun."

The wizard was burly, with hair the hue of dirty straw, and pale gray eyes like chips of ice. His greeting was a blunt question. "You are alone?"

Glarond smiled faintly. "Hardly."

The mage's hands moved in hurried gestures, shaping a shielding magic that would foil those who watched and listened both from a nearby chamber or by spell, from afar. Its flowering became a sudden flurry of flamelike radiances in the air around Corloun, a sign that it was clawing vainly at an already active shielding magic that would prevent it from forming. The wizard lifted his head to give the Baron Glarond a frown. "You work magic?"

The baron gave him that same faint smile once more, and said almost gently, "Evidently."

Corloun's face darkened with irritation and he opened his mouth to speak, but Baron Maerlin put a hand on the wizard's arm in what was evidently a command for silence. His neat goatee and round face gave him a feline look as he advanced a step and asked, "You've heard the latest, I presume?"

Glarond nodded. "My eyes at court are as attentive as yours. I was spellspoken no more than a few breaths after our Risen King finished shocking the assembled."

"As was I," Maerlin said, turning to pace across the room. "Fresh oaths for us all—fresh insults—and a recrowning that must not be allowed to happen."

Maerlin's wizard took a smooth step to one side, to where he could face both men clearly. Corloun kept his hands out of sight in the folds of his robe, doubtless holding some magic ready, but neither baron spared him a glance.

The Lord of Glarond folded his arms calmly across his chest. "Making this meeting rather more urgent."

Maerlin shook his head in mounting anger rather than disagreement, and let bitterness creep into his voice. "He'll put his toadies into Silvertree, Blackgult, and Brightpennant, and probably Phelinndar and Tarlagar, too, cow Adeln and probably Loushoond into doing whatever he says—and we'll never have room or coin enough to whelm swords against him."

"Whelm we must," Glarond replied, and lifted his lip in a sneering smile as he added, "as any prudent Vale ruler must do forthwith, with Serpent-priests on the move again, bustling here and everywhere with blades and dark spells and hired cabals. Defending our land is but our duty."

Maerlin let a smile devoid of mirth pass across his face. "Excuse enough," he agreed, "because it's true. Without the Scaled Ones, our vigilance could be much less—and any of us recruiting hireswords would sound a clear warning of war. Whereas Ornentar's desperate entreaties reveal that one of us has already in secret hired the famous Swords of Sirlptar . . . and this news leaves us all unsurprised." He fixed the other baron with a level gaze and asked, "Think you any of us are foolish—or desperate—enough to try to take the Serpents as allies?"

Glarond shrugged. "Ornentar, perhaps. Stripped of his wizards and his warswords, he may prefer holding a treacherous blade to facing us all empty-handed."

"The Serpents rise and fall, but I've never heard them saying the Snake itself will roam the Vale before," Maerlin said, pacing again. "Is this them merely using fear as a sword, d'you think?"

Glarond shrugged. "The tales say if the Sleeping King is awake, so is the Serpent. True or not, it forces us all to hire and train and warm our armor-forges—and when we're all excited, our ears are ready for the whispers of priests seeking to set us at each other's throats."

"Are they mad?" Maerlin snarled. "Why destroy Aglirta? How does that win them anything worth having power over?"

Glarond shrugged. "Wizard," he asked the watchful Corloun, "why do mages strive ever to work new and stronger spells, when they could far more safely work within the known arsenal?"

The look the mage gave his host was venomous, but his lips remained firmly closed.

Maerlin filled the silence with the jovial words, "You bring us to the traditional crazed-wits of importance in the Vale. Are men not wizards because they desire to wield great power in their own hands—and are such men not always defiant of others? I take care that my mage benefits from his service to Maerlin, just as I take shelter within the cloak of his spells. Others have not been so careful."

Glarond nodded. "Who is undeclared for baron or tersept just now?"

Maerlin smiled. "I doubt my agents see other things than yours do."

Glarond wordlessly gestured to him to continue despite that, and his visitor set to pacing again. "If you mean those truly of the Vale, and of proven power, leaving aside all the rainbow-cloaks who swagger the streets of Sirlptar working trickeries for fistfuls of coins . . . there's Tharlorn of the Thunders, and Bodemmon Sarr. Oh, yes—and Embra Silvertree."

Audeman Glarond lifted one elegant eyebrow. "What of this 'Band of Four'?"

"The king's ragtag blades and backstabbing spellhurlers," Maerlin sneered dismissively. "A handful of louts hired by Silvertree's dainty daughter, hoping to worm her way into the royal bed and thereby keep her head on her shoulders."

Glarond frowned. "I'm not so sure." He moved for the first time, striding slowly to his bookshelf and back. "Silvertree was the strongest of us all, in both blades and spells—and his daughter slew both him and his Spellmaster after the Four fought their way through all of Castle Silvertree's guards."

"Bah!" Maerlin replied. "She used magic to take herself past all those guards, and somehow caught them both unawares. Probably with wands or the like they'd stored in some room or other. What have she and her three bedmates done since then, eh?"

"Undertaken this oh-so-secret royal mission," Glarond replied, "that seems, if certain watchers are to be believed, to be bringing them to Glarond right now."

Baron Maerlin's eyebrows rose, and then descended as his eyes narrowed. "Is this why you contacted me?" he asked softly. "You fear four vagabond fools?"

"Rather," Glarond replied calmly, "I believe the secret your wizard has crafted will serve to destroy them just as readily as it should—and you hope it will—fell the Risen King."

"And just what secret would that be?" Maerlin asked, even more softly, as behind him Corloun lifted his hands into view, his eyes dark and steady as he glared at the Lord of Glarond. The hungry glows of roused magic were licking and flickering up and down the wizard's hands.

Awakened magic licked and flickered like shadowy flames up and down the Lady of Jewels' hands. Things had moved—with the slightest of dry scrapings, to be sure, but certainly moved—in the dark shadows and tumbled stone ahead.

"I don't like this," Hawkril muttered, in a deep, unhappy rumble. "Things are not as we left them. The roof is restored, and much that was fallen raised again; someone's used a lot of magic here. . . ."

"Perhaps it restores itself," Sarasper said slowly, trying to peer past the six silent shafts of light, into the dimness beyond. "Still, I'd be happier if I really believed that."

Craer nodded grimly. "So," he agreed, moving ahead like a lithe and crouching shadow, his blackened throwing knife a dark fang ready in his hand, "would I."

In the darkness not far away, two skeletal hands made a last gesture. The dark red glows around them were overwhelmed by a sudden, boiling rush of dark fire, the cold black flames of a finished spell whirling away into nothingness.

It was the second spell to whirl away from those brown and bony fingers in swift succession.

A sudden, eerie roaring echoed around the riven library, shouting back from every wall and rubble-heap. The four intruders halted tensely, darting glances in all directions.

Dark red and black fires blazed balefully as Phalagh heard the din of his first spell—the noise that was all that it did—roll around him, cloaking the unavoidable noises his second magic would make.

Now. The skeleton in its tatters of robes shuffled forward to confront the intruders. Now, while the bones of the many who'd perished in the library were drifting and slithering together amid the tumbled stones, wreathed in crawling red and black spell-flames.

Their eyes were fixed on him, yes, and not on the two darkly flickering skeletal hands rising up from the dust and wreckage behind them, almost as tall as the thief in the forefront—gigantic hands made up of the floating bones of the fallen . . . now drifting forward to strike, fingers spreading wide. . . .

The shuffling skeleton spread its arms in a dramatic flourish, and they saw spell-glows raging up and down its bones.

"Horns!" Craer cursed, hurling his blade and then diving to one side.

It's never good to stand still when a mage—bag of bones or not—is hurling spells your way.

"Bebolt!" Hawkril echoed, dodging in the other direction. They both saw the procurer's blade spin harmlessly through the skeleton's ribcage and clink down into the darkness.

Then they both heard a faint, strangled "urrk!" and scuffling sounds from behind them. Armaragor and procurer whirled around in startled unison.

Sarasper was gagging in the bony grip of a floating hand, its fingers made of many floating, tumbling bones, that was tightening around his head, chest, and throat.

Embra was held by many smaller clusters of bones, tugging at her like a dozen or more hands. Their grip had plucked her from her feet, up into the air, where she was thrashing and shuddering in a frantic fight, kicking her legs helplessly.

"Sargh!" Craer and Hawkril gasped together, and sprang to help their friends.

Behind them, Phalagh's bony smile widened, and he raised his skeletal hands to weave another spell. . . .

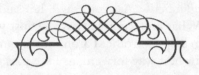

3

So Melting a Secrecy

aron Audeman Glarond leaned forward with an easy smile on his face. If he felt any fear of being struck by a spell, it did not show.

"The secret," he told Baron Maerlin calmly, "that at least four of our fellow barons know—so destroying me won't keep it. I speak of flames, and melting men."

His two visitors stiffened. The wizard Corloun hissed like an enraged viper, but his master asked coldly, "And just what do you know of fire and men who melt?"

The Lord of Glarond shrugged. "A fire, built in part by Corloun's spells, whose flames burn a bright blue and green. Men forced into them aren't scorched or cooked, but their flesh melts like wax . . . and they seem to fall under the wizard's control, as if commanded by a spell." He spread the one hand that was in front of him in a wave that echoed a shrug, and added, "So much is all my knowledge. I'd like to know more."

There was a little silence as his visitors glared at him, faces white with rage and fear. Then, almost reluctantly, they turned to look at each other.

"If he knows . . ." the wizard hissed, when the silent language of their glances failed.

That made Maerlin's head snap back to regard his host, eyes narrowing. "Which four other barons know of the—melting men?"

Glarond's response was a regretful shake of his head. "No," he said softly, "that little secret is my only armor against the two of you, just now. If we're to trust each other, let me keep it." The ghost of a smile passed across his face before he added, "So that's five barons who can betray you both to the Risen King. I hope our little conspiracy can strike swiftly, whatever we plan to do to Snowsar."

Maerlin's eyes glittered. "As you say," he said furiously, "you're armored against us. What protection have we against you?"

"Nothing that can stop four other barons at the same time," the Lord of Glarond replied. "Your best way forward, as I see it, is to unfold everything to me now—making me just as much a traitor if a king's wizard peers into our minds with his spells."

The looks traded by the two visitors were longer this time, but just as silent. They ended with a sharp nod from Maerlin; in response, the wizard Corloun stepped forward and told Glarond bluntly, "Specifics of my spells you shall not know, now or ever. That is *my* armor."

The Lord of Glarond nodded, saying nothing, and the wizard continued, "The fire enchantment is as you say; so far as I know, save for illusions specifically crafted to ape its hues, it is the only magic that makes flames so vivid, green and blue."

He stepped idly forward, rubbing his hands together as if lost in thought. If he noticed a cat stirring just a little under a chair, he gave no sign of doing so.

"Rather than dying and falling to ash, men burned in it become what I call 'the Melted.' Their flesh melts on their bones, running and sagging to grotesquerie, their bones become rubbery and very strong—and they fall under my will."

"When you sleep, do they roam free?"

"No," the wizard answered flatly, and instead of elaborating, he added, "At any time I desire, I can 'burn' one of my Melted from afar. It blazes up like a torch as I send a spell to it. The magic passes into the Melted, and is emitted from its fingertips when it touches the right someone. Then it collapses into ashes and dust, and the full fury of my magic is visited on the being it touched . . . such as the king, or one of his precious Band of Four."

"Or a treacherous baron, perhaps?" Audeman Glarond murmured mildly, examining his fingernails. "Warning duly noted, most subtle of wizards."

Oh, most subtle. Lying tongues, and traitors, and the craven.

The Risen King of Aglirta smiled grimly as courtier after splendidly garbed courtier slipped in through the arched and gilded doors, to join the swelling throng already milling along the walls of the throne room. None of them approached the River Throne itself; he sat alone amid a goodly stretch of bare tiles, his only companions the young pages sitting, hidden from him, against the carved, kneeling stone knights that flanked the throne itself.

King Kelgrael Snowsar flexed his arms and quelled an urge to shift sideways in his throne and throw his feet up over one of its massive carved marble arms, a pose he remembered as far more comfortable than sitting upright and staring down from his height upon the assembled people. It was even harder to quench the urge to yawn.

He should be excited—angry, or more amused, or eager for what was to come. Instead, the King of Aglirta felt a little weariness, a tinge of sickness at what he knew was to come, and a great, gloomy emptiness. His grip on the scepter across his knees had already melted away to become a row of lightly resting fingertips on the old, smooth metal; firmly he halted the beginnings of rhythmic tappings on the scepter, and gripped it tightly again.

Some of the watching eyes, of course, would see that grasping as something born of fear. A sign of weakness—nay, *another* sign of weakness.

After so many years asleep, perhaps he was getting too old for this. Kelgrael smiled a little at that, and touched the hilt of the sword at his side, quelling the urge to draw it forth and check its readiness (which he'd already done, earlier and in private; doing so again now would send all sorts of forewarnings and messages he didn't want to share with the growing, excitedly murmuring throng), and watched more and more strutting merchant lords and self-styled "lords of the court" arrive, glancing swiftly at him and then away as they slipped into the room without approaching the River Throne where one man sat all alone. As usual, the only person staring up at his king with anything that resembled admiration was that young lad with the staring black eyes—the son of the dead bard Helgrym Castlecloaks. There he was now . . . Raulin, that was his name . . . giving Kelgrael a tentative smile. The Risen King smiled back, warmly, and the young lad almost darted to his usual place against the wall, seemingly embarrassed.

Gods, but Flowfoam Isle could be a crowded yet lonely place. It had not always been so, but Aglirta had been shattered while he slept, the proud rich land he remembered swept away into legend, leaving behind too many fearful folk cowering under too many fierce and cruel barons and tersepts.

Such as the one coming here now. The king was sitting court this day to pass royal justice upon the Tersept of Rithrym—a man known to do just as he pleased, often and with brutal consequences for anyone who stood in his way. These courtiers, wastrels and scavengers and opportunists among the few good folk and those simply drawn to power, were here to see the confrontation . . . here to see if the man-legend on the throne was a dotard or weakling, or if Aglirta truly had a king again.

There had been *so* many such testings, as the months passed. Baron after baron had come to Flowfoam Isle with bluster and pomp and show of arms, to make their own separate peaces with the man out of legend, come so inconveniently to life. They could not ignore his summons because of the hope his mere presence had lit in the suffering people of Aglirta, but none of them was eager to lose his own swaggering power—and much coin—in return for a justice none of them recognized, and a peace none of them trusted.

Some had been openly defiant—and why not? What wizards had the king, and what army, save those too old or weak to find service elsewhere, or too young and green to yet have anything to their names but hope and—if they went unslain—years ahead of them to spend?

The Tersept of Rithrym was Augrath Naerimdon by name, but he could just as well—and fittingly—have been called "Defiance" or "Overconfidence." He was summoned to court this day to account for certain seizures of merchants' goods that traders in Sirlptar had called "tyrannical," and King Snowsar had already grimly labeled "brigandry" before his court. He had no doubt that his judgement had reached ears in Rithrym long since, and neither did his court—which was why they were all gathering to watch the fun.

The main doors boomed, far down the hall: a heavy knocking of spear-butts, by the sound of it. No slipping in to join the chattering throng for Tersept Augrath. In the space of instants the sounds of the courtiers rose in sudden high excitement, and then fell deathly silent.

Into that sudden stillness broke the loud crash of the doors being flung wide, to rebound off the wall in spaces wisely vacated by experienced courtiers. It was a sound punctuated by the shrieks and then moans of a few less worldly guests, who'd been in the way and were now crumpled on the floor in the wake of those lofty and glided doors.

The King of Aglirta stared calmly down the empty length of his throne room at the new arrivals: half a dozen tall warriors, gleaming and impassive in their full battle armor, ranged in a line abreast, at the head of others. They bore no shields, and their swords and daggers were scabbarded, but their visors were down, and they gave no greeting—and did not kneel—to their king.

At some signal Kelgrael Snowsar could not hear, the six warriors split into two trios, wheeling to either side to face the courtiers. Their swords flashed out, and there was a murmur as splendidly garbed men fell back before brandished steel. The warriors did not advance, however, but stood guard in their places as other armored men, the black diagonal arrow across a golden shield of Rithrym bright upon their breasts, strode forward between them.

The cortahars of Rithrym strode into the throne room not in unison, but like fighting men advancing on a broken battlefield: warily, with swords and maces in hand, seeking foes and perils in their paces ahead.

In their midst walked one man who was helmless, his hair like an orange flame, and his dark eyes gazing hard on the king from beneath scowling brows. Augrath Naerimdon, Tersept of Rithrym, this must be—for Rithrym had no wizard to magically force the guise of its ruler on another man. No mages, but warriors in plenty. Over a hundred of them here now, crowding into the throne room as the courtiers shrank back along the walls, real fear in their murmurings now. So many swords, and men eager to use them . . .

Men shouldering their way through courtiers to every side door of the hall right now, as the tersept waved his arms in an imperious signal. Securing the doors, putting broad armored backs to them, and standing with ready steel to stare at any who strayed near. There were fearful words, like the squeakings of disturbed mice, as this courtier and that tried to leave the throne room, and was prevented; the Tersept of Rithrym smiled grimly as the jaws of his trap closed. He raised his hands, and his army of warriors halted, several hundred strong.

He stepped forward perhaps half a dozen paces more and took a broad-legged stance, crossing his arms over his chest. It was not the pose of a supplicant, or a loyal subject, or a man who felt fear.

"You label me brigand, Snowsar," he said abruptly, "and call me hence. I come not to kneel, but to see what manner of man dares style himself 'king,' and claim to be the Sleeper of Legend come to life. I look, and see a man alone . . ." His voice rose to let that last word ring around the chamber, before he added in a lower growl, "And am *not* impressed."

"I do not require your awe," the Risen King said calmly, "but I do command your obedience. No tersept holds office save by leave of the king; you have no authority but what I lend you."

"Ah, but I do," the Tersept of Rithrym replied, with a mirthless smile, and spread his gauntleted hands. "My swords are my authority, and they are all the authority I need. Something that every Aglirtan understands, and none dare dispute. More trustworthy than wizards, and stronger and less open to dispute than any claim to be 'royal,' or do anything 'rightful.' Look, O man who claims to be king. See the men who stand with me?"

He peered past the throne, smiling more easily now, and said, "I mark but children standing with you now, and two spearmen cowering in the rearward corners. Those two added to what I passed coming up from the river I mark at a dozen armsmen in all. Not a mage of note to be seen, either—certainly none to match the Sirl wizards I've hired to fend off baronial mages in the months to come . . . more than you've thought to do. All in all, Flowfoam has managed a regrettably meagre muster against my much larger force. To put it bluntly, Risen King, you can choose to surrender your crown, here and now—or die."

He waved one hand lazily. At this signal a cortahar near the south wall casually slashed out with his warblade, cutting open the throat of the nearest courtier. Blood fountained and the man staggered a few steps, gurgling, before sprawling to the tiles to choke on the last of his own blood.

Screams went up from all sides of the throne room, and suddenly the room was alive with frightened courtiers, bolting in all directions like panicked rabbits.

"Stop!" the tersept bellowed, his voice sudden ringing thunder in the high-vaulted room. "Stop, all of you—or die!"

Sudden stillness fell, and in its hush Augrath Naerimdon gave King Snowsar a smug and brittle smile, and made another signal with his fingers.

Two warriors with cocked and loaded crossbows glided forward out of the press of warriors to flank the tersept, menacing the king with their weapons. Augrath of Rithrym's mocking smile widened.

The King of Aglirta answered it with a wintry smile of his own, and barely lifted the scepter in his hand.

As its aged metal burst into a brief blaze of winking lights, there was a grating sound—and a floor-tile gave way, plunging one bowman down into nothingness with a startled yell.

There were rumblings—and the cries and scramblings of the pages—as the two carved stone knights kneeling on either side of the River Throne rose stiffly into the air. Stone groaned like a living thing as they straightened up, shuddered, and then lumbered forward, shaking the tiles with their tread.

Into the din of startled curses from the warriors of Rithrym broke screams and shouts from outside the hall, cries from their fellow cortahars and the courtiers who hadn't dared to enter the chamber, that heralded the awakening of other stone knights, here and there in the passages.

King Kelgrael Snowsar kept his eyes on those of the tersept, and saw the man's face go slowly white. The crossbowman beside the Lord of Rithrym hurriedly fired his quarrel at the king, who moved not a whit. Its whistling flight ended in an instant with a sharp crack and the bursting shower of tumbling splinters, as the bolt struck an unseen barrier and shattered.

"Magic shields him!" a warrior growled fearfully, falling back. In smooth, unhurried calm King Snowsar arose, set his scepter down on the throne behind him, its ends still winking with magic, and slowly drew his sword.

The crossbowman turned on his heels and fled, his bow clattering to the floor. The Tersept of Rithrym watched him go, glanced back at the advancing king, and then backed away, turning to flee after only a few steps.

Armored men were jostling each other, shoulder-plates ringing, as they sought to stream out of the double doors they'd thrown so rudely open not long before. Men cursed and shoved and punched—until something dark rippled in the stone of the door arch, and became the looming arms and head and shoulders of another stone knight.

Arms that swept up—and then down, dashing warriors to the floor in bloody pulp.

Shouts and screams fought for supremacy as the cortahars of Rithrym tried now to turn and move away from the doors. The tersept came to a helpless halt in front of their surging, trampling chaos, cast a look back at the king striding tall and terrible towards him, and fell to his knees.

"Mercy, O King!" he cried. "Spare me!"

"Mercy," Kelgrael Snowsar told him almost sadly, as he took one slow step forward and swept his sword around in an arc that would lop Augrath Naerimdon's head off, "lies beyond what I can now afford. You leave me needing you too dearly as an *example*—" there came a wet, solid thud as the blade bit home "—O idiot of Rithrym."

Blood spurted and flailing-armed armor toppled.

The Risen King looked past it, at the rush of warriors stampeding out the side doors, and found himself staring into the frightened faces of many cowering courtiers.

He lifted his hand and pointed at one he'd seen sneering earlier. Holding the man's eyes with his own, he let his pointing finger descend to indicate the slumped body on the floor in front of him. "Clean this up," he said shortly.

The man wavered, licking pale lips, and the king added quietly, "That's a royal command."

The man swallowed, stepped gingerly forward—and vomited violently, pitching onto his knees. As his tortured eyes met the royal gaze once more, the king pointed at the mess on the tiles and added, "That, too!"

The man went gray and toppled facedown into his own spew, in a dead faint. King Snowsar sighed, and pointed at the next courtier.

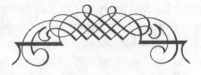

4

The Sword Settles All

*C*oldly clawing fingers were climbing her cheeks, only moments away from blinding her forever with cruel gougings. Tears were near blinding her already, streaming from her swimming eyes, and the world was spinning crazily as a dozen hard hands pinched and tore at and throttled her. Embra thrashed helplessly in a sea of pain, everything slowly darkening as the hands at her throat tightened. Mighty sorceress she might be, but she couldn't even touch the floor, or grab hold of *anything*, she couldn't . . .

Feebly she struggled against tugging fingers, trying to lift her arms so she could reach the spiderlike bones climbing onto her face, and pluck them away before they—*before they*—

As a helpless scream rose up in her and the first bony probing caught at her eyelid, despite her violent headshakings, Embra's fingers brushed the Dwaer at her breast.

Power surged through her, pouring forth in a wave of blinding-bright magic before she quite realized what she was doing.

Golden air roiled in the wake of the surge she sent forth, a shielding spell that swept away bones before it, shattering and crumbling them like sand struck by an angry sea. Skeletal fingers tumbled through the air, shredding the hand of many bones from around Sarasper's struggling body.

On and on her magic howled, born of her fear and revulsion and urgent need. So suddenly had Embra Silvertree been thrust to the brink of death or disfigurement, through much pain, that it all hardly seemed real. Through staring, swimming eyes she saw bones smashed into dust and shards—and the same roaring magic slam Sarasper and Craer aside, tumbling them through ruined bookshelves. Hawkril took the full brunt of the shield-wave, bones pattering off his armor in an angry stream, and was hurled away through the darksome air—to smash right into the robed skeleton that had menaced them all with its magic.

Brown bones clawed at the air desperately as the armored warrior spun among them—and abruptly two bony legs were standing alone, joined by pelvic bones but staggering like a drunken man, as the cursing armaragor rolled on rubble-strewn stones beyond it, bony arms shivering under him, and a skull snapping its teeth into his face ineffectually.

Solid stone was under Embra's boots again, and she tottered thankfully forward, bracing herself to stand straight and speak the enchantment she needed.

Her throat was raw, and ached as if those bruising fingers were still tight around it, but she husked out the words somehow, letting her pain and disgust give them force as she spread her hands and desired of Aglirta that no bones walk in this place.

There was no roaring wave this time, no wash of light, but only a chorus of small sighings, as bones collapsed into dust here and there. The bundles of bones that had scuttled and leaped and shaped themselves into hands crumbled and were swept away, Sarasper coughed weakly and started to curse—with just enough vigor to tell her without looking that he'd live—and the half-skeleton Hawkril was struggling against suddenly became a disjointed cluster of separate bones thrashing and bouncing away in dozens of attempts to flee.

The armaragor rose snarling among them and lashed out with his fists and boots and blade, seeking to smash every bone he could see into dust. Embra saw the two bony hands a little way beyond him, wriggling as they sought to shape a last, desperate spell, and opened her mouth to cry warning.

She closed it again a moment later, her shout unvoiced, as Hawkril's blade slashed through those spell-glowing fingers. He flung himself forward on the remnants while they were still falling, and rolled around on the ancient stones, grinding and lashing out with his gauntleted fists. The flickering red and black radiances soon died away, and stillness came to the ruined library—a stillness broken only by the swift, ragged breathing of Four who were grimly taking in yet another warning of just how swiftly death can reach out in Aglirta, and harvest the unready.

Even as the eyes of four panting adventurers sought each other out in the grandest surviving chamber of Indraevyn, red and black radiances blossomed somewhere not far away in that ruined city. Somewhere deep, dark, and dripping.

The spell-glows blossomed like dark stars in the void, pulsing and dancing above eyes that widened in alarm . . . and then narrowed in fury.

Those golden orbs belonged to a wolf-headed beast as large as a horse. It clung spiderlike to a ledge in what had once been a cellar. Its long and powerful legs were thickly cloaked in reddish, grayish fur, cruel bony spurs jutting from the joints that on a human would have been elbows and knees.

Even in bards' tales, few longfangs were as big as the one now shrinking back from the ruby and ebony lights, snarling in a vain attempt to scare the radiances into flight.

Instead, they swooped and settled—and the large golden eyes of the shuddering longfangs dimmed, until two cold and tiny points of light glittered out at the world from dark sockets.

The longfangs had fed not long ago, and hadn't planned to move from its ledge until the gloom of night was dark upon the land. That which now rode it, however, had a hunger to hunt.

The wolf-headed, spiderlike predator stretched its hairy limbs like a cat, arched itself, and then advanced at a steady pace. For something so large, it moved in uncanny near-silence, its feet falling upon the stones with velvet softness and almost fastidious delicacy. Crossing one cellar, it turned without hesitation into another, sparing no time for scuttling spiders and palely glistening cave-snakes. It was seeking rather rarer prey: humans.

Four humans in particular—four who stood in a riven chamber somewhere above. Patiently the longfangs began to stalk. . . .

"Done yet, Gurkyn?"

"I'll let ye know, Mararr," the man bent over the fire said sourly into the flames that were threatening to blacken his nose. "I'll let ye know."

Mararr bent over the sizzling meat, peering. "Aye, it's right dead, Gurk," he said calmly. " 'Twill be done soon now."

Gurkyn Oblarram hissed in irritation. Careless parents might have given him a name that sounded like a drunken man spewing up a meal of live frogs—but it was not the deed of a friend to remind him of it. A swift and biting tongue never makes up for strong-shouldered good looks and height.

"Why don't ye go somewhere and conquer a kingdom, hey?" he snarled accordingly, without looking up from the swiftly charring rabbit he was holding in the flames. "This'll be done soon. . . . Ye'll have just enough time!"

The armaragor wearing the baldric of many short swords stepped a quick pace back, to be quite clear of any sudden jabs with a hot cooking-fork, and chuckled. "I'd miss that tongue of yours, if I wasn't around to hear it." Mararr lifted his eyes to fix the cook with a calm, level gaze, and added, "I'd let it cool for a bit, if I were you. . . . Even after all that wine back in Sirlptar, you've not quite made leather of your lips and tongue yet."

Gurkyn grunted. "It'd take a bebolten longer list of feasts to wear out my mouth than we've enjoyed since seeing Aglirta again. A graul and bebolten list!"

There were several growls of sour agreement from the dark forms drifting closer to the fire on all sides. Several empty stomachs raised complaints of their own as an echo, and their owners huddled their cloaks closer around themselves and out of hard habit glanced around at the night. They had left the Vale as proud and mighty soldiers of Blackgult, every man of them, tasted bloody battles and defeats on the isles their master had hurled them against, and found their weary ways home from the ruin of Black-gult's dreams only to find their master dead or fled, his barony fallen, and themselves declared outlaw by Blackgult's greatest foe, the Baron Sil-vertree.

The moment they'd set foot outside Sirlptar—and an honest warrior's purse doesn't last long in that crowded, expensive city—every barony had hunted them. Scores had found swift graves in as many days, and the rest had learned to flee and lurk.

As they were lurking still. The returning men of Blackgult had been treated as vermin and brigands until even those sickened by having to behave so became sneak thieves and slayers in the night, brutal and savage in their bladework and swift to seize what was not their own. The Vale was alive with baronial troops, barons' mages in risen power, and Serpent-worshippers armed with poisoned blades—and those who'd survived all these had become hardened men indeed.

Wherefore many of them were huddled here this night, around an upland—and carefully shielded with ramparts of now-scorched turf—campfire in Silvertree not far from Flowfoam Isle, gathered to hear some hope.

One of their number, a bold armaragor known to all as "Bloodblade," had sent word around the lurking outlaws that he had a plan that might mean a brighter future for them all. Some of them guessed what choosing this spot to tell them might mean . . . but they'd been desperate men long before a man had stepped out of legend to declare himself the Risen King of Aglirta, and they were beyond desperate now.

A much-scarred giant by the name of Lultus lifted one bushy eyebrow. "Be that rabbit done yet? Iffen I wanted to eat fire-black, I could rummage old firepits, I'm thinking, without the daring of coming down here, right onto the points of this new king's blades!"

Gurkyn growled wordlessly and turned his fork from the fire, letting the carcass on it trail aromatic smoke into the night. The shadows that were men moved closer, drawn by the smell, and there were low rumbles of hunger from many throats as they saw his knife flash.

"A piece for every man," he said, "but some'll have to wait for the second one to cook."

"Ye've *two*?" another man asked, hunger making his voice thick. "Where's the other?"

Gurkyn squinted up at him. "I'm sitting on it."

There were some halfhearted chuckles, but they didn't last long.

"How much longer are we going to be standing here, while some wizard or other sends bowmen to ring us in, eh?" another warrior snarled. "Where's Bloodblade?"

"Duthjack's up on yon ridge, seeing to it that no one's creeping up on us," Gurkyn told him. "When we've all had something to chew, he'll be down."

"To lead us in a charge clear across the water," someone said sarcastically, "treading on the very waves as if he were a wizard himself!"

"Sargh to that!" someone snarled fearfully, and another man hissed, "Be *still*! Wait, and hear Bloodblade, and spare us what you *think* he might say! I've not yet seen proof that ye *can* think!"

"We've all seen battle, Gloun," a warrior nearby said wearily. "We're not fools. Why else call us here, if not to try to seize the throne?"

"Oh, aye?" Gloun asked witheringly. "And who of us would make a king, eh? *I* knew Sendrith Duthjack when he was a lad ducking his wood-chopping tasks, long before ye knew him as 'Bloodblade'—and if he were sitting on yon throne right now, with a crown on his head and *two* lady wizards giggling in his lap, he'd *still* be no more a king than I am!"

"Oh? And you'll tell him so, just as loud as that, when he's standing here with his sword out glaring at you?"

"Aye," Gloun said, a little more quietly. "Will any of the rest of ye, though, I wonder?"

"I will," said a voice that was as deep as doom and as sharp as the edge of a woodsman's axe.

Heads turned. The speaker was shouldering out of the shadows, a head taller than most of the men there, little gleams of fireflicker shining here and there on his armor where the soot and mud he'd caked it with had rubbed away. Hard emerald eyes, a white moustache . . .

"Kalarth?" Gurkyn asked, peering up from the flames.

"Aye," the man replied, never slowing his stride, and then added a word: "Rabbit."

The word was a flat command. A dozen hands went to hilts, and there was a shifting and a hissing of indrawn breaths as a dozen men readied themselves for battle.

Kalarth had once held a bridge alone against a Silvertree patrol, and slaughtered them—four-and-ten warriors in all. In the Isles, his blade had emptied boats and villages with swift and glistening ease, and in Sirlptar only a few months back, he'd faced down and fought a mage of note—Arliiryn of Carraglas—in the street . . . and won, leaving the wizard huddled on the cobbles with his lifeblood pooling in the gutters.

Kalarth turned as he chewed, and his sword was suddenly in his hand. The warrior who'd taken an angry step forward shrank back again, and Kalarth tossed him the rabbit with a smile, fork and all. "One bite, mind," he said, the promise of death bright in his eyes, "and then pass it on, or . . ."

He didn't bother to say the rest. Nor did any of the warriors make the slightest sound of dispute. The fork was passed around in silence, men striding idly away as they chewed, hands ready on their scabbards, hardly daring to trust that they'd have time to swallow before some foe or other would strike. There were fresh sizzlings from Gurkyn's careful crouch by the fire, and as if the sound had been a herald's trumpet, a man strode out of the night with two others at his back, drawn swords in their hands.

Kalarth spun smoothly to face the newcomer; the glances they traded might just as well have been their swords crossing to begin a duel. The newcomer raised an eyebrow. "All the way from Starn Rock, Kalarth? I'm impressed."

"I don't intend to be hunted down by wizards and dogs because you've roused all Aglirta trying something overbold, Duthjack," Kalarth said flatly. "Things're just beginning to settle down in the Vale—"

"Aye, as we starve," the man who liked to be called Bloodblade interrupted. "When we're all gone, then the barons'll turn on our new king . . . but we'll all be too dead to watch the fun."

"So you're proposing—?" Kalarth prompted, staring around into the night as if he expected baronial armies to suddenly sprout among the trees on all sides.

Sendrith Duthjack lifted his voice a little, so that it carried clearly across the hollow. "An attack on Flowfoam this very night. Slay this so-called king, sword any barons, tersepts, and wizards we find, and seize the castle. Get our bellies full, search the place on the morrow, and decide then whether to hold it and put a new king on the River Throne, or take what we can back into the wilds."

"A new king by the name of Bloodblade, perhaps?" Kalarth asked, turning his head a little to one side but never taking his eyes from Duthjack's.

Bloodblade lifted and dropped his shoulders in an easy shrug. "Perhaps. The important thing is to slay Snowsar, and benefit however we can from what will follow, as one baron lashes out at another, up and down the Vale. I was thinking more of defending the Isle over hiding in the Wildrocks or taking to the forest."

"That's no choice," Gloun growled. "Trees are a poor cloak against rain and snow."

Bloodblade shrugged. "On the other hand, if wizard after wizard sends spells—or armies—against us because they know we're standing over the River Throne, we could simply be choosing a grander grave than elsewhere. Lurking again could let us seize a barony with but a few swordthrusts, once its strength is spent fighting some rival baron."

"Pretty talk," Kalarth said, "doesn't distract *me* from seeing that you're planning on leading us on a cold swim in the river, to an Isle defended by the Three alone know how many guards and—if half the tales of Baron Silvertree are true—some deadly guardian beasts or waiting spells, or both, to hack our way through an unknown number of wizards, all to butcher one man sitting on a stone chair. A dozen mages have been hunting us these long months past, and here you're planning to do something bold with us all gathered together, on display like tavern dancers for them to blast and twist into monster shapes and torment with mind-pains! I've followed idiots all too eager to spill my blood to buy their victories before—once or twice too often. Are you another of them, I wonder? Just how well have you thought this through, Duthjack?"

"Well enough to have a boat ready for us," Bloodblade said coldly, "and precise places for each of us to head for, the moment we set foot on Flowfoam. One of those places will be the kitchens, crammed with food simmering for morning meals right now, but with most of the cooks asleep."

There was an involuntary murmur—from some of the men, almost a moan—at those last words, and Bloodblade let it rise and fall as a little smile grew across his face. It was a smile that didn't reach anywhere near his eyes.

"And then again, hearken," he added sharply. "If this strike is to fall as swiftly and as surely as we'll need it to, to have any hope of staying alive, I'll need to be obeyed as if I was baron over us all—or better than that!"

There was a ripple of humor, and then sudden stillness, as all eyes fixed on the two men facing each other.

"Well, Kalarth?" Bloodblade asked softly. "Will you obey me? Or shall we have it out between us now, blade to blade?"

"There are no other choices?" Kalarth asked almost mockingly. "Such as simply stepping back into the dark and letting you go to your doom without me?"

There was a rustling then, as one of the warriors who'd walked with Duthjack drew a cocked crossbow out from under his cloak, and carefully laid a quarrel in its firing-runnel. He lifted it almost slowly and aimed it at Kalarth.

"I'm afraid not," Bloodblade replied mildly. "I dare not treat all our lives so lightly. You could, after all, go straight to some wizard and warn Flow-foam of our coming."

"Whereas you," Kalarth's deep voice came right back at him, "could have done that already, and be sending us all to our deaths, while you wait here in safety for a reward."

Duthjack's smile vanished. "I think all of us here know me better than that."

"No," someone who hadn't spoken before said, from well away from the fire. "No, it's knowing you well that makes me fear just that."

"And makes me expect it," Kalarth added quickly, as Bloodblade tried to peer around him and identify who'd spoken.

"The second rabbit is ready," Gurkyn announced suddenly. As heads turned to look at him, Kalarth moved.

His hand whipped down and then up again, and something flashed in the firelight for a flickering instant as it spun through the air. The man with the crossbow gave a queer cough and turned his head sharply to the west, blood spraying from his opened throat. His crossbow fired its bolt high into the night somewhere over Gloun's shoulder—and the night was suddenly full of fast-moving men, thudding feet, and drawn swords.

Bloodblade Duthjack and Kalarth charged straight at each other, unflinching, blades sweeping up as they ran. Their steel met so hard that sparks flew, and clanged aside—as Bloodblade threw a handful of sand into Kalarth's face.

The tall warrior shook his head frantically, slashing the air viciously as he sprang blindly back, trying to prevent Duthjack from striking—but by accident or design, Lultus stumbled into him, and as Kalarth whirled around to deal with this new foe, Bloodblade swept the tall warrior's feet from under him with a vicious swordcut, ran after the rolling, cursing Kalarth, and pounced, stabbing viciously and repeatedly down into the man's face.

Kalarth was dying after the first thrust, but Duthjack thrust his wet blade home four or five times more before springing free—almost decapitating Mararr, who was crouching in guardianship over Gurkyn, in the process—and racing to where the fire was between him and most of the gathered warriors.

"Are you with me, men of Blackgult?" he snarled, raising his crimson blade. "Or do you stand against me, buying the fate of Kalarth for yourselves? Hey? Speak now! The night draws on, and I'd rather spend it swording barons on Flowfoam Isle than cutting down my sword-brothers here! What say you?"

Gloun raised his sword to the stars—a little unhappily, Mararr thought—and cried, "I am for you, Bloodblade!"

"Aye!" Lultus echoed in his bearlike roar. "For Bloodblade!"

Swords and cries of support were going up all around now, laced with Gurkyn's sour, "Do you want to warn *all* the idiots on yonder Isle—or just the deaf ones?"

His voice carried. All at once, the shouting warriors fell silent. Bloodblade turned to regard the man by the fire with eyes still ablaze with fury, and whispered, "Are *you* with me, Gurkyn Oblarram?"

The cook rose slowly, kicking clods of earth back over the fire, and in the sudden, spark-swirling gloom replied, "I am. I just hope your schemes extend to ruling Aglirta—and not just conquering it."

Sendrith Duthjack regarded him without expression for a few seconds, hefting the bloody sword in his hand as if aching to use it on the little man, and then said calmly, "As things befall under the watching Three, it does. Are you ready to free the realm, Gurkyn?"

The cook took a bite of rabbit, passed his fork to the nearest warrior, and drew his sword. "Lead me to a baron who has an urgent need to be more my size," he growled.

The gathered warriors chuckled, and the man they called Bloodblade commanded, "To the river!"

"Right, your bold and bridling plot it is," Lultus growled, as they moved forward together. "Now, where's that boat?"

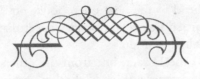

5

Spells and Mirrors

ow, where's that book?" Craer joked, his voice barely above a whisper, his eyes turned upwards. "Let me see. . . ."

The open books floated in midair high above the ruined floor, hanging motionless and silent in the eerie shafts of light, as they might well have done for centuries. Just what magic that light was, none of the Band of Four quite knew, but it had kept the books unharmed by fire, lightning, snows, rain, and the collapse of the huge, arching dome of stone that had once enclosed the shafts. Now the upper ends of the radiant columns simply faded away into empty air, and the weather howled unabated through the library as it did through everything else in forlorn, overgrown Indraevyn.

Three necks had grown tired of craning to look up at the unchanging show the columns afforded the world; their owners were strolling rather warily about the library with swords drawn, looking for things that might move or try to keep hidden—in particular, bones. Thankfully, they found no such lurking attractions.

There came a time when one of them sighed and glanced back up at the silently floating books. "Lady Embra," Sarasper called, "does it really take this long to read a few lines?"

The woman who was floating above the books frowned almost fondly down at him, her eyes twinkling, and then crisply began to read aloud, " 'Four are the Worldstones, none of them master of the others. They seem quarry-stone, brown and gray, but lighter, and are fashioned into spheres that fit the hand. Nothing known can break them—to sunder them would beyond doubt shatter their magic, and pour forth such fire as to make the world tremble.' "

She turned her head to the next open book, not looking down at the three faces now upturned below, and read what it displayed to the world. All of the men had halted to listen.

" 'You may know the Dwaer, one from the other, by the deep-graven runes they bear. If the rune is thus—' " Embra dropped her declamatory tone, and said in her own, gentler voice, "Like a barbed fishhook." Then she gave Sarasper a glance, made her voice loud and crisp again, and continued, " '—you look upon Candalath, the Stone of Life. If the stone has this rune—' " Again she dropped into her own voice. "A circle with four star-points radiating from it."

Craer was grinning up at her now, and gesturing grandly that she continue.

She nodded in imperious acknowledgment, and resumed her lecturing tone. " '—it is Hilimm, the Stone of Renewal, that you hold. A rune thus'—a row of fangs," she interpreted, and continued, " '—marks Mlarr, the Stone of War, and if the symbol be so'—a turret, or tapering castle tower—'you hold Quarlar, the Stone of Building."

"So it was the Stone of War that the Spellmaster held, at the last, when we fought him," Hawkril said slowly. "What makes it suited for War, where yours, Lady, is for Life?"

Embra shrugged, spread her hands in an "I know not" gesture, and drifted a little to one side, to read aloud from the next book. " 'Mages may use them to source spells, but the Dwaerindim have great powers of their own, whose awakening is more subtle, but lies within the grasp of those who have no gift for magic. Each Dwaer-Stone has powers unique to it, each has some powers shared with the others, and there are also powers that can be called upon only when certain of the Dwaer are used in combination—and placed properly.' "

"As usual," Craer murmured to his closest friend, "swords are simpler."

Hawkril's face split in a slow smile, and he nodded. Above their heads, the Lady of Jewels was already drifting to the next book.

" 'Unless willed to give power to a magic, or redirect and augment or alter a spell cast by another so as to touch or affect a Dwaer or its bearer, Dwaerindim drink in most known magics, swallowing such tracelessly and utterly. In this manner they can be employed to protect an alcove, an item beneath or behind them, or their bearer from hostile magics, though the warning must be given that certain magics resist the control of a Dwaer.' "

"It neglects to list just which ones, of course," Sarasper guessed aloud, his voice as confident as it was dry. Embra gave him a nod and a rueful smile, and then turned to the next book.

" 'All of the Dwaerindim can be made to glow,' " she read aloud. " 'The intensity and hue of their radiance can be controlled—and varied—by an awakener who possesses a fierce will, or by a wizard used to employing magics that control radiances. Any of the Dwaer can be made to hover in the air silently and for as long as desired, though the means of directing this must be learned. All of the Dwaer can, when so employed by one who knows how to so command them, purify of taint or poison any waters they are immersed in. Care must be taken, for strong drink is made as water by this power, and the enchantments borne by potions likewise banished forever.' "

"Three above, it sounds like a courtier outlining a treaty," Hawkril growled. "*This* is going to help us save Aglirta?"

Sarasper gave him a look. "Know thy weapon, warrior," he quoted the old maxim, "and live a little longer."

Hawkril nodded and sighed; overhead, Embra reached the last book, sat herself on empty air, and announced almost primly, " 'One who knows can call upon a grasped Dwaer to provide them with life in conditions that would otherwise slay or disable. Where blazing sun would scorch and there is no shade, or winter snows freeze where there is no warmth, and where one would perish, parched, with no water to drink, the Dwaer can sustain and serve. More than this: one who holds a Dwaer can see in darkness as well as creatures of the night. There is even more: a wizard who grasps a Dwaer can call on it to give force to any spell he can mentally frame and control, though the Stones do not give the ability to wield magic to those not having the talent for it.' "

"I believe we're all quite familiar with that last power," Sarasper said wryly. "These writings seem straight and simple to me, Lady; I ask again, what kept you so long?"

Embra descended her own height or more, to hang close above the old healer's head and glare at him. "What I read you is what these books *now* say; there were different words on their pages the last time we were here. I can't recall all of what I read then—'twas in much haste, with battle below, remember—but so far as I can recall, that end one then told me, 'Then did the Golden Griffon rage/At his forever foe enthroned/In the splendor of a nest new and strong-raised,' until I turned its page and so uncovered the words 'The place of fallen majesty, its master and namesake now gone, with all his strivings, to a pearl upon the fast Silverflow, an upthrust prow of shields for to cleave the winter waves.' In other words, they then spoke cryptically of where the Dwaer could be found. There was more than that, something about the Dwaer sometimes having wills of their own, or at least doing things their wielders don't want, and didn't call forth . . . and *that's* what I really wanted to read properly."

She sighed deeply. "Yet I couldn't touch the books then, and I can't now. By using the Stone and my will, I turned the pages of the end one *then* . . . but I can't do that, no matter how often I try, now. Nothing happens. Something has changed. Trying to puzzle that out, healer, is what had kept me. That and trying to memorize these new words."

Sarasper lifted one eyebrow. "Memorize them? I *can* write, you know."

Embra Silvertree made a face at him, and then sighed, rose up to hang above the books again, and as Sarasper set to work with his quill pen and parchment-press, began to recite what she'd read aloud again, slowly and clearly.

Craer and Hawkril divided their time between glancing at the ruins around for any sign of approaching danger, and frankly admiring their lady companion.

There were advantages to being one of the richest ladies in all Aglirta. There were also advantages to being the daughter of someone as breathtakingly beautiful as Tlarinda Silvertree had been. Of course, that had to be weighed against the drawback of having Faerod Silvertree as a father—a drawback that had slain Tlarinda, forced Embra into slavery and spelltorture, and driven her to flight, and hard adventure . . . and here.

Embra Silvertree was wearing leathers and boots as soft and supple as those that seemed to be Craer's second skin, and as dark as her hair, though its usually glossy flood was gathered and bound at the back of her neck. A faint, pulsing glow of magic surrounded her, centered on the hand-sized mottled brown and gray stone sphere hanging in a harness of fine chain upon her breast: Candalath, the Stone of Life. Its awakened powers had girt her about with a web of magics that let her fly and hover, shielded her from spell-strikes and the bite of anything metal—like the tip of a crossbow quarrel— and should foil all magical spying from afar, preventing it even from finding her here. In particular, turning aside all probings made using other Dwaerindim . . .

"So the Dwaer can do all sorts of wonderful things if you learn how to force them into obeying you," Hawkril rumbled slowly, watching Embra read and thinking he'd seldom seen anything in his life so beautiful as her face, "and have a will of iron."

"In other words," Craer agreed, waving up at the Lady of Jewels, "we leave playing with Dwaer-Stones to *her*."

"But the king bade us find the other Stones, and bring them back or at least learn right clear who held them, and we swore to do so," Hawkril said, looking down at his friend with sudden soberness on his face. "I'm good with a sword, but that means nothing against such as *that*." He waved one large hand up at the glow under Embra's shapely chin, and growled, "It'll be a long time before I forget watching a *castle* fall on us!"

Craer shrugged. "I think we'll get so fed up with wandering around searching that it'll be almost a relief doing battle with anyone we do find holding a Dwaer! Anyone with the brain of a bat who has one isn't going to just show it to us . . . and anyone of less brains probably won't hold on to a Dwaer—or his life—for all that long, with wizards and Serpent-priests and the Faceless Ones all out looking for them."

"Thanks for the reassurance," the hulking armaragor growled, looking around the ruined library for lurking foes one more time. "I was trying to forget the latest crisis looming over all Darsar, in hopes that—for once—someone else would take care of it."

"If we tarry here much longer," Sarasper put in sourly, setting aside his pen, "long years will gather in all our bones and someone else will *have* to take care of it!"

"Whine, whine, growl," Embra said mockingly, as she drifted down to join them. "Do men who go adventuring ever say anything else?"

Craer winked. "Well, yes," he replied, "and they usually precede such utterances with, 'Ho, wench!' Shall I give you a sample—?"

Embra wrinkled her nose and waved him to silence, her nimble fingers twisting the gesture into a rude signal. Craer put his hands on his hips in arch mimicry of an affronted lady of high station, clucked in mock disgust, and rolled his eyes.

"I've an idea," Sarasper said in a dry voice. "Strut *him* up and down the Vale until anyone who has a Dwaer gets exasperated enough to try to blast him to ashes. Then, of course, we'll know who has one."

"And if their attempt to blast me doesn't miss?" Craer inquired, in injured tones.

The old healer shrugged. "The armies of Blackgult had no shortage of procurers, as I recall—and almost any of them would have to be less annoying."

Craer turned to face Sarasper and imitated Embra's rude gesture, with several elaborate flourishes.

"Shall we be off, then?" Sarasper inquired, ignoring the procurer.

"Whither, exactly?" Hawkril rumbled. "I've little stomach for parading down the entire Vale, given the love various barons seem to have for us."

"I wanted to talk about that," Embra said, nodding. The Stone at her breast pulsed brightly, once, and she frowned down at it. "Someone's trying to find us again."

There was a little silence as the three men drew in close around her, peering hard at the silent ruins around them as if expecting wizards, beasts, and bowmen to spring up triumphantly from behind every stone.

"Speak, lass," Hawkril grunted, hefting his warsword and keeping his eyes on what forest he could see through the riven walls. "I think Craer's left off being clever for a moment or three."

"That was a subtle hint, right?" the procurer murmured. "Yes, Embra, we're listening: talk."

Embra collected all of their gazes calmly, and said gently, "I do not want to say this and have you inwardly think I'm forcing you into something. For love of the Three, grumble now, and—"

"Save it not for after one of us has been killed," Craer murmured.

The three men watched the sorceress draw a deep breath, close her eyes for a moment, and then say in a voice suddenly close to tears, "Yes. Yes, that's exactly what I mean. We don't know who has the other Stones, but they must know who we are. There's a very good chance we'll die before we've done what the king asked of us."

"Can't a Dwaer bring us back to life?" Hawkril growled in a near-whisper, glancing around as if the crumbling walls themselves were listening.

Embra shrugged. "Perhaps, but I don't know how to make this one do that, so the answer is no. But hear my thoughts on your task. Blundering about the countryside trying to winkle out where the Dwaerindim lie by prying news out of every talkative carter and farmer in every tavern will just make foolish targets of us all. So will spying on barons, tersepts, and wizards—all of whom have something to hide or keep safe from thieves even if they've never even heard of a Dwaer, and will assume we've come to seize. So. I'll use my magic, if you'll aid me, to trace the other Stones."

Sarasper gestured at the Dwaer hanging at her breast. "And how will you succeed if spell-searchings can be so easily blocked?"

The Lady Silvertree nodded and leaned forward, impatient in her eagerness. "I won't try the open prying others have used, like that you saw me block here and when we were speaking with the king. That way can be blocked easily by those who know how and are awake and alert. If it does succeed, it shows both Stone-holders to each other and opens a way between them—a doorway whose threshold can span miles, from one edge of known Darsar to the other, if need be, so that a single step takes one across territory it takes months to traverse. Monsters, missiles, and the like can race or be hurled through such a door, as can spells. Nothing and no one near either end can be deemed safe by any prudent person."

"So instead—?" Craer prompted her, thoughtfully tapping the flat of his dagger blade against the nails of his curled fingers.

"Instead," Embra answered, "I'll work a subtler, ongoing magic that seeks unleashed Dwaer magic like a hound sniffing for the scent of a hare. A slow 'this direction feels better' spell that should escape detection."

Those words brought a crooked smile to one face in the room. It was not one of the three men gathered around the sorceress, nor even a face any of the Four knew was there. It adorned the gray visage of a head that hung unnoticed in the shadows: a floating, disembodied human head whose lips widened into a soundless chuckle—just before it vanished, winking away silently.

Nor did that exit go unnoticed. In deeper shadows well behind where the head had been, around the sagging end of a collapsed shelf, another face smiled in its turn. This one had a body beneath it and a beard adorning it— all of which withdrew behind the shelf in soft silence moments before Craer lifted his head to glance in that direction.

The bearded man did not reappear after the procurer glanced else-where—but something else moved, even farther back in the gloom. A small bat took wing from where it had been clinging to the ceiling, swooped out one of the rents in the walls, and flapped away across the ruins. It, too, seemed to smile as it went.

Another bat flapped past the windows, free to come and go in the night as he was not.

The man sat alone in his chair in the deep, waiting silence, and swallowed his rising bitterness.

The voice seemed to come out of the darkness right beside the Baron Loushoond's elbow. "You are alone, and seated in shadow?"

He almost cursed, and did flinch, but fought down the urge to jump out of his chair and snarl in his fear, and instead said slowly, making his voice as calm and deep as he could, "I am. Loushoond keeps its bargains."

"That," the voice said dryly, "is good."

The Baron Loushoond's right hand closed around the comforting hilt of the short sword he wore under his robe before he asked, "Shall I unhood the lantern?"

"Do so," came the reply, and as the light flared forth the Lord of Loushoond found himself staring at the robed and cowled figure he'd expected, its head bent forward to shield its face entirely from his view, the wide sleeves of its robe folded over its hands so they, too, could not be seen, and his eyes found interest only in what was held between them: a sphere of greenish-clear glass larger than a man's head.

The sphere he had not expected. It could only be some magic or other, and could not bode well, but Berias Loushoond kept his face serene and his tongue still as his mysterious visitor moved fingers beneath the concealing sleeve in an intricate pattern, seemed to listen intently for a moment, and then said, "We are alone. This is well. I had no doubt of your honor, Lord Baron, but I had feared your idiot of a tersept would spy on us."

Loushoond smiled thinly. "So he would have done, had I not sent him to the far end of the barony with hints of a brigand raid."

His visitor nodded in satisfaction and took a swift step closer, to stand well in the light of the lantern. Then it threw its head back, the cowl fell away—and the baron found himself staring into a darkly beautiful female face. No scales, and certainly not a man.

"You're not—" he said sharply, hand darting to a bellpull and grabbing for his sword.

The woman did not move, even when the tip of his blade was gleaming near her breast. The alarm-gong did not sound; he pulled again on its cord, and found himself holding a severed length of tasseled rope. His visitor smiled, but made no move.

The baron's eyes narrowed. "Who *are* you?"

"The one you expected is—elsewhere. I, too, serve the Serpent," she said, her voice now lighter than before. A slender hand slowly drew open the robe, to reveal bare flesh beneath. Unhurriedly she showed him herself, from throat to ankle. "Look well, and see: I bring no weapon here against you this night but the truth. There'll be no need for guards and wizards and alarm-gongs."

The baron swallowed, his throat suddenly dry. Dark, glistening eyes melted into his with an unspoken promise, and shapely limbs caught the lantern-light as his visitor glided a few paces back, to lean against his decanter cabinet in a pose that swept the robe behind her to display all . . . and smiled.

"For now," she purred, "I ask you only to watch."

Almost lazily she tossed the glass sphere up into the air—where with a flash of silent spellfury it became a shimmering mirror. The fires within it became shaped—the shapes of people, as if seen through a window. Loushoond bent forward in his seat, peering.

He was looking into a dark-paneled chamber very much like his own, at two figures he knew. One was an old rival, the Baron Eldagh Ornentar, and the other was the man he'd expected to meet here this night. . . .

"Unfold to me, then, your concerns," the hooded figure commanded softly.

Baron Ornentar's fabled face of stone had cracked hours ago; the many-ringed hand he waved at his hovering scrying-sphere trembled visibly. "All of my mages are lost!" His shout rang back off the ceiling and the polished shields on the walls. "Ornentar now stands unprotected against the armies of Silvertree and all the other roused, whelmed baronies!"

"Sssoftly," the Priest of the Serpent hissed. "I, too, have been watching the battle of Indraevyn and elsewhere, besides. Ssso impressively have the ranks of mages in the Vale been thinned these last few days that you need not worry overmuch. More ssserious is a gathering of minor wizards from many baronies, in Sirlptar. They meet to agree on what to do about the peril of Silvertree's runaway mages."

The baron sat frozen in his high seat. It was a long and uncomfortable time before he whispered, "We weren't invited. Ornentar wasn't even told of this."

The cowled priest nodded his head. "Even ssso," he granted, his voice calm and flat.

"All of the baronies risen together against me," Baron Ornentar whispered. "We are doomed."

The priest shrugged. "Not if aid is forthcoming."

"Aid?" The baron gaped at him. "From where?"

The Priest of the Serpent spread one hand in a slow gesture.

The baron stared at him. "You would? Yes, yes," he said, voice rising almost to a babble of relief—and then pausing. "And your price?"

"The aid of the Ssserpent ssshall be yours," the hooded figure said solemnly, "in return for the turning of Ornentar to the worship of the Ssserpent."

The baron sat silent in his high seat for a long moment, and then nodded slowly. The priest strode away from the wall towards the ruler of Ornentar, swaying slightly, and said, "There is a ceremony. Remove your tunic, and the chains of gold you wear."

The baron's eyes narrowed, but he did so, slowly and with increasing reluctance.

When Ornentar's white, heavily hairy torso was bared, the priest slowly brought one hand into view from behind his back. It seemed to hold nothing, but when he extended one finger to the baron's sagging breasts and the paunch beneath, his touch was cold. Cold and slimy; as that finger traced a complex figure on the baron's chest, it left a glistening trail . . . a trail that began to glow a dull greenish-white.

The priest blew out the nearest lamp, leaving only the flickering light of the sconces on the wall. In the dimness, the glow coming from the baron shone more strongly. The ruler of Ornentar looked down at himself in consternation.

"Kneel," the Priest of the Serpent hissed. The baron stared at him, but the priest said and moved no more than a stone statue as long, silent moments passed.

The baron frowned, looked away at nothing for a while, and then, slowly, crouched down out of his chair onto his knees. Tapestries stirred between every shield then, all around the room, and figures robed and hooded just like the priest glided into view, smoothly taking places in a circle around Eldagh Ornentar. They kept silent, hiding their features in the bent cowls of their robes and keeping their hands drawn up into their flaring sleeves, but he could feel their eyes upon him.

The baron stared up at them, wild fear and suspicion rising in his eyes like kindling flames—and then the design on his chest flared into white fire, and in its bright radiance he saw them all bare one sleeve and thrust that arm out at him. They took a pace closer in unison, and knuckles brushed him on all sides.

There was movement then, on twenty shoulders, as serpents came slithering out into full view to glide swiftly down every arm. The baron stared in horror at their coilings, and then up into the cowls at a row of calm, confident faces—and then fangs struck, and struck, and struck.

The baron swallowed—it was almost a sob—as tongues flickered and serpentine heads turned to fix him with glittering eyes. The venom was a burning, surging numbness in his veins. . . .

The figures drew back in unison, their sleeves falling to hide the snakes within, and the Priest of the Serpent strode forward to stand over the master of Ornentar Castle.

As the shadow of that dark cowl fell upon him, Eldagh Ornentar looked up in horror and gasped, "Poison! I—I live only at your whim!"

The priest pulled back his cowl to let the baron see the smile on his scaly serpent-face. "That's right," he said triumphantly, his voice seeming to echo down from impossible heights as darkness surged and spun, and Eldagh Ornentar's world whirled away. . . .

The scene in the mirror faded with the fainting of its baron—and a moment later, the mirror itself seemed to melt and run, losing its shape and slumping in midair like a fistful of icicles dripping floorward.

Horrified, the Baron Loushoond stared up at the Serpent priestess. Her smile was broader now.

Suddenly the ruin of the mirror undulated towards him, like a glass snake swimming through the air. Something as cold as he'd ever felt slapped around his wrist, and his sword clattered from his hand. Loushoond snarled a wordless oath and struggled to heave himself up out of his chair—but by then the glass that had been a mirror and before that a sphere had now become shackles, clamping him into the seat, and the priestess had let her robe fall to the floor and come striding right at him, moving fast.

"By the Three—!" he gasped, voice rising in sudden, real fear.

"They watch, to be sure," she purred, eyes shining in triumph as she lowered her lips to his, "but I'm afraid that's about all they do."

Fingers like iron drove into his cheeks, forcing his jaws wide as her mouth descended—and from out of its warm depths glided a small green serpent, its eyes glittering at him in a tiny triumph of its own, fangs parting. . . .

In Loushoond's last, gurgling moments, he was dimly aware that he was choking on the thing as it wriggled right down his gullet, and that a warm body was pressing against his, and that there wasn't anything he could do to avoid joining Ornentar. . . .

6

Paved with Stones Enchanted

They'd stumbled away from Indraevyn for hours before finding it: a green hill in the endless forest, a huge clearing in woods furnished with very few open spaces. Embra had declared it ideal, but her three companions had squinted and sniffed their ways around it suspiciously, as if they expected cave mouths to yawn open in it without warning, or the entire hill rear up and be revealed as the armored back of a wakened dragon. The lady sorceress had stood watching them with her arms folded and a sympathetic smile on her face as they searched, never uttering an impatient word as the time passed, and the three men shook their heads and growled and announced in their various ways that they could find nothing wrong with it—but that it certainly didn't *feel* right!

Yet time passed without alarm or attack, and Craer circled the clearing well out in the trees and found nothing of menace, and at last they gathered by Embra's tree and admitted with varying degrees of gruffness that there seemed to be nothing amiss with the place. Nothing but a feeling of being . . . watched.

"We're in the Loaurimm, gentlesirs," the Lady Silvertree reminded them gently. "It's alive, crawling with more creatures than ever carried sword for my father, or marched in Blackgult's army. There must be dozens of little eyes on us right now. Yet I see a shortage of bowmen and wizards, and am content. Let this be the place, and let the time be now."

She spread her arms in a gesture that urged them back into the trees, and stepped forward alone onto the mossy flanks of the hill, asking over her shoulder as she went, "Are we clear on this? Sarasper covered all?"

"Aye," Craer and Hawkril admitted reluctantly, more or less in unison.

"We know what to do," Craer added, and they saw her nod as she reached the crown of the hill, just before she closed her eyes and turned to face west, towards Aglirta.

The procurer leaned close to Sarasper and murmured, "I *am* clear on what we're to do, but I'd like to know this: just how much magic—besides healing; I mean spells, like Embra's castings—do you know, anyway?"

The old healer thrust his head close, so they stared at each other with noses almost touching. "Enough to know I shouldn't be meddling with such," he muttered darkly. "I wish a few more young and eager wizards would achieve the same knowledge." Then he stalked away around the edge of the clearing, waving at Craer to take up his own position.

From across the open space Hawkril cast the moving men a glance. His sword was in his hand, and his eyes seldom strayed from the trees around the hill. He seemed as tense as a hound straining on a leash, aching to explode into battle, as the three men of the Four took up positions equidistant around the clearing.

No foe came. Embra knelt, chanting something, set the Dwaer-Stone between her feet, and rose slowly, hands moving in intricate, air-weaving gestures. Then she spread her arms, fingers down, with the air of a contented crafter finishing a long task.

Silent white fire sped out from each fingertip, to strike the ground and cling, sputtering without scorching. Embra closed her eyes again and seemed to shudder, tilting her head slowly back until her face was upturned to the sky. Pulses of brighter fire traveled down the lines of light to the ground and back up again, washes of radiance that seemed to wink back off the trees around and set up a gentle rustling of leaves.

Sarasper watched, eyes narrowing, and waved one hand until he caught Hawkril's attention. He frowned and pointed at the armaragor's blade in reminder; the hulking warrior nodded slowly. Satisfied, Sarasper slowly lifted his hand, ready to signal. What they'd agreed to do would weaken them very swiftly—they'd have no time to spare, and all too little extra ere their endurance ran out, so things had to be just right. . . .

The Stone had to be removed from the magic, to prevent it—and thus this place—being traced by anyone with a Stone that Embra might happen to "see." And that would leave this washing white fire with only one place to take energy from . . . a healer, an armaragor, and a procurer. There was a rude old rhyme about such a trio, but the Three cast down if he could remember it now. . . .

In a slow, grand sweep of fire-wreathed motion, the Lady of Jewels floated up into the air, arching over backwards as she rose, until she was perhaps twice the height of a tall man off the ground, flat on her back with her arms spread, linked to the ground beneath by a web of restlessly silent magical flames.

Sarasper's hand swept down. "Now," he growled, not knowing if either Craer or Hawkril were close enough to really hear him. "Just as I showed you, mind."

Hawkril thrust his drawn sword carefully into the soil behind him, leaving it standing upright like a sentinel, and strode forward, up the hill. As he reached the steep part of its slope, he crouched forward until he was almost advancing on all fours.

Fires snarled and dipped towards him, whirling near his head and shoulders, and their light flashed back from sweat glistening on the armaragor's face.

Hawkril Anharu, Sarasper realized suddenly, was terrified. Well, he wasn't exactly cheerful himself just now. Both he and Craer had thrust their hands into nearby streams of magical fire—and were staggering.

It was like trying to walk into a flood of water racing the other way, an endless, tireless stream that dealt no pain, but sucked life out of one with every step. . . .

The fires were surging through and around them both now, taking energy at every ebb. Sarasper vaguely became aware that he was staggering sideways with slow, aimless steps, like a drunken man, the hair all over him standing on end and dancing in time with the pulses of the spell's fire. . . .

Hawkril had grimly crawled through flames that seemed to reach for him and rake at his face and arms and armor—which seemed to be growing hot, judging by the smell and the redness and creases of pain on the armaragor's face. Yet as Sarasper watched, the armaragor's hand was steady as it reached out with no trace of hesitation or fear, to close around the humming, glowing Stone of Life, from whence silent fire was roaring up in a column to Embra's body, and thence from her fingers to the ground—and to two fools staggering around the edges of the hilltop.

He and Craer were facing each other now, driven by instinct to balance the flows of fire between them. The little man's face was as dripping as Hawkril's, and his hands were trembling, but his flesh was as pale as bone. Sarasper swallowed and tore his gaze away, back up to Embra hanging unseeing in the sky above them, her body trembling in the flames of her own making. Gods, but they'd all die if this went on too long. . . .

Hawkril was crawling back down the hill now, not quite daring to turn around, the Dwaer firmly clutched to his chest. The surges of fire were growing swifter now, and deeper, draining more as they fed on Sarasper and Craer, as if knowing the Stone would soon be lost to them.

Fire washed over his eyes, dazing him, and rolled away again. Dimly Sarasper became aware that he'd fallen to his knees. Embra's spread-eagled form was rippling, as if blown in a gusty breeze, mere feet off the hilltop now; Craer must have fallen to the ground.

From where he was, the trembling healer could just see Hawkril's slowly moving body back up against his own sword. The armaragor sat against the steel as if in a chair, threw back his head and gasped for what seemed like an eternity—and then crawled around the blade to its far side.

Fire sprang back as if severed, howling in soundless rage through Sarasper until he was blinded, his eyes full of white flame that did not sear, but stole his breath, his strength, his . . . everything. . . .

On his left, leaves—deep, many-clustered, and green, with faint birdcalls in the distance. On his left, sky—blue and cloudless. Beneath him, soft earth with its damp smell of old leaves, decay, mushrooms, and little shoots—accompanied, somewhere under his spine, by a few very hard roots or rocks.

Hawkril groaned. His insides felt weak and empty, as if someone had slit him open and spilled all his strength away. It took three heaving, snarling attempts before he made it up onto one elbow, panting like a man who's run for miles, and looked around.

His rising had spilled the Stone onto the ground; he caught it out of habit before it could roll away, his eyes seeking but one thing: Embra.

The lady he was, gods help him, coming to love. More than his own skin, more than Craer's friendship, more than the beauties of Aglirta. For all her waspish tongue and unhesitating use of her sorcery to rule him . . . by the Three, but she was beautiful! When she looked at him—

She was staring at the sky right now, her unseeing eyes a cloudy gray. She lay on her back on the crest of the hill. . . . She was lying very still. Sudden fear for her had Hawkril scooping up the Stone and trying to scramble up the hillside without even sparing time to frame an oath.

He fell on his face, the world going very dim around him. What was *wrong* with him?

Her magic. Her magic must have drained him as well as Craer and Sarasper. They were huddled on the hilltop too, as motionless as a couple of rocks, white and sweat-soaked faces staring at nothing.

Hawkril swallowed, set his teeth, and crawled up the hill, cradling the Stone awkwardly as he went. His arms felt like hollow things, bending like flower stalks, and he was shuddering. If she was dead . . .

He forced himself not to think of that, to dwell instead on the cursed pain each reaching and clawing motion brought him, each . . .

He'd reached her, he was looming over her now. She lay so still, not breathing, her eyes two burnt-out candles.

"Lady," he whispered, setting the Stone carefully on her breast. "Oh, lass, live!" Gently he drew one of her hands up to her throat, and curled its fingers around the stone, and then did the same with the other, not for the life of him knowing what he'd do if nothing happened.

A tiny white flicker of cold flame stirred around the Dwaer, seeming to rise from her throat beneath it. A throat that rippled as her breast slowly— oh, so slowly—began to rise and fall. Three be praised!

He held her hands cradled around the Stone, a strange creeping, prickling feeling stealing up his arms. "Oh, lass," he growled, "come back to me!"

Dark blue eyes flickered open and fastened on his. Tears welled up in them, her hands clung to his arms and a sudden shudder went through her, like a dog shaking itself, and then she was gasping, "Hawk!"

Her eyes drew him down. Hawkril's lips closed on hers before he quite thought about what he was doing. Their mouths met and melted together. Her tongue brushed his mouth in a caress, and she moaned under him. Moaned and then moved under him, eager—

—to throw him off. Hawkril's heart plunged as those slender hands shoved at him. As he sat back, world suddenly grim, he admitted it to himself; aye, he was smitten.

"Later," the Lady Embra gasped impatiently up into his forlorn face, shaking free of his grasp. "We're in danger here!"

"Lass?" he asked, looking wildly about and then back to where his sword stood.

"Help me," she hissed, climbing up him with fingers as hard as claws in her haste, until she was tottering on her feet, her pelvis against his head, clutching at his shoulders for support. "Get me to Sarasper," she moaned, trying to shake the armaragor.

She might have been the wind trying to shift a boulder, but after a moment he rose ponderously to his feet—and swayed.

Fear rose into her throat, both for him and for herself—if he fell on her and crushed her, who would come to her aid? What could save them all? Wh—

Strong arms plucked at her shoulders, cradling them, and the familiar deep voice that she could feel as much as hear, with their bodies pressed together, rumbled, "Hold to me, lass—haste it is!"

And the world whirled crazily and she was being set down lightly beside the sprawled, blankly staring body of the old healer. She knelt in haste, the Stone of Life pulsing as she held it out and down to touch a wrinkled, age-spotted hand.

Sarasper's grizzled jaw hung slack, and he looked very dead. The Dwaer flashed almost angrily as it touched him, and Embra found herself suddenly close to tears. They'd have given their lives for this, these three trusting men . . . the first three men she'd ever dared trust.

Only three. Some might never muster that many trusted friends in their lives, but it did not seem so large a host that she could afford to lose any of them. Dark misgivings rose within her in the moments before the healer groaned, threw up a feeble hand to wave away the world, and muttered, "Gods, what was I drinking?"

She and Hawkril exchanged a startled glance. It was enough to send them both into helpless sniggering laughter, bowed over and shouting mirth until the tears came.

"I don't find it all *that* funny," Sarasper grunted somewhere in the middle of it, in just the tones necessary to set them going all over again. Thus it was some time before Embra found herself bending over the crumpled body of the procurer, and losing all laughter in fresh foreboding. Gods, but he looked so *small*. Could such a body, whatever its sardonic spirit, have survived the draining? Could—

Craer coughed the instant the Stone touched him, grimaced, and then mumbled to the world, "No more hurling spells for me!"

"He's awake," Hawkril growled, waving his retrieved warsword above their heads in a flourish of relief. "Now tell us why all the haste, lass! *What* danger?"

Embra looked up at him with eyes that were large and grave, and then met the gazes of the others. "Well," she said, drawing in a deep breath, "the magic worked, but I could sense only one other Stone—because it's so close to us that it almost blinded and overwhelmed me!"

"How close would that be?" Sarasper asked, his eyes narrowing.

Embra shrugged. "About a mile or so . . . no more."

"No more cold courtesy, I pray. Well met, sirs," the Tersept of Sart said briskly, as they touched palms together. He swept out his arm in a gesture that bade them sit in the tall, arch-backed chairs drawn up like proud swordguards around a large and gleaming table. Its ornate carving and the small and shining forest of decanters and goblets it held shouted the wealth of Sart to any eye that beheld it and the darkly splendid ranks of highboards, tallchests, and great orlors that loomed along the walls behind it. "Pray take wine, and eat. We have no care here for spilled food, nor ceremony—eat, drink, and be at home!"

"If I was at home," a man with dark and scowling brows and a hard-weathered face replied bluntly, "I'd feel a lot safer than I do right now and right here. How do we know that the king's wizards aren't listening to our every word?"

"The wizards of Sart hired to prevent just that tell me so," the tersept replied smoothly, "and assure me further that they far outstrip, in both numbers and puissance, the few bonfire-wizards who serve the River Throne. No less a warband than the feared Swords of Sirlptar defend our gates from hiding, behind the guards you saw. Be at ease, my Lord Factor."

"Oh?" The Factor of Gilth's tone was derisive, but he was lowering himself into one of the grandest seats and reaching for a goblet as he spoke. "The Lady of Jewels is a bonfire-wizard now, is she?"

"And if they call her so, what says that for their judgement?" asked a Sirl agent whose dark green silks, adorned with dozens of filigreed gold medallions, looked as if they cost more than six such tables. As he sat and reached for wine, he chimed where the others rustled.

"So far as we can tell," the tersept told his own goblet as he reached for a decanter and nodded to the three Factors of Sirlptar to take seats of their own, "the Silvertree sorceress has left Flowfoam with her three lovers on some private mission for the king. Some at court whisper it has to do with slaying the Serpent—who's also said to be Risen, though Snake-priests have been saying that ever since I was old enough to talk—while others say the Band of Four is off to find the treasury of fallen Blackgult, to fund the River Throne in buying an army to subdue us all."

"*That* I believe," said Daragus of Gilth. "If Silvertree seized it ere he died, and his mages failed to make off with it ere they perished, his daughter is best suited of all in Aglirta to be its retriever."

"We know Silvertree's dead?" the tallest of the Sirl agents asked, raising an eyebrow. "His body's not been found."

"Nor," one of his fellows—the shortest and most stout, a bearded man in red velvet adorned with cords and tassels of gold—pointed out, "have those of his wizards."

Daragus shrugged and spread hands that gleamed with many massive gold rings. "The months pass, and there's no sign of any of them."

"Might I remind you," the factor in green responded, "that wizards can change their faces and all, far more easily than most men?"

Daragus gave him a sour look. "And might I remind *you*, Factor Phelodiir, that fireside tales are one thing, and what wizards actually take the trouble to *do,* day by day in the real Aglirta, is quite another. It costs trouble and coin and the stuff of life to cast spells, and more to maintain them. Why bother? If you've magic enough to spare some to spin such a spell, you've enough to see no need for hiding. Act openly, and blast down all who come riding to do you harm—that's the wizards' way."

"What thickheaded mages you've met with, I must say," the tall factor said to that, shaking his head.

"Gentlesirs, gentlesirs," the Tersept of Sart said in swift and slightly overloud soothing, "let our brawl be where it truly lies, with the so-called Risen King, and not with each other. We all stand in the same peril because of him. We all face the loss of our freedom, because of him. The Snake-priests connive and stab with poisoned blades up and down the Vale . . . because of him."

"Glarsimber," the Factor of Gilth growled, "spare us the grand speech. Only fools and tyrants expect rivals—and let's be blunt, that's what we are—to speak with one voice, in sweet accord, in the first instant they catch sight of a common foe. Fireside tales again."

"Has he really demanded that all baronies and towns surrender their armies to him?" the bearded factor asked. "What were his words, exactly?"

"He wants to be 'recrowned,' Carthel, and have us all swear oaths to him," Daragus of Gilth replied in a near-snarl. "Whereupon he'll promptly issue orders to all who serve any of us, bidding these swords be here and those lances hie themselves *there* . . . well away from we who whelmed and trained them. He need not speak plainly to make his intentions and destination clear. Not a—"

"Wait a bit, wait a bit," Factor Phelodiir interrupted. "Nothing of this is news to any here. My Lord of Sart, there's more riding you than this—I could tell so when you called for this conclave, and I can see it waiting in your eyes right now . . . and more than that: waiting impatiently. What news?"

The Tersept of Sart, aware that he had the full attention of his guests for the first time since inviting them to sit, unhurriedly selected a decanter, held it up to the light to gaze at its contents critically, and poured.

Into the silence the Lord of Sart was building, Factor Carthel murmured, " 'Tis true. I can see it in him now, itching to be free. Speak, Belklarravus."

Tersept Glarsimber Belklarravus of Sart looked up over his glass at the four factors—his old rival Daragus and the three from Sirlptar: Phelodiir, Carthel, and the tall one . . . Telabras, that was his name, yes—and found rage rising in him once more, just as it had when he'd first heard the news. He set down his glass so they wouldn't see his hand tremble, knowing he could do nothing about the redness that must now be washing across his face, and said crisply, "I have discovered from a source at court whose words I've learned to trust—"

"Tell us who that might be," Daragus growled, "for if he's truly a trustworthy courtier, he's the first!"

Belklarravus almost shouted in fury at the interruption, but the urge passed in an instant, and he found himself glad of the moments of dry chuckles around the table that let him regain some calm.

When silence had fallen once more, he gave them all a thin-lipped smile and began again. "I've discovered from a source at court whose words I've learned to trust that the king is going to restore the barony of Brightpennant, stripping Sart and Gilth of our standing as independent towns."

"Towns that would lose their tersepts," Telabras murmured. "Wherefore you are determined to prevent this at all costs."

"I—exactly," the Lord of Sart sputtered, finding the words he'd just been about to say spoken for him. "Gentlesirs, the Vale must be rid of the Risen King!"

Excitement made his words rise into what was almost a shout, and they rang back echoes from the decanters as his guests sat silent, nodding, before Phelodiir of Sirlptar said mildly, "Well, that's certainly an aim clear enough to keep us from charges of 'sly intrigue.' If we're to talk treason, we'd best have something useful to say; 'twould be a pity to be drawn boneless and spitted in the sun to die for empty words."

"Then let us be done with empty courtesies and disputes both," Daragus said fiercely, "and speak! Let us begin thus: the rise of an Aglirta ruled by a strong king can't help but be a real threat to the present prosperity and independence of all of us. Agreed?"

There were nods around the table. The Tersept of Sart opened his mouth to take control of the converse once more, but the Factor of Gilth snapped, "A moment more, my Lord. Before we begin the wild scheming, let us consider the players in this game. Barons and tersepts up and down the Vale sit in the same chairs we do: hating to give up their sway and the swords who obey them, and not quite daring to openly say so or defy Flowfoam. All of them are waiting for a chance to somehow come that will free them of having to submit to Snowsar; if we give them one, they'll take it."

"And plunge the Vale back into bloodshed," Telabras muttered.

"Undoubtedly," Daragus said quickly, "but let us not stray down such ways yet. The other traditional players are the wizards, who are of three sorts: those too puny to matter, those not strong enough to stand alone and so standing beside this baron or that tersept, and the few of real power who survived the slaying spells of Silvertree's Dark Three."

"Those would be Tharlorn of the Thunders and Bodemmon Sarr," the Lord of Sart put in, "plus Embra Silvertree and any of the Three who yet live."

"Oh, but—" Carthel began to protest, but was interrupted by the Factor of Gilth.

"Grant that one or more of them *may* still live," Daragus said fiercely, "and consider with them any outlander or other hidden mage who might stand forth, and move on to the players we're not so used to: the Serpent-folk and the Faceless."

"More empty legend!" Phelodiir spat. "Now who's dealing in fireside tales?"

The Factor of Gilth gave the man in green silks a cold look. "Consider, then, any who wield a Dwaer-Stone, whether they be Koglaur or not, to stand as this last group of players. Consider also that we know not the real powers of the Dwaerindim, but that they're quite possibly great enough to win the realm for whoever can wield most of them."

"Seize Aglirta with an enchanted stone one can hold in one's hand?" the Lord of Sart scoffed. "Hold back a little harder on your drinking now, Daragus!"

"Reports out of Indraevyn," the Factor of Gilth snapped, "vary wildly, but all agree that buildings were shattered and wizards—several at least—slain in the time it takes a man to draw a few breaths. Wizards with spells to defend themselves, standing ready in known danger, mind. Now see such a Stone in the hand of a man placed where he can blast an army on a road, or a wizard caught unawares . . . hmm?"

"You talk sense," Factor Telabras agreed quietly. "What's your measure of the Snake-priests?"

"Worse tyrants than the king," Daragus said promptly, "hence unattractive as allies—but if their power grows apace, perhaps deadly to retain as foes, or defy for too long."

"Well, your words certainly cheer me immensely," Phelodiir of Sirlptar said sarcastically. "I grant that you've identified the players facing us quite well—but I heard no indication of a shining road to victory in what you've said. Surely you have a plan in mind."

"No, Factor, I do not," Daragus said flatly. "Half-considered dreamers' schemes for Aglirta are in part what has given us far too many years of warring barons, and let wizards become the tyrants of whim we know them as. I see no clear leader for the Vale, and no one likely to win, save perhaps the Serpent-priests—only as lurkers who survive to pick up the shards after we've torn each other apart, and not victors on battlefields or in the hearts of Aglirtans."

"So we've talked and talked," Carthel of Sirlptar said heavily, "and stand now just where we did when we first crossed the threshold of our good Lord of Sart: troubled by the state of the Vale, resolved to strike down the grasping reach of the king—and with not a step along that road agreed upon among us. So, my Lords, we're still just where we've all spent tens of years: watching the Vale torn apart by one dispute after another, while we dream of what might be, and watch our own coin and power slip away. . . ."

"I have no great scheme," Daragus told the others. "I came here hoping the Lord of Sart had one. I find myself too unsure of the real power of the king—and wanting to see what befalls when a baron defies him. Then, perhaps, we'll know if a lion rules us, or an empty voice, or someone who can call down lightnings out of the legends that spawned him."

"Too early to declare ourselves, yes," Phelodiir agreed, "but far from too early to make preparations. . . . We should agree on something, Lords, or all our time and daring is wasted."

"Well, then," the Tersept of Sart said, leaning forward. "Let it be thus: we agree, here and now, on another meeting—and between that day and this, we craft such schemes as seem to us to have merit, to share with each other at that moot. In the meantime, any royal herald, envoy, or messenger who comes to Sart with a hand-count or less of bodyguards will, I fear, vanish; the turmoil created by the king's own decrees and lack of law-swords has made road-brigands *so* bad of late. I can hardly credit that the rest of the Vale—Gilth, for example, and even Sirlptar—might be much safer. So many folk of Aglirta, after all, fear the fingers of a king they barely know. . . ."

The three Sirl men chuckled as one. "Silken words as sharp as a sword," Telabras murmured, "and as sweet as good minstrelry. Where shall we meet, then?"

"Sirlptar," Daragus of Gilth said promptly. "Gathering there evokes the least suspicions—and I'm sure three of us at this table have power to spare, to make the meeting-place secure against royal prying. That leaves 'when.' "

Phelodiir of Sirlptar looked at their host with his brows raised in silent query, collected a silent nod from the Tersept of Sart, and said, "Well, then, let it be a month hence, the night *before* the Feast of Dragonfall, on the upper floor—I'll see that rooms are held—of the Windmark Wyrm inn, on Semble Street. That's just below the Tower of Lanterns, on the seaward side, nigh Orthil's Spoon."

"I know it," the Factor of Gilth said, setting down his goblet. "We're agreed, then?"

Their host nodded, and said formally, "Let us part. Be welcome again in this house."

"You truly mean that?" Factor Carthel murmured, as they rose in unison.

The Tersept of Sart regarded him for a moment, unsmiling, and then said calmly, "No. No, I don't."

"No." The wizard lifted a face adrip with sweat and murmured, "No, they left no magic behind, Lord."

The Tersept of Sart nodded and snapped, "Leave us."

After the scrape of the old mage's crutch had been replaced by the deep thud of the entry door closing, the tersept went to the window. The Factors of Sirl and their twoscore clerks and bodyguards astride their magnificent matching mounts were just trotting out of the gate amid their own dust. He watched them dwindle out of sight along the river road before asking the empty air, "You heard?"

A large and dusty chased metal bowl stood atop one of the dark, glossy highboards along the back wall of the room. Something rose out of it, upwards in silence without wings or hands to lift it.

It was a severed human head that had left its body long enough ago that the flesh cloaking the skull was gray and mold-mottled . . . but not so long ago that the jaw had fallen away. A thin line of drool was spilling from that sagging jawbone as the head turned towards the Tersept of Sart, the light of fell, cold life glowing in its eyesockets. The jaw worked for a moment before tightening into a smile. "Yes," the skull hissed. "More than enough."

The tersept nodded, not knowing what more to say. He'd feared the Spellmaster of Silvertree when Ingryl Ambelter had been alive and whole and in distant Silvertree; he feared this head, floating mere feet from him right now, infinitely more. It flew to and from the ruins of Indraevyn, somewhere in the forest east of Silvertree, with apparent ease and swifter than any falcon—and it seemed to be able to wield magic at will.

The dry, rasping voice of the Spellmaster's skull sounded again, a little closer to him. "When you do attend that meeting in Sirlptar," it advised, "try not to act unsurprised when all of you seem to have hit upon almost exactly the same plan."

Tersept Glarsimber Belklarravus did not look at the gray head as it drifted nearer, its smile broadening. Icy fear was tightening clutching fingers around his heart, and he was too busy trembling uncontrollably. . . .

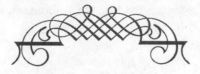

7

Battles and Bodies

*H*awkril looked around at every tree as if it was a foe glaring at him with sword drawn. "Did the spell not say what direction this Stone lay in?"

"No," Embra said shortly, "it did not. 'Twas like a blinding light, overwhelming my sight."

Bristling brows drew together in a frown. "So we almost died . . . for nothing."

The sorceress let out a long sigh, and sat down on the mossy hillside. By the Three, but she was weary. "You could say that," she admitted. "On the other hand, it tells us we're very close to a Stone we seek—and almost certainly that an enemy of the realm is near, for I can't believe any of the Dwaerindim remain unclaimed, or that anyone now holding one, after all this strife, will be a friend of the king . . . or anyone who stands in their way."

The armaragor nodded as curtly as if she'd rebuked him, stamped his feet, hefted the blade in his hand, and strode a few steps away before wheeling and tramping back.

Embra made no move to rise, despite Hawkril's obvious restlessness and the feeling of tension that hung over the hill. The Stone throbbed in her hands, yet she could tell from the faces of her companions that they felt just as she did—dazed or brain-mazed, like a wizard who's hurled spells half a day without rest.

Hawkril gave the trees another suspicious glance, turning on his heel to look around in all directions, and asked slowly, "Do all spells drink that much life, to cast?"

The Lady Silvertree shrugged. "Many take far more; that one was mild, for I crafted it with the Stone, and sourced it in you three only after it was begun."

The armaragor frowned. "The spell: just what was it?"

"A mistake," Embra replied crisply. "Hush, now," she added, pointing. "Craer's heard something."

The procurer was crouched beneath the leaves of the nearest tree, head low to the ground, hand raised to give a signal. He'd been poised thus for a long time, as Sarasper moved slowly along the hillside to look and listen in another direction. There was something about this hill that made for uneasiness; there seemed to be a watchfulness, a tension in the air. Perhaps some foe was standing right behind them now, using a Dwaer-Stone to hide its true shape and seem a tree. Or perhaps—

Craer's arm swept down. An instant later, the procurer was whirling around and sprinting up the hill, shouting, "Longfangs! Big as a horse— bigger!"

"Where?" Hawkril growled, as his friend raced past him. The armaragor was staring hard at where Craer had stood. The procurer had set branches whipping and dancing in his haste to be elsewhere. Those branches dipped, rose, rustled—and flew aside as the hunting beast burst forth from them, trailing a cloud of torn and shredded leaves.

"Wolf-spider," some called it for its looks, though it was neither of those things. Its many limbs moved like a spider's legs, but it had fur and a wolf's head with dripping jaws as wide as a doorway.

This one was twice as big as Sarasper when he took the longfangs-shape, and its shaggy gray shoulders were thrice as large across as Hawkril's. Bulging gray-furred muscles rippled along its back and neck as it came on in an uncannily quiet charge—for all the world as if it was drifting over the ground rather than touching it, like an arrow flying slow enough to watch, yet terrifyingly too fast to outrun.

Hawkril growled, set his feet, and held his warsword low and behind him in both hands, swinging it back and forth and humming wordlessly as he waited for the beast to charge up to where he could cleave it. Craer had spun about, panting, and was snatching out the daggers he had strapped to himself here, there, and everywhere, until he held three splayed in one hand and a fourth ready to throw in the other.

The eyes of the longfangs were cold, white points of death, not the golden blaze they should have been, and Embra was already crying a warning to Sarasper to make ready for magic as the monster stormed up the hill and hurled itself on Hawkril.

Strangely, it made no attempt to avoid his blade, but took a mighty slash that shortened two of its legs and laid open its breastbone without slowing or flinching—and bowled the armored warrior over, blade and all. Hot black blood drenched Hawkril and smoked on the moss as the long-fangs clutched him and rolled over and over, trying to bite its way through his armor.

Craer sprang after it, driving home one dagger hilt-deep and using it as a handle to reach the beast's neck, where he clung desperately, unable to reach the eye he wanted to sink his second fang into. As he dug his fingers into reeking fur and set his teeth amid a din of gnawing and roaring, he shouted aloud what he was thinking, " 'Tis as if this beast doesn't know *how* to be a longfangs!"

"It's . . . doing . . . well enough," Hawkril snarled from somewhere beneath it, panting under the weight that buffeted him.

Embra had murmured something over the Stone and then stepped back to watch the results.

Bone teeth shaped like giant rose-thorns jut from the joints of all but two of a longfang's limbs; those two bare forelimbs end in little snapping jaws. This longfangs was so large that its "little" limbjaws were larger than Craer's head—and one of those limbs was now reaching back past the beast's head to snap at the man clinging to the back of its neck.

Craer shrank away, wincing and stabbing at those thrusting jaws with his dagger. Growls told him that Hawkril was straining to do something below, and Sarasper darted past with blade drawn, heading for the beast's rear, but the procurer hadn't time to see more: the second limbjaws was reaching for him! The longfangs, it seemed, was at least momentarily aban-doning its attempt to eat through Hawkril's armor in favor of removing the stabbing annoyance from its back.

Ducking frantically away from swooping fangs, Craer felt a burning pain and wetness as a tooth laid open his forearm, peeling back his worn leathers as if they were made of mist. He twisted away from those jaws and then saw the other limb rearing back, teeth gnashing and biting the air before diving down at him like a gleaming battering ram. . . .

He wasn't going to be able to avoid them, he was going to be—

In the last moments before striking, those jaws gaped wide—impossibly wide. The teeth were growing, curling inwards as they lengthened with blinding speed. What was happening? What could—

The limbjaws bit down. Teeth clashed together inches in front of his face, and jammed. They were caught on each other in a tangle that grew thicker as Craer watched . . . and the teeth continued to grow.

The longfangs gave the world a startled roar and shook its limbjaws. When that helped not at all, it struck the entangled jaws against each other in mounting fury and frustration, trying to strike off whatever was binding them half-shut. Their glistening forests of fangs were two wild tangles now, both limbjaws growing shut—but the head of the longfangs, with its own larger snarling, drooling maw of fangs, was unaffected.

Fear and frustration joined rage in the beast's roaring; in the midst of the squalling tumult, Craer heard Embra laugh triumphantly, and knew who'd saved his hide. The longfangs reared up, like a mountain suddenly deciding to touch the clouds, and then plunged its head down to bite, tumbling the procurer helplessly off.

He was still bouncing and rolling through his own cloud of moss, still clinging desperately to his dagger-hilt and being dragged along the hillside as the beast's head swung, as he heard Hawkril curse weakly from somewhere beneath it—growled words that ended in a wet gurgling.

"Hawk?" the procurer called, kicking himself back onto the shaggy neck and then ducking low down its far side to avoid being clubbed by the furiously flailing limbjaws. The fur glistened dark red in more than one place, and Craer heard Sarasper make the sort of grunt that meant the healer had swung his sword hard, and it had struck something that nearly numbed his hands. Craer snatched out another of his daggers, twisting himself almost into a ball on the neck that was rearing up again, and shouted, "Hawk!"

Somewhere under the furry, heaving bulk, the armaragor groaned. Craer drove the dagger he wasn't clinging to deep into the fur beside him, struck a bone fairly deep inside, and watched black blood gush forth, burning his hand before he could get his blade free. His friend was hurt, and—

Something struck Craer so hard that his eyes saw only darkness slashed across with a scattering of winking stars before the world rushed, swimming, back. He blinked away enough tears to see something large and dark moving above him before he was smashed again, a blow so hard that his teeth rattled as he was torn free from his dagger and hurled away, propelled by a furry forelimb that broke a rib in the doing.

Pain stabbed at his right side, a searing that flared fiercer when he landed, skidding through yielding moss until he came to a sneezing stop, chin to the damp earth halfway down the hillside.

Embra was shouting something, her voice high with fear and urgency, and from behind him came the horrible cracking and gnawing noise of the longfangs biting on something, like a dog with a bone, that was slow to yield under its jaws. Hawkril's armor, no doubt.

Craer scrambled to his feet, wincing—oh, to be sure, a rib or worse was broken—doubled over to hiss out a long curse and set his teeth to face what he'd what he'd have to do next, and took one of his long knives from his boots. The longfangs was throwing back its head to tear something apart, and for one heart-stopping moment Craer thought it was one of Hawkril's legs. Then he saw the tatters of cloth and mangled metal, and knew it was just a leg of the armaragor's prized armor, with no flesh inside it.

Hawkril lay sprawled and bloody, staring unmoving at the sky, beneath the wolf-spider. "Three preserve!" Craer gasped, breaking into a ragged, desperate run.

Embra's hands were spread, a winking wash of light arcing between them as her latest magic faded. Whatever it had been, the longfangs didn't seem bothered—and as he ran, Craer saw her dart in under its descending head and offer herself to those hungry jaws, to keep it from biting open Hawkril's defenseless body. Sarasper was crouched a little ways off, feverishly plucking small items from within his clothing and spilling them out on the ground in front of him. He was seeking what he needed to weave a spell—but would he be in time?

Craer knew a certain sprinting procurer wouldn't be—even if a thin, foot-long knife could somehow stop this man-eater at a touch.

The longfangs bit down. Embra skipped aside, leading its reaching head to one side, away from the pinned and senseless armaragor. "Gods," Craer gasped, "deliver us from this—this *thing*!"

He left the Three no time to answer his prayer before he charged to the longfang's neck and sank the steel fang in his hand hilt-deep. The thing roared in pain, almost deafening him, and swung its head wildly back his way. But he was in behind its jaws, right against the heaving side of its head, and there he danced, moving with it so it could never turn to reach him, hacking and stabbing.

Hawkril was being trampled beneath his boots. Sudden rage rose to clutch at his throat and make him shout. Craer stabbed and stabbed until sweat was almost blinding him, and the pain in his side was making him sob. He pummeled the beast with his fist whenever he could, circling with the longfangs as it left the sprawled armaragor behind, smashed a gasping Embra aside, and tried to slap down the little dancing man who was stinging it again and again. . . .

Kneeling not far away, Sarasper Codelmer found the three tiny figurines he was seeking: the last handful of the enchanted fripperies he'd taken from the Silent House. Scooping two of them back into his belt pouch, he snatched a scrap of ribbon he'd found earlier from his lips and bound it around the statuette with trembling fingers, eyeing the looming wolf-spider as furry limbs crashed down very near.

All of the Four had once licked the ribbon at his insistence, leaving behind traces of themselves. The Horned Lady willing, he should now, by a spell he thought he remembered wholly, be able to snatch the king's most pressingly imperiled—and not so mighty after all, by the Three—heroes away from this beast of the backlands, across miles upon miles of Aglirta in the blink of an eye, to his favorite chamber in the Silent House. His longtime lair in his own time hiding in longfangs shape. Sarasper smiled grimly at that thought as he raised the statuette and murmured an incantation that seemed to flow into his mind from some comfortable corner of memory as if it had been just waiting to burst forth behind a door he'd kept locked for too long.

Sudden warmth surged through Sarasper, a prickling flood running up his arms and across his face, radiance leaking like sparks from his eyes and mouth as it reached up and *out.* . . .

He hissed the last words of the magic and spread his arms, the better to let the spell flow forth. Its power surged and seared him, tugging at his insides, making him tremble on the dark edge of weak oblivion, the gently curving moss seeming to rise up to meet him. . . .

An instant before Sarasper's face ploughed into the earth, the world whirled through a sudden cloak-swirl of flashing light and utter darkness—and he was suddenly elsewhere, dank stone under his knees and dust pricking his nose in the instant before it struck cold stone and skidded painfully forward. As he turned his head to one side, eyes swimming, a gray bulk reared up in the ale-hued light of the familiar cavern, and a fresh roar of pain smote his ears. A bestial roar that almost drowned out Craer's softly gasped cursing.

He was back in the Silent House, and his companions with him. Unfortunately, his spell had somehow brought the longfangs along, too. . . .

Courtiers prefer to dwell in luxury. This demands sumptuous apartments, servants' quarters at a discreet remove, feast halls and other grand chambers, and a sufficiency of kitchens, pantries, and wine cellars. It does not demand, when the king they are there to obey, advise—and keep watch over—has not a strong count of warriors to call his own, miles upon miles of spider- and rat-roamed cold stone bunkrooms, armories, and corridors. Wherefore much of what had been the lower levels of Castle Silvertree before the return of the Risen King now lay dark and silent, behind doors that were never opened. Free of torches or lanterns and wary humans bearing them, abandoned to tiny, dark, beady-eyed creatures that scurry, and the patiently gliding snakes that hunt them.

In one such room, made gloomier than the passages around by still-splendid dark paneling, something suddenly appeared in the air.

Something round and grinning, which floated eerily in the air as it spun around, seeking foes that were not there to make menace.

It was a severed human head, gray and moldy flesh cloaking a skull whose eyesockets harbored the gleam of fell, cold life. "Well, well," it said, into the empty darkness. "Not the welcome a minstrel would have sung about. . . . but fitting, for horror come home again."

Its jaw worked in soundless laughter for a moment or two as it turned once more to survey the chamber, found what it sought on a high shelf, and glided thither.

Just as he'd left them: the never-finished, restless enchanted scepters of the mad mage Ladazzur of Arlund. Completing them had been one more project a busy Spellmaster hadn't ever been able to find time for. Ah, well. They never would be finished now.

The floating head of Ingryl Ambelter hovered above the two chased silver scepters and hissed a word that seemed to crawl through unpronounceability and out again. Green fire awakened in the crystals within those silver sheaths, winking and pulsing, and ran in two lines of cold fire the length of Ladazzur's slender, unfulfilled dreams.

The ghostly lights of the skull's eyes seemed to glow more brightly as it murmured something over the scepters—and then opened its jaws to accept the sudden rush of rising green flame that roared up from darkening, crumbling silver.

Green fire wreathed a laughing skull, scorching the ceiling, as the scepters collapsed into ash. Then Ingryl spun away from the wall and descended to the height off the floor that his head would have been in life.

There he hung as green fire faded into pale wisps of mist or smoke that tumbled out of the skull, streaming down to the floor, to coil there and ascend once more. For a long, silent time they rose and fell, streaming back and forth in a writhing column that slowly dwindled, seeming to coalesce into solidity here and there.

Solidity that spread, shaping shoulders and elbows, until a last wash of mist died away and a ghostly body hung beneath the skull. It took its first tentative steps, toeless feet scraping dusty flagstones, its legs churning formlessness for an instant. The skull dipped and then rose again as the body beneath it rose taller and darker.

Wraithlike mists cloaked the skull in skin that hid nothing of the mold-ravaged grayness beneath, the bared patches of bone, and the cold lights where eyes should have been.

Ingryl's new body shuddered, tottered as thickening weight shifted within it, and drew its first breath. He used it to sigh, loud and long, recalling his real, ravaged body, lying twisted and crumpled in a dark river cave atop the tangle of rocks and rusting blades and the many enchanted things that had kept him alive when he should have died.

Broken, rotted, and without hands or feet, one blasted away and the rest eaten by the cray-crabs and blood-eels of the Silverflow. Without a head now, too . . . history. He'd find that cavern again for its magics, when needful, but for now he had to make this new, spell-spun body truly alive and whole. For that he'd need to devour his own flesh: a cantle carefully hidden, long ago, in a vial of enchanted elixir not far from here in the castle cellars. Then it would be time to visit his onetime tutor, and gain the vitality he needed.

It would not do to be found now, still stumbling and vulnerable. Ingryl fought down his eagerness and forced his weak, clumsy beginnings of a new body to move slowly and carefully. His first act was to lean against the walls, in a corner where two came together, and his second was to force his essence slowly out to every fingertip of the trembling, shuddering form, making it truly his. Doors were waiting ahead that would only open to the touch of Ingryl Ambelter. To say nothing of the traps . . .

There was a smeared scattering of ash on the floor. Ingryl's lips tightened in a mirthless grin. So the baron had sent a hapless guardsman to try to break the spell-lock, and then had the remains dragged away. Again. Barons are such predictable, brutish idiots.

Ingryl kissed a stone door in a certain place, murmured a word that mattered and a slightly louder one that was nonsense, and laid his hand on the door in another certain place. The door melted away, and in the brief moments before it became solid again, the Spellmaster ducked through its frame into the curtains.

He hated their wet and waiting slime, but they were necessary: nets hung thickly with a curtain of little slithering slime-worms, pale and bulbous and with eternally twitching, questing ends, like giant maggots. His little slithering guardians, their slime harmless to him, but deadly to all others. Still alive after all this time, as patient and as deadly as their master.

Beyond was a small, dark stone chamber, its walls lined with shelves of battered old caskets. One held potions and spellbooks, all the rest skeletal things that would clutch and grab at anyone foolish enough to open them. In their midst stood a low table with a coffin on it—whose touch would dash lightnings through any hand but that of Ingryl. The Spellmaster wondered briefly if the baron had ever known who truly ruled Castle Silvertree, behind his back.

Not Ingryl Ambelter ever again, if he didn't hurry. The burning agony was rising into his chest now, his breath acquiring a rattle. Ingryl lifted the coffin lid, looked down at the skeleton in its wooden frame, and laid his hands on the three stout cross braces that would take his weight.

The flaws of the magic he'd worked—or the ravages of time, on Ladaz-zur's scepters—were greater than he'd thought; the effort to clamber up onto the table and then into the coffin left him trembling. Draped on the cross braces that kept him from crushing the bones so close beneath, Ingryl embraced the grinning bones and hoarsely gasped out a spell.

An eerie light grew and pulsed along the bones, washing over the Spell-master ere it faded away again. Ingryl lay still, listening to the tiny sounds that accompanied a finger crumbling and dropping off the skeleton into the bottom of the casket, and smiled.

He was whole and vigorous once more. Beware, folk of the Vale, for Ingryl Ambelter strides forth again! Or would do, once he raised himself out of the coffin.

Ingryl took time and care over it, and when he was done stood silently looking down at the bones of Gadaster Mulkyn, most famous and—thus far—most feared of Silvertree mages. None but Ingryl knew they lay here . . . or Gadaster's true fate.

After a moment, the Spellmaster stiffened. "A gathering of magic around my . . . Sirl portal?" he said slowly, and raised one eyebrow. "My thanks, Gadaster."

He turned to go, recalling the sequence of spells he'd crafted to steal Gadaster's power (and ultimately the old mage's life), with no one—including Gadaster—being any the wiser. Satisfying, and still secret. Brilliant spell-craft that he'd never dare to tell anyone about.

Ah, well. By the sound of things, 'twas high time to work brilliant spell-craft again. . . .

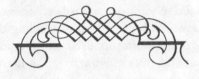

8

A Swordsman's Home Is His Castle

The wolf-spider towered over her. Embra spread empty hands, knowing she couldn't weave any useful spell in time, and dodged away, hair swirling wildly around her shoulders as she cast glances here and there, seeking ways out and the whereabouts of her companions. She knew this room; they were back in the Silent House, dragged there by Sarasper's desperate spell. . . .

Hawkril lay sprawled and bloody in his gnawed armor, Craer was darting around furred limbs, slashing and stabbing with a long knife, and Sarasper was sagging wearily against a wall, face ashen. Embra's precious Dwaer-Stone was somewhere in the wolf-spider's innards, swallowed whole when the thing had bitten down on her upflung arm, back on the hill.

The Band of Four was in no state to win this battle.

"Flee!" Embra cried, more to learn Sarasper's condition than anything else. His eyes were closing as he sagged back against the wall, but his lips were moving. She tried to hear his words, but—

"Stagger is more like it," Craer called back to her. A moment later, she heard him grunt in pain as a flailing limb struck him sprawling, his knife clattering away. He rolled over once and then rocked back and forth, moaning in pain and twisting on the cold stone floor. The longfangs growled in triumph and stalked forward.

Without thinking, Embra ran towards it, waving her arms. The shaggy head lifted from looking at the fallen procurer, to fix her with hungry golden eyes. That buttery stare sharpened, as she met it, into a white glitter, until those eerie, spell-spawned orbs of death were staring at her once more. A deep rumble came from its throat, and it surged towards her.

Embra frowned. The pain they'd caused the beast must have weakened the bone-wizard's hold over it, so that sometimes it was a longfangs on the hunt, and sometimes the servitor of a wizard outlasting death to struggle for control over it. Just now, the bone-wizard was riding the wolf-spider's own angry mind . . . for which, Embra supposed, she should be grateful. Thanks to the wizard, the longfangs was moving to strike her down before snatching up Hawk or Craer to wrench off their heads and make sure they were dead . . . or to feed.

Embra backed away, shouting wordless defiance at it—and then turned and ran. If she could get to Sarasper's pouch in time . . .

"Lady," the old healer hissed, his face a mask of sweat and his teeth clenched, "get back. Give me *time*!" One of his arms was longer than it should be, and had gone a strange yellow color. Gray fur was sprouting here and there along its thickening length, growing thicker as she raced up to him.

"*No*, Sarasper!" she cried. "It's twice your size—if you can even *make* fangs-shape before it gets its teeth into you!"

He shook his head as if to sweep her words away, his body shuddering. As Embra snatched at his pouch, the old healer's eyes rolled, his mouth went slack—and he fell over sideways, dragging her along. Embra wormed her way desperately atop Sarasper, raking through the pouch between their bodies by feel. He'd had no time to shift his shape—but she really didn't have time to work any sort of battle-spell. As the old ballad went, "Too little time and too much need."

Even as Embra sighed out her exasperation, her fingers closed around the smooth hardness of one of the figurines. She clutched it hard and rolled furiously away, not caring if she tore the pouch to shreds.

The longfangs loomed above her, its eyes still those cold, cruel white points of light, and its drooling jaws opening. Its limbjaws, now two bristling fists of broken, ridiculously overgrown teeth, were raised high in the air like clubs, waiting to crash down.

Embra kept on rolling, trying to get past it before it could smash her against the stones of her own palace, knowing she couldn't possibly get clear.

The floor boomed right beside her, and the Lady Silvertree felt sudden, sharp fire in her scalp as her frantic tumbling tore pinioned hairs away. Showers of fang-shards peppered her face as the limbjaws rebounded from the great blow, and the wolf-spider turned to face her squarely, those gaping jaws lowering and thrusting towards her. . . .

She barely knew six rooms beyond this one, and almost nothing of the unsprung traps of the Silent House. Sarasper was the only one who could use its defenses against this beast—and Sarasper was lying senseless or dead right behind her. It was up to the Lady of Jewels to defeat this beast that could bite and rend them all to blood and bones.

It was always up to the bloody Lady of Jewels.

She hadn't realized she'd shouted that aloud until Craer's voice came mockingly out of the dimness on the far side of the longfangs. "Of course. Some people take *so* long to grasp life's little lessons."

The stream of furious obscenities she shrieked at him then awakened echoes all around them. The wolf-spider paid no attention to the procurer, who was on his feet and stabbing again, but kept after Embra, smashing into a pillar she rolled behind as if it wasn't there.

The pillar was four feet thick, and had held up the lofty ceiling of the hall for centuries. The fine network of cracks clawing their meandering ways across the runes graven into it did not widen as the room shook and the dust fell in clouds, nor did the pillar move an inch. The longfangs roared its pain and lurched away, seeking to go around one side of the pillar and bite down on the rolling, dodging sorceress.

She still had all of her limbs, and still had hold of the figurine, but she wasn't getting even time to breathe, much less call a spell to mind and cast it. Embra roared out rage of her own as she rolled to her feet and sprinted away, the beast's great jaws snapping shut on empty air far too close behind her.

"Lady Embra!" Craer called, from somewhere off to her right. "Can your magics heal? Use the Stone!"

The longfangs crashed into another pillar, and smote the stone floor beside her with one of its useless limbjaws; Embra sprang out of the way and shouted back, "It's inside this beast! Hawk's hurt, isn't he?"

The procurer surprised her. "He's bad," Craer called, after a few soft curses, "but we need Sarasper more. I can follow the way we took down to Adeln—but I don't know how to get to it from here . . . and this end of the House is all traps!"

"Claws of the happy dancing Dark One!" Embra spat. "Will *nothing* go our way?"

"And if things did, where then would be our adventure?" the procurer called back cheerfully. "Our heroics? The exploits of the mighty Band of Four that the bards could sing about?"

"Craer," Embra snarled at him, as she panted her way up a short flight of steps to a balcony whose rail had already broken away and shattered, some time ago, "bards will sing about *anything*. If we did nothing, they'd just make it all up!" Teeth shrieked along stone as a limbjaws tried to sweep her off her feet. "I'd rather see them all here, now," she added, thrusting herself between jagged stones where a hole had been broken open in the balcony wall, to get as far from the longfangs as she could, "to help us fight this thing!"

"Lady," Craer shouted, "remember when you conjured up that nightwyrm, in the ruins—when you were thralled? Could you do that again, now, and fly it down the beast's gullet?"

"Sargh it, Craer," she almost screamed, "it takes forever to . . ."

The wizard-tamed longfangs was trying to haul itself up onto the balcony, thinking it had her trapped—and the crumbling stones, weakened here by years of water seeping through the stones and freezing each winter to form iron-hard fangs of ice, were breaking free under its weight and tumbling down with it. She might just have time enough.

Bracing her shoulders against broken stone, Embra held up the figurine, set her will, and began to hiss out an incantation that was frighteningly simple. . . .

Forgotten and ignored by the wizard-driven monster, Craer made his way carefully around the chamber to where Sarasper lay. It was no wonder, given all the humans with bows and the delight nightwyrms have of dining on men and their cattle, that the batlike hunting horrors were rare in the Vale these days—but why hadn't wizards made war on each other with swarms of the things?

Sarasper lay on his back, twisted awkwardly amid shards of stone long fallen from the vaulted ceiling above. Craer stroked his hand as gently as any hesitant mother might, to awaken a sick child. "Sarasper?" he whispered. "Do you hear and heed?"

There came a faint groan from the old man sprawled on the stones, and he turned his head a little and mumbled something. Craer bent over him like a lover, moving his ear to keep it always just above those muttering lips.

"Seems like we've always been . . . running . . . fighting. . . . Aglirta in our hands, to save or let fall," Sarasper told the darkness. "So tired . . . let it fall. Just let it fall . . . to shatter and be done with all striving. . . ."

Craer shivered. He'd heard a man speak so just once before. The man had let go of life and just shrunken and died, in a day and a night, with no wound or mark on him. But was Sarasper spent, or thralled again by the spells of some lurking wizard?

They needed him. They needed his wits, his healings, and his fire to fight . . . or they might all die here. But how to call up that fire again?

"Embra?" he called, looking up in time to see the longfangs scramble at last up onto the balcony amid a clattering cascade of dislodged stones. "Embra, I need you here!"

The longfangs was questing this way and that, shuffling and peering hesitantly, seeking—

Finding. From out of the darkness thrust a torrent of dark wings, striking as swift and keen as a swordblade, right into the wolf-spider's maw, overwhelming its roar and hurling it right off its feet, neck twisting as it tumbled. Its shriek of rage and alarm became a cacophony of choking gurglings; black wings beat and flapped furiously—and by sheer determination the conjured creature drove the longfangs into the break in the wall and stuffed it into the space beyond in a tangle of raking, scrabbling limbs.

The nightwyrm was already fading away as Craer watched. "By the Three," he told the chamber fervently, "I'd not want to have any mage hunting me!"

Embra staggered out of the darkness then, sobbing. She fell heavily to her knees, clutching her head in obvious pain, and gasped, "Whatever *now*, Craer?"

"Lady," Craer hissed, "I need you here. It's Sarasper! He's—"

The Lady of Jewels flung back her head, pain sharp on her face, and said wearily, "Still dying, yes?"

Craer scrambled to his feet. "Yes," he snapped. "Yes, he is. Can you help . . . or are sorceresses only good for blasting and burning and deceiving?"

Embra Silvertree crawled a little way along the edge of the balcony on her hands and knees, lifting dark eyes to look across the many-pillared chamber at him. "If you're goading me, Craer, please stop. If you truly want an answer, I'd have to say . . . yes." She closed her eyes and sank down onto the stones.

"Gods above!" Craer shouted, "is *everyone* going to lie down and die on me?"

The longfangs answered him with a wet roar that bespoke pain but more fury, and he heard furious scrapings as it sought to untangle itself from the cleft into which it had been thrust, and win free once more. To stalk, Craer supposed, the only thing still standing in the Silent House: procurers.

Desperation made him swift. A few gasping moments of plunging across stones that turned underfoot, and he was reaching up to touch the Lady Silvertree's face, where Embra lay huddled with her head half over the edge of the crumbling balcony.

"Lady!" he said, shaking her as vigorously as he dared. *"Lady!"*

"Craer," the sorceress murmured, "if you want me to see to Sarasper, you're going to have to carry me to him."

"I *can't*," Craer snarled into her face. "I'm not big enough!" And then he set his teeth, reached up to catch hold of her shoulders, and hauled.

She came over the edge like a full grainsack, smashing him flat to the floor, and they groaned in unison. The longfangs roared in angry answer, and Embra squirmed atop Craer, her knees and elbows bruising him as she struggled unsteadily to her feet.

"Help me, Craer," she husked, staggering forward. "I . . . can't . . ."

"Strangely enough," he said, wincing and limping his way to where he could put an arm around her shoulders, "I've noticed that!"

A smooth and shockingly firm breast was pressing against his cheek. Craer drew in a deep breath of the fragrance Embra wore, sighed it out again, and guided her forward. As the longfangs roared again, louder and more eager this time, the thought came to him that if he started to hum, she couldn't help but be made a little more awake; she'd feel the thrumming in her chest, and . . .

He hummed as they picked their way across rocks, until Embra chuckled into his ear and said warningly, "If you set me to laughing, I won't be able to do whatever it is you want me to do before the longfangs devours us all!"

"I'll risk it," Craer told her happily. "Anything to get you away from just lying there waiting to be eaten, like Hawk and Sass."

His determined words brought them to the healer. Sarasper was still lying on his back amid the stones, very much as they'd left him. Embra looked down at him and sighed. "I'm not a healer, Craer."

"Lady, we need what he knows—where to get you more family magics to drain for your spells, if nothing else," Craer said fiercely, almost forcing her to her knees. "He's got one of those gewgaws left—just one—and I need you to heal him with it, to get him awake and alert again!"

"Craer, I *can't*," Embra told him. "I don't know how. Undoing burns or sword-wounds that I've just seen caused, yes, but . . ."

"Lady, he's lost the will to be here with us," the procurer told her, gripping her shoulders so hard that the Lady of Jewels gasped and looked at him with eyes wide in pain and alarm. "I need you to give him that back, and make him heal himself. Can you take the magic from that gewgaw in his pouch and feed it to him, for him to heal? And can he help *Hawk,* graul it?"

Embra nodded. "Sargh, Craer, let go," she said, wincing. "Give him back his will to live?"

"Kiss him, Lady," Craer said, his face still fierce. "Hold him, and stroke him, and murmur his name like a lover. Make him feel needed, remind him what it feels like to be held—by the Three, lick the end of his Serpent-damned nose!"

"And while I'm swarming all over Sarasper, just what will you be doing?"

The procurer bent to his ankle and then straightened again in one smooth motion. Something bright flashed up into the air—only to be plucked into stillness in midspin by nimble fingers. Craer waved the knife he held with a little flourish, using it to point at the balcony. "I," he announced grandly, indicating the rise and fall of questing legs that marked the monster's attempts to drag itself out to freedom once more, "will be holding off a longfangs. Alone."

Embra shook her head and gave him a rueful smile. "Procurers," she said. "Centuries it's taken them before one of them found something useful to do. And I was here to witness it."

"Lady," Craer growled, "you may not be familiar with all of the rude gestures used by us lower ranks in the Vale, but—"

He performed one for her, with enthusiasm, and then bowed with a solemn flourish, before turning and racing off across the chamber again, dagger drawn.

Embra shook her head and leaned forward, fingers probing in Sarasper's pouch for that last figurine. "This is not," she told the still form of the healer beneath her, "how lady sorceresses of this or any other realm are supposed to behave. I hope you feel honored."

From the lips of the old man came a muted noise that was probably a groan, but might have been agreement.

It was echoed, an instant later, by a roar from the longfangs, embroidered by Craer's ringing shout. Somewhere far across the chamber, there was a scrape of metal on stone as the din roused Hawkril Anharu. He moaned in pain.

"Gods above," Embra asked the vaulted ceiling above her, "can't a girl get a little privacy? Well?"

The Lord of Glarond turned from his window. "Well?"

His Court Wizard did not bother to smile. "You were right, Lord Baron. They did return to the ruins, and read something from the books there before they were attacked."

"Attacked?"

"By a bone-wizard, and later a longfangs. They vanished—whirled away by a Silvertree spell, no doubt—and I've thus far been unable to trace them."

"A task you will return to, forthwith," the baron observed in the dry, flat voice that meant he was giving an order.

Rustal Faulkron inclined his head. "Of course," he replied, and turned to leave an instant before adding, "My report concludes, Lord. Is there anything else?"

The Lord of Glarond smiled. "No, Faulkron." The Court Wizard was already beginning to stride away when he added, "Well, one thing, perhaps. Why is it that the Lady of Jewels—sheltered lass that she is, the spell-slave of her father—can read these floating books while all the rest of you wizards of the Vale cannot? Have the gods marked her for favor?"

Faulkron's face tightened. "To your first: I know not. To your second: Lord Baron, those whom the gods mark seldom know more than brief favor. More often their fates are dark dooms that bards outdo themselves spinning tragic ballads about. I'd not want to be marked by the gods for anything."

He looked back, and they stared into each other's eyes expressionlessly for what seemed a very long time, still and silent, before the baron ran his tongue slowly along his lips and said, "Faulkron, your wisdom frightens me. Again. Perhaps the gods *have* marked you."

The Court Wizard of Glarond made no reply before he strode away, but Baron Audeman Glarond had known him for a long time, and did not fail to notice the tiny gesture of warding that the wizard made before he moved.

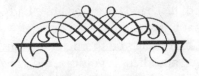

9

A Nightguard Unsleeping

Sometimes Sarasper Codelmer thought the gods had marked him, and took particular delight in playing tricks on one old, lonely, fugitive healer. No dream could give him this warm sweetness of the lips on his, the tongue darting tentatively into his mouth between purrs of, "Sarasper, come back to me. Come back!"

No dream indeed. The tingling in him was the risen fire of magic, swirling around and through him from a dwindling hardness on his chest—one of the figurines from his pouch—pressed against him by the warm, soft weight of . . . of . . . *Embra?*

"L-Lady Silvertree?" he said disbelievingly, into the mouth that was questing for his. He tried to sit up, pushing against stones that rocked and turned over, and in his scrabbling for balance he closed one hand on something warm and soft that was definitely not a rock.

Something bare. Shocked, he stared into the eyes of the Lady of Jewels from mere inches away, snatching his hand back as if he'd grasped a burning branch.

"What, Lady—?"

"Sarasper," the sorceress said firmly, "I need you awake. Do I have your attention now?"

The longfangs chose that moment to roar—and they heard rocks clatter and Craer curse. Two heads turned as one, in time to see the procurer tumble helplessly from the balcony to the floor, the wolf-spider swarming angrily after him.

Their heads turned again, noses almost touching once more, and the old healer's mouth crooked. "Well, Lady," he said, "you *did*, but—"

Embra caught hold of his fingers and guided them once more to her breast. "Now?" she murmured.

Sarasper snatched his hand away again. "Lady—lass—stop this," he growled. "Tell me what it is you'd have me do!"

"Use the magic I'm feeding you through our skins' touch to heal yourself," Embra told him, "and then, if you can, aid Hawkril so he can move and stand." She gave him a brittle smile, and added swiftly, "After that we need you to lead us away from this longfangs, clear of all traps, and get us more magic that we can both call on—"

Sarasper was nodding almost frantically. "Lady," he snarled, trying to thrust her away, "sargh it, list your needs *later*!"

The longfangs was coming across the stones in a hungry flood, ignoring the dancing form of the procurer as he stabbed and sprang away, rushed in to stab again and ducked away once more. It was heading straight for the sorceress.

"Heal yourself," she hissed, as she calmly rose, readjusted her bodice, shook out her sleeves, and faced the onrushing monster.

Sarasper gaped up at her as the magic rushed into him, soothing and invigorating at the same time. By the Three, but it felt good. A cleansing, enlivening surging, forcing his changed arm back into human shape, driving away the sick, empty feeling of exhaustion . . . but he needed a few moments more, just a little time, and the longfangs was so close.

Embra Silvertree flicked her fingers and fire spat from between them—a brief, searing bolt that lashed at the wolf-spider's eyes. The longfangs squalled but kept coming.

The sorceress was already moving purposefully away, wearing a tight smile of battle excitement, drawing the longfangs after her.

Sarasper lay still as the last tongues of magic lashed him into full and tingling wakefulness, watching the Lady of Jewels dance gracefully in the distance. She dodged and circled as the longfangs, snarling now with its head lowered and its parted jaws slavering menacingly, pursued her doggedly, its eyes sometimes a lionlike gold, and sometimes cold white lamps of all-too-wise light. Where was the Dwaer-Stone? She held up one of her hands warningly, cupping empty air as if she could grasp and throw it, and from time to time called almost carelessly, "Oh, Sarasper, take not all day! I've almost no magic left to entertain this beast!"

Had they lost the Stone? It seemed like an eternity before Sarasper found his feet, waved a wordless reassurance to her, and set out across a small forest of loose rocks that turned underfoot treacherously to where the armaragor lay. Staggering awkwardly, waving his arms for balance and cursing softly and often, while keeping one eye on the stalking longfangs, the healer finally reached Hawkril—and winced at what he saw.

The hulking warrior lay on his back, sprawled and bloody, his armor gnawed and twisted where it wasn't missing altogether. No healer in all Darsar had power enough, alone, to set all this harm right and snatch the armaragor back onto his feet, fresh and hale. But perhaps, for a start, a little less would serve. . . .

Sarasper set his teeth in a grimace and hauled at torn edges of armor plate here and there, prying tortured metal away from bruised flesh beneath. As he forced broken bones gratingly back into their proper places, Hawk murmured and moved beneath his fingers.

"Well?" Embra called, her voice high with excitement and fear.

Sarasper shook his head at her. "Patience," he muttered. "A little patience!"

"Hand that sage advice to this longfangs," the sorceress shot back, "not to me!"

Sarasper gave her a mirthless grin and bent back to his task, feeling himself grow weak and tired again as vitality flowed out through his fingers into the warming flesh beneath. He had to get from this part of the House, all broken and crumbling furnishings and traps, to certain rooms east and south of here, in those depths of the Silent House never reached by looters or overbold hired adventurers foraging for earlier Barons Silvertree. One chamber he recalled, its walls sheathed in glossy green marble, held a great-front cabinet bristling with some long-vanished Silvertree's collection of music boxes, every last one of them enchanted—some so lavishly as to glow and pulse where they sat, down the long and waiting years. He had to get there, to have the makings for healings and give Embra the stored fire to power her battle-spells, but a score or more of traps awaited betwixt here and there, and . . .

"Lady Embra!" he called, excitement making him shout. "Remember you Thaalen's Nightguard?"

The Lady Silvertree lost her footing in calf-deep loose rubble and toppled helplessly sideways, sobbing out a curse as gray-furred limbs swept down at her.

A knife flashed and those limbs flinched back. Craer sprang over her, humming something merrily as he stabbed and slashed, his dagger a bright and slicing fang. Embra rolled to her hands and knees, snarling as stones tore at her desperately clawing fingers, and shouted back, "*Yes,* sargh you, and what—"

As she gained her feet, full remembrance of the Nightguard—an inner fortress within the Silent House that a certain particularly fearful-of-slayers-lurking-behind-every-face baron had built, and retreated to, nightly—came to her, and Embra added in a very different voice, "Oh."

"Exactly," Sarasper called, as Hawkril groaned under his hands and made his first feeble struggle to rise. "If you, as the Silvertree heir, know the words that call up the power of the Nightguard—"

"I do," the sorceress shouted back. "Those enchantments—taught to all of the blood Silvertree as amusing family lore, because the curse was always thought to make them useless—gave my father the beginnings of his 'Living Castle' spellchains for me. But we have to get there first, and there're the traps. . . ."

"Leave those to me," the old healer cried, "and behold! Your favorite Hawk is with us once more!"

With a growl, the armaragor rose ponderously upright, trying a smile. It was obviously an experiment, and wavered alarmingly as he staggered in a half-circle, swinging his arms and wincing, ere he caught sight of the long-fangs once more. Hawkril stiffened and growled, one hand darting to where his warsword should have been.

"Steady," Sarasper growled, plucking at the torn and bloody thews of the armaragor's other arm. "A charge right back into those jaws right now would not be a glorious, effective, or even particularly useful thing! I need you to lure and run away just now!"

"Oh?" Hawkril grunted, tugging his warsword free from the shards and tangled padding of the armor across his chest and down his right side, whence it had been driven deep by the bulk and smashing blows of the longfangs. "And how am I to lure it if I have not its attention, hey?"

"Gods above if you haven't found *another* unassailable reason for brainless battle," the old healer snapped. "Well, just mind you lead it through *that* archway, mind—d'you hear?"

"But of course, Lord of Battles," the aramargor growled. "Yon archway 'tis!" And at that he raised his voice in a wordless bellow of rage that became a trumpeted, echoing challenge, and launched himself across the chamber.

His charge banished the bone-wizard's control for the nonce, and the longfangs roared back its answer as it spun around to face him, ignoring both the procurer it had already been scorning and the sorceress it had been trying its utmost to slay. They both turned startled faces to the charging Hawkril—but were distracted by the wildly waving healer.

"Here, to me!" Sarasper called. "Through here!"

The sorceress and the procurer exchanged glances, and then Craer gave Embra a shove towards the door and growled, "Go! It's not as if there're any minstrels watching to see what a mess we're making of being bold heroes, now—get going!"

"Without you?" Embra replied teasingly, over her shoulder. Craer demonstrated another rude gesture of the Vale to her in reply, as they broke into a run together. Hawkril burst between them with a savage grin, going the other way with speed and enthusiasm, and the wet thud of his first blow landing—and the pain-laced squalling of the longfangs it provoked—sounded clearly over the scrapes of their hurrying boots on the loose stones.

"Hawkril!" the hurrying pair heard Sarasper call warningly. "Don't get enthralled in battling it, now—just draw it back here!"

"Healer," the armaragor grunted back, between gasps for breath and the snarls that marked him swinging his blade hard to strike aside reaching limbs or striking limbjaws, "do I tell you how to heal?"

"Hawk," the old man replied reprovingly, "I was swinging a sword before you were—"

"A gleam in the eye of the unborn granddaughter of the lass being born as you picked your first blade up by its wrong end, I know," Hawkril called. "Just one more—*unnhh!* There!—and I'm your enthusiastic lure!"

"Whatever became of warriors who just grimly and silently followed orders?" Embra wondered aloud, as she gasped her way up a short flight of steps to the archway where Sarasper stood waiting—and barring the way beyond.

"They all got killed unquestioningly following the orders of utter idiots," the healer grunted back, "meaning no offense, Lady Baron."

"I'll take none," Embra told him, "if you refrain from calling me that." As Craer joined them, they turned together to watch the armaragor, his blade dark and wet with longfangs gore, lumbering across the stones towards them, the wolf-spider lurching along in pained pursuit.

"Are you all enjoying the sight?" Hawkril called. "Or placing bets, perhaps? Or just standing in my way like utter idiots?"

"There're traps ahead, bone-for-brains," Sarasper told him. "Through this arch, swing hard and fast to your left, and run ahead until you come to a room lit by a faint glow. Enter it not, but put your hand on its entry arch and turn hard right, ducking down the passage then before you. It descends to a room of many pillars. Wait therein for me—but don't, if you would cling to your life, touch a single pillar!"

"In, left, right before light, touch no pillars as we tarry," Embra chanted.

"Indeed," the healer agreed, at the same time as Craer, watching the chase hurtle across the room towards them, said quietly, "The beast's eyes just changed again. Your instructions may aid it just as they do us."

"Graul and bebolt," Sarasper snarled. "Why can't wizards just stay dead?"

Embra shrugged. "I know not—but if they did, we'd have no king to serve, no Serpent would imperil the realm, and we'd all be cowering under the sword of whatever baron was most brutish."

"I'm glad *you* said that, Lady Baron," Craer told her, as Sarasper touched their arms in a signal and then ducked through the archway into darkness.

They sprinted after him, turning hard left as bidden. The passage was dank and smelled of earth, seeming both colder and damper than the chamber they'd left. Behind them came a clang and curse as Hawkril struck his warsword off the unseen stone wall and feared for its edge.

The way was as clear as Sarasper's description. The hard-racing Band of Four found it hard not to brush up against any of the forest of identical smooth stone pillars as they brought themselves to a variety of clumsy halts—particularly Hawkril, who could hear the scrapings of the wounded wolf-spider hastening close behind him.

As the armaragor lumbered into the room, Sarasper snapped, "To this wall, by me!"

The healer was standing between two narrow arched openings. As his companions came up to him, he pointed and said, "This one. The other holds sure death."

As the Four plunged down the passage Sarasper had chosen, there was a sharp explosion of sound behind them—a violent din of clacking and clattering, broken by a shrill, ragged shriek of pain.

"It touched a pillar," Sarasper said in satisfied tones, as they emerged into a smaller room with faded scenes painted on the walls. It contained a single central pillar, painted to match the walls, and several small heaps of ruin that had once been furniture. There were three closed doors in one of its walls.

"This gives us time," he added, voice low and swift. "The left-hand door is the safe way on. Leave it open behind us to lure the beast; the other doors lead to rooms that may or may not slay it, but—"

"The Nightguard lies this way?" Embra asked eagerly.

"Yes," Sarasper told her, "but don't expect to find a luxurious sanctum or even an armory and furnished stronghold." He led the way up a rising, rough-floored passage into a large, echoing chamber adorned with crumbling balconies, dozens of dark windows high in the walls opening into unseen chambers, and many doors around the walls. Two were set high enough to be reached by railless flights of steps; Sarasper went up the rightmost of these.

"Right here," he panted, pointing upwards at the arch at the top of the stairs, "is where I need you to utter the word that raises the Nightguard!"

"Just as the longfangs is passing under it, no doubt?" Embra said with a smile—that faded as quickly as it had come. "And if I misjudge, and it gets into the stronghold with us?"

The healer looked at Hawkril. "After we're up the steps," he said, "you have to be the crawling wounded victim. . . ."

A slow smile spread across the armaragor's face. "Is that Old Hungry I hear coming now?"

None of his companions bothered to answer as uneven, halting scrapings grew louder down the passage behind them. They were too busy swarming up the steps.

"It's safe, beyond," Sarasper called. "Hawk?"

"Ohhh," the warrior groaned convincingly, collapsing onto the bottom step and smearing it with three fingers of blood daubed from the wounds on his chest. He clawed at the next step with trembling fingers, and cast a despairing glance back over his shoulder at the longfangs as it scrambled unsteadily into the room, its fur dark with gore and its eyes two lamps of chill death. "Three defend me," he gasped, clambering weakly up a step.

"Hawk!" Craer snapped warningly. "It's coming fast!"

"Don't," Hawkril gasped, "interrupt great minstrelry! I may not be the actor Halivaerus of Sirlptar is, but . . ."

Roaring in mock pain, the armaragor clawed his way a step higher—and then sagged back in mock agony, listening to the ragged scrapings becoming rapidly louder behind him. With an apparent titanic effort, Hawkril heaved himself back up onto the step, and then immediately up to the next one.

"Hawk!" Craer snapped again. "It's—"

"Some procurers find themselves utterly unable to trust the abilities of others," Hawk growled, "or, for that matter, anything at all. That may make them good procurers, but—"

"Some armaragors," Craer called back, "find themselves utterly trusting their own battle prowess, far beyond all sense. This may make them good corpses, but—"

"All right, all right," Hawkril growled, reaching the top step. The long-fangs rose up behind him with menacing speed, reaching with its limbjaws for a man-shattering blow.

He rolled abruptly aside as a limbjaws crashed down, and then back again to avoid the second blow, launching himself to his feet and into a sudden sprint through the arch.

Eyes two chill points of light, the longfangs surged up the steps in uncanny silence, reaching out a forest of furry limbs after the racing warrior.

Embra took a deep breath, and said loudly and precisely, *"Cathkaratha lamarratha thauriïr!"*

And the air caught fire—cold, crawling blue fire that stabbed across the dimness in a webwork of sudden and dazzling complexity. The radiance faded swiftly, its brightness yet blinding the Four as rushing stone descended with a roar, a deafening boom shook the room—and there was suddenly a huge stone slab filling the arch. A door whose lower edge was dark and wet, in a spreading pool that held the feebly twitching front half of the wolf-spider.

As the Four watched the limbs sag and slither to the floor, the cold lights in the eye sockets of the severed head slowly faded—and Embra let out a long, shuddering breath.

"Worry not," Craer joked. "The lower half of the thing is probably raging around on the other side of the door, fairly dancing with impatience to get at us and kick us to death! Why, I wouldn't be sur—"

His jaw dropped as his wandering gaze chanced to travel to the top of the arch. The fall of the door had revealed a dark cavity above the arch: a hitherto-hidden room. The procurer started forward, asking quietly, "Embra, just where did the Silvertrees like to hide their treasure?"

"No, Craer, I really don't think—" the Lady of Jewels began, and then fell silent as she watched the procurer swarm up the smooth stone doorslab as swiftly and easily as if he'd been walking up a staircase, and disappear into the dark opening.

"If there's treasure, he'll find it," Hawkril growled, shaking his head with a smile. "An old boot here, a cracked chamber pot there—"

"Treasure's what you make of it," Sarasper agreed, "and—"

Craer reappeared in the hole—or rather, vaulted out of it in a swift plunge to the floor, his eyes wide and staring. "Three defend!" he cried, as he landed with a roll.

Skeletal arms appeared in the opening—human arms whose rapidly moving bones ended at the shoulders, swarming down the door like snakes racing across level sand.

Hawkril hefted his warsword and squinted sourly at the approaching bones. "Kin of yours, Lady?" he growled.

Embra shrugged. "More likely apprentices to family mages from before my time."

Hawkril nodded, eyes on the dozen bone-arms that had now reached the bottom of the door, and handed her his sword. Its weight made her curse and catch hold of its hilt with both hands as it crashed floorward.

With two swift strides the armaragor crossed the room, plucked up a huge, dark table, and turned, hurling it, in one smooth motion.

It hurtled across the room like a great, tumbling warrior's shield, and struck the floor so hard that its slide into the door shook the room. The great crash sent shattered bones flying up into the air in shards, even as a wall of choking dust fell like a heavy curtain.

"Do you *mind?*" Sarasper and Embra snapped in unison. "This *is* . . ." They trailed off, looked at each other, and then finished uneasily, "My home." As the Four gathered to share glances, they started to chuckle . . . mirth that built into a roar of shared laughter.

In a chamber of pillars not so far off, the echoes of mirth awakened something. Something that moved inside cold stone, descending until it shimmered forth, melting out of the pillar it had been hiding in for centuries.

Something hard-shelled and large-clawed that shuddered in silence for long moments as it gained bulk and solidity, before rousing itself to prowl forth and feed on these noisy victims-to-be . . .

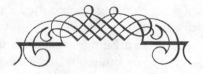

10

To Kill a King

The end of a rope slithered down out of the night, brushing so close by Gurkyn Oblarram's face that the surly old warrior almost jumped back with a shout—and did dig steely fingers into the shoulder of the man beside him, and hiss like a startled rocksnake.

"Sargh, let go!" Mararr snarled under his breath fiercely, twisting free. "I'm no foe—or *wasn't!*"

"Pardon, by the Three, pardon," Gurkyn muttered hastily, watching the many short swords on Mararr's baldric sway and jostle in a dappling of moonlight. "Thought it was . . . a snake or something."

"Something it *will* be," Mararr Guldalmyn promised him in a harsh whisper, setting his boots against the wall and hauling himself an arm-length up the rope, "if it should happen again. Depend on that, O master of pots!"

Gurkyn gave him a deep growl, of the sort a hunting hillcat makes deep in its throat, but said no more. The armaragor who wore a small forest of short swords walked up the wall and into the darkness overhead with powerful, steady pulls on the rope. Gurkyn watched its end dance for a time, and then gave those around him a slow and sour survey. Lultus was far larger and heavier than one old and often drunk cook, and Gloun was even less of a climber. The other two, Peldrus and Tathil—no, Tathtorn, that was his name—Gurkyn barely knew. They'd come late to the baron's service, mere days before the sailing. Then, as now, they moved as one, not needing to speak or even gesture, seeming guided by the same thoughts. They'd prevented the boat from grating against the jetty, they'd held it while two sevens of men—Duthjack's blades now, every one—had clambered out . . .

and they'd made the moorings fast, their eyes never leaving the line of warriors slowly climbing the walls of Flowfoam, first with clawlike hands and
then using the rope let down by the brave first few. Duthjack himself, his
eyes large and dark with excitement, had already ascended, his personal
bodyblades Calargh and Naor before and behind him. No alarm had risen
as warrior after warrior had struggled up onto the wall, invading the royal
isle unseen.

A good beginning, for a foray to kill a king. Too good, Gurkyn feared;
how could they not have been noticed? This had been the castle of Baron
Silvertree, infamous in the Vale for his cruelty—were there dozens of death-
traps ahead? Or watchers on the walls loading and aiming bows even now,
awaiting only the ascent of the last intruding warrior, so as to have all gathered for easy slaying? Or was this Snowsar really so lax or overproud or
powerless as to have no guards on the walls of Flowfoam?

Gurkyn shook his head. Sixteen men in all had crossed the cold waters
of the Silverflow crowded shoulder-to-shoulder in Duthjack's stolen boat.
Sixteen to hurl against the whelmed swords of a castle.

Not many. But then . . . what whelmed swords? Flowfoam seemed to
sleep this night, with not even a torch to be seen on this side of the Isle, and
no one walking the ramparts where desperate men had climbed, to crouch
now, plotting together, like rats gathering at the same scrap of meat.

Aye. Just like hungry rats sharing a meal. Wherefore it was to be hoped
that the meal was large enough for all, and would not become a battlefield
for desperate men tearing at too meagre provender. Gurkyn stared thoughtfully off into the night, watching moonlight make the moving river into a
bed of winking silver stars, and wondered what would go wrong—and if
he'd see morning, or end his long and hard road choking in darkness with a
sword through his guts.

The end of the rope fell into his view again, dancing wildly, and the
dark mountain that was Lultus reached out a ponderous arm and touched
Gurkyn's shoulder. The cook gave the shining river one last glance, sighed,
and set his hands on the rope. The moment his boots touched the wall,
someone above started hauling him up.

His climb was a swift and easy walk, not the laborious, arm-tiring haul
he'd feared. In a few hard-breathing moments he was standing on the battlements some sneering Silvertree baron had built, in the midst of a hushed,
wary crowd of warriors all peering down into the trees beyond.

A moonlit wood seemed to stretch a goodly way in from the wall, giving way in the end to moonlit spaces—gardens, for pools glimmered here
and there, and small, arched stone bridges could be seen. In the far distance

rose the dark bulk of Flowfoam itself, all stone balconies and turrets. A few lights were twinkling in its windows—but the scene before the hungry warriors seemed otherwise empty of awake, aware life.

"This is going to be like butchering babies in their cots," someone muttered, as the growing cluster of Dutchjack's men hefted their swords and tried to measure the distance to the unseen ground below.

"Never say that," someone else grunted sourly. "Whenever I hear those words, it's just before things go wrong. *Badly* wrong."

"Lultus, you the last?" Mararr asked, and when the wordless growl that meant yes came back to him, he added, "Then swing the rope around—leaving it tied up, just as it is—and toss it down this side of the wall! *Move*, man!"

"Battle obviously presses us into an urgency I've not noticed a need for," Lultus observed in a deep, sarcastic purr that made more than one man chuckle, as he did as he was bid. "Pray forgive my shortcomings, O bold Mararr."

"Enough chatter," Bloodblade said coldly, before the armaragor of the many shortswords could make reply. "I doubt even an idiot king would use deaf sentries."

"Something's not right," Gurkyn said abruptly, striding towards Duthjack until he found himself about to step onto the point of Naor's ready blade. "I can feel it."

"You can *feel* it! Well—" someone began jeeringly, but Bloodblade whirled and snapped, "Enough. Something *is* . . . not right."

"Aye," Calargh agreed, shaking his own sword as if it were a minstrel's rattle, "I feel it too. It's as if—"

He froze, dropping into a crouch, as fifteen warriors watched him alertly. "The stones," he said suddenly, stamping one of his boots. "They're alive!"

"What?" came from several incredulous throats, but Bloodblade snarled, "No—be *still!*"

In the silence after his words they all felt it: the slightest of ripples beneath their boots, as if the stones of the wall were breathing, or gathering themselves, in a stealthy shifting of some gigantic muscle, to—

"Off the wall!" Bloodblade snapped. "Jump! Into the trees!"

The battlements erupted into a tumult of rushing, leaping men, sped on their frantic ways by Calargh's sudden scream. Fingers of stone had risen unseen to encircle his ankle; his charge towards the gardens became a headlong topple to the walk along the wall—where his face crashed down into the rising, cruelly piercing fingers of another stone hand. Naor looked back in time to see his fellow bodyblade's face being torn off; as blood burst out across the stones and he opened his mouth for a cry of horror, he was

already in the air, crashing down through leaves and branches already dancing in the wake of plunging warriors.

"Three above!" someone gasped, as the thuddings of landings died
away and they heard Calargh's blood gurgling forth above them. "What's
that?"

"Claws of the Dark One," another warrior cried, pointing at the wall,
"What's *that?*"

The stones were bulging forth, in a shape that looked as if a warrior
with sword in hand was striding stiffly forward through a curtain. With the
faintest of groans, stone parted from stone—and a warrior *was* striding forward: a man of stone with blank smoothness where his face should have
been. A stone sword swept up to hack, and the lumbering stone knight
turned swiftly to face the nearest gaping human warrior.

"Sargh!" Gloun cried. "It's alive!"

"There's another!" Lultus shouted, his voice almost a sob of fear.
"Over yon!"

Where his shaking hand was pointing, the stones of the wall were flowing like mud, thrusting forth in a huge prow that became two knights of
stone, striding forth ponderously as someone shouted, "A wizard! The king
has a wizard! We're doomed!"

Someone else—Gloun—shrieked and ran.

"To me!" Bloodblade shouted, silencing the warrior who was crying
doom and discovering wizards with one mighty blow of a mailed fist. "We
mustn't—"

Even as the man whose jaw he'd broken reeled and fell, leaving behind
only wine-dark blood dripping from his gauntlet, the man who led the ragtag warriors saw that half a dozen of them now were pelting away through
the woods, and the others were wavering. A stone sword struck the ground
hard enough to set the nearest trees rustling, and the man who'd rolled frantically aside from its strike shrieked like a terrified child and scrambled up
through a bush, to race blindly away into the night.

To the Dark One with stealth now—and with standing and fighting, too!
"To the castle!" Bloodblade cried, pointing ahead into the dark trees and
seeing the faint glows of moonlit glades in the distance. "Charge!"

No one waited to question his orders this time. Duthjack's blades
whirled away from striding stone warriors with ragged cries of horror, and
ran. Fear made their feet fly, fear kept them crashing crazily through shrubs
and sliding across wet flowerbeds where prudence would otherwise have
made them creep and skulk—and in a very short, gasping time, they were
pounding along paths and across bowers increasingly open to the cool silver
moonlight, and leaving the trees behind.

"Not such a wondrous idea," someone lamented, as they raced along. "If the king has more wizards than a baron, we're—"

Bloodblade swerved and lashed out at that babbling warrior with all the force of his running feet, taking him to the ground in a vicious two-handed smash into the man's face. He felt something give under his gauntlets as they bounced on the ground together. Rolling away from fresh wetness, he found his feet again, and ran on. This had not been a wondrous idea, no. . . .

Six or seven stone knights were striding patiently along through the trees after them, swords raised. Gods! They had to find the mage compelling these things, whoever he was, and fast. If only the Blackgult ranks had yielded up a few more good bowmen, th— But no. That sort of thinking was for fireside blustering, not staying alive while kingslaying. Sendrith "Bloodblade" Duthjack set his jaw and waved his blade in a circle above his head. "To me!" he shouted, as loudly as he dared. "To me!"

If they blundered on like this, they'd reach the palace and take the arrows of its bowmen, if there were any, right down their throats. He had to rally his men—there! That little folly-tower!

"Whelm yonder!" he cried, pointing with his blade. "To me!"

The tower was no more than a three-sided room, open to the air on the side nearest the castle. Its other walls were all pierced with large, arched windows—bare, empty openings without shutters or draperies—and it narrowed swiftly to a shingled spire, perched on a little hillock amid floral beds like a castle turret set down on the ground by the grasping fingers of a passing giant. It wasn't quite a bowshot away from the palace walls, but it would have to do.

They hadn't much time. Those stone things might walk with comical grace and swing their swords as slowly—but they kept on striding, and he had no idea if they could be stopped or shattered or even fought. They couldn't fit into the palace, though, if it had doors of the usual size. A handy door was something they had to find in a hurry. Aye, this was turning into a nightmare of running and desperation and—

Abruptly a door opened in the palace wall, thrusting a bright, flickering ribbon of lamplight into the night with the flash of a drawn sword blade, and heads were peering out. Their shouts had been heard.

No orders were needed to make all of Dutchjack's warriors crouch to the ground and then keep still; they might have been so many dark rocks amid the night-gloom as three cloaked and silk-shirted courtiers lifted glimmering lanterns and peered into the night, blinking. "Haroo?"

These were not the tactics of men used to war, expecting attack, or even . . . possessed of prudence. They hadn't even drawn their swords, though high-polished, silvered blades glittered at their hips. The doomed courtiers took several tentative steps outside and called again. Moonlight caught the gleam of earrings amid perfumed and shaped side-whiskers, and breastplates sculpted like birds with wings upswept in flight.

"Is anyone there?"

"Haroo?"

The courtiers exchanged glances, and then walked a little apart from each other, peering more carefully at their surroundings.

On all sides of the man who called himself Bloodblade, warriors trembled with eagerness, only their eyes moving as they looked to him for a signal.

The ground trembled. Stone knights were treading nearer.

"Strike!" Duthjack barked, thrusting himself bolt upright and waving his sword so it flashed in the moonlight. Courtiers gawked at him, lifting their lanterns a little higher.

For two of them, as dark shadows boiled up from the ground and thrust blades right through them, it was the last thing they ever did.

The third courtier, a little behind the others, gave a little shriek, like a terrified mouse, and whirled into flight. A warrior sprang after him, racing right at his back, overtaking swiftly, blade raised to strike at the throat.

The courtier threw his lantern back behind him; it burst full in the warrior's face. Gloun Ummertyde fell screaming, his hair afire, flames streaming between his fingers as he clawed desperately at his eyes. Dark shadows raced past him, sprinting to reach the howling courtier as the man ran, half-cloak flapping behind him and stumbling in his gibbering haste, for the open door.

Gauntleted hands reached, and notched, blackened blades stabbed desperately, biting only empty air. They were not going to reach him in time.

"What befalls—?" a grand voice rolled out into the night, as fresh faces appeared at the door. The speaker got no further, his words ending in a startled grunt as the terrified courtier smashed into him and sent him flying, both men rolling on a tiled floor within and upsetting something that fell with a crash and a clatter.

"Get in there!" Bloodblade roared. "Before someone can close it! *In,* horns to you!"

Mararr reached the door first. He flung it wide and darted within; the converging warriors saw him slip on something, and then thrust viciously with the shortsword in his left hand—once low, and once high. Someone tried to scream, but ended up choking wetly instead.

And then they were all streaming through the doorway, blades held straight up to avoid swording each other as they jostled through the portal.

Bloodblade cast a swift look back at the moonlit wood and saw blank stone faces regarding him—five, at least, plodding forward patiently. He cursed and swung the door shut with a crash.

Naor already had the door-bar ready; he dropped it into its cradles and gave Duthjack a nod of reassurance as the man who sought to slay a king this night spun away from the door to glare around the room they'd stormed.

Three men of the palace—one wasn't much more than a boy, and wore servants' livery—lay sprawled and dead on the floor, and his warriors were already darting in all directions, flinging open doors and peering here and there. Bloodblade swallowed a curse—gods, had they *all* forgotten to keep together and heed orders?—as he saw faces turn his way.

"That way," he snarled, waving at a door that led in the right direction, "and keep *together,* bebolt you!"

They streamed through the doorway, moving quickly but more quietly now, and along a lamplit passage of closed doors that opened into a cross-way in one direction and an archway into a grand chamber in the other. Startled faces regarded them across an empty realm of polished marble floor.

"In at them! Let no alarm be raised!" Bloodblade bellowed, and then caught at a sword arm and snarled, "Mararr—take two sideblades and find stairs up—wizards always like to look down on the world from up high!"

The armaragor saluted, his baldric of many blades swirling, and stormed along the cross-passage with two men at his heels. Bloodblade looked to Naor, in his usual place at his master's side, and muttered, "Watch our rear—if you see any crossbows, yell!"

His warriors were already pelting across the grand chamber, an echoing place of lofty vaulted ceilings, huge paintings of stags being hunted through green-glimmer woods, and curving lounges from which white-faced men in silks were rising, goblets in their hands, and grabbing vainly at slender swords dangling from their hips.

Duthjack's men struck with brutal efficiency, slashing faces and breaking necks with almost magical speed. Some of the courtiers didn't even have time to cry out before they were falling; the one who went to his knees to plead was cut down without hesitation.

There was a clattering crash as a white-haired liveried servant who'd backed into the room with a tray of filled goblets turned, saw the butchery, and flung down his burden in terror. As the man spun around and caught at the handle of the door he'd just come through, Lultus threw his sword with care and precision.

It struck the old man around his ears, spraying blood. The servant threw back his head, fell against the door he'd been trying to claw open, and slid down it without a sound.

"Good wine," Gurkyn said with a gasp, setting down an empty goblet with a heavy thunk.

Bloodblade opened his mouth to rage at such idiocy—and then closed it again. Eight goblets were already being drained, their stems raised to the ceiling as warriors tossed back the contents with swift jerks of their heads. Horns of the Lady, what was the use?

At least no alarm had been raised. "Drag the bodies against that door," he said, pointing at where the servant had fallen, "and let's be on—back out the arch and along the other passage, where I sent Mararr!"

With both hands, his warriors were scooping up pastries and what looked like river-oysters in sauce, spread on palm-sized loaves of bread, but they were looking at him and nodding; Bloodblade rolled his eyes in disgust and set out back across the marble, striding swiftly. The stone knights might follow them inside, after all. . . .

The cross-passage climbed a short flight of steps, widening into a gallery lined with statues, and gave into another passage that climbed a few more steps and opened out into a room from which two passages ran off north and northwest, a broad flight of steps ascended to the west, and a large, ornate, and closed pair of double doors awaited in the south wall. The body of a servant was huddled on the lowest three steps, thin ribbons of blood descending along the white marble from it; Bloodblade smiled approvingly at this sign from Mararr and led the way up, gesturing at the floor with his blade to urge stealth as he heard their first footfalls echo back from a high and unseen ceiling somewhere above.

Three look down on all, but this place seemed deserted! *This* was the court of the King of all Aglirta? It had the empty, echoing feel of a grand house shut up for the season, with only a few servants left behind. On the obverse, of course: sprawled corpses rarely rush about screaming. Bloodblade smiled tightly, and ascended.

More bodies were strewn in the grand chamber at the head of the stairs, sprawled around a crackling fire in an outthrust fireplace. Most were richly dressed, none of them women, and some of them had tried to fight; one of those slim, useless needle-swords lay broken underfoot on a rich manyfurs rug, amid many bloody bootprints. Duthjack looked this way and that, seeking another stair and seeing none.

He shrugged and crossed the room to a far archway, where Mararr had left another body with one arm outstretched to point down the passage beyond. The warriors crowding around Bloodblade eagerly followed its guidance, moving ahead almost like dancers with their bloody swords held ready, low at their sides.

More bodies lay ahead, and more archways, leading through a succession of rooms—one a library of sorts, another a room bristling with antlered heads and other hunting trophies—to a last door, flanked with lit torches: a chapel to the Lady.

Bloodblade's eyes narrowed. This had been Castle Silvertree, and many a baronial family used their House of the Huntress for trysts and more: if this king had ladyloves, he might well be found in curtained, dimly lit chambers somewhere beyond here. A sprawled guard—the first man in armor they'd seen in the palace—gave weight to the supposition, showing that Mararr had shared it.

They entered the chapel warily, finding the usual Horned Altar and the expected row of dark, curtained-off doors beyond. A priestess of the Lady lay sprawled on her face in a spreading pool of blood in front of one of them, her fingers clutching the curtain. Bloodblade's lips tightened. The gods did not look well on those who waged war in their temples.

The door beyond stood open, and—Mararr had good instincts. A dark, narrow stair ran upwards, every third step faintly glowing with magic that doubtless warned someone, somewhere, of ascending feet. It was to be hoped that no one was still alive, above, to heed such warnings any longer.

Naor laid a warning hand on his master's arm for the instant he needed to slip past and lead the way up the stair. There was another body in the room at its top—a servant in much grander livery, draped over a lounge with empty hands dangling. Bloodblade smiled. They must be nearing the king, or the wizard, or both.

Time for prudence. He stopped and waved men past him with his sword, telling Lultus and Gurkyn, "Stay and guard this stair, you two—bottom and top. Call to each other and to us if anyone crosses blades with you . . . or hurls a spell."

He went on then, Naor at his side, with the rest of his warriors now ahead of him. Let spells or crossbow bolts find their chests, and not his.

They passed through three more chambers of death, and never noticed the carved face high up on the stout central pillar in the fourth room whose sculpted eyesockets held real eyes—the eyes of Ingryl Ambelter, Spellmaster of Castle Silvertree once more, though as yet unheralded. Those eyes gazed narrowly at the intruders, and then drew back into the depths of the pillar and vanished.

· · ·

" 'Ware!" Lultus called, eyes narrowing, as he drew back onto the bottom step. "Look!"

Gurkyn peered down the stairs and saw a glimmering below, in the chapel. "Magic," he snarled unnecessarily.

The light had burst out of nothing, into a wash of tiny golden stars, like sparks from a fire that were somehow refusing to wink out—and in their heart a man was standing. A little man in leathers, short and slim and staring around himself in bewilderment, a slender sword leaping into his hands.

Lultus did not wait to see if this apparition was friend or foe. He snatched one of the long knives from his boots and threw, hard.

The slender man's head snapped up at the sound, and he dove aside, his sword stabbing out in his wake. There was a musical clang as the hurled dagger struck it and went tumbling aside. Then the newcomer was charging forward.

Gurkyn started down the stair slowly, his blade held ready. Lultus would not appreciate aid he did not need, and—

"I'm pleased to make *your* acquaintance, too," he heard the little man say merrily, as Lultus surged forward and steel met steel. "However briefly."

Blades sang and darted—and Lultus was toppling, blood fountaining from his throat, and the little man was bounding up the stair. He gave Gurkyn a wide smile, and waved his bloody blade.

"Craer Delnbone, at your service," he said jovially. "Are you going to try to kill me, too?"

Gurkyn Oblarram took one look into those dancing eyes, and then turned and fled up the stairs as fast as he could.

As Bloodblade's band strode across yet another room, Mararr Guldalmyn burst through an archway, fleeing as fast as he could. He panted as he came running towards them, blood on his face from a slashed cheek, and more dripping from the hand that dangled uselessly, several of its fingers almost severed.

"Hold!" Peldrus barked, speaking for the first time that night. "What—?"

Mararr sobbed and brushed him aside, twisting desperately past. The others fell back to let him go, and saw that several swords were missing from his baldric.

As the armaragor gasped his way on, Bloodblade saw who it was and snapped, "Guldalmyn, stop and stand! I command you!"

Mararr slowed, caught at a pillar, and swung himself to a stop, panting.

"What is it?" Duthjack growled. "Who did you meet with?"

There was a commotion in the room ahead, and all eyes went to it, in time to see two grim courtiers hurl the body of Skuldus—one of the men Mararr had taken on his foray—into the room, and follow it. A tight knot of courtiers moved forward behind them, blades in their hands and faces tight with fear and determination. At their head strode a man in full plate armor, his visor down and a sword in either hand. There was blood on both blades.

Mararr pointed wordlessly at the courtiers.

"Slay them," Bloodblade commanded bleakly, raising his voice just a trifle. As his men moved forward, he took two steps, plucked up an ornate chair, and hurled it down the room. It crashed into kindling amid the courtiers, making several hop aside and curse, but not downing a man.

Then blades met with a crash, on all sides, and fighting began in earnest. Duthjack's warriors were blooded veterans, desperate outlaws not so long away from battles as to forget tricks of the fray, and they faced obviously frightened, unarmored men years past desperation on battlefields. Yet in the midst of the defensive, overly careful courtiers strode the armored giant, his blade biting like a serpent, sliding past a parry to take Peldrus in the throat, and then Braerim, in as many breaths.

"Take the armored knight!" Bloodblade barked, plucking up another chair. If he could hurl it over everyone's head, and hit that helm at the right moment . . .

His throw caught on a shoulder, and spun aside, serving only to make one of his own men reel and stagger. A courtier's blade leaped in to kiss a throat, and that was one fewer blade to obey Duthjack.

A courtier fell, and then another. Then the armored knight, his blade flashing in a knot of foes, hewed down Nluthkin and Tathtorn, sending a third man—Earlevus—reeling back. Earlevus gave Bloodblade a fear-filled glance and then bolted past, fleeing the room.

"Stop, sargh you!" Bloodblade shouted, reaching out with his sword to stop the man or cut him down—but finding his reach just short. *Horns and bebolt!*

Others were fleeing now, turning and pounding back down the room. "Stand, you dogs!" Duthjack raged, clawing one man to a halt but missing the rest. "Stand and fight! We've a kingdom to win!"

"Three forfend," came a voice from within the closed helm, "*more* idiots seeking to seize Aglirta with their swords. Lady, aid me."

Bloodblade spun around again to the fray, and ran a courtier through with some satisfaction, kicking another savagely in the crotch as the first man groaned his bloody way to the floor. There was a scream behind him, and he turned his head in time to see Earlevus reel back into the room and fall, his slayer yanking his blade free. It was a darting little man in leathers Bloodblade had never seen before—a procurer, by the Three, not a courtier!

Gods, was someone *else* trying to slay the king this night?

Bloodblade whirled around again, made a desperate parry, and danced away from a stumbling courtier. Blades skirled on both sides, another of his own warriors ducked aside—and Bloodblade found himself blade-to-blade with the armored knight.

His lip curled. The helm of the mysterious swordsman was of olden design; a swordtip could easily slip into its visor-slits. Sendrith Duthjack raised his bloody blade and snarled, "Meet death, man!"

"Oh?" The deep voice rang within the helm. "I've been seeking the Dark One for a long, long time—yet I never seem to find him when a warrior tries to show me the way."

"Then let this day be your day of finding," Bloodblade snarled, springing up into the air to put all of his weight behind a sweeping swordcut that should burst through his foe's guard and strike home into that visor.

Steel shrieked, and locked—and held. Two men strained, their blades bound together, faces almost meeting. Then Duthjack spun away and struck, low and swift: his best trick-of-the-blade, which had slain old Sarnor six summers back, and the outlaw Largrath before that.

His steel was turned aside by steel that seemed to spin out of nowhere to meet it. That same parry slid dazzlingly into a strike that smote Bloodblade's ribs sorely, tearing away an armor plate to clang and dangle by its remaining strap.

"Who *are* you?" Duthjack gasped, reeling back from his foe's swift steel.

The armored knight lifted his visor. Cold eyes stared at the outlaw.

"Your king," came a voice that was even colder.

Duthjack swallowed, uttered what might be a sob—and fled.

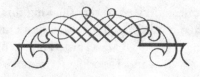

11

Of Snakes and Stones and Wells

Gazes met for a fleeting instant, each seeing hope dawning in the other. This just might be the chance they were awaiting. The two apprentices did not have to smile to share that thought—which was good, because neither quite dared to. This might, just might, be the day when the mighty and widely feared Tharlorn of the Thunders fell—dead, or twisted into endless torment and imprisonment by two unknown novices at sorcery.

There'd be plenty in the Vale to thank them for that. More than once, Tharlorn's dark magics had cracked like a slaver's whip over those he deemed his enemies. His spells had eaten men alive from within, or turned their limbs to tentacles to leave them flopping vainly until slain by revolted neighbors, or sent flying eels to devour the eyes of those who dared stand against him.

Wizards of note had been among Tharlorn's foes—a few, at first, and then pairs and cabals of them, driven together by increasing fear of the man who could call down lightnings from the sky, and turned men who intruded onto his lands into helpless statues, their muscles locked, until they perished of thirst or the creeping cold . . . or were devoured alive by scavengers.

Not so long ago, Tharlorn of the Thunders had been served by three apprentices—young, eager sorcerers of accomplishment who leaped to serve their master with absolute loyalty. Daring to do no less. The younger two were men, but the eldest and most skilled was a woman, and Tharlorn's bedmate: Cathaleira Bowdragon, of the Bowdragons of Arlund. Her family were famous in magecraft, and she was not the least among them—but a day after their first meeting, she was Tharlorn's willing slave.

That had been twelve summers ago, and a little more, and the time had come when Tharlorn had tired of willing slaves and their slyly ambitious little treacheries. Wherefore only two apprentices were standing in the chill deeps of the outermost spellcasting cavern beneath hidden Thundergard this day, and both of them were men.

"There," Tharlorn said suddenly, lifting his arms, the great sleeves of his robes billowing open by themselves as power streamed forth from him, in an invisible flood so rich and so sudden that the air itself seemed to ooze and shudder. " 'Tis done."

They were the first words the archwizard had spoken since muttering the last of the ten incantations that had transformed a tiny groundsnake into Tharlorn's masterpiece: a mage-slayer. Cathaleira's body had still steamed then, gutted and laid open on the worktable like a hog on a butcher's slab . . . before the many-times-enlarged snake had fallen on it, the snapping jaws of its many heads biting down in hungry unison, and devoured every last bone of the youngest Bowdragon. Tharlorn would face the enmity of a family of sorcerers when they learned her fate—but then, he would probably welcome it. Even archwizards need entertainment.

Tharlorn's fingers clawed the air in deliberate half-circles, and he could be seen to tremble. The two apprentices exchanged glances, and then the taller of the two took a cautious step forward to where he could—just—peer at Tharlorn's face.

The Master of the Thunders was sweating, and veins were standing out on his neck like dagger-blades. His lips were writhing soundlessly, his face contorting in a silent struggle that seemed to intensify as the snake across the chamber rose slowly, like a great, swaying pillar, and locked its gaze with the archwizard.

Thick it was, its shoulders as huge and heavy as a horse. "Shoulders," the apprentices had dubbed them, because they could think of no other word for the huge, corded mass of muscle where the shimmering scales ended, and what was sinuous and serpentine bulged out into a gigantic fist of flesh. A dozen slender, eel-like necks sprang from those shoulders, each ending in a golden-eyed head that was little more than an impossibly large set of jaws. Those sharp-fanged maws snapped at air, gaping in an endless, hungry, vain reaching for the wizard who'd shaped them.

The mage-slayer quivered. Great rippling spasms ran the length of its body as it tried to undulate forward, strove to wriggle its coils into movement— and failed, fighting the wizard's will.

Its golden forest of eyes glared at Tharlorn with a hatred that could be felt. Cathaleira was trapped behind them, awake and aware now—and silently screaming at her imprisonment, raging against his tightening control.

Locked in the mad depths of the monstrous body Tharlorn had shaped, twisting living flesh and bone as he fused several creatures together with spell after hissed spell, growing them into something out of nightmares, Cathaleira Bowdragon was damned as few humans had ever been. Her only crime had been ambition, her only mistake being too handy to her master's reach.

A thrumming that was deeper than growling droned about the room as the struggling mage-slayer tried to roar, or even hiss. No matter how many dripping jaws she'd been given, Cathaleira couldn't even scream.

The two apprentices stood like stone statues. Their faces were expressionless, two careful masks, as they watched Tharlorn of the Thunders tremble.

Their master was trying to bring his creation under his will as surely and as completely as he controlled his own hands. The taming, it seemed, was not going well. The snake hadn't managed to move any closer, but its tremblings hadn't eased, either—and now Tharlorn was trembling, too. His robes were sticking to his sweat-drenched body as he mind-wrestled in an invisible web of magic, seeking to overwhelm and conquer Cathaleira's mind as he so often had, betimes with tenderness as well as cruelty, her body.

Neither apprentice dared move for fear wizard or monster would notice them and lash out. Breathless and trapped, they swayed, fear-filled eyes glittering. They dared not move—but they dared not stay. If their master failed, would the many-headed snake bite and crush them in her haste to rend Tharlorn, or in triumph thereafter, before Cathaleira realized she'd need their aid to have any hope of inhabiting her own body again—or mastered her own red rage?

Their master, on the other hand, had sacrificed his most loyal and capable apprentice without warning. Would they be next, once Tharlorn controlled the mage-slayer, and desired to let it practice striking down prey—or wanted to feed its hunger?

The Lord of the Thunders straightened, and a smile spread slowly across his face, revealing clenched teeth.

"That's better," he gasped, his voice a strained parody of its usual casual arrogance. "You're mine, Cathlass . . . as you always were. Mine. Never forget it!"

He threw up a hand, and the great bulk of the snake reared over backward, its many heads snapping in unison at the ceiling, their darting tongues a brief, flickering forest. Tharlorn watched the heads fall back to regard him in baleful chorus, and smiled.

Without warning the mage-slayer whirled around and thrust its jaws at the two terrified apprentices. Golden eyes glared into their brown ones from about a foot away, glittering with malice—ere turning away in swift unison, as Tharlorn's smile broadened.

"Yes," he told them, "I think, and she obeys—without pause or demur." As he made the many-headed snake hasten in front of him, tracing a tight circle on the tiles like a minstrel showing his juggling to a crowd on all sides, he added, "Her scales are my most inspired innovation, I think: they reflect spells back at their sources."

He smiled at their tight, white faces and added lightly, "Try to remember that. It gives pause to harmful ambitions, I find."

Without waiting for a reply, the most feared wizard in all the Vale turned back to his circling mage-slayer. "I made you to destroy persons of my choosing. Let the rage you feel for what I have done to you goad you and guide you—as you slay the one whose image you now see."

Tharlorn waved his hand, and many golden eyes widened as one. Slavering jaws hissed in a rustling chorus, "Bodemmon Sarr!"

"Of course," the wizard replied, turning on his heel. He strode out of the room without another word or a backward glance.

The mage-slayer swung its heads to regard the two stock-still apprentices. The massed gaze of many glittering golden eyes, the two men found, carries a curious weight. Ere a few silent breaths had passed, they were both trembling.

Abruptly the serpent stiffened, turned its head with what might have been sneers twisting its many mouths, and slithered out of the chamber. It, too, did not look back.

Two faces that were pale with fear turned from fascinated contemplation of its undulating body to look at each other. Dry lips were licked, but neither of Tharlorn's surviving apprentices spoke.

In each other's eyes, each saw the same horror at Cathaleira's doom—and the grim knowledge that similar fates might not be far off for them.

The Lady of Jewels stretched long, shapely arms up over her head, swung them slowly down as her unbound hair stirred restlessly about her shoulders, and said to the men walking with her, "Ah, but it feels good to be saving the Vale with you three again!"

Craer merely grunted, but both Hawkril and Sarasper cast her looks and murmured variations to the effect of feeling the same way about her. Rested and restored, the Band of Four did feel at ease as they strolled along the winding farm lanes of upland Aglirta. They were in the poorest, most sparsely settled backcountry of what had once been the barony of Phelinndar—a land of many small farms, fenced with rocks and tangled gray giants of old tree stumps, where woodlots were many and their trees deep and dark, as if the Loaurimm was reluctant to draw back its fingers and let go its grip on the fallen barony.

Craer had almost decided to trust Embra again. She'd certainly seemed as bewildered as the rest when he'd found himself back with them in the Silent House again, after that bewilderingly short bout of running and slaying his way through Flowfoam against some outlaws bent on kingslaying—and she'd sworn up, down, and by every last oath of the Three that she'd cast no spell on him, and knew nothing about his sudden relocation. Craer knew the feel of Dwaer-magic by now, though . . . and if it hadn't been Embra using a Stone on him, who had it been? Hey?

Yet she'd offered to have Sarasper truth-tell her denials, and insisted almost to the point of tears that she'd had no hand in his sudden journey, and . . . and by the Three, Craer believed her. Which meant that someone with a Dwaer was watching over them.

Well, *that* shouldn't have been surprising news. After all, they were here, now, with the matter argued to a standstill and wearily set aside, to resume their hunt for Dwaerindim.

Embra had used her Stone to take them back to the clearing where she'd cast her seeking spell (a long time ago, it seemed). Now that place lay perhaps a day's journeying behind them. A small, swiftly banished prying spell that had nonetheless consumed an enchanted lamp of surpassing ugliness had told her that the Stone they sought now lay somewhere ahead of them, close by.

That lamp had been one of the few fragile items among the scores of enchanted oddities—old treasures from a grander, more magic-rich time—that now bulged in carrysacks and baldric pouches and even undergarment slings on each one of the Four. Though Embra's Dwaer-Stone was slung once more beneath her breast on a carry-chain (recovered after Hawkril had performed particularly bloody surgery on the upper half of the dead longfangs), they would need magic against the wizards and scheming barons and Serpent-priests; lots of magic. Besides, there were spells and spells—and use of a Stone this close to another of the Dwaerindim couldn't help but attract attention.

And a reaction that could only be two things: hostile and deadly.

"Lady Embra," Sarasper asked suddenly, "isn't it high time for our disguises? Wizards may sit unawares for heroes to burst in on them in min-strels' tales, but I've never found them to be quite so careless in real life—my life, at least."

"So it's you, is it?" Craer joked, firmly setting aside memories of being snatched to the Palace in midstep and then back again, several rooms and slayings later, just as abruptly. By the gods, he was Craer, and he would *be* Craer, merry tongue and all. "Without the walking ill fortune you bring, healer, we'd still be able to dance right in and pilfer hairs right out of the noses of sleeping mages without even interrupting their snores! Three take you! How long is it going to take me to steal enough for an early retirement to a life of idle leisure?"

"Judging by the mountain of coins and gems necessary to meet *your* needs for 'idle leisure,' I'd say about another sixscore years," Hawkril grunted. "Naetheless, Sarasper's right. It's time. Farmers' poacher-bows put quarrels through you that are just as hard as a guard's sword—or a hedge-wizard's farknife spell."

Embra sighed and spread her hands, palms downward, in a "stop" ges-ture. "You've the right of it," she granted, "and I've got to stop thinking of this as some sort of pleasure outing. Aglirta is in truth still ruled by no one. Stand still, all of you."

Craer made a brief, muted sheep's bleat at her, but all three men obeyed.

"Are we to be the Lady Baron and three courtiers, lost after losing our horses, or—?" Hawkril asked, his mouth lifting in the not-quite-grin that meant that his query wasn't serious.

"Why stoop to such a lowly rank? Why not be the Risen King himself," Craer asked, "and the three of us all barons? I'd quite like to be a sneering, mincing bar—"

"If it's to be left alone we want," Sarasper said sourly, "and you two can stop playing clowns-of-the-manor for a moment, we'd do better to be four Serpent-priests. *Everyone* will give us wide sword-room then!"

"And hiss in fear, and remember our passing, and not lift a hand to help us, should we ask," Embra Silvertree told them. "Nay, I think we'd do better as pilgrims seeking a relic of the Lady."

"No," Hawkril put in, "that will have us having to ask questions every-where about hunting cats or white falcons or suchlike. Pilgrims of the Huntress always seem to be seeking unusual beasts, remember? Better to be of the devout of the Forefather."

Ignoring Sarasper's wince, the armaragor rumbled on, "Then it's just us seeking flowers or seedlings in reverent silence, peering everywhere and speaking only to pass on soft blessings on everyone."

"Blessed Hoaradrim," Craer murmured, "that'll do. It's been years, though, since I've seen pilgrims dare to walk the Vale."

"Ah, but the king has returned," Embra said triumphantly. "A new peace dawns, we spread confidence by showing our trust in the king's guarding hand, and I spell-spin those long brown 'leaf-loving' robes for us all and need not worry about reshaping every last one of Craer's hundreds of daggers."

"Or Sarasper's hundreds of worries," the thief murmured in agreement, ignoring the dark look the healer gave him.

"Faithful of the Oak worries me not at all," Sarasper told them. "Do it, lass."

That earned him a twirl of Embra's hips and the mock-breathless reply, "By your command, Lord." Craer and (a little more slowly) Hawkril chuckled.

The old healer rolled his eyes and asked disgustedly, "Do none of you idiots take anything seriously? Anything at all?"

"Our meals," Craer said quickly. "Hawk's concerned most with belly-filling, whilst I apply myself to best filling flagons with *quality* dr—"

"Oh, belt up," Sarasper growled. "Three preserve me, it's like traveling with two minstrels who can never stop yammering. Two *bad* minstrels."

Craer put his hands on his hips in mock outrage. *"Well!"* he protested in scandalized tones. "Across half a kingdom we come to give thee succor, deliver thee from the lonely darkness that is Silvertree House, show thee the thrills of several lifetimes as we battle sorcerers, monster-beasts, and evil barons from one end of—"

"Craer," Embra said crisply, poking a statuette of Forefather Oak hard into the thief's leather-clad crotch, "be silent. Now, and for a reasonable time thereafter. You wouldn't want my spell to go wrong and you end up as a toad with uncontrollable flatulence, now would you?"

"Nay, Lady, you know him not," Hawkril said hastily. "He'd *enjoy* being a toa—"

"You'd almost have to kick an endlessly farting toad, wouldn't you?" Sarasper interrupted, rubbing his hands. "Do it, Lady."

"Silence, all of you," Embra said, turning her head to include all of them in her glare. Her eyes stopped, and lingered most fiercely, on Craer—who gave her a quick, impish little smile and said nothing. Very loudly.

Embra held up the statuette warningly, and without further ceremony began to whisper an incantation over it. A white, sparkling mist seemed to well up from nowhere to coil around her hands as she chanted, touching each of her companions with the figurine as it started to dwindle within her cradling fingers.

As the spell spun on, Hawkril turned his head slowly to survey the fields and trees all around them, seeking anyone—or any beast, however small—that might be watching. Embra had chosen her spot well. They were standing under the sheltering leaves of a huge old oak, in a spot where the dirt track they'd been walking along turned a gentle corner, around the bulk of a hill planted with barley, that rose steeply on one side of them. On the other, a dry brook had carved a little gulley that was almost completely cloaked in thornvines and broad-leafed woodmallow bushes—a small scar of broken ground out of which soared the oak flanked by a few strangled, sickly trees of other sorts. They were standing in a little hollow, walled away from prying eyes. Anyone spying on them would have to be standing very close.

Or using magic.

That thought sent a little chill through the hulking armaragor, a coldness that lasted through their slow, silent transformation into Faithful of the Oak. Embra became a fat, shuffling matron of cheerfully buxom manner, missing teeth, and copious warts; Sarasper became her even fatter counterpart, his face almost hidden in folds of drooping flesh; Craer became a thin, pouting-faced lass of boylike bonyness, and Hawk himself became a—a—

"Gods," he muttered, looking down. "You've made me a woman!"

"Quite fetching, too," Craer said, "if you like thighs like cows and bosoms like carters' potato sacks. Come to me, ravishing beauty of my drea—"

Sarasper calmly took the shapeless leather hat that had materialized on his head and thrust it smoothly over Craer's, pulling it down to well below the sallow girl's chin. Tangled locks of hair curled up here and there around its edges, but nothing else of the transformed lastalan's face could be seen. Hawkril snorted and Embra sputtered with mirth as Craer struck a pose and declared in muffled tones, "*He's* going to say it's an improvement, but I hold quite firmly to another view."

"I'm not so sure," Hawkril told him, straight-faced. "Leave it on for a time, whilst I think on this, hey?"

"And what might your name be, good matron?" the still-hooded Craer asked sweetly, crossing his arms beneath a frankly nonexistent bosom.

Hawkril drew himself up and declaimed with dignity, "Call me Vordra."

It was Sarasper's turn to double over in mirthful sputters, echoed by Craer from within the hat.

Embra raised an eyebrow. "There's something howlingly funny about 'Vordra'?"

"Vordra," Sarasper told her, "was one of your father's most prized breeding cows. A very good milker." He frowned. "He kept you *that* locked up?"

"Gods, yes," Craer agreed, emerging from under the battered hat. "I thought you knew."

Embra sighed and shook her head. "In all seriousness, remember this, gentlesirs: what I know is dwarfed by what I pretend to know."

Craer winced. "Words too well chosen to forget. A pity they aren't more often uttered by those whom they most closely fit."

"Such as—?" Sarasper asked meaningfully, leaning forward with a scowl.

Craer handed him his hat. "No, no, healer; none of us. I was thinking more of barons and suchlike rabble."

Embra shook her head and smiled. "We can be all day trading tongue-thrusts," she told the nearest branches overhead, "or we can settle on names for each other and be about this, hmm?"

"Well said," Hawkril growled. "Let's walk." He spread his arms and shooed his companions along the road, so forthwith they became Olim, his wife Vordra, their daughter Rendree, and Vordra's friend Lassa—who in her sweetest and most haughty Silvertree tones advised Hawkril to say nothing if all he could manage was his usual deep growl, and Craer to say nothing at all, ever, unless he wanted Lassa's boot well up his backside.

They were still chuckling at that when Olim saw the signboard, and pointed. Craer's eyes were still the best among them all; he squinted and announced, "Tarlarnastar. A small village—and proud of it."

"It does not," Vordra growled, "say that. Lay by your cleverness for a time, Crae—Rendree. I've never heard of Tarlarnastar."

"And I'm sure its folk have never heard of you, either, *Mother*," Rendree said sweetly, dancing swiftly out of reach.

"I thought you were going to kick him," Olim said to Lassa—who smiled back and then took two running steps and punted the young lass head over heels into the nearest ditch.

Rendree came up spitting frogs and snarling, "That's not so funny." His comment was swiftly belied by shrieks of laughter from his three companions. "I'm not sure Faithful of the Oak walk about hooting like drunken tavern lasses, either," he said sullenly.

Those words were true enough to abate the shouted laughter somewhat, and it faded away completely when Embra stiffened. She put her hand on Craer's wrist, just for a moment, warning him with her eyes. A moment later, that part of her magic that had let them see their new guises, instead of the true shapes beneath, started to fade.

Whatever he liked to pretend to be, the thief was no fool. An unseen alarm could only be magic that Embra had felt . . . and since no fire or flying sword or dancing bones were racing up to smite them, it must be a spying spell. They were being watched. The lastalan spun around and skipped back to Sarasper. He could see his companions as their true selves again, which meant that Embra had stopped working magic, and was trusting in her finished spell to show the world their disguised shapes.

"Does it still hurt you, Father?" Craer asked, frowning as a young girl might. "I heard you groan."

Sarasper met Craer's gaze for the briefest of moments, and said, "Aye, lass, you've the right of it, as usual. The Forefather delivers me not from the pain." His next step was a pronounced limp.

"Yet it does me good to hear us laugh, all together," he rasped. "Let us press on, for it may be that this Tarlarnastar holds my healing, or some sign from the Father."

Craer rolled his eyes, just once, to let Sarasper know he was playing the part of a pious pilgrim all too well, and turned away in his girl's body to run ahead a little, and peer—and sigh, and come pack kicking at stones. "I see no towers, Father," she said. "Only huts."

"And can you see all there is to see from one run and look?" Vordra said severely. "Walk with us, girl, and we shall enter this place together. It may be that hope, and help, and even salvation lie in other places besides *towers.*"

"Aye, well said, Vordra," her friend Lassa agreed, linking arms with the goodwife, who in turn leaned on her husband. "The Father loves trees and growing things, not the stones of men—and what is a tower but a man's pile of stones trying to be a tree?"

The look young Rendree gave her in response held a large measure of wrinkle-browed, eye-rolling incredulity. It ended abruptly when the thief within the girl saw Embra struggling not to sputter with fresh laughter. "We're not very good at this, are we?" she asked innocently, skipping away again.

"Some of us are *very* poor at heeding—walk *with* us, girl!" Vordra snapped. And so it was that four pilgrims walked or limped arm-in-arm into the small village that must hold the Stone Embra had felt.

Tarlarnastar was a small, pretty village. A few war dogs barked, straining at their neckchains, but only chickens ran underfoot in the mud of the lane. As Rendree had said, there were no towers, but only a few small cottages set close together along the road, their gardens running back into trees. Flat, displeased bleatings told of sheep somewhere nearby behind those shuttered houses; the ringing of a smith's hammer met their ears as they came down between the houses, and saw a wider space ahead, where the road widened to circle a stone wellhouse.

The smith was working outside, in the shade of his own shoeing cradle. No oxen were in it, and what he was hammering looked soon to become an axehead, or perhaps the blade of a frow or a big man's handhoe. He was a sweating, rough-bearded man who'd known battle, if the scar across his shoulder could be trusted, and as was the way of smiths and villages everywhere, he was working in the midst of an audience of lounging older men.

Curious looks and narrowed eyes measured the four travelers as they approached. If the smith heard or saw them, he gave no sign, but went on shaping his work with hard, ringing strokes.

Rendree started forward, but Vordra pulled her firmly back. It was Lassa who went to one of the seated men.

"Peace be with you, man, and with the Vale," she said, looking down into his guarded squint. "We are four Faithful of the Oak, and the man among us is hurt. Is there a healer, or a herbalist—or even a wizard—anywhere about, to see to him?"

The question earned them more curious looks, but the men staring at them kept silent for a long time, as the smith swung his hammer and then turned back to his forge, before a reply came. The man Lassa had spoken to worked his jaw as though chewing, looked at her and thoughtfully at the anvil, and told it, "Best go into the wellhouse, yon. The lord's there; he'll say."

"Forgive me," Lassa said, "but who is lord in Tarlarnastar?"

The man spat thoughtfully into the dust between his feet and told her, "Turnhelm, he calls himself. A great warrior, or was."

A few folk glanced out of windows or looked up from picking and weeding as the four pilgrims passed, and favored the four with more curious glances.

"Have these folk not seen pilgrims before?" Vordra rumbled in what was intended to be the faintest of whispers.

"Are you sure we haven't grown bat-wings and tails?" Rendree muttered in reply. "It *can't* be that they get no visitors—woodcutters are always going up into the Loaurimm, and floating down what they can't cut and pile on their carts."

Olim shrugged and held up his hand. They could just see the head of his dagger hilt in the curl of his closed fingers; the rest of the weapon was hidden in his grasp and up his sleeve. "Trust in the Forefather, as I do," he said pointedly, "and *be ready.*"

Tarlarnastar did have a tower, after all. The wellhouse was a large, round cylinder built of huge stones, though its walls barely overtopped Vordra's head; the space inside had to be as large as three cottages, or more. Its one door was wide enough for a cart, and stood ajar, with a single lantern or torch glimmering fitfully somewhere within. Lassa pushed the heavy wood

until it gaped wide, and stepped inside—only to be jostled aside by an excitedly skipping Rendree.

The young girl saw a round, open well with its bucket-hoist lost somewhere in the darkness of the rafters, hard-packed dirt and straw underfoot,
an untidy pile of rotting buckets to one side—and a dozen men or more in
the room: armaragors, in armor and with drawn swords in their hands.
Their smiles, as they started forward, were not friendly.

"So lastalans skip into battle like young lasses now, do they?" one of
them sneered. "Well, well, always a new tactic to bedazzle us."

A knife spun from him, flashing towards Embra, but Craer flicked out
a hand almost casually and struck it aside. Four magical disguises, it
seemed, had abruptly vanished.

"*Don't* kill the wench!" someone shouted. "We need her alive! The rest
don't matter!"

"Now, that," Craer said, springing at an armsman who was trying to rush
past him and driving his dagger hilt-deep into the man's ear, "annoys me."

The man made a strangled, gurgling sound as Craer pushed him away,
using the falling warrior to propel himself into a leap at someone else. As he
sprang, the thief added, "It always annoys me when folk dismiss me as
someone who doesn't matter. Know this, dolts: we *all* matter. Even your
deaths diminish me . . . a little."

By then the wellhouse was a chaos of charging warriors, blades glinting and clanging off friendly armor, walls, and the well-rampart as they
were waved wildly. Behind Craer, Hawkril growled like a bear and
strode forward to meet the armaragors. There was a sudden flash from
between Embra's hands, and by its light the Four saw that the large
round room held even more men than they'd thought. Craer planted
both of his boots hard in the gut of a warrior who folded up around the
thief, groaning out his pain as he let a sword fall from one hand and a
dagger from the other—and the light between Embra's hands was suddenly a raging bolt of snarling brightness that danced across the rear of
the chamber like a restless snake, leaving men gasping and staggering in
its spark-strewn wake.

"Get her!" one of the six warriors facing Hawkril shouted. "Take the
witch down!"

Armored bodies surged sideways, bursting past a tumbling Craer and
beyond the reach of Hawkril's blade. Sarasper spun away from one swordcut with blood fountaining from the side of his head—and the next warrior
lunged through the space where the healer had stood and put the tip of his
blade through one of Embra's moving, spell-weaving hands.

Light leaked out of the wound as she shrieked, and as dark blood streamed forth in its wake the sorceress looked up with fire in her eyes and cried out an incantation that made the very air shake. Figurines burst along her belt in a row of little flames.

Something unseen but heavy rippled in the air, rolling out from her. It moved like a huge wave crashing ashore, sweeping men off their feet and hurling them back against the stone walls in a clatter and shrieking of armor. Men shouted in fear and pain, and Embra snarled back her fury at them.

Hawkril grimly hoisted a man into the air like a hog on a spit, slowly raising his blade as the man transfixed on it convulsed like a wriggling eel, spat forth blood in a great spasm, and then fell limp.

Beside the armaragor, Craer found his feet and reached down to haul up a crawling Sarasper. Between them and the far wall was nothing but emptiness—living and dead, the warriors of the wellhouse had been swept back against the stones.

The old healer clawed his way upright, swayed, and caught hold of Craer for support. For just a moment then, no one moved. Embra stood with her hands raised, holding the men who'd attacked them pinned against the wall, straining and snarling, their sneering smiles changed to fear and fury.

Abruptly she noticed that one man—a man without armor, but who wore a cowl and ragged shoulder-cloak, his face lost in its shadow—was stepping forward, as if her spell wasn't touching him. He walked with one hand thrust into the breast of his tunic, as if hurt, but he moved like doom coming for Embra—slow but inexorable.

She slashed at him with the last of its force, an outpouring that should have sent him tumbling away helplessly. Yet he strode on, limping as he came, slow but somehow . . . confident.

With a shock Embra became aware of something else: the Stone she wore against her ribs was thrumming and swiftly growing warm. Soon, she knew, it would sear her flesh, and begin to cook her. Another Stone was doing this.

"Who are you?" she hissed at the man, digging into her bodice with frantic hands. Even the chain-sling was growing hot.

Craer, Hawkril, and a staggering Sarasper were closing ranks in front of her, swords raised and ready, to meet the advancing man—and, she now saw, a handful of warriors who were following on his flanks, as if he was the tip of an arrowhead coming at her.

A voice spoke from behind the advancing man, a voice she'd heard somewhere before. "Bow down before the rightful Lord of Tarlarnastar: Turnhelm the Mighty!"

Craer hooted in open mirth at that title, but none of the other Four joined in. Their eyes locked on the gleam of a Stone held in the breast of a tunic—and on the face above it, eerily lit by its growing glow.

It was a face Embra had known all her life. A face whose very sight awakened cold fear. Sickened, Embra laid her bleeding hand on her own Dwaer-Stone, hearing her spilled blood sizzle, and tried to force it back to coolness. She'd never be able to do it, this shaken and with so many swords coming for her. Swords in the hands of warriors she knew, too, from too many fear-filled years.

"Welcome, Daughter," said the Baron Faerod Silvertree, his smile as cold as a deep, white winter.

A spell she did not recognize erupted from behind him, racing past Embra's shoulder in a green arc to burst behind her, filling the wellhouse doorway with green raging fire that sent stabbing pains through Embra's back and thighs until she scrambled forward, cursing. They were walled in.

Her father had dabbled in magic, but this was something beyond her lore; Embra's eyes narrowed. There was a mage here, hiding behind the man who'd birthed her . . . the man she hated more than all other foes put together.

Yet it was her father—Turnhelm indeed; a very apt name he'd chosen himself—who held a Dwaer-Stone, and was making hers turn traitor on her.

She closed her hand like a claw around the Stone at her breast, regardless of the pain. She would wrest control of it back from him, or die in the trying. She'd hold it until the last bones of her fingers crumbled to ash and let it fall. . . .

The moment her mind was in the flow between the Stones, Embra knew she was the stronger. Easily she thrust her father's influence away from her, until their wills strained in midair, closer to him than to her. Hasty spells had been cast to aid him—and only their force kept her clenched will from striking out through his Stone.

Faerod Silvertree had come to a halt, barely beyond the reach of Hawkril's blade, but all of his warriors were slowly staggering forward from the wall, fear and hatred of Embra warring on their faces, to stand beside him. Some of them had been his bodyguards in Castle Silvertree; one or two of those had been Embra's tormentors. When they stood in a long, menacing line—minus the few who'd never move again, lying still along the wall in awkward tangles of armored limbs—they took a step forward, in unison.

Behind the Four green fire raged, a wall of needle-thrusting death at their backs.

"So you found a Stone, Father," Embra remarked, almost casually, letting her eyes bore into his.

Faerod Silvertree's mouth crooked, a little. "An outlawed tersept had been hiding it for years," he said, "using it for nothing. My need was greater—particularly after his life so abruptly and regrettably ended—and since then, I've been healing myself. I'm almost whole again." His trace of a smile faded. "Almost."

Sudden fingers of fire burst into life behind the Lord of Tarlarnastar, reaching around him in a bright and deadly halo to stab at the Four.

Stab, and strike home, amid four gasps. It felt like heated daggers were being driven through the Four. They staggered, and Sarasper sagged slowly to the wellhouse floor.

"Old bones," Faerod Silvertree remarked. "Throw them aside, Daughter; your fondness for lesser beings remains a weakness. I need you to be a strong blade in my hands once more."

As Embra bared her teeth to snarl "Never" at him, the wizard stepped out of hiding from behind the self-styled Lord Turnhelm, wearing triumph like a swirling cloak.

It was the Master of Bats.

"Surrender, and live," the wizard whom Embra thought she'd slain laughed at her, his eyes cold and cruel as he let his hard gaze range across the Four, "or defy us, and . . ."

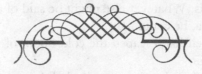

12

Aglirta Beset

"D ie," one of the warriors muttered, so low that only the man beside him could hear. "Defy the king, and die. . . ."

The hollow around them was like many others in the heights: a small, fern-choked cleft overhung by the spreading boughs of massive blackbark trees. A place of moss-girt stones and dappled shadows, where birds whirred from bush to bush, or trilled briefly from high perches.

In one place, the birds shared leafy boughs with two grim and silent men—warriors, by their garb, who sat huddled in dark cloaks peering tirelessly out across the Vale below the heights, where the woods of Silvertree gave way to farms and lanes and shops, falling away to the silver ribbon of the river winding in the distance.

The hollow below these sentinels was also unlike most others in the heights. It held not darting birds and furtive furry things, but a grim and ragged handful of men. Four warriors in well-used armor, three with drawn swords ready across their knees.

All of them sported bandages dark and stiff with dried blood. The standing, restlessly pacing one whose bindings were across his brow and around his arms was the one called Bloodblade, who'd lately dared to try his hand at kingslaying, and found it a harder sport to master than he'd thought.

The men around Bloodblade had followed him on his foray with eagerness, but there was little that could be termed "eager" in the hollow now.

They had run miles to reach this place, sprinting and stumbling even more desperately than they'd fled from barons' patrols since their return from the Isles. They'd run panting, the screams of dying fellows in their ears, as they stumbled over uneven ground and before that fine things that broke underfoot on the tiled floors of the palace—routed by one man and a few scrambling guards. Whatever else might be said of the man who called himself king in Aglirta, he could fight.

Bloodblade himself had escaped the cold doom of the king's swordtip only because of a chair.

A gilded, overstuffed chamber seat, hurled through the fray by Mararr in a timely manner. It had swept Snowsar and his blade aside from Sendrith Duthjack's throat long enough to let an overmatched rebel leader scramble away from the spot he'd begun to think he'd die in, and flee like a fearful child through the palace, abandoning all in his hunger to be well out of reach of a blade he could not parry, that leaped through his guard time after time to kiss flesh and spill Duthjack blood.

Those wounds burned and itched now, and fear lay on Sendrith Duth-jack like an ever-present heaviness beneath his snarling anger. Bloodblade had never been afraid before, and he was discovering it was a feeling he hated more heartily than anything else.

King Snowsar had to die. Not to put Sendrith Duthjack on a throne now, but to shatter and banish this fear forever.

He was half-expecting to see the glitter of speartips and armored men on horseback bobbing up the slopes below, guided by wizardly prying to slay the handful of men who'd escaped the king's blade and Flowfoam's stone guardians to reach this place.

That was what he'd have done, were he king. Give no time for finding far lairs or calling on aid, but fare forth and sl—

"Claws of the Dark One!" one of the sentinels in the trees hissed, leaves dancing as he leaned forward for a better view.

Every head lifted to look at him, but he held silence as long minutes passed. Mararr finally growled, "What is it?"

"I know not," the man above him muttered. "Some sort of—beast."

Mararr squinted up at the sentinel. "*What* sort of—?"

The man pointed. "Look for yourself. I've not seen such before."

The men on the hollow shared frowns and questioning glances—and then, as one clambered cautiously up out of the cleft and forward, between shrubs, to crouch on the rocks at the edge of the heights.

Something that might have been a lizard and might have been part cow was trudging along a field not far below them, dragging a stumpy tail along in its wake. It was gray, and held two huge claws or pincers low beneath its outthrust head—a feature as bare and as ugly as the bald, snapping-jawed, leathernecked head of an Isle sea turtle. Its body, as large as a wagon, was humped but smooth, stretching out into thin wings that looked for all Darsar like the edges of a shell. . . .

"Three defend!" one of the warriors swore. "It's a huge crab of the deeps, come up on land!"

"A land crab?" Mararr snapped in disbelief. "What could make a crab come this far from the sea?"

"Magic," Bloodblade snarled. "A wizard meddling with what's better left alone, as usual. Bringing it to hunt us, I'll wager."

The lumbering gray land crab came to the edge of a field, where stones turned up in ploughing had been heaped man-high to form a fence. The men on the heights, weary of running away, watched closely, in case the beast should turn along the line of stones and come closer—and to judge how agile it was by seeing it climb and clamber.

The beast neither turned nor ascended from its plodding progress upriver, but without pause or ceremony trudged forward, *into* the stone. In silence and without any flash of spell it stumped doggedly ahead, dragging its heavy tail. Bloodblade's men crouched in the rocks like so many statues and stared at the land crab intently as it trudged ahead, melting into the stones like a shadow, until it was completely gone.

The field beyond the fence of stones held a few cows. They were grazing, heads down, their only movements lazy flicks of their tails against buzzing flies. Bloodblade and his men watched the land crab emerge from the pile of stones, still lurching along at the same slow, deliberate pace, and cross this next field.

The nearest cow lifted its head for a moment, chewing thoughtfully— and a long gray claw shot out, closing on a bovine leg but continuing in its forward thrust. The suddenly struggling cow was hop-walked awkwardly across the grass for a few moments before the other claw reached forward to clamp on to another leg—and the cow was heaved over onto its back with a crash.

Claws closed, severing the legs within them, and the cow screamed in pain—raw, high bellows that ended abruptly when the land crab's jaws bit through its throat. Blood fountained, and the men on the heights watched the land crab feed patiently amid the red glistening thrashing. Its bites were deliberate and unhurried—but the cow was reduced to a tangle of bones in the time it might have taken a weary warrior to yawn his way through the unbuckling and kicking aside of his armor and walk away, leaving everything strewn where it had fallen, for servants to see to.

"Gods above," one of the watching warriors said roughly. "What can it be?"

"I'd say," Mararr replied slowly, as they watched the crab-beast resume its slow journey upriver, "that it's a rock crab or some other small lizard thing, twisted and made huge by the spells of wizards obeying the Risen King: a monster born of his commands, sent forth to slay all his foes."

"Is that so?" Gurkyn asked darkly. "It'll be busy for years, then."

Mirthless chuckles greeted this sally, a grim ripple of sound that died away as suddenly as it had arisen, lost in astonished gasps.

"Sargh," someone whispered, fear making his voice tremble—and another of the warriors among the rocks actually whimpered.

Coming across the field of cows from another direction was another monstrous beast. It was in a hurry, this one, surging ahead in a continuous, impatient undulation, and paying no heed to either cattle snorting and hastening out of its way or to the doggedly disappearing land crab. It was the largest snake any of the warriors had ever seen—and it glared at the Vale through golden eyes that gleamed on a dozen long-fanged heads, each at the end of its own coiling neck.

Men crouched as low to the rocks as they could as some of the heads turned to look at the heights, jaws snapping hungrily—but the snake never turned or slowed, gliding downriver with frightening speed.

"May the Three take all mages," a warrior whispered, "bebolten *soon!*"

"Before sundown," Mararr agreed fervently, as the many-headed snake disappeared over a distant rock fence. He shivered then—and he wasn't the only one.

She set her teeth and shivered, knowing what she must do. *Now!* Now, while they were still gloating!

Embra abruptly dropped her furious wrestling with her father through the Dwaerindim, and shivered again, knowing the pain that would come.

Even as the ravening fire of his Dwaer-Stone stabbed at her, the Lady of Jewels lashed out with the roiling energies of her own to twist the green fire behind her—forcing it into Sarasper in a cooling, healing flood, so that it was a barrier no more. Then she whirled the fire of her Stone around in a great, ragged shield to parry the flood sent by her father's fury.

She almost managed it, deflecting much of the howling tempest aside to claw along the walls. The rest of it thrust through her like a dozen ice-cold swordblades, shocking a scream out of her that made her father and his wizard both wince.

Then she was hurtling away, arched over backwards and rigid, turning slowly in the air as she went so that her thighs struck the wall first with teeth-chattering force, and she slid down it onto the floor, face-first, with her mind awhirl, power roiling numbingly through her. *The pain, oh gods, the pain!*

As her trembling, convulsing body fell on its side in the dirty straw, Embra tugged at the flows of force and hurled them at her father and his mage, seeing them both stagger back with something akin to alarm mingled with dawning respect on their faces.

There were startled shouts from her father's armsmen, and through swimming eyes Embra saw the huddled form of Sarasper boiling up into the furry, spiderlike bulk of a longfangs, Craer and Hawkril taking up stances before the healer to shield him during the transformation.

The Baron Silvertree knew what the healer's changed shape was in an instant. "Sword it!" he ordered his men, pointing at the trembling bulk, and then turned to the Master of Bats with a snarled, "Wizard!"

The sorcerer Huldaerus gave the baron a tight smile and spread first his hands, and then his cloak. From its inky depths welled up a great flood of chittering, flapping darkness: a cloud of bats, sweeping up to the ceiling like impatient smoke seeking a chimney. "It shall not climb out of reach," he remarked almost casually. "Nor will these two bladesmen last long with their eyes torn out by my little ones!"

Embra tried to crawl to her feet, but the wellhouse whirled crazily around her. She sank back into the straw with a helpless gasp, clawing at her breast to try to touch her Stone and draw on it. Her father's warriors were charging forward in a grinning wave, blades glittering, so many that Hawkril could not help but be overwhelmed—and once he was gone, they'd all be swept away, the Band of Four gone forever. . . .

"Gut them with your blades," the Baron Silvertree said with a cold smile. "Let their deaths be slow and painful. We'll let my daughter watch; perhaps, at last, she'll learn something."

The man who ran into tiny Dlaenriprel was gasping and staggering, groaning too hard in his fight to breathe to form words at first. He clutched at the sleeve of an astonished carter and gasped something wordless but urgent as he sank to his knees.

"What, man?" the carter snapped, staring into the man's panting face. "What news?"

"Behind me," the man gasped at last. "Coming . . . here soon. Monster!"

The carter's eyes narrowed. "What sort of beast?"

"Crab claws . . . huge crab-thing! Move . . . your cattle! Eats cows!"

The carter stared into the man's face for a moment that banished all disbelief, and then whirled, letting the gasping man fall, and ran for the horn by the well, to rouse Dlaenriprel.

And to think some folk liked to rouse trouble. Flowfoam was like an anthill kicked open by a farmer's boot.

King Kelgrael Snowsar leaned back on the River Throne and tried to hide a sigh. A moment later, his jaws were aching as he fought down a yawn.

Another day beset by intrigues. And to think some stoneheads *wanted* to be king.

The throne room today was truly the heart of the anthill, with courtiers scurrying this way and that, cloth-of-gold finery swirling and glinting, and the scheming chatter risen to a ceaseless din that echoed back from the ceiling in its restless, urgent fervency. His stewards of the chamber had been on their feet since dawn, fending off men who tried to rush the throne like besiegers storming a breach—and they were still at it now, stiff collars quivering with the force of their indignation and insistent commands.

One at a time they let the yammerers come to him, and one after another he heard them out, a bleating flood of fawning, now menacing, now oh-so-unsubtly hinting faces and reeking scents and glittering finery.

"Surely, Your Exalted Majesty," the latest one was saying, a patronizing sneer creeping across his face as if he judged Risen Kings too blind to notice such little details, "you must see that the family Halidynor has the elder, better claim to Phelinndar! Onthalus Halidynor should be standing before you as the most loyal of your barons right now—and can be, by this time two days hence, if you but—"

There was some sort of commotion by the doors. Voices raised in anger, heads turning in annoyance, stewards converging.

A man who wore more mud than shimmerweave thrust aside a steward and snarled loudly, "I care not if these folk have been waiting *three* days and nights through! My news cannot wait! The king's ready arm is needed *now*!"

More stewards rushed to that spot, and there was more shoving. "Aglirta stands in peril!" the man shouted desperately, as high collars hid him from view and started thrusting him back to the doors. "A rescue! My King! A rescue!"

King Snowsar came to his feet in a bound, dismissing the smoothly sneering courtier in midword with a curt wave of his hand, and strode down the steps from the River Throne with one hand upraised. *"Hold!"* he bellowed.

Silence fell in the chamber. All eyes were fixed on him but those of his struggling stewards, as they sought to move a man who, it seemed, would soon need to be dragged away.

"My stewards," the king added quietly, "desist. Bring that man to me."

Outrage was born on dozens of faces, most of his stewards' among them. A few managed to keep their faces carefully impassive; Snowsar almost smiled as he watched others struggle to seem loyal and eager to serve—and fail miserably.

"Keep me not waiting," he prompted, as the stewards seemed to hesitate, almost as if conferring amongst themselves in a flurry of silent glances. "Many concerns press us; many good people stand here . . . waiting."

The stewards had, it seemed, been arranging themselves into a formal escort around the intruder, for they now turned to face the throne in unison and marched forward, impatiently pushing the crowd of curious courtiers aside.

The man in their midst was red from his struggles, and looked more weary than triumphant. "Speak, goodsir," the Risen King bade him, hands on hips as he stood at the foot of the steps. "The concerns of all Aglirtans are welcome here."

The man bobbed his head in acknowledgment, caught his breath, and said in a rush, "A fearsome beast is come to the realm, Your Majesty—the like of which no man has seen before. A crab-beast as large as a haywagon, that walks the land and devours cows where they stand! It rends and devours farmfolk and even armaragors who stand against it, but otherwise ignores all, and will not be turned aside from its journeying—straight upriver. 'Tis in old Phelinndar by now."

The man paused for breath, and the court erupted in derisive chatter. The mud-caked man glared around for a moment, shook his head at the open disbelief he saw on many faces, and added loudly, "I am sent from Garthrail. We've no tersept or lord, but I speak for all—and for the farmers of Aundlestone, Brethrithyn, and Klaendor. Silvertree has no baron for us to turn to, no one to defend us against this beast born of fell sorcery—so we turn to the king."

The Risen King drew himself up to his full height, and took a step backwards without looking, up one step of the stair to his high seat, the better to be seen. "The Throne shall provide," he said loudly. "Stewards, make ready my Swords of the Castle, ready-armed for war. Bid them bring along a wagon of lances and a barrel of pitch. Let all be ready on the barge by sunfall."

There was a moment of shocked silence—and then the chamber erupted into a positive roar of excited, indignant, and incredulous talk.

Gods, was this Risen King to be a hothead forever wild-riding to the excitement of the moment? He dared to send his paltry bodyguard, or go with them! Who, then, would rule Aglirta while he was gone? Was this some trick of a baron, to gather in the king to a swift death by arrows in the woods upriver from Silvertree? How dare this clod of a farmer burst in with such a wild, obviously false tale! Was he hoping to capture the king and demand a ransom of Aglirta? Well, he'd get not a single copper wheel from *this* purse, no, nor—

"Tell me more of this beast," the king said more quietly, stepping down again to take the mud-covered man by the arm and guide him up the steps to the table by the throne where two stewards guarded decanters of wine and a platter of biscuits and cheeses. The roar of converse fell instantly to a ragged hush, as courtiers strained to hear every word exchanged by the king and the man from Garthrail.

"It's, ah, gray, Your Majesty," the weary envoy began, gratefully accepting a goblet steered into his hand. "And slow, with a hard shell on its body. Were it not for its claws—which are like a crab's, but as long as you or me with us laid down, y'see—you'd probably think it a great turtle come out of the river. It, ah, stumps along when it walks, like they do, and has a bare-skinned head like a river-snapper. It may turn aside to fight or dine, but goes right back to the line of its travel, and proceeds. Men with pitchforks tried to get it turned around, and did—but after it ate their forks and the hands of one who was too slow to let go, it went back to its old heading, as carefully as a matron at her knitting."

"And how," the old and impressively bearded steward Ranthalus asked severely, "do you know it was, as you put it, 'born of fell sorcery'?"

Ranthalus was the eldest of all the stewards of Flowfoam, and spoke first—on the strength of the paltry few spells he'd mastered, though none at court had actually seen him do anything more impressive than make all the torches in the throne room catch light at once, and soar their flames high or dim them to guttering in silent obedience to his will.

"It was the rocks," the man from Garthrail said simply, not knowing what title to give this scowling old man and so essaying none.

" 'The rocks'?" Ranthalus asked, quoting with a fastidiousness that was equal parts derision and irritation.

"Rocks, aye. The beast, y'see, walks through them. *Through* them, like they aren't but clouds or mist, be they stone barn walls or rocks of the field."

Ranthalus raised an incredulous brow—an action in which, across the crowded throne room, he was not unaccompanied. "A land crab, that walks as straight as a shot arrow up the Vale, eating men and cows, and strolls through stone. Man, have you been drinking?"

The reply was swift and firm. "Many a time, oldbeard, and much since we fought it—but there's nothing wrong with my eyes, nor with those in six villages I know of!"

"You fought it yourself? That is, man: 'twas solid, that you could feel?"

"Numbed my hands on my best fork when it broke the end off it," the man from Garthrail said. "And I dragged old Nurgar—dead or dying, by then—away from it after it snipped his leg off. Got his blood all over me. It's real, all right—no wizards' crowd-dazzle spell, if that's what you're after."

"May the Three strike you down, man, if you say false," Ranthalus began severely, "and the right royal justi—"

There came another commotion, even through the now-rising babble of the court, and the old steward lurched around to peer with the growl, "*Another* beholder of beasts?"

It seemed the stewards of Flowfoam learned swiftly. They were escorting another travel-stained man across the room briskly, ordering aside increasingly angry courtiers with brisk authority.

The king laid a hand on his eldest steward's arm, keeping Ranthalus silent, as this new arrival reached them and went to his knees. "Great King," he gasped, looking up with remembered fear in his eyes, "I bring word of a fell beast!"

"A crab that eats cows?" Ranthalus asked with a frown, pretending not to see the sharp look his king gave him.

The man looked puzzled. "Nay, Lord," he said, " 'tis a snake as large as a cottage, with many heads!"

"Gods above!" the old steward snarled, looking to the ceiling as if he expected the Three to be hovering there with glowing holy scrolls of guidance held out to him in their hands. "Is there—urrrkk!"

The gods weren't waiting by the ceiling, but someone was.

A someone clad in dark leathers, who'd just finished swinging the domed skylight back into place with stealthy care, and was sitting in a hook-sling dangling from a none-too-solid stone gargoyle ceiling boss, contemplating how best to strike. Someone who was wearing a tusked and grinning "battle ghost" mask, of the sort used in the masques of hot summer in the many-terraced city of Houlborn, and holding a long, needle-thin sword naked in his hand.

Someone who, as First Steward Ranthalus stared up in open-jawed amazement and dawning horror, sprang lightly from his perch and dropped down through the air with a whirring of tether-line, sudden smoke billowing from something clutched in a dark-gloved hand. The grinning mask loomed up very suddenly as the source of the smoke was tossed into the courtiers—but Ranthalus had eyes only for that glittering blade, extended point first and coming down at him very, very fast . . . right into the heart of the steward's rough, croaking attempt at a scream.

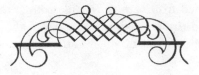

13

Some Surprises; Nasty

*A*s his spice-smoke plunged courtiers into helpless fits of coughing, the man who called himself Velvetfoot launched himself calmly down into the shouting, gaping tumult of their midst. He had, after all, a reputation to maintain.

He'd whispered energetically for some years, spending more than a few coins in the process, to succeed in attaching the murmured words "a deadly success" to his name. He'd managed to keep that linkage intact during recent reverses only because of a timely death that, thankfully, he'd had no hand in. The deceased was a secretive mage who'd hired him to find a Dwaer-stone in the ruins of Indraevyn and bring it back for use in a ritual to awaken the Serpent In The Shadows. Velvetfoot had said more than one fervent (though silent) thanks to the wizard's slayer—before in turn killing him. A reputation, as has been said, must be maintained.

The highly useful fact remained that one cannot be seen as a failure by a dead man—nor do mute corpses spread word to others. Wherefore Velvetfoot had soon been suggested to someone else as the perfect man to slay an inconveniently Risen King.

Personally, Velvetfoot held the view that it was unwise to kill King Snowsar at this time, and so plunge Aglirta into a bloody struggle for power before the royal court had grown strong and settled enough to hold the realm together through the violent death of a king and subsequent coronation-by-force of an usurper. In a lawless land, deaths come easily, and **slayers-for-**hire command only paltry fees. In a settled realm, slayings are **harder** and more expensive . . . and *that* was the sort of Aglirta Velvetfoot wanted to dwell in.

Wherefore he'd brought no crossbow and poisoned quarrels with him this day, and Snowsar stood not far from him right now, very much alive. Moreover, he'd learned from a very reliable source that a rival slayer-for-hire, a Sirl man called Andalus who wore a battle ghost mask when he did his killings, had already been hired—by other interests—to end the life of the king.

Andalus had been the man who'd so conveniently slain Velvetfoot's Dwaer-seeking employer, and in turn been removed from the ranks of the living of Aglirta by Velvetfoot. That latter obliteration had been very private, so it was no risk to one desiring the blame for a clumsily public attack on the king to fall on the wrong slayer-for-hire to wear a mask that said "Andalus" to those in the know, as one dropped down out of the shadows to try to slay a king.

So Andalus would fail to slay the King of Aglirta here today. It was not the first time that the man plunging through the air with sword stretched forth to slay had disagreed with an employer as to the wisdom of a slaying. And among professional slayers and those who hire them, disagreements have a regrettable habit of ending in sudden deaths. . . .

Velvetfoot's blade plunged deep into the open mouth of an old and arrogant steward who was reputed to be something of a mage—and who, therefore, would serve Aglirta infinitely better as a corpse.

Blood fountained amid frantic garglings, and as Velvetfoot's boots smashed the bearded old body to the floor, shattering ribs like dry twigs, the slayer tore his sword free and swung it in a wild arc around himself, almost casually laying open the throat of the second travel-worn envoy.

Dark blood sprayed forth. As he plunged through it at the king, drawing his sword back to strike, Velvetfoot noticed that his blade was dripping white, green, and gold with the brains of the old steward. Hmm: the colors of Gloit. Interesting. Now, how to keep from killing the Risen King of Aglirta without being obvious about it?

He'd have to stumble, allow the man—who seemed agile enough, leaping back now to gain room to swing the royal sword, and drawing it with swift grace—a chance to flee, and also give him good reason to; in front of his court, at least, this Snowsar seemed to want to play the noble hero. Perhaps maiming his sword arm would suffice. . . .

The royal sword flashed a bright blue-white, and there was a sudden, intense chill in the air. Magic. Velvetfoot sprang to one side as the other messenger from the country made a grim, unarmed grab for him, and then ducked smoothly under the man's outstretched arms and punched him hard up under the ribs.

Winded and staggering, the man from Garthrail stumbled back where

Velvetfoot's blow sent him—right into the heart of the flickering web of magic that was fading into visible life around the king. The man stiffened, gasped, and froze—toppling to the floor wild-eyed and helpless, his body immobile in midconvulse.

Failure here would not be difficult in the slightest, after all. Horns and gongs burst into sudden life, and were echoed in the halls behind the throne room, as stewards finally found something useful to do in their diligent service to Aglirta.

Wearing the faintest of smiles behind his mask, the man called Velvetfoot whirled and fled. He doubted this square-jawed royal hero would have gone around this palace rapping and prying on things to find the hidden ways—and he doubted even more that any of these other dolts would think to look for secret passages even if they were hurled bodily into one.

Wherefore lurking to learn things that could enrich should be easy. Boots were already pounding along distant passages as Velvetfoot vaulted over one would-be foe—or, more likely, just a courtier who'd learned how to strike a dramatic pose with his sword, and didn't want to waste a chance to use it in public—put the toe of his boot into the face of another, and whirled out an archway and around a pillar into oblivion, all in a few frantic instants.

It was a handful of frantic instants more before the first shouting guards pelted past the pillar, arriving in haste to aid their king.

They were in time to see an unfortunate courtier stray too close to the royal swordtip, and discover that the king had found a sword somewhere that, when its magics were awake, paralyzed those it touched. Enthusiastically they raced across the polished tiles to hack at the stiff and helpless bodies—only to be waved grimly away by a king who looked profoundly annoyed.

And no wonder. This was the second attack on him, in the very heart of Flowfoam, in as many days. They hastened to obey his curt orders, removing the fallen, both alive and dead, the slit and empty fruit that had held the spice-smoke, and the swords strewn here and there. "Be sure my armor's on that barge," was the last royal order.

The guards needed no orders to decide to stand flanking the throne as King Snowsar beckoned to the nearest steward, and the audiences resumed.

The distractions of plunging assassin and swordplay and claims of fantastic beasts—the one going downriver, and hence work for barons, but the other enough to make the king abandon his court to make war on it—would provide rich fare for the avid gossips, but they were still annoyances to courtiers desiring to be busy getting the king to recognize or outlaw this or that baron, or decide on half a hundred little matters of trade, preferential treatments, and treaties desired with this outland city or that.

"I'm both pleased and proud to see Your Majesty unharmed in the wake of these unpleasantnesses," the sixteenth smooth voice murmured, "and confess myself impressed by the bold and heroic figure Your Majesty presented, in the fast-closing teeth of danger. May I say how fortunate all Aglirta now is, to have such a pillar of noble might wearing our crown."

Indeed. Boldly and heroically, Kelgrael Snowsar managed neither to roll his eyes nor to yawn.

"Under your wise rule, Majesty," the courtier murmured, leaning as close to the king as he could, "Aglirta should rise to be greater than ever before. Perhaps to rule the Isles beyond the Vale, and the lands beyond our mountains. You might be King Kelgrael of all Asmarand in but a few years."

The king crooked an eyebrow. "If I–?" he muttered.

"If you do the boldest thing of all," the courtier almost whispered, "and keep peace with the folk of the Serpent, rather than fighting them as your barons do. Let them worship, know their friendship and support, and grow stronger as they do—rising together to greatness!"

For just a moment, the face of Kelgrael Snowsar was like stone, his eyes two hard gems that did not sparkle. Then he lowered his eyebrow and murmured, "We'll talk more of this later."

"Majesty, depend on it," the man said, straightening and stepping back from the throne with a smile curling his lips and a flash of triumph in his eyes.

"Oh, I shall," the king said, so quietly that not even the steward standing beside the throne could hear him.

Swiftly, as the courtier bowed and strode away, the steward bent to the royal ear and said hesitantly, "Majesty, I fear I heard you poorly. How may I serve?"

The king murmured, "Mark you the man who was just speaking to me?"

"Yes, Majesty."

"Follow him, and see where he goes and what he does. Enlist others you trust in this watching upon my pleasure; try not to be seen by him. When he leaves Flowfoam, do not follow."

"Shall I begin now, Majesty?"

The king nodded grimly, and the steward slipped away. Another steward stepped into his place; the next courtier was already sidling up to the throne, sketching the briefest of bows, and arranging a dazzling smile on his face.

The bold and heroic Crown of Aglirta let a somewhat smaller smile touch his own lips, and asked in a voice that just managed to avoid weariness, "Yes?"

Many small, hungry smiles, biting . . .

Bats poured down on Embra in a blinding, chittering flood, nipping at her face and hands with needle-sharp teeth, blotting out her view of . . . of . . .

Her companions being slain!

Desperately Embra tried to sweep stinging claws and leathery wings aside, to see, to breathe, to be able to reach her Stone and—and—

The bats were raging above her bodice so thickly that they formed a solid, writhing mass she couldn't reach through. They were tugging at the Dwaer, lifting it away from her flesh so that all she could still feel of it was the carry-chain she'd slung it in. She couldn't touch it, couldn't call on it, couldn't help—

A baron and a wizard watched the black pillar of flapping, shrieking bats that held Embra Silvertree somewhere in its depths, and smiled identical cold smiles.

Then they turned their heads, more or less in unison, to watch their armsmen cut down the armaragor and the thief. In a matter of moments, only a longfangs would be left of their foes in Tarlarnastar's wellhouse . . . and the Master of Bats had spells enough ready to smash twenty longfangs to blood and tatters.

Helms and armored shoulders surged and heaved, gleaming blades swept up—and abruptly the baron's swordsmen were stumbling to one side, crying out and staggering.

"What—?" Faerod Silvertree snarled, blinking in amazement. Plates of armor were flapping or flying aside, steel was ringing loud upon helms and vambraces and upflung gauntlets, and—blood was flowing!

Unseen blades were striking his armsmen down! The baron got a brief glimpse of Hawkril, fencing with a few of the foremost, and saw astonishment to match his own on the hulking armaragor's face. He swung his head to glare at his daughter—and saw the bats swirling and biting unabated, the feeble and bloodied fingers of one hand briefly and ineffectually showing through the flood. Embra was helpless to call on her Stone; the cloud of phantom swords hacking his men down was coming from somewhere else.

As the last of his bloodily diced swordsmen fell, the baron turned his raging glare on his wizard, only to find the Master of Bats staring openmouthed at Embra. "But that was Dwaer-work!" the wizard gasped. "Who—?"

He was answered by a blast that rocked the room, hurling Hawkril and Craer back against the wellhouse wall. It plucked the longfangs from the ceiling like a dangling leaf whirled away in storm winds, and left Embra gasping in his place, smashed into a tangle of shattered boards and beams—and cloaked in a wet, sticky flood of crushed bats. Groaning timbers slowly gave way as she shuddered . . . and the Lady of Jewels fell to the floor, senseless before she hit.

Ears ringing and eyes swimming, Hawkril clung grimly to consciousness, dimly aware that his foes were gone.

Faerod Silvertree had been reduced to splintered bones around a wildly flickering Dwaer-Stone . . . and all that was left of the Master of Bats was a cloud of frantically flapping bats fleeing boots that stood empty of all but smoke.

After a few groggy moments, the numbed armaragor saw something else. A glow from the depths of the far shadows, a softly growing light by the back wall of the wellhouse. It was coming from a round stone about as big as a small cabbage—a stone that was being gently juggled in the hands of a man standing in darkness.

A Dwaerindim! Its shadow-shrouded holder stepped forward, and the last thing Hawkril saw, as he struggled to see the man's face and failed, was the gently bobbing Stone bursting suddenly into blinding brightness.

The Dwaerindim pulsed again after the armaragor's face went slack—and the fluttering bats convulsed in midair, froze, and sagged senseless to the floor. The man who held the Stone looked carefully around at all the death and the sleeping things who clung to life, and smiled.

He took another step forward, banished the spell-spun shadows from around himself with his Stone, and reached down to seize what he most wanted.

"Inderos Stormharp," he introduced himself jovially to the senseless Four, "at your service . . . but mostly, I must admit, at my own."

Flowfoam was an interesting place. Some of its secret ways, choked with dust and cobwebs and shriveled spiders, were obviously unused and forgotten. Others served hurrying servants as carry-ways between dining halls and kitchens. Velvetfoot lingered in the darkest corners, a stone with eyes watching the palace bustle around him.

There were a lot of cooks and errand-lads and chambermaids, but only a handful of guards—none of them standing sentry. The king seemed to have no chancellor or chatelaine or Master of Swords; this was a court undefended. If all the courtiers milling about in and near the throne room were swept off the island, the Lion of Aglirta would be left with fewer servants than many a grand merchant's house, let alone the household of any one of his barons. Entire wings of the palace were dark and dusty, and there were even disused rooms among the chambers around the throne.

The man called Velvetfoot—his grinning mask long since discarded, and his face acquiring its own thoughtful frown—looked and strolled until he found the royal bedchambers at last. Unguarded, unless one counted a young girl setting out bowls of flowers and retrieving the fallen petals of their predecessors. Unbelievable!

There was even a guardless passage that ran from a reception hall adjoining a main stair to a closet in the royal bedroom!

Shaking his head in disbelief, Velvetfoot crossed that room, stepped around a large potted talathtria, and set his fingertips against a panel of polished marble that was of a lighter hue than the surrounding stone. *Now, if I was stupid enough to trumpet to all that I'd constructed a secret passage, I'd mark the door thus. . . .*

His lightly tracing fingers found the catch, and the panel sank inwards without a sound. Hmm; in recent use, at least.

This way should run on to just above and behind the throne room—and doubtless, thereat, to a private royal stair. Obviously the Barons Silvertree, whose house this had been, feared no one, and cared not to defend themselves overmuch, or conceal their vulnerabilities. Unless, of course, the tales he'd heard of a "Living Castle" that watched intruders and struck at them on its own were true.

Now, *that* was a thought to send ice down one's spine. . . .

Velvetfoot stood for a moment, listening to utter silence, and then went on. He was not surprised to find what was underfoot just inside the passage—but the muted thunder of hurrying strides in the dark way beyond did make him draw back into the reception hall, leaving the panel open, and hasten to acquire the habits of a patient statue behind the nearest hanging.

Gods smile, but the hanging even had eyeslits cut into it by some spying predecessor! Velvetfoot watched through them as King Snowsar came to a sudden halt at the mouth of the passage, sword in hand, and stared down at the body sprawled in its own blood there.

The light from the reception room showed both king and lurker who the dead man was: the steward Snowsar had sent to spy on the Serpent-loving courtier.

As Kelgrael Snowsar lifted the man's wide-eyed and staring face in his hands, a bat left its perch high on another hanging and flitted away.

Velvetfoot watched it go with his heart pounding. Bats just didn't flap leisurely around at midday. This was . . . wrong.

A moment later, he almost gasped aloud. The surface of a wall-buttress near the king had swirled and spun in the silent grip of magic, to reveal two eyes in the depths of the stone that regarded the king with cold, dark, and unfriendly amusement. The face in which they were set could be seen for just a moment, and Velvetfoot felt cold fear worm its way through him for the second time in a handful of breaths. Hadn't the Spellmaster of Silvertree died?

Evidently not. The slayer was still quaking behind the hangings, knowing that the mage in the pillar, legendary in the Vale for cruelty, could quite well know that he was there, when a panel farther down the wall slid silently open—and *another* face peered out, this one belonging to a bearded man with bright green eyes, who wore stained travel-leathers . . . and whose features melted, like the wax of a collapsing candle, as Velvetfoot gaped at him.

King Snowsar noticed none of these. He was staring down at the crumbling ruin of his drawn sword as it dropped, shed flakes that vanished ere they hit the floor, and then sighed into dust all at once.

Where the dust struck the floor tiles, smokes arose, trailing away down the dark passage the king had used. Kelgrael Snowsar hefted the useless hilt in his hand, watched the last wisps of smoke stream away as if in a hurry to be out of the palace and away from Flowfoam, and murmured, "It's failing so fast—and for such trifles! This can't go on, or Aglirta is as doomed as if no one stood against the Serpent!"

14

Debate, Decisions, and Death

*I*t was cold and dank in the tomb, and smelled of old earth and creeping mold. Olden-work; a single stone room set into a hillside, with the crypt reaching back into dark oblivion from the center of the back wall. Daylight, reaching in through the gaping arch that had no door, stabbed only so far as the mourning benches and the plain stone block where the dead were laid while priests chanted the Farewell of the Three over their unhearing ears.

The man standing in that doorway peered around the room suspiciously. He was fleshy, and wore fine clothes, but no one had ever dismissed him as fat or stupid. He could see some evidence that followers of the Serpent had recently used the gigantic stone as an altar for rituals involving snakes and candles and blood. He'd seen a brief glimpse of such a rite, through a window in a place no respectable tersept would want to be seen in: naked servant girls lying on their backs with snakes slithering all over them as robed and hooded men chanted and swayed. Idiots. No, make that dangerous fools.

Thankfully, there were no Serpent-folk here now, only old Gelgert shuffling out of the rear of the tomb, where—under a heavy stone lid, thank the Three—the dead lay mouldering in their pit. It was to be hoped that the folk of the nearby hamlet of Waendaster lay deep and content in the eternal sleep . . . for the rest of this day, at least.

"You're sure?" the man in the doorway asked sharply, waving a hand at the darkest depths of the tomb. Without waiting for a reply, he sat on the bench closest to the door and settled his weathercloak more closely around him.

The tall, thin man in threadbare robes inclined his head politely. "Lord Tersept, I am," Imbert Gelgert replied, in his slow, earnest way. "The dead stir not, and no magic is awake in this place."

"Then get you gone, mage," the Tersept of Sart snapped, "but be ready at my call. Don't let him see you."

The old wizard inclined his head and shuffled out. Tersept Glarsimber Belklarravus, called by some the Smiling Wolf of Sart, favored his mage's back with the slow, soft smile he was famous for. Some dogs respond best when kicked often and with enthusiasm.

Through the entry arch, the tersept could see the rolling lip of the hill that hid the road below from view, a line of trees marching away beyond it that marked the meeting of two fields, and—in the distance, where a death-wings circled lazily in the sky, looking for carrion—the silver glimmer of the river.

He was crazed, meeting in a tomb to plot a royal slaughter with only his favorite handful of magical tricks and one old, bumbling wizard to protect him from brigands or Serpent-folk or agents of the king or . . . treacherous barons.

The man appeared quite suddenly over the brow of the hill, trudging as if tired, even reeling a little—but he was alone, as agreed, and wore only a belt knife that the tersept could see, and he was, unmistakably, the Lord Baron Berias Loushoond.

If any of the farmers hereabouts got curious about why a tersept and a baron were meeting in a remote hillside tomb, such curiosity would swiftly be their last misfortune. The ruler of Sart resisted the temptation to go to the door of the tomb for a wary look around, and instead got up and moved away from the light, to the darkest of the benches.

The baron thrust his head into the tomb with no sign of hesitation or even alertness, and lurched forward almost as if he was drunk.

"Loushoond?" the tersept snapped. "What ails you?"

The baron turned stiffly toward the source of the voice that addressed him, blinking. It seemed a long time before a reply came to his lips. "Nothing, Sart," he said flatly, in the deep voice he used when trying to impress.

Tersept Glarsimber smiled in the darkness. So even bold barons get nervous, and drain a flask or two before going to plot treason. A weak shield, then—but he only had to last until the turn of years, and Snowsar's recrowning. After that, King Glarsimber the First would have need of bumbling servitor barons. Good ones were so hard to come by these days.

"Sit, then. We've much to discuss."

Baron Loushoond shrugged and sat, stiff and clumsy. Aye, he must be drunk, though whatever it was he'd imbibed didn't have the reek of ale or some other throatslakes. "The lances of Loushoond are utterly loyal to me," he said abruptly, "but I can see no peaceable pretext for whelming them and marching them up the Vale unless it is to attend Snowsar's recoronation—and then only if he invites us all to come in armed array, or if other barons choose to bring their war-might."

The Tersept of Sart smiled tightly. "I think you see things very much as I do in this," he said, "but I also know that the fields of Loushoond yield much provender for us all, and have done so for many a year—wherefore trees are regrettably few in your fair land."

Somewhere dark, where the image of two men sitting in a tomb glimmered in a pool that glowed, a woman stiffened and hissed, "Trees?"

She turned swiftly to seek guidance, disturbing the two dangling serpents that were her only garb. Their fangs tightened on the tips of her breasts, and fresh streams of blood, mixed with the purple foam of their spittle, ran down her flesh. She shivered, her eyes half-closing.

"Lose yourself in venom-dreams later, Sssister," the serpent-headed man said sharply. "This is more important than even the fool of Sart believes. Have our good puppet now speak thus. . . ."

The baron's brow wrinkled. Again his response came very slowly. "This is so," he said, in tones of obvious puzzlement. "We buy barges of firewood every harvesttide."

"And would it not save Loushoond much coin if its strong warriors could fell and cut wood freely?"

The baron frowned. "It would—but that entails war with the lands around, to gain forest ground . . . and I count the spilled blood of my armaragors and the mistrust of all my neighbors as a high price indeed, not a road to 'free' wood."

The Smiling Wolf of Sart held up a hand. "What if," he purred, "the far-seeing and bold Baron of Loushoond remembered the news of wild battles in the ruins of Indraevyn, and thought not of magical Stones or ruling kingdoms, but instead of . . . miles upon miles of trees for the taking?"

The baron peered along the benches at the tersept. "Send men with felling-axes on their shoulders walking upriver, through all the baronies of the Vale? An invading army just strolling through? How happily d'you think our fellow barons and tersepts will look upon *that*?"

The tersept shook his head, still smiling. "What if they went by another way?"

Baron Loushoond frowned again. "What, up into the Wildrocks and stumbling through the hills? Some barons would still see that as invasion—and I'd lose scores of men with broken legs and necks, with more of them lost and still more gone outlaw or stabbed by outlaws! Three above! Are these idiocies the 'schemes that cannot fail' your wizard's message promised, Sart?"

Tersept Glarsimber's smile never wavered. "Barges float firewood down to you every year—and you sell the bargemen crockery and ground-nuts and cheese to take back with them, do you not?"

"Aye, of course, but what—"

"You've many lances and strong men to wield them, do you not?"

"Aye, and wha—"

"Well, what are lances but long poles? The bargemen of Adeln and Brostos pole their barges back home each year; what's to stop Loushoond sending a barge or six all the way to the Loaurimm? From whence, when they're done cutting and—at just about the time of oh, say, the glorious recrowning—have grown restless to don armor and swing swords again, it's but an easy drift downriver to Flowfoam?"

A baronial jaw dropped, and its owner sat blinking at the Tersept of Sart for long moments, goggling like a fish out of the Silverflow.

A room away—in the dark rear chamber of the tomb, where he sat slumped—a small, slender man in tattered leathers shook his head in disgust at this treason. He was still too weak to move, even if he'd dared to, too wracked with pain to trust his limbs . . . and still bewildered at being snatched from a wellhouse acrawl with battle-magic to this place. Whoever it was who enjoyed hurling Craer Delnbone up and down Aglirta with a Dwaer-Stone, Craer fervently wished he'd choose someone else for his attentions.

On one of these trips, he was going to get killed.

"I . . . see," Loushoond said at last, in the outer room. "And what would their restless swords harvest, in your view?"

"Heads," the tersept purred, "both royal and baronial."

"Baronial? How many?"

Glarsimber of Sart smiled and nodded. "As many as possible, of course."

The Lord of Loushoond frowned again. "And tersepts? How many of those?"

The Smiling Wolf shrugged. "A few. Not all. Some will be needed, to kneel before Aglirta's new king—His Majesty the Lion, Berias Loushoond."

The baron blinked in the gloom, and then, slowly, smiled.

. . .

"Sssss!" The priestess bending over the pool hissed out her scorn. "Not very subtle, is he?"

"Sssister," the priest reminded her with a slow smile of his own, as he stroked the heads of her snakes to make them bite down, and slid an arm around her shoulders to support her as she shuddered in ecstasy, "he doesn't have to be. This is, after all, Aglirta."

"Realm of fools," she murmured drowsily, as her head lolled back into venom-driven dreams. The priest smiled even more broadly and took over the spell, to guide the good Baron Lackwit of Loushoond through the rest of this meeting. It probably wouldn't take long; the Wolf of Sart had gloated so much in his life that he'd acquired the knack of doing it swiftly.

As swiftly, perhaps, as the Sacred Serpent would soon rise over Aglirta.

Gods above, Hawkril thought dazedly, as pain stabbed through him like blades of fire, but he must still be alive, to hurt this much.

He groaned before he could stop himself, and then cursed inwardly at his foolishness. That noise might just earn him swift and sharp death from someone nearby who'd thought him a corpse—that man with the third Dwaerindim, for one.

And just who, by the glory of the Three, could that man be?

The Three declined to answer. Hawkril smiled without mirth, tried to move . . . and discovered that he still had a left arm, at least, because he was leaning on it—and gods, did it hurt!

Slowly, wincing and clenching his teeth at the red blaze of agony that shot down to his fingertips, he moved the fingers of that hand, curling them, making a fist, and finally reaching out to plant them on the ground.

Rough straw and dirt. He was still in the wellhouse.

Ah, yes—the battlefield of their latest bard-pleasing victory. Sargh.

Hawkril fought next to open his eyes, fearing that he'd find himself gazing at the dung-smeared tines of a pitchfork, and the angry face of a Tarlarnastar farmer glaring down from the other end of it.

Instead, when he'd finally blinked the glimmerings of tears of pain away, he found himself looking around at stillness, lit by daylight coming in the open doorway by his left shoulder—and down through a splintered hole in the roof above. There was a sword—not his own—in the dirt by his hand; he took hold of it, hefted its comforting weight, and risked twisting around to look out the door.

The pain almost made the armaragor collapse on his face, weeping, but he settled for a roar of pain and a swift return to sitting in his tangle against the wall. The villagers were out there, all right, standing a good dozen wary paces back from the door—and his sudden appearance and grimace had made them draw back hastily, and exchange anxious murmurs.

Hawkril struggled to sit up, hampered by both his hurts and the diced, fly-swarming meat lying across his legs that had once been four or five swordsmen. More lay in a long, butcher's-floor heap off to his right. He tried to free one of his legs from under the wet, stinking heaviness, and couldn't.

Alarmed, he clawed at the carrion with both hands, almost whimpering in his urgency. Gods, to have his throat slit by villagers, after all this!

When he could sit up, and gasp properly, and look around again, Hawkril saw—Sarasper! The old healer was lying on his back, mouth agape and a fly crawling idly around his cheek; he looked very dead.

Graul. Graul and bebolt. Where was Craer? And the lass?

Was that—? Yes! With a roar of mingled anger and pain Hawkril heaved himself to one knee, wobbled there for a moment before desperately using his sword as a crutch, and—sent himself sprawling on his face in the dirt across the doorway.

There were more murmurs from outside. Well, at least they sounded more wondering than angry. Hawkril snarled and heaved and struggled to drag himself upright on his knees again. Leaning on the sword, he could now see Embra lying sprawled on the floor amid splintered roof timbers. She and they were shrouded in crushed bats—little wings upthrust at crazy angles, tiny jaws forever agape—and dust. Her face was white and still, and his heart froze ere he could get to her and clumsily, as gently as he could, turn her this way and that, to make sure no splinter had impaled her, or there wasn't some other gods-cursed wound on her, somewhere.

He found nothing like that . . . and soon after he'd begun his fumbling examination, she acquired a frown, stirred a little, and put out a soft hand to his cheek, like a sleeping child reassuring itself by touching its mother bending over it. Her touch was as gentle and fleeting as the brush of a falling feather, and her hand fell away to her side almost immediately, but Hawk found himself following it, tears in his eyes and catching at his throat, to plant a kiss on those fingers before he could bring himself to heave himself away from her and begin the struggle to find his feet.

Claws, but he was supposed to be a warrior! The first on his feet, the last to go down, fighting hard . . . The wellhouse spun crazily around Hawkril Anharu as pain shrieked through his side and his swordarm, and he crouched hastily back to his knees before he might fall. When he looked up again, it was straight into the face of a villager edging cautiously forward to peer in the wellhouse door.

He smiled at the man and waved his sword suggestively. The man bolted like a rabbit under the shadow of a hawk.

"Well," Hawk said roughly, after him. "Well, well. It seems I'm still alive."

"Really?" a faint voice answered him. Its fine thread of mockery was familiar. "I'm still alive over here by the well, too . . . but I can't say as I'm all that well."

"Craer!" the armaragor roared, scrambling across the wellhouse and rolling his friend over.

The procurer hissed in pain. "Gods, Hawk! D'you have to be so . . . hearty?"

"You're alive!"

"I'm not so sure," Craer told him, clawing his way up Hawkril's arm until he was sitting up. "Being dead hurt a lot less than this."

Hawkril chuckled and slapped the hilt of his found sword into his friend's hand. "If you're joking, you're alive. Can you get up?"

"I'll let you know," Craer said, wincing, as he rolled gingerly to his knees and reached to catch hold of the wall around the well, for support. "What happened?"

Hawkril shook his head. "Someone else was here—someone who had a third Dwaer."

Craer's head snapped up, and then he shot glances all around the wellhouse.

"No," the armaragor told him, realizing in an instant both what his old friend was seeking and what one Hawkril the Bruised hadn't really seen until then. "They're gone. All three Stones *and* the mysterious man who had the third. He blasted the baron and the wizard of the bats to bones and smoke."

"Bones and smoke," Craer muttered, looking around and shaking his head slowly. "I don't doubt it." Something caught his eye, and he leaned forward and plucked something out from under a red, glistening pile of what had until recently occupied a human belly. It was Hawkril's sword. "A man, hey? Then he's the one who sent me to the palace . . . and the tomb full of talkative traitors, just now."

The armaragor frowned. "What's that?"

Craer shook his head and waved a hand in dismissal. "Later, I think," he said dazedly. "*If* I can think later, that is."

Sarasper chose that moment to cough, choke weakly, and then groan. "What happened?" he asked the ceiling rather wearily. Hawkril put a hand on his shoulder.

"You're familiar with our usual triumphs in battle?" he asked dryly.

Sarasper groaned again, rolled over, and put a hand over his eyes. As he did so, the last tufts of longfangs fur on it dwindled back into his skin.

Craer cast a look out of the wellhouse doorway—and promptly began retrieving swords and planting them in a point-down row in the dirt, never taking his eyes off the villagers for long. "Hawk?"

"I know," the armaragor growled. "Just smile at them until I get the lass awake, will you?"

"I," Sarasper announced weakly, "am going to drain a *lot* of the Silvertree family magics to heal us all, starting now."

Hawkril barely heard him. "Embra?" he was asking gently, leaning over a face smudged with bat gore. "Embra?"

Her lips moved slowly, and he had to bend close to hear her faint whisper: "Hawkril."

Then Embra's eyes opened, her face tightened in pain, and she added, "Just let me lie here for a bit—and tell me what happened."

"Someone I never saw properly," Hawkril told her, "a man, was here with a third Dwaer-Stone. He did something with it that made invisible blades carve up your father's armsmen—and then blasted your father and the bat-wizard. Utterly. I know not if any bats got away, but you're wearing most of the rest of them."

Embra's face started to twist into an expression of disgust, and then she decided she couldn't be bothered, and merely nodded. "And then?"

"He did something with it that sent me to sleep. Now he's gone, and all the Dwaerindim with him."

Embra nodded again, slowly. "I felt that. . . . I knew it when you woke me. How is everyone?"

"Sarasper's hard at work destroying Silvertree figurines and salt-dishes and glow-at-will doorknobs," Hawkril told her. "He's almost ready to work on you."

"Good," Embra growled, letting her head fall back. "Something's broken—my right shoulder—and I can't remember when I've hurt so much."

"So can you devote some time, Lady, to thinking about what we do next?" Craer called. Embra turned her eyes to meet his and smiled ruefully.

"Am I now our leader?" she asked. "I thought some among us were a mite weary of being led around by a lady mage."

"I didn't say you'd be the only one thinking on such things," the procurer replied, "or that we'd leap to do your bidding . . . but you *are* our closest thing to a Dwaer lore-sage."

Embra closed her eyes and sighed. "If you knew how little I know," she told them, "you'd not say that."

"Lady," Hawkril said awkwardly, "Craer and I can manage without anyone to tell us what to do, but we'll manage as foraging warriors, who know magic—and Dwaerindim—as something to be feared and destroyed or fled and hid from . . . just as most of yon farmers and village folk would. We'd fight for the king, and die well for him, too—but he'd best not look to us for saving the kingdom and hurling Dwaer-magic and all. That's your work."

Embra nodded faintly, without opening her eyes, and then said, "Help me up, sitting upright against something that doesn't touch *this* shoulder. If I scream, stop moving me."

Hawkril looked at her a little helplessly for a moment, and then reached forth large and tentative hands and gathered her up.

She stiffened once, and hissed in pain, biting her lip, but she did not scream. Not even when the battered armaragor slipped and deposited her against the stone wall around the well a little more precipitously than he'd intended.

"Embra?" he asked anxiously, as she shuddered under his hands. "Are you—all right?"

She smiled wanly. "I'll live, you great ox. Get me a figurine from Sarasper."

The healer came with it, proffering it with a growled, "Craer's hurt worse than I'd thought. Are you sure I shouldn't heal you before you try . . . whatever idiocy you're going to try?"

Hawkril winced, but Embra smiled at the old man. "Well put, Sarasper—and no: if I trigger some sort of mind-blasting trap whoever now has my Dwaer has left waiting, that'll be that much more of your healing, and the Silvertree family magic, wasted. But tarry here, as I try, and watch my eyes; if they glow red or bright and I speak as if I was someone else, slap me senseless—and don't hesitate in doing it!"

"This sounds very dangerous," Hawkril growled.

Embra shot him a look. "Whereas your assaulting Castle Silvertree wasn't? Either the first time, after an armful of my gowns, or the second, when we knew the Spellmaster was waiting for us with a Dwaer?"

Hawkril sighed, and it was in tones of defeat that he asked, "So what must we do right now?"

"Watch me," Embra said crisply, "from far enough away that you'll have a chance to get out if some magic or other bursts forth from me. Oh, and draw me a bucket to drink."

Wordlessly Hawkril offered her his flask; she shook her head. "I don't want anything stronger than water in me when I try the tracing."

"You're going to trace the Dwaer-Stone you carried," Sarasper said grimly. "A wise thing, when you've no Dwaer to protect yourself with?"

"None of this charging about the realm fighting mages and hurling Dwaer-blasts is 'wise,' Lord Longfangs," Embra snarled at him. "It is, however, necessary . . . unless one prefers to sit drinking in a chair somewhere and watch doom charging up, ruining Aglirta as it comes, to sink its claws in one!"

Sarasper shrugged. "She's well enough to try it," he told Hawkril and Craer, lips almost twisting into a smile. "Stand back."

They exchanged wry glances as Embra watched them, shook her head, and held up the figurine. She closed her eyes and murmured something— whereupon a crackling, humming webwork of tiny bright lightnings burst into raging being around her closed hands, spitting bolts that coiled down her arms almost hungrily. The light between her fingers flared and the bright radiances suddenly washed down over the lady sorceress, causing her limbs to shudder and spasm . . . and faded away.

Embra's head lolled to one side, and wisps of smoke rose from her empty palms.

"Lass?" Hawkril cried. "*Embra!* Embra, *speak!*"

"Clever remark," she mumbled. "Arch observation, airy comment about it being nothing and another to the effect that I feel fine, sarcastic declaration about Aglirta never feeling safer around me, followed by a light-hearted quip, and . . . Craer to supply all the words, because my brain just won't."

Hawkril almost shook her. "But are you all right?"

"To use my most hearty lie once more," she said slowly, looking up at him with a twinkle in her eyes, "I feel fine."

"The trace failed?" Sarasper asked, his eyes on Craer—who was crouched behind the row of swords, watching the villagers and hefting a dagger in one hand, ready to throw. By their mutterings and strategic withdrawals, it seemed that they were watching him, too.

"Yes," Embra sighed, looking around at the gloomy wellhouse in exasperation. "Whoever has the Dwaer has used its magic to make it untraceable by my spells, at least. Without an altar or some other thing with a powerful, permanent enchantment to 'boost' my magic, I'll never be able to gain the slightest hint of where any Dwaer-Stone might be unless I happen to be so close to it as to already have it in sight."

"So we've failed the king?" Hawkril growled slowly.

"Call it, rather, a small defeat," Sarasper told him. "A setback worth a rest by a fireside to brood over—and then on again come morning, with blades out and fresh merriment to lend us wings!"

Craer's head turned. "Gods above," he said, "you sound like a courtier!"

"Sir Slytongue," the old man replied gruffly, drawing himself up in mock pomposity, "I once *was* a courtier."

"Well, that explains some things," Embra told the ceiling innocently.

Hawkril stared at her for a moment, and then shook his head. "If you've all finished being clever," he growled, "there remains before us the problem of what do we do *now?*"

"Well, then," Craer replied, holding up a calming hand, "I see two choices before us. We can blunder about Aglirta trying to find a Stone by spying on Serpent-clergy and any wizards who make unusual trips—an approach that's likely to fail at anything but getting us slain in any ambushes barons, tersepts, or Serpent-priests care to mount."

"Or we can follow the clever advice of Craer Delnbone," Embra put in, "and—?"

Craer smiled and sketched a courtly bow. "Or we can set a trap of our own by choosing a defensible place to fight in, going there, and loudly but 'inadvertently' discussing at the nearest inn or tavern to that place how we must 'use the Dwaer we have' to summon the legendary Swords of the Lost, or the Risen King's favorite wizard-tutor, or the Jewels That Never Were—and then see who shows up to attack us."

"Well, that seems simple, safe, and sane," Sarasper said sarcastically. "Gods, why didn't we just do that first off, instead of coming here and fighting bats?"

"I knew Longfingers'd see the best way," Hawkril said triumphantly. "He always does!"

Embra and Sarasper exchanged glances—hers amused and his incredulous—and then the Silvertree heir smiled and said, "Crazed it may be . . . but I can see no other road to take."

The healer blinked at her. "Well, there's the small matter of finding a place to defend," he said heavily, shaking his head.

"The Silent House," Craer told him innocently. "Where else?"

Embra nodded at the old man. "You're the only living expert on its ways, and what they hold," she pointed out.

Sarasper rolled his eyes, shook his head, and then waved one hand in a gesture of resignation. "Well enough. The Silent House, we hope the Doom won't claim Embra, and if no one comes calling, we at least have a place of our own to shiver the next winter away in. So that's it? We're just going to walk out of Tarlarnastar, after slaying its lord and all his men and shattering the wellhouse? What if these villagers attack us?"

Craer acquired a wolfish smile. "I'd almost welcome that, right now," he said, and there was suddenly a dagger gleaming in his hand.

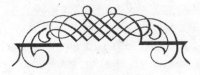

15

A Bad Day for Wizards

The scorched and wild-haired man had only one hand, but that wasn't stopping him from using it vigorously—nor from cursing in a constant harsh hissing.

He clawed away thick green cloaks of dangling moss from stone after stone like a man spell-driven. The very air was green in his wake as he stumbled along the cliff, snarling oaths at the sky.

From time to time a tatter-winged bat would flap and tumble down out of that much-profaned sky to settle on his shoulders—and after a few moments of chittering and clawing its way to just the right spot, it would melt into the dark weave of the man's cloak.

He paid these arrivals no heed, though each made him a little stronger, a trifle larger and taller than the bent and wrinkled shadow of a man that had first risen here. The stone-cleaner's mind was fixed on one thing alone: finding what he was looking for under the thick clumps of moss. An observer, had anyone been standing nearby, might have been forgiven for thinking that the burnt man was devoting most of his energy to raging as he searched.

"Idiot sword-swingers, that's all they are!" the Master of Bats snarled. "Standing alone, I'd watch behind me, cloak myself in armor-wardings so none could catch me unawares with arrow or blade . . . but oh, no—barons must have their secrets!"

He shrieked in a sudden outburst of uncontrollable fury, snatching and flinging away moss like a madman—until with a sudden gasp of satisfaction, he found the hollow he was looking for, plucked forth the yellowing human skull he'd left there long ago to keep curious fingers away, stared into its empty sockets—and with a growl of sudden decision, jammed the relic down over the stump where his right hand should have been. He spat into its eternal grin, "No need to let faithful old Huldaerus—only the man who made you whole again, only the man who showed you how to *use* your precious magic Stone!—know that you had *another* Dwaer at your command. After all, can't trust mages! Better to leave the great Master of Bats unawares, so you can laugh at him behind his back—and he can be the first to fall when this *other* trusted servant turns traitor!"

Waving the skull beside his ear as if it was a hand puppet and he a minstrel reaching the climax of a comedic masque, the wizard thrust his hand into the hollow, turned something unseen—and suddenly grinned with a fierceness that almost matched the wide smile of the skull as he heard a deep groan from the rocks to his right.

The Master of Bats turned to watch a boulder there quiver as it came to a stop a handwidth farther out from the hill than it had been. He nodded his head in satisfaction, and the smile fell off his face.

Glaring at the boulder, he snarled in fresh fury, "Oh, no! Barons trust none, and throw away wizards in droves before it's time to empty their next goblet! And always—*always*—they must have great armored dolts standing around to menace serving wenches and their fathers, the old farmers . . . oh, yes, and every last passing wizard, too! Mustn't let men of real learning and skill forget their place! So it's lumbering stoneheads in my way, jostling past every few breaths with their sneers and their cold looks, hefting their swords meaningfully as they scratch themselves and belch and cover me with their stink and their foul breath and their flatulent, brutish *arrogance*! *Garrrrghhh!*"

The furious wizard dashed the skull against the nearest rock, snarled at the bone shards that burst up into his face as it disintegrated, and shook the stump that should have been his right hand at the sun.

Then he fell silent, breathing heavily, and glared around at the trees falling away down the hillside below him. Birds mewed and shrieked farther along the cliff, but there came no shout or footfall in the wake of his outburst. He was alone in the wilds of Aglirta, high in the rising hills above what had once been the barony of Blackgult, trembling in the weak aftermath of his fury.

So rarely in their lives did wizards dare to lose their tempers so. To let control slip, with every last stableboy fearing and hating you, and leave yourself so unguarded . . . it had been years since the Master of Bats had let rage take such firm hold of him. Now, shuddering at his folly and in winded exhaustion, he stared at the raw end of his right arm and gathered his will, letting resolve grow slowly cold and hard within him.

He raised his stump to the sun once more, and with slow, deliberate care pronounced words over it. His will was as iron, or harder—as durable as the cold, hardened flows of stone that surround smoking mountains. Huldaerus *would* prevail. His will had always carried him, from sullen boyhood to mastery of magic, through firespells and treachery in plenty, to here.

Here and one more defeat. Not his, the blame for this one—and that was good, for it was a defeat born of utter stupidity.

Careless, arrogant stupidity. About the only good side of it all was that the wellhouse walls had hidden his fall from the villagers. Letting the common clods know just how quickly and easily a mage could be struck down—with a pitchfork, say, or even a hurled log from the fire—would not have been a wise thing.

Magic rose in his throat as the wizard Huldaerus spoke the last words of the incantation, surging up warm and clear, pushing aside the sick feeling and wavering resolve that the pain had brought. The spell reached out . . .

. . . And suddenly the Master of Bats had a skull adorning the ruin of his arm once more. It was fresh and still slick with blood, a little larger than the one he'd just shattered, and there was nothing about it to tell the eye that this was not the discarded brain-bones of a commoner nor yet a wizard—but was instead the spell-restored last leaving of Baron Faerod Silvertree.

Huldaerus snarled fresh curses and rebukes at it in a quieter, almost weary voice, as he reached out with his good hand and tugged the boulder open a little more. The skull, as he'd expected, replied but little.

A crack appeared as he strained, a revealed space behind the pivoting stone that grew wider as the wizard set his shoulder against the stone and shoved, clenching his teeth to keep from groaning aloud in pain.

The crossed branches within were sagging a little, and so rotten they crumbled at his touch, but they'd been just as he'd left them; nothing larger than, say, a fox had passed this way. Not for the first time, the Master of Bats gave thanks for two things: that there were no mines in the rising mountains above Blackgult, and that he'd been the one to find this old mage's tomb.

It made a perfect hideaway, and the magics he'd cached here over the years would sustain him, let him replace his missing hand and banish his burns, weariness, and pain—and give him shelter. He was surprised to find that keeping hidden seemed suddenly attractive.

Prudence was not a force that Huldaerus, the Master of Bats, had hitherto allowed to govern or even feature prominently in his life. Yet he was willing—even eager—to give in to it now, lying low for the nonce and using spells to spy on the land around.

"I'll just sit here," he told the stone seat inside the door, "watching history unfold, and await the right moment to charge forth and seize whatever advantage might present itself—after the others have had a good time slaying each other."

The stone seat did not reply, so the wizard sat down on it, put his feet up on the end of the tomb, and started awaiting.

There was a sudden flash of light from around the bend in the road before them.

"Magic!" Hawkril snapped. "Craer? *Craer!*"

The procurer had been scouting ahead, keeping to the trees. Three above! If some lurking—

The armaragor went around the bend in a fury, running hard with Embra's shout to halt ringing unheeded in his ears. If anything had befallen his old friend . . .

The land before his eyes had been scorched by a storm-fire some years back; a hill or two stood bare of trees, cloaked with naught but tall grass and creepers and thornbushes. They might have afforded hiding for a skilled procurer seeking to crawl and lurk unseen, but not armsmen or a wizard, or—

A bewildered boy, standing alone in the road with a few fading, shimmering motes of light drifting around him. A handsome, almost lass-beautiful lad with great dark eyes, now frowning in puzzlement, who wore well-made boots and hose, topped with a tabard such as bards wear.

"You!" Hawkril snapped. "What have you—ah, boy, did you see a man here, just now? About your height, in leathers? He'd have had a sword in his hand, or daggers. . . ."

His voice trailed away as the boy shook his head, fear and wonder warring in those great dark eyes, and asked, "W-Who are you, sir? And where—what is this place?"

The lad was staring around at the road and burn-scarred hills and trees as if he'd never been outside a house before. Hawkril looked hard at him, and his fine clothes. All right, make that a castle.

"My name is Hawkril," he said curtly, peering everywhere for some trace of Craer. "Yours?"

"Raulin, sir. Raulin Tilbar Castlecloaks. My father was the bard Helgrym Castlecloaks."

Hawkril's only reply was a grunt, but there was respect in his eyes as he glared at the boy, and Raulin recognized it. He tried a wavering smile at the glowering armaragor.

Almost reluctantly Hawkril lowered his blade, as Sarasper and Embra came up on either side of him. "How came you here, lad?" he asked.

"Dwaer-magic," Embra said a little grimly, before the boy could reply. "I know its feel now. That's what I was trying to tell you, Hawk."

Sarasper eyed the boy narrowly. "A breath or two ago you were in the palace, am I right?"

Raulin nodded, almost eagerly. "Yes," he said, "and then . . . then I was just—" he shrugged, and turned slowly to look behind him, pivoting around to face them again "—here."

The old healer looked at Embra, and they nodded in grim unison. "And at the same time, Craer was taken there—or somewhere."

Hawkril gave them a dark look. "Snatched again? Three above, if I lay hands on whoever's playing with those Dwaer—"

"You'll be trampled in the charge of everyone else who wants to do him harm," Embra said ruefully, "or just wants to relieve him of the Stones." Her eyes finished their slow appraisal of the boy standing in the road in front of them, and saw that he'd begun to blush under her scrutiny.

"Raulin," she said, "Sarasper's going to work a little magic on you; if you are what you seem to be, it'll do no harm, and you'll feel nothing. The son of Helgrym Castlecloaks is welcome with us, though we seem to wear danger like a cloak these days. Will you walk with us?"

"Of course," the boy said, as happily as if she'd given him a gift. Then he shrugged and added, "Where else would I go?"

There were two reasons why the hard-eyed, raven-bearded man in purple was riding along the muddy back roads of the Vale. The first was that Bodemmon Sarr disliked wasteful, needless spellcastings. Magic should be a deft sword, not a castle-shattering bludgeon. Though magic seldom sped from his elegantly gloved fingertips, and few things disturbed the easy smile he customarily wore above his pointed, curled beard and between his glossy gold earrings, he never hesitated to strike when spells were needed.

The second was that Bodemmon Sarr liked to ride. Few dared challenge or impede him for long, or lived to attempt such folly more than once; he traversed Aglirta as if he owned every tree and hedge of it, wending his way among rolling fields and green forests at his own pace, taking what he fancied and changing what he desired to change.

Hulking bodyguards in the best battle-plate armor—black and adorned with his symbol, the spread amber wings of the sunset hawk—rode in pairs before and behind him, and his ever-nervous apprentice, a cook, and two serving wenches who were kept busy assisting with Bodemmon Sarr's meals, bathing, dressing, and bedsport rode astride four of a tethered string of ten pack-mules, between the second pair of bodyguards and the rear guard of four identically equipped warriors.

From time to time the man who knew himself to be the most capable wizard in all the Vale—whatever that upstart Tharlorn might claim—drew on a pair of crimson gloves from his saddle-prow, and spoke the word that made a hunting hawk issue forth from one of them. It had been years since he'd uttered the word that made a javelin spring from the palm of the other; these blasted barons had hunted the Vale boar until there were almost none left. Bodemmon Sarr was almost at the point of yielding to his growing desire to hunt a new quarry as he rode: barons of Aglirta.

Even they had fallen on hard times of late, he reflected, his easy smile never changing. In many places, he'd have to settle for hunting tersepts.

In the interests of greater sport, he'd probably have to hunt this self-styled Risen King ere long—but in the meantime, there was entertainment to be had in participating in the various scrabbling conspiracies that had become the life of Aglirta in the wake of the falls of Blackgult and of Silvertree, the war of wizards at the ruin of Indraevyn and the nightwyrm attacks on Sirlptar, the return of King Kelgrael Snowsar, and the rise—one of many such risings, down the years—of those foolish enough to worship the Serpent.

Ah, but the Vale was fairly aflame with whispered offers, covert knifings, and dark speculations—wherefore he was riding quite openly to a certain inn, to meet with some crudely disguised conspirators even now engaged in whelming an army to seize Cardassa or cow its baron into joining them in a bid to seize the River Throne. Others might want to rule from Flowfoam for the power or their own delusions of royal fame and glory, but Bodemmon Sarr wanted to help an endless succession of ambitious ladies onto that throne, purely for the amusement their loving—and inevitable treacheries against him—would bring.

Boredom. Anything to banish the empty dullness of his days. The wizard in purple sighed and glanced back at Glarth. Receiving his apprentice's usual too-quick, uncertain smile, the mightiest mage in Aglirta looked away and sighed again, more heavily this time.

By the Three Who Watched Over All, life was becoming a gray, empt—

Ahead, a guard shouted a warning and turned in his saddle to give his master an urgent signal.

Bodemmon Sarr leaned forward in interest. That circle of the man's hand, always granting that he hadn't been so fatally stupid as to use the wrong gesture or seek to amuse himself by exaggeration or deceit, meant "monster."

A dangerous or, at the least, an unfamiliar and threatening beast. Hmm. The mightiest mage in all Aglirta made the signal that told his men to move aside, and spurred his charger forward to investigate.

He found himself looking at something slow and gray that was plodding towards him behind two huge pincer-claws it had thrust out in front of its humped shell of a body. It looked like a crab out of water—though he'd never seen a crab the size of a small wagon before. Bodemmon Sarr sat in his saddle calmly, watching the beast come for him. Or rather, watching it march east regardless of what was in its way.

On sudden impulse he conjured a shining wall across its path. The beast neither slowed nor hastened as his spell took effect—and a hard, clear barrier sang into glowing life across the road. Force-solidified air, unbreakable without extensive spellwork, its radiance stretching from a rocky outcrop on the south side of the road to a tangle of broken boulders and old stumps flung up together when the road was made, to the north.

The land crab, or whatever it was, struck the wall with a crash—ramming it obliviously, the watching wizard thought, rather than attacking it as a foe. Those huge claws scraped and tore at the shining wall until the magic shrieked aloud—but held.

Bodemmon Sarr folded his arms across his chest and smiled just a trifle more broadly. In a moment it would either draw back to mount a charge at the wall, or turn to go along it and seek a way around . . . and he'd learn a little more about what he was facing. A small part of him thought it must be a conjured beast, brought from a far land by magic or twisted by spellwork from something smaller and different. The Vale just could not have held something this large for long, without his knowing of it. . . . After all, he *was* Bodemmon Sarr.

The land crab turned slowly to the north and lumbered along the wall, letting one claw squeal a line along it to tell the beast that the barrier persisted. The wizard saw that it was dragging a heavy, stumpy tail as it trudged along, and awaited with quickening amusement the spectacle of its labored clamber over the tumbled rocks.

His eyebrows lifted when instead it turned at the end of the wall and strode through the heaped tangle of stones as if they were pure spell-spun illusion. A moment later, Bodemmon Sarr found himself staring into a large, dark, and furious eye as the land crab lifted a head as bald and as ugly as that of a carrion-vulture or sea turtle, and turned it to one side to regard him fixedly.

What by all the hidden whims of the Three *was* this creature?

Abruptly it ended its glaring at him and began to move again, turning slightly off the road, to the north—and straight at the nearest of his guards.

For a moment, as the man's helm swung towards him in a quest for his instructions, he was tempted to just let it go. And then he saw that its chosen route, thanks to the curve of the road here, would take it right into the pack-mules, the food they carried, and his cook and pleasure-wenches. He gave the guard the signal to attack.

The armsman spurred his war-mount to one side, seeking to pass by the nearest claw and lean in to put his swordtip through one of the land crab's eyes. His blade flashed out of its scabbard, his eyes never leaving the beast, and he—

Screamed in surprise and pain, as that bald head suddenly shot out with blinding speed, the corded neck extending like a lance, and bit through his swordarm.

"Gods above!" Bodemmon Sarr gasped, jaw dropping in utter amazement. Blood was spattering as arm and sword bounced amid dead leaves and hard-trampled wildflowers, and the convulsing warrior bent low over the neck of his horse, which was snorting and trembling almost as much as its injured rider.

Those jaws had pierced armor without pause or effort. The beast was moving with sudden speed now, advancing to block the flight of the armsman's horse as it turned, not having much room among the trees. One of those great claws thrust out.

It was the horse that lost a limb this time. As it went down, screaming, Bodemmon Sarr snarled three clipped words, spread his hands, and sent spell-spun arrows of purple fire sizzling through the air at the humped shell of the thing's rear.

They struck, flared, and . . . faded away. The crab-beast stiffened, its claws full of flopping, blood-drenched warrior, and turned to give him a look of flat, dark menace.

All this, and it could pass through stone . . .

Enough—more than enough! Bodemmon Sarr barked the order that would send all of his guards into action and turned his own mount, heading for the mules and Glarth's none-too-reliable assistance. Now that they'd all seen its speed, that many blades should make swift work of its eyes—for he could see no place for its head to retract all the way into, to avoid seeking steel—and he'd yet to see a beast, however large, outlive for long the loss of its head.

Of course, magic could persist where flesh failed, and the crab-thing *had* passed through stone. So this just might be the work of Tharlorn of the Thunders, sent to weaken and annoy. Wherefore he'd make ready to blast and rend it utterly, while thinking of a suitable response to send back to the hedge-wizard who dared to think of himself as Bodemmon Sarr's rival.

The rear guards whipped past their master, grim-faced and with their blades already drawn. He let them pass before making his own gallop back along the road to the milling cluster of mules and frightened faces, the wenches and his apprentice kept from fleeing only by the sharp tongue and ready reins-grabbing of the cook. Ugly and wrinkled as an old boot, but worth her weight in ten armsmen. There was another scream from behind him, and then a hoarse, ragged shout. Bodemmon Sarr permitted himself a soft curse as he hauled hard on his reins, slowing his charger from what seemed almost panic-driven swiftness, and sprang from his saddle.

"Glarth, I'll need you. The wyvern-head chest."

"Master, what—?"

"Questions later, chest *now*. Here, on this rock. Brithra, my thanks—see that the lasses tether all the mules to the trees, and join us. I'll need you to pour out some powders."

The cook merely nodded and turned to do as she was bid, with none of the stammering and fumbling of his apprentice. Bodemmon Sarr turned his head to see how his men had fared—and was in time to see one of them flee on foot through the trees, crashing and stumbling in terrified haste.

Not just one of them; the fleeing man was the *last* of them! The mightiest wizard in all Aglirta cast a last look at the slaughter—and the land-crab spitting out armor as it bit and chewed at the heart of it—and then calmly bent to his boot, drew forth a dark and slender wand that thrummed as he muttered a word over it, and sent death leaping through the trees to behead the man who'd dared to flee his service.

The dark-armored torso danced headless past a tree before it toppled; Bodemmon Sarr watched it fall from sight before he looked again at the crab-beast.

It was almost upon him, its claws and jaws slick with dark, wet blood. The wizard swallowed, spat out a word that made the runes up and down the wand flicker—and fed the land crab all of the fire in the wand in one swift, air-splitting burst.

His own skin tingled, the air blistered and roiled around him, and the snarling of rushing magic almost plucked him off his feet—but then, quite suddenly, the wand sputtered and died.

The crab-beast loomed up over him, shuddering in pain but very much alive, and whole, and—

Furious. Its first bite almost took off the right foot of the mightiest mage in all Aglirta, but Bodemmon Sarr leaped for his life, planting his face in road dirt, and the beast contented itself with devouring a pack-mule—the one carrying most of the food—instead.

The horrible wet sounds were loud in Bodemmon Sarr's ears as the wizard angrily wiped his eyes clear and snarled out a spell that filled the air with crackling green lightings, made one of his pleasure-wenches topple with smokes curling from her nose, mouth, and the holes that had, mere moments before, held her eyes—and left the Thrice-damned crab-beast unharmed.

Glarth was sobbing with fear and clutching blindly at the ankles and legs of Brithra the cook; she was beating at him with her fists in a vain attempt to get him to let go. Even as their master reached them, she snatched a black firepan from the saddle of her own mule and brought it down hard on his head. The apprentice went limp.

Brithra's face was white with fear as her eyes met her master's. "Lord, I'm sorry!" she gasped. "I—"

Bodemmon Sarr clutched her shoulder with fingers of fierce iron and snapped, "No, no, you did nothing wrong. Help me turn him over!"

A horrible scream and even more horrible wet, crunching sounds heralded the passing of another mule—or perhaps the other pleasure-lass—as the cook and the wizard bent to their work with feverish haste. "Back!" Bodemmon Sarr hissed at Brithra, and then shouted out a spell without waiting for her to scramble aside.

Glarth's staring body glowed a sudden sickly yellow—a hue that faded with agonizing slowness as Bodemmon Sarr knelt over him, tensely watching the crab-beast tear apart the last of the mules and turn its head towards a cook and two wizards. At last the yellow was gone from all but the apprentice's eyes; Bodemmon Sarr stammered out another spell and sprang back, even as that horrible bald head bent down.

Glarth's head and one shoulder were gone in the first bite, steaming blood pouring forth in a torrent that made the crouching cook moan and put an arm up in front of her eyes. The other arm and most of his right side vanished in the second; Bodemmon Sarr put a firm hand on Brithra's shoulder and towed her back and away, biding his time in cold calm.

The crab-beast's next bite left nothing of the apprentice but trembling, spasming legs and a blood-drenched remnant of pelvis joining them. By the sudden lift of its neck and its brightening glare at Bodemmon Sarr—the wizard could have sworn it was *smiling* at him—the crab-beast seemed to be finished dining on apprentice, and finding its appetite for the master.

Bodemmon Sarr let it lunge one step along the road at him—a step that the thing took with terrifying speed—and crisply spoke a single word: the sound that would trigger the last spell he'd cast on Glarth.

Then he turned and ran, abandoning Brithra and all in a frantic sprint away from—

The wet, sickening blast that shook the road under his pounding boots and sent slimy cantles of crab-beast spattering through the trees all around him. He felt the warm heaviness of its gore slapping across his shoulders, just before the main force of the blast plucked him off his feet and sent him rolling headlong through a needlethorn bush.

And then, but for his panting, the gods gave Bodemmon Sarr blessed silence.

He dragged himself slowly out of the remnants of the bush and turned to look at the slaughter, seeing nothing moving but a feeble, blood-drenched figure that could only be Brithra. The crab-beast was quite gone.

Bodemmon Sarr smiled grimly. Tharlorn's cleverness may have kept it from harm under the lash of most of Bodemmon's spells, but Glarth had enjoyed no such protection—and even that huge humped shell hadn't saved the beast from the ravages of a devoured man exploding in its innards.

As some forgotten mage had once remarked, there's more than one way to spell-dice a dragon.

Brithra and her moans could wait. He had to retrieve a certain something from his own saddle-pouch, to whisk himself across the Vale from here to safety. If another something was still in its place, he'd bring her with him. Good and trustworthy cooks are hard to find.

Bodemmon Sarr retrieved both somethings and stood grimly above the torn remnants of the crab-beast. "Tharlorn," he said calmly, "you are a—"

The gigantic, many-headed snake dipped its shimmer-scaled body out of the trees in eerie silence, swaying forward to let a dozen jaws gape open and then snap shut.

Eleven closed on empty air, but one harvested the head of the mightiest mage in all Aglirta in one gulp.

A headless Bodemmon Sarr danced spasmodically along the road for a few moments, risen but unhurled magic sparking and spitting from his fingers—and then toppled, twitching, into the dust.

The many-headed serpent bent, its jaws tore the writhing body apart—and Tharlorn's mage-slayer stiffened and rose like a wary pillar to look all around.

It seemed to gaze up the Vale for a very long time before suddenly descending again, to glide swiftly and purposefully away westwards along the road.

When it was quite out of sight, a blood-caked woman slowly drew her knuckles from her trembling mouth. Then, and only then, Brithra the cook permitted herself to scream.

.   .   .

Craer Delnbone sighed, sat on a handy stone, put his feet up on the stone beside it, and started waiting. Creeping through ferns in the roadside shade one moment, and then . . .

He'd obviously been whisked here for a reason. That much was certain from the unfamiliar, hulking body his own slender form had somehow changed into. He flexed large and hairy hands for the first time in his life and shook his head in bewilderment. He was evidently a warrior of impor- tance, by the armor and cloak and all—and by the looks of things, he was somewhere far downdale, on the other side of the river. Cardassa or there- abouts.

Hmm. He just hoped the plans of the mysterious wielder of the Dwaerindim involved Craer's continued survival for the next little while. And the continued health and happiness of whoever he'd now become.

He was not a devout man, but a moment later, Craer found himself silently praying to any and all of the Three who might care to listen, as he closed fingers that felt awkward around the hilt of an unfamiliar sword.

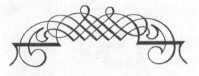

16

Flagons Aplenty, and Blood Enough to Fill Them

The first soft shadows of evening were stretching forth from the trees to shroud the road in gloom as four travelers, on foot, trudged out of the heart of outlaw-haunted Deep Hollow and came to where the war dogs were chained, to give ears in the Flagon their first warning of visitors—honest or unwanted.

The Flagon and the Gauntlet was an old inn, but a prosperous one. The only stop on the road through the woods that linked the steadings of Phelinndar with the farms and mills of Silvertree, it sprawled away from the road like an old, comfortable, and gigantic sleeping hound through three clearings that (but for a lone fenced gap) were safely walled against bears, hunting cats, and other creeping creatures of the night—such as outlaws with sharp knives in their hands—with a palisade of old and stout fire-hardened logs.

Men with ready crossbows guarded the road-gate that let wayfarers into the innyard, and they were not used to regarding folk who came afoot out of the deep forest in a kindly manner.

They grew even more wary, standing in their archers' booth above the road, when they saw the armored giant of an armaragor who led the four, sword drawn and face hard. Yet the woman who strode behind him looked every haughty inch regal or at least highborn, for all her road dust, and the man who leaned on her was undeniably old—while the youngest of the four, an almost beautiful boy who brought up the rear, walked with a limp and a face twisted in pain.

"My foot hurts," Raulin complained, as they drew nearer to the gate. "Is all this acting really necessary? If they shot down or turned away every traveler along this road, they'd soon starve!"

"Lad," Embra cooed back over her shoulder at him, "humor me just a few moments longer, will you? I can, of course, say a few words—a very simple incantation—and that overpronounced limp of yours will become very, very real."

Raulin's reply was a mutter that sank into a growl as one of the guards at the gate barked, "Crave you welcome within? Your names, then, and business!"

The first soft shadows of evening were stretching forth long fingers, and hiding much that was unlovely in these back streets. Even some things that moved.

The dung-carter had not been lovely at birth, and a hard life had done nothing to improve his appearance. So many white and thick-ridged scars crossed his head that his face thrust forward into a doglike snout, and what little hair was left to him grew in awkward clumps, leaving much rough and puckered bare flesh between. He whistled tunelessly as he came down the dark steps into the full stink of the sewers of Sirlptar, the sack of rotting refuse on his shoulders heavy enough to make him stagger.

Dusk was coming down the steps even more swiftly. It would not be long before these dark underways came to life—and there were some in proud Sirl city who'd stick a knife into even an ugly, stinking dung-carter in hopes of winning a few copper coins ... or just for their own dark amusement.

The carter shuffled a little faster, though the steps under his boots just here were wet with something dark and sticky. The general reek and gloom were too great to tell what the spill was, even if he'd cared to bend and peer. It would be good to be gone from this place—and next time *he'd* choose where they met.

Something moved in the darkness behind a stone pillar. The dung-carter froze, swung his dung-sack in front of him as a shield, and growled, "Who be there?"

The something moved softly forward into what little light there was, and he could see that it was a woman, bared to the world but for a half-mask and a cloak she wore pinned up on one hip, in such a way that it could swiftly be let fall to cover all.

"No danger," she purred softly, "but only Oblarma."

That name seemed to make the dung-carter relax. He set down his dung-sack with a grunt, kicking it to let its contents spill down the nearest swill-chute. "Oblarma," he said in the curiously formal Sirl trade manner, with a grin that displayed many black and broken teeth, "know that Indle am I. Are you alone, but desirous of being less so?"

"Yes," the ivory-skinned woman said softly, as she came forward to let him see that her hands were empty, before she reached forth to stroke one of his arms, "and yes."

Indle the carter gave her a wordless growl as he reached for her, holding up two fingers. She responded with four, and instantly lowered one to leave three. He grinned. "Three 'tis."

Together, arms around each other, they swirled through a dark doorway. Oblarma broke away to unhood a lamp with one deft snatch of an old helm, and let fall a door-bar with her other hand, before anyone else who might have been lurking on the sewer stairs would have had time to do more than blink.

"Nice breasts," the carter murmured, in a low and quite different voice.

"Nice scars," was the reply, as the pleasure-lass snuffed the lamp, plunging the room into smoke-threaded darkness. "The teeth were good, too."

Her voice changed as she spoke, becoming at once deeper and softer, almost buttery. In the darkness, her flesh was flowing. Oblarma's face melted into blankness first, and the breasts Indle had praised slid away into smoothness moments later.

Indle was also changing—dwindling into something thinner and blank-faced. Each featureless Koglaur face then sprouted a mouth like a long tube, and grew a single ear as deep and as cupped as a flower blossom. The two tubes stretched forth into the waiting ears, and no other ear in the room— had there been one, in that noisome, dripping, door-barred darkness—could have heard the conversation that followed.

"Have the Serpent-folk placed anyone in Flowfoam yet?"

"Esabras says not. Their march through the baronies, however, continues unabated."

"Are the townsfolk growing fearful, or are the Serpents deft and quiet?"

"Barons," came the reply laced with dark amusement, "never go quietly."

There was a sound that might have been a chuckle. "All of us can now withstand their venom?"

"All but Tlalash—who I fear can never stand against any Snake-worshipper."

"Then we are as ready as we can be. I would know your thoughts on this, Ashene's plan . . ."

The words that followed did not take long. When the door was unbarred at last and the Koglaur slipped out, they wore quite different faces.

. . .

"Belgur," Weldrin murmured, pressing some coins into the hand of a man he'd already bought many times over, "how many gold coins are you holding?"

The ratlike man looked down at his palm and then up again, in a brief, swift glance that gave no one time to strike while his head was lowered. "S-Six, Wel."

His swordsorn smiled. "That's right. There'll be another four to join them if you bring Artheld or Nimmor back before the next hearthfire's lit."

Belgur did not have to look out through the screen at the Flagon's busy hearth to know how long that gave him—which was a good thing, because he was busy frowning at his superior. "Serpent-priests? You want me to bring Serpent-priests *here*?"

"It's most important," Weldrin murmured, "that I speak with either of those two without delay—in this booth, and alone. Outside this curtain, neither you nor they know me. If they're suspicious and want to come in force, let them, but say that Weldrin bids them tread softly and hide their faces."

Belgur gave him an uncertain look, so he added, "Four coins more, Bel. Remember that."

The ratlike little man nodded and ducked out of the booth. Weldrin waited until the next log rolled over in the taproom fire, sending forth its spray of sparks, before he followed. He did not go far.

The booth he left was at the end of a row of six that all looked into the taproom through shuttered screens, but opened not into that roaring scene of drinking and dining and warm fires, offering their curtains instead to a dim, quieter passage.

The passage held a booth-boy, who took coins from those desiring to use the booths, and—at the end, across from the one Weldrin had been using—an armed and alert warrior who made sure that no one refused to pay the booth-boy, or disturbed the occupants of the most expensive (and private) end booth. He and Weldrin ignored each other; it was the professional thing to do.

The booth Weldrin went to was at the other end of the row, a larger and better-lit room right beside the cross-passage that let scurrying tankard-lasses and hearth-boys stream from kitchens to taproom and back again. The Flagon might stand alone in the woods, but on nights as busy as this one, its guests made it almost its own village. One peopled with folk uniformly loud and hungry.

The booth Weldrin entered was almost as noisy as the taproom—which was abuzz with the news, brought by the high lady, her tutor, and her two bodyguards who'd come in just at dusk, that the Band of Four who serve the king were taking the legendary Dwaerindim Stones to the Silent House, curse of the Silvertrees, there to summon much long-hidden magic from Aglirta's glorious past, to defend the realm in this dark time.

Just as the prophecies said, some hissed, and fell to arguing whose prophecy was best, and what else those cryptic sayings foretold.

A dark plot hatched by the sorcerers of the Vale to gain access to the River Throne and seize it, others insisted—a claim amended by still others, who held that the plot belonged to barons and not world-witless wizards.

"World-witless wizards," Weldrin purred to himself as a particularly angry shout cut through the booths to echo down the passage. "I like that."

"Weldrin," one of the warriors hissed, the moment he'd shouldered his way in through the curtains, "that high lady out there—she's the Lady of Jewels!"

"Aye," another of the men said, setting down his tankard, "no doubt over it; she's the baron's brat, all right. What'll we do, Weldrin? Hey?"

"Run a sword through her?" the first warrior burst out.

"Huh," a fierce-whiskered man said with a leer, "I'd like to run something else *into* 'er, first. Then we'd see what sort of a sorceress she is!"

Weldrin held up his hands for silence. "Easy, lads," he snapped, his voice low but his tone clearly that of a man giving orders. "These are screens here, not wizardglass window; she can hear us as clearly as we hear her. Let's have no more names."

The warriors nodded and fell silent, their gazes fixed on him. Weldrin gave them a slow smile and took a wedge of nut cheese from the platter with one deft thrust of his belt-knife.

He'd been their commander before the baron's fall, and would be again—swordsorn of what had once been twenty Silvertree blades, now sadly reduced to eight. Weldrin of the Sixth, he'd been, among the Baron's Best. His men had thought so, too, or they'd never have stayed with him, following him all the way out here to the wild hindquarters of the Vale—and another fallen barony, Phelinndar. They'd been here twelve nights now, raiding east into the fallen lands with impunity, bringing back all they could seize and carry off, rutting and butchering at will among thick-witted farmfolk and their gormless young. Two farmgirls were waiting upstairs, gagged and bound ready on his bed, right now.

But this, laughing out in the taproom right now, was a prize beyond all that Phelinndar could yield that they together could carry—even with the wagon they'd have to steal in another night or so. The Serpents would pay him a hundred gold coins, or more, for her brought to them alive . . . but his men knew nothing of Weldrin's fondness for Snake-worshippers, nor theirs for him. They'd leave him if they did—and might even put their swords into him at that leave-taking.

But the Serpent-priests, he knew, had more than deadly venoms in their pouches. They had fang-juice that brought sleep, not death, and could as easily send Silvertree blades to slumber as slay them. When his blades awakened on their wagon, their captive, the Lady Embra, would simply be gone. He'd have to listen to their snarls all the way to Sirlptar, of course, but that was a small price next to what the Serpents would pay. Best to get it in gems, though—he'd have a hard time lifting his feet with a hundred gold filling his boots.

The Band of Four had taken rooms here, of course. Later, when they'd gone there and a lot of folk had fallen asleep at the tables or grown too drunk for their wakefulness to matter, the fun could begin.

"First off," Weldrin told his blades briskly, "stop drinking *now*. We need to be awake and sober later—unless your guts feel ready to welcome quarrels fired from every Flagon-helm's crossbow!"

There were some growls at that, but no serious cursing; their heads were thrust forward to hear his plan. Weldrin gave them a big smile as he put his foot up on a bench, and asked, "How'd you all like to be rich?"

They waited in silence, without roars of approval or questions. Good lads.

"I, too, recognized the Lady," he told them, "and was checking on her lodging just now, using Belgur as my scout around the back and the stables. They've two rooms, but I know not yet if she sleeps alone, or if we'll have to use our swords to separate her from one or more of yonder dolts. Yes, the big one knows how to use his blade, but wait a bit. I've paid a young lad to watch and see on the stairs who goes where. By and by, we'll strike."

"And—?" Turstrin burst out, impatient as always. Weldrin gave him a thin smile.

"Dead, the Lady's worth nothing. I want her unharmed, though we'd best bind her hands, stop her mouth, and blind her with a blanket bound over her head and right down to her wrists; she *is* a mage, after all—but as a captive, presented to our Risen King in chains as a 'traitor sorceress,' she might be worth quite a reward."

There were nods around the table. Weldrin spread his hands. "Even if we don't get coins," he added, "rightful ranks among the swords at his court, and the lands in Silvertree and Blackgult that go with such honors, are nothing to be spurned. We can all be Lords of the Vale yet."

"She just yawned," one of his blades said excitedly, turning his head from the shutters.

"Right, lads," Weldrin said with an eager smile, spearing himself more cheese. "It won't be long now."

Well, at least it wouldn't be long now.

Belgur trotted through the woods as quickly as he dared. The faster one went, the harder it was to keep quiet—and along these trails, snares were set for men as well as for little scurrying beasts.

Either might doom him, he reflected wryly—for what was he but a little scurrying beast? He kept to the deeper gloom, well away from the light of the rising moon, so as not to be seen—at least, not before he got a moon-dappled glimpse of whoever was trying to see *him*. His dagger was ready in his hand in case that happened.

By the Three, but he hated the Serpent-priests and their snakes. No good would come of Weldrin doing business with them, of *that* everyone could be sure, and he'd just as soon be done with this dark errand and safe in his bed under the eaves, in his favor—

The hand that slapped the knife from Belgur Maerbotham's hand came, he swore, right out of a dark tree trunk.

It all happened so fast. One moment he was ducking under a low branch and stepping to the left to avoid a shaft of moonlight on the trail, and the next he was struggling in the grasp of what seemed like a dozen strong arms—or were they tentacles?

He couldn't move, couldn't breathe, fingers jammed into his mouth and somehow growing *larger* in there! He was struggling just to gasp, and the horribly strong grip that had him trapped was tightening. . . .

And that was when the knives slid into him, six or more, so velvet-soft and so utterly, utterly cold.

Belgur shivered, and tried to scream, or sob, or plead, or do something to stop the horrible wetness bubbling up inside so chokingly . . . he couldn't breathe . . . he couldn't breathe . . . and as the night suddenly seemed darker and the silence whirled up around him, Belgur Maerbotham stared up in horror at his slayer, now bending over him to make sure of the kill.

His last terrified thought was that the head caught in the cold moonlight above him had no face!

"Brigands are *so* bad these days," a voice murmured in the darkness, as the waters of a sucking bog closed over the little man's body. "Regrettably, another message to the Serpents goes undelivered."

"Gloat later," another voice purred, rising in tone as its owner's throat shifted in height and shape. "We're a long way from the Flagon now—and if we deliver them from the Serpents, they still have the Silvertree wolves to contend with. Hurry!"

The reply was a growl—as a great cat bounded into the air, flapped the wings it was still growing, and strained to reach the stars. The falcon that shot past it sighed loudly as it did so, a sound that was strangely human.

Yet somehow . . . different.

Embra yawned again, almost dipping her nose into the drinking-jack that the fat and bustling tapmaster had insisted on bringing her. Then she threw back her head, long and dirty hair swirling in a shining flood over her shoulders, and gasped, "Gods, but I'm tired! Someone show me the stairs to bed."

Half a candle ago, those words would have brought ribald and enthusiastic responses from a dozen men or more around the warm and roaring taproom . . . but it had grown very late—or early, if one took another view—and the stairs had seen more than a little stumbling use already. Other drinkers snored at their tables, or had slumped back in their chairs and begun the slow slide to the floor that might or might not awaken them. At least one booth was still occupied, because someone had just snapped distinctly in its unseen depths, "Whoever you're waiting for, Weldrin, they're not coming, so stop *prowling*."

The few tables still occupied by waking patrons tended to be those shared by pairs of furtively muttering merchants who'd long since finished and shoved aside their ale and river trout on hot toast to begin dealings best done with few ears around to hear. These twosomes were tucked into the farther, darkest corners of the cavernous room, far from the sleepy coals of the hearth and the lanterns hanging nearby.

The Four were seated almost under one of those lanterns, over the wreckage of a huge meal of mint-buttered boar and roast pheasant and a dozen sorts of fiery pickles. Three empty decanters and a hand-keg stood like weary sentinels amid the bowls and platters and longforks, and Embra wasn't the only one yawning.

"Lady, *please*. Stop that," Raulin snapped at her sleepily, clinging to a half-full tankard as if it could hold him up, as the Lady of Jewels threw back her head and yawned again.

"We'd best go up," Hawkril growled, looking at Sarasper. The old man was sitting silently over his tankard, fast asleep with his eyes open. The armaragor nudged him—and then had to grab for him wildly as the healer toppled over sideways, still sitting neatly. Even when large and desperate fingers closed around his elbow with bruising force, the old man never awakened. As the snarling warrior hauled him back upright, Sarasper turned his head, still fast asleep, and emitted a single dainty snore—almost a belch—into Hawkril's face.

Raulin sputtered with mirth, choked, and doubled over, nearly knocking his forehead on the table. Embra raised her eyebrows, and then looked at Hawkril and said crisply, "Indeed."

Without waiting for his reply, she swung her legs around the side of her high-backed chair so she wouldn't have to go to the trouble of pushing it back from the table and stood up, reeling a little in her weariness. "Raulin," she said, "leave the rest of that, unless you'd like to spend the night down here."

"Lady," Hawkril told her, hoisting the healer in one hand and reaching for the still-coughing lad with the other, "that'd more properly be 'what's left of the night.' We're down to the last two barmen—even the tapmaster's gone—and it's but three candles to dawn."

"Wonderful. Woe betide the chamber-wench who tries to wake me in the morning," Embra yawned warningly.

Hawkril chuckled at a sudden vision of a sleepily furious Embra turning a cheerful, buxom chamber-wench into a toad, and led the way to the stair.

They'd taken rooms at the end of the overpassage, which would no doubt be cold, drafty, and dark, but quieter than the chambers nearer the stairs. The passage-door of one was locked and barred, but its connecting door to the other room was unlatched, so the way for any intruder to reach Embra was through the room where three men would be snoring—with Hawkril lying across the passage-door, sword to hand, and Sarasper sleeping right across Embra's door.

Embra looked around her little chamber in the gloom. She had her bed, her chamberpot, and icy wash-water for the morning . . . and that, right now, was all in Aglirta that mattered.

It *was* cold, and the bed doubtless had its share of tiny biting bugs. For a moment Embra considered just wrapping herself in her cloak and falling onto it and into welcome oblivion, but then she thought of spending days being bitten—and scratching, with Craer's leeringly enthusiastic offers of help ringing in her ears, if he reappeared from wherever he'd been snatched to, again—when she could bundle her clothes in that cloak and hang them as far from the bed as possible, and just scrub the bugs off in the morning. So she sighed and started tugging and unbuttoning.

Bare and shivering beside the bed as she shook her tangled and dirty hair out and ran her fingers through it as best she could—gods, *that* would end up full of bugs, too!—the Lady Silvertree was reluctant to step out of her boots; once her feet touched the threadbare rug, the chill would really strike home.

So it was that, straightening up from blowing out the bedside lamp, Embra was far more awake that she'd hoped to be, and still wearing her boots, when there came an almighty crash from the other side of the door. She whirled around. "Hawk? Sarasper? What's—?"

The sound was followed by a snarled curse that a man makes when he's both startled and doing something that tries his strength, and the unmistakable sound of a sword ringing as it was drawn.

Embra reached for the door-latch—only to hear a whispering voice she did not know from the other door: the barred one that opened into the passage. "Lady Embra?" it quavered. "Lady of Silvertree? Are you there?"

Cautiously she stalked across the room, halting a good three paces away from the door, and called back, "Who is it?"

The answer was sudden. Steel stabbed for her, gleaming in the moonlight: the thrusting blade of a long, slim sword driven with vicious force through the seam between door and frame.

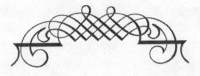

17

Nice Boots, and Battle

Embra stared at the swordblade, flashing at the level of her midriff as it caught the moonlight coming in the unshuttered window . . . and found herself far more furious than scared.

She did not even think of screaming. Instead she gave a gasp, and a moan—but had no time to further mislead the bladesman on the other side of the door; the sword was withdrawn before she could toss the bed-blanket over it or do anything else to make its wielder think he'd wounded her.

From the other side of the door came the furious snarl, "You *fool*! We need her unhurt!"

A year ago, the Lady of Jewels would have raised her hands and blasted the door, passage beyond, and all to ashes, not caring if the Flagon then caught fire and burned to outshine the stars. Now, however, she was much more than a year older than she'd been then. She whirled around, marched across the floor, and flung open the other door, not caring if her three companions—and every other man at this end of the Vale—saw her skin. "What by all the Three Blazing Gods is going *on* ou—?"

She ended her question in midshout when she saw Hawkril shorn of his armor, a hairy muscled colossus in sweat-soaked leather breeches, hacking for all he was worth with the blades he held in both hands at three thrusting swords, or more, that were stabbing into the room from the dark passage outside. The armaragor was standing just inside the doorway, with the splayed shards of the room's outer door tangled around his feet. He, too, hadn't gotten around to taking off his boots.

How had they—? The door must have been riddled with rot, to collapse at a single blow that hadn't shaken both rooms. But—

And then something twisted on the floor nearer Embra, drawing her eye down.

Sarasper was sprawled senseless on the floorboards. A huge splinter of wood from the shattered door had burst through his shoulder like the blade of a halberd, and a white-faced, trembling Raulin was scrabbling to stanch a dark and swift-spreading flow of blood over the old man's chest, whilst snatching from time to time at the flickering bedside lamp on the floor beside him, to move its light where he needed it to be.

As she watched, he whimpered in rising fear. He shuddered as he stared down at the man dying under his hands, looked up at Embra in startlement—and then stared at the bare-skinned sorceress in gaping earnest as she strode deliberately forward and murmured the lone and feeble healing spell she knew, pressing her fingers into Sarasper's gore.

Magic flowed over the old man in a wash of spidery radiance, light that faded almost before it began.

Embra smiled almost fiercely into Raulin's astonished face, and said to him, "Whatever you're going to say, don't. Say something else instead."

The young man's mouth opened, and then shut, as his bone-white face suddenly went as red as Sarasper's blood. "Uh," he said finally, "nice boots."

Embra rolled her eyes, bent to lay two bloody fingers across his mouth before he could say more, and snarled into his face, "Find me all the little figurines and coffers and suchlike that Sarasper carries—I need them *now*!"

Raulin blinked, nodded, and started to scrabble again, this time among the healer's discarded belt and pouches. "Is this for your magic?" he murmured, not looking up from his frantic snatching and unlacing and unbuckling. "Do y—"

He sensed, rather than saw, the lady standing over him tremble suddenly—a scant moment before she spat out a single word that echoed in his head like bells jangling amid thunder.

Wincing, Raulin stared up at Embra, just in time to see fire race from her mouth like the bards said dragons could do. The flames snarled over him like a hurled lance, and he twisted around in time to see them race past Hawkril's busy shoulder and burst right in the face of one of the men out in the passage.

That man screamed, high and shrill, like a young girl scalded—and incredulous about it. Raulin saw him stagger back, sword clanging to the passage floor, with fire leaping up from his face. The man's eyes could not be seen in the bright inferno; the flames seemed to stream from his mouth upwards, to lick at the ceiling.

"Raulin," the Lady of Jewels said with terrible, gentle care, "please find me those little figurines."

The lad's head snapped around. He gave the glowering sorceress an emphatic and very swift nod, and set to work even more frantically than before.

In a handful of seconds he slapped a figurine into Embra's waiting hand, and followed it almost instantly with a little pinch-pot that she plucked up between thumb and forefinger to stare at curiously.

After a moment of scrutiny, her face clouded as if she was trying to remember something that would not come to mind, Embra shrugged and closed her hand over its tiny beauty. Murmuring a few swift words, she opened her hands again, cupping them to cradle the Silvertree relic, and snapped an incantation that rolled and echoed in Raulin's ears, and made Hawkril turn his head from the whirl and ring of steel for just an instant.

And light blossomed above her palms, swirling blue and green, softer and more gentle than any tongue of flame. As the radiance flared, the figurine and the pot were gone.

Embra pointed her cupped hand like a claw at Sarasper's shoulder, as if her fingers were daggers, and then drew her hand slowly back almost to her shoulder . . . and the great shard of wood in the healer's shoulder trembled, shuddered, and slid slowly and stickily forth.

A great gush of dark blood followed it, and Raulin clutched frantically at Sarasper's wound to try to stanch the flow. Blue-green light licked around his fingers, and he drew back with a wondering look at Embra, shaking his hands to drive away a sudden tingling within them. Radiances swam in from the empty air to circle the old healer's wound . . . and then rush into it.

Light flashed and was gone. In its wake the blood stopped coming, though the shredded flesh remained bloody and torn, and the mask of agony that was Sarasper's face did not ease or show any signs of awakening.

"Guard him, Raulin," she murmured, trailing just the tips of her fingers along his shoulder as she stepped past the kneeling procurer.

"L-Lady, is he–?"

"Guard him," she said without turning. "I've done what I can for now. Hawk needs my spells more, and–*Hawk!*"

Her last word was almost a scream. Raulin spun around, the old man under his hands momentarily forgotten, to stare at the doorway.

Hawkril Anharu was doubled over in pain, facing the door with his great warblade trembling in his hand. Another sword was standing out of his guts, and only the still-raging firespell Embra had hurled in his aid was keeping the slayers in the passage back from charging through the doorway. They were cursing and trying to stab past the spinning balls of flame that roiled and bobbed above the threshold, but the swaying armaragor was just beyond their reach.

Embra plucked at Hawkril's arm, bending with him to peer at his wound—as the balls of flame in front of her flickered and began to fade. Her head turned, dark tresses swirling, and she screamed, *"Raulin!"*

The youth launched himself up from the floor in a running leap that carried him past the sorceress—another figurine slapped into Embra's palm as he swept past—to a chair near the door. Snatching it up, he ducked to his knees so as to be under the failing flamespell, and threw the chair wildly out into the passage. There was a brief tumult of thudding boots, men stumbling back into each other, and startled oaths.

Snarling, the bard's son snatched up another chair and held it in the last of Embra's dancing fires—until it caught alight, and he was holding a mass of flames. Grimly, biting his lip, he held the blazing chair in the doorway, crouching as far and as small behind it as he could.

Embra spared the lad not a glance. She'd knelt in front of Hawkril, heedless of the blood, to look up grimly into the clenched teeth of the warrior's sweat-soaked grimace. Gently she said, "This is going to hurt, but try to stay standing right here—and *don't* fall on me."

Eyes like flame burned into her as he nodded, once. Embra set her teeth, put the figurine in her mouth, and hauled the sword out of him.

Hot blood almost blinded her as she let the blade clatter down beside her, but she thrust two fingers into the wound before it could close, replacing them with the figurine in sobbing haste. Holding her hand over its small, rough base, she shouted the words of the healing spell she knew by heart now . . . and another Silvertree relic melted away to nothing under her fingertips as tingling light surged and flowed through them.

Whatever this statue had been—she'd not bothered to look at it closely—it had held more magic than any of the Silent House relics she'd handled thus far. There was a sudden roaring surge of light from under her fingers, and Hawkril was hurled back and away from her, his body arched and spread-eagled in a halo of white fire.

Gasping as the icy searing of a *lot* of magic surged through her, Embra was plucked from her knees and hurled out the doorway into the passage, where she fetched up against the wall in a curled heap, her ears ringing, atop a stunned Raulin.

Thankfully, the burning chair had flown from his hands to crash and bounce from wall to passage wall, and none of their increasingly fearful night attackers was close enough to put his sword through the tangled limbs of a nearly naked sorceress and a bewildered youth. Embra shook her head dazedly, trying to move swiftly, and slapped at the wall in frustration when her legs seemed made of slowly drooping mud.

Yet she *could* move, and hastily too, though her limbs felt numb and monstrously clumsy, like clubs of flesh without joints. Embra was still uncoiling herself when Hawkril grinned at her on his way by. Seemingly completely healed, he pounded out into the passage waving his warsword like a child impatient to use a new toy.

The Lady of Jewels found her feet, swayed unsteadily, and then put out a hand to the wall to steady herself as she snarled, "Raulin! *Raulin!*"

The young lad she'd landed on was groaning and reaching blindly for the wall, and showed not the slightest sign of having heard her. That was no wonder, given the noise Hawkril was making as he battered his way through the parries of his foes with huge sweeps of his blade.

The door of a room opened a little way down the passage, and a sleepy, frowning, and heavily stubbled man in a dirty nightshirt peered out.

"Can't you—" he began, before he got a good look at Embra Silvertree leaning against the wall glaring back at him, with her unbound hair framing her, wearing only her high-topped boots.

His eyes widened, he smiled—and Raulin's foot unintentionally smashed that door shut, driving the man from view with a loud, meaty smack that was followed almost immediately by a heavy, tumbling thud, as the boy scrambled up, trying not to look at the sorceress, and gasped, "Yes, Lady?"

Embra shook her head, grabbed his arm and tugged him vigorously back towards their rooms, and snapped, "Stop trying not to stare at my skin for a moment, and get in here! I need you to hide and guard Sarasper!"

Raulin stepped back and gave her an incredulous look, while swords clashed and rang behind him, and they heard Hawkril's exultant growl rise into a bark of low laughter.

"While you, uh—while you go to war with—ah—that?" The boy waved in the general direction of her body, his scarlet face turned firmly away. "No, Lady, I can't let y—"

Embra sprang forward and caught hold of him with clawlike fingers. "Raulin," she snarled into his ear, "do you truly think you can stop me? And is this not a weapon, with all the goggling that men do? And just what good, by all the loving Three, will I be standing in there with a blade if a dozen men rush me in the dark, hmm? I probably couldn't even lift it before he'd be dead and I'd be on my back for a few moments of pleasure—theirs— ere I followed him to the grave. Raulin, I need you to do this! Find another room with a door you can bar, and get Sarasper into it, and you with him! I *can't* guard him!"

Raulin looked at her wildly, and sprang for the door. Then he turned in the doorway, banging his shoulder with a wince and a gasp, and asked a little wearily, "I suppose you'll be wanting some more figurines and gew-gaws?"

Embra struck a pose, bare as she was, and smiled sweetly at him. "If it's not too much trouble . . ."

Raulin's reply, as he ducked back into the room, was surprising, vivid, and inventive. Embra was even more surprised to discover she could still blush.

Hawkril swung and hacked with a fierce smile on his face and exaltation in his heart. A few breaths ago he'd been in agony, the fire of slow death spreading from his belly and his strength seeping away with his every gasping breath—and now he felt as strong as a rutting ox and more fresh and energetic than, well, than he'd ever felt in his life! His sword seemed as light as a willow-wand in his hand, he was easily fast enough to hold off four—now three—blades seeking to slay him, and . . . and he couldn't tear his mind away from the image of Embra's curvaceous behind, and the little row of bumps that marked her spine as she lay twisted in a ball against the wall, staring up at him through her hair.

The eyes of the closest of the three surviving attackers—men he'd never seen before, though they had the look of veteran warriors—widened as the man's glare lifted momentarily from Hawkril's face. The warrior was looking over Hawkril's shoulder, and the armaragor lost no time in ducking his sword-hilt in under the man's elbow and heaving. As the man staggered back, Hawk took a single stride forward and drove his right boot into the man's gut—right about where this same man had left a sword in Hawkril, not so long ago.

The man tried to shriek as ribs cracked and he began his helpless journey towards the ceiling, but all of his breath was leaving him explosively, and he managed only a strangled whistle. The eyes of the next attacker, too, strayed for a moment to something behind Hawkril, but the armaragor did not turn his head to look—not even when Embra purred from beside him, "Hail, Boar of Blackgult. Have you missed me?"

"Lady—lass—I *have*," Hawkril told her, stepping forward across the passage as the man he'd kicked crashed senseless to the floor, to engage the blades of the two remaining men. "And you . . . are you still missing your clothes?"

"Yes," Embra replied cheerfully. "Raulin says I make a most fetchingly effective distraction. Among other things."

Hawk made a sound that was part snort and part chuckle, and drove one man back a pace with a furious slash whose backhand swing almost put his swordtip in Embra's face. She dodged behind him with easy grace and without delay, hissing a wordless comment at how close he'd come to carving her.

The armaragor took another step forward. He was carrying the fray along the passage, step by hacking step, to the head of the stairs. Swords were striking each other so hard that the steel was ringing like bells and spitting sparks. More than once Embra winced and ducked away from a particularly noisy clash.

The Flagon was an old and creaking inn, but it was a wonder how few folk had awakened and peered out into the passage to see the reason for all the tumult—or perhaps they were awake, and cowering behind their door-bars with knives clutched ready in their hands, hoping that sharp-edged battle wouldn't come looking for them.

Or perhaps, Embra thought, she'd misjudged the up-country Vale, and guests at the Flagon were quite used to the ring and clatter of swordplay in the halls through the dark hours.

As they drove their attackers to the head of the stairs and down, a third man rushed up the steps to join them. He was just in time to bump and jostle with his two sweating fellows as Hawkril's scything blade swept them another step down the stairs.

"Weldrin! Where *were* you?" one of the bladesmen snarled at the newcomer, as a desperate parry left his blade momentarily stuck in the stair-rail (which, he now noticed, bore many older notches and sword-scars) and his hands numbed with the force of clashing steel.

"No *names*, you dolt!" Weldrin snarled back. "And I was cutting the alarm-cords! Or did you want all the night guards outside—and all the other guards sleeping around us, too—out and on top of us the moment we first drew steel?"

"Huh," the other bladesman growled, twisting aside from Hawk's reaching blade, "you mean they're not?"

Nortreen Jhalanvyluk had been tapmaster and proud part owner of the Flagon and the Gauntlet for the better part of two decades, and its tapmaster and second flagonman for another two before that. The worn old beam above him, with its tiny carving of a watchful owl and its wandering sweep of darker wood, was as familiar to him as his own right hand.

What was not so familiar, awakening here in his broad bed in the low-ceilinged room at the end of the passage, was the clang and shriek of swords striking other swords *inside* his inn, in the—he looked over at the unshuttered end window, and saw only deep darkness—very heart of the night.

Worse than the sounds that had awakened him was another sound that should have been there, and wasn't: the gentle rise and snore-laced fall of Margathe's slumbrous breathing. He glanced quickly in his wife's direction, and saw a large and ominous silhouette on her side of the bed that could only be Margathe sitting up, very much awake.

Tonight she'd been asleep before his arrival—curses on travelers who liked to sit up half the night, drowsing over their cups but expecting fresh ale and even hot food at all hours!—and, as was her wont, had welcomed him to bed without waking by a volley of snorts, and the persistent warming of her cold feet on his backside, keeping him on the drifting edge of slumber for too long before proper sleep dragged him down.

Once, carrying out slops to the hogs behind the stables, he'd heard an old merchant describing them, all too accurately, to a younger companion: "Both large folk—like two trundling mountains, but Nortreen's the jovial and bustling sort, and his wife is pure viper venom. Always sour, doesn't miss a thing, rules her kitchens like a cruel swordsorn. Smile, say nothing you don't have to, and keep away from her—like her staff do, as much as they can manage!"

Nortreen had winced at that flat, pointed accuracy then. Half a score seasons later, the merchant's words were just as true. Margathe dreamed of a grander life in a baron's town, with coins in plenty and fine gowns and a life of hosting other fine-gowned ladies for afternoons of wines and gossip . . . and as she grew older and fatter and Nortreen had shown no signs of leaving the "ramshackle backwater" he saw as home and she saw as a step on a stair that they'd tarried on for far too long, her tongue had grown steadily sharper and her manner colder and more bitter.

The Flagon *was* his home, with his partners dwelling two baronies off and visiting once in the last seven summers. Fighting would mean broken furniture, broken heads, and mayhap even a fire! He had to get up and go see, but not, please the gods, under the driving lash of Margathe's tongue, and—

"Well, it's about *time* you woke!" Her voice stung like a lash. He flinched and ducked his head away, but every word descended on his head arrow-sharp: "Three above, I swear I could've been murdered thrice over before you'd hear or feel a thing! And there you lie, snoring like a sea turtle while our squalid roof burns down over our heads, and reavers hack apart every guest and stick of furniture in the place, brutalize my girls, and *cook* every animal in the stables in the flames, spearing the carcasses on their belt-knives! I wonder if you'd wake up if they trussed you up and hauled you out to the cooking-spit—or if the Risen King himself came in here with all his knights and shoved you out of bed onto the floor, so he could have his way with me!"

Nortreen's head was whirling at that last vision as he gave a wordless growl in reply and swung himself out of the bed, slapping his bare feet deliberately down on the cold floor rather than into his slippers, to jolt himself awake.

Still, he blinked at nothing and sat scratching for a few breaths, as the creaking of the bed subsided under him, mustering the will—and the energy—to heave himself upright and go to see what the trouble was.

"By the Three! We'd all be murdered in our beds before you even got *up* out of yours!" Margathe was truly angry now, fury no doubt born of the fear beneath. The bed creaked as she rose and stumped angrily to her boots by the firegrate.

"Must I do everything myself?" she snarled, hefting the poker in her hand. "You chose to stay here, Norr—*you* chose this over our bright future in town! This is your inn!"

"Yes, yes, my treasure," Nortreen said wearily, finding his feet—and the old war-axe on the wall—at more or less the same time. "I'm going. Bide you here, an—"

"Ohhh, no!" she snarled in scandalized horror. "Oh, no! I'm not lying here in the dark, alone and unguarded, waiting for some outlaw to burst in and assault my charms! How dare you expose me to such danger! How dare you leave me in such peril! How dare you waste my talents, when I could rouse all the kitchen girls—and send *them* to wake the guards!"

Nortreen gave her a look as he hopped awkwardly, pulling on his boots. Slippers be damned—if he was going to go out and get killed, he wouldn't break his ankles and slip onto his backside a dozen times while he was at it! "You'd trust our kitchen lasses with the guards?" Perhaps he could distract her from the thunderous catalogue of his own faults by raising the possibility of someone else's scandal.

Margathe gave him an even colder look. "You think I haven't trained our girls to know better? You think I don't watch over them, to be sure such doings don't befall under our roof? Norr, you wrong me! You wrong me deeply!"

Claws of the Dark One, the tapmaster told himself silently, his inward voice searing in its bitterness, *but someday I just might. I just might.*

A moment later he was stumping out into the dark passage, axe in hand. When Margathe upbraided him for not taking a lamp, he growled, "I left it for you, good wife," and roused himself into the lumbering equivalent of a charge, forward into the night. Anything to take himself out of reach of Margathe's tongue.

Her reply was a seething snarl. Nortreen Jhalanvyluk winced. Right now, he would assuredly not want to be one of the Flagon's kitchen girls.

Not even at his own weight in gold coins each year.

Not unless roast Margathe was the first dish on the morrow's table.

Steel sang and bit, and another bright wedge of the bladesman's sword flew into the air and tumbled to the floor, winking in the dim lamplight. The man moaned with fear as Hawkril slashed even harder on the return swing—and the man's blade bent visibly in his desperate parry.

His elbows had already driven his fellow bladesman crashing into the far stair-rail, and kept him there, wincing and crouching in a series of ineffectual lunges that just wouldn't reach up the stairs to the armaragor.

"Take him *down*, curse you!" Weldrin snarled from behind them both, shoving at Murgin's backside. To the Dark One with his stupid little play-lunges! Oh, his men were good sword-swingers, far better than most, but this armaragor was fast, very fast—and somehow they couldn't get past the wall of steel he wove with that huge sword. No one should be able to lift a blade that size, let alone swing it about as if it were a needle! And the sorceress didn't help, either, showing her flesh mockingly at every third or fourth blow, taunting them with the chance that she might hurl fire down their throats, as she'd served Uirgurr.

Jalard cried out in fear as his blade broke right off at midpoint, the shards flying into his face. Weldrin slapped his own sword into Jalard's hand and snarled, "*Hold* your ground!" even as the hulking armaragor above them hacked his way a few steps down.

Weldrin stared at his two frantic bladesmen, winced as their foe's next swing almost beheaded Jalard—and wheeled around, bounding down the stairs with Hawkril's deep laughter stabbing after him.

"Weldrin!" Murgin sobbed, fear winning out over anger, "come back! You bastard! You utter reeking bastard!"

He'd have to see to it that those two didn't survive this night's battles, Weldrin thought grimly as he raced down a dark passage, his heart pounding in his ears. They'd never trust him again.

He almost fell in the darkness as his boots found a step down in the passage—or rather, for one sickening moment, found no floor beneath them. The landing hurt, and Weldrin groaned as he thought grimly that he probably wouldn't have to see to the deaths of Jalard and Murgin. That armored giant on the stairs was all too likely to attend to it for him.

There was suddenly a door opening in front of him, and flickering light from behind it. Weldrin was running too hard to stop even if he'd wanted to. "Three above," he gasped, "let there be no sword to the fore!"

Boots thundering on the floorboards, he wondered if the gods would even have time to hear that prayer.

"Roldrick," the husky voice by his ear said urgently, "wake up."

That seemed an odd thing for his old swordsorn to say, now that Roldrick had run him through with six swords and was strangling the furious old man for all he was worth. Old Deldroun was refusing to die, snarling defiance through his white moustache and growing ever larger, no matter how hard Roldrick throttled him. . . .

"Roldrick!" The voice was insistent, and—female!

Roldrick whirled around, there on the purple plain with the red sandstorms blowing and the huge skeletons of things that had perished ages agone rising over him like the burned timbers of ruined houses, and found himself gazing into the golden eyes of a dragon, impossibly close. . . .

He blinked. He *was* gazing into golden eyes! He was in his bed, in the dark, and Jelenna of the kitchens was bending over him, lamp in hand and wearing nothing but a shawl that had slipped to lay bare one breast and shoulder. He stared at a tiny brass ring in her nipple until something crashed across his face and she said crisply, "Enough drooling, man—*up!*"

Roldrick blinked at her, and then grinned sleepily and put a hand around her shoulders to drag her down. "Don't lasses believe in kissing first and suchlike, anymore?"

She slapped him again, her blow turning his head over his left shoulder and leaving his eyes watering. "Harrr!" he snarled angrily. "What's th–?"

"Get up and bring your sword," she snapped, stepping quickly back out of reach of his angry grab. "There's fighting going on by the main stair."

"Why me?" he protested. "There's a duty guard, look you!" Putting a hand over his eyes to shut out the lamplight, he turned over and hauled the blanket she'd pulled aside back over his shoulders. Gods, no wonder he felt cold—she must have laid him bare to take a look, the wench! Well, well . . .

The slaps fell like the blows of the last man he'd fought in a tavern, jolting him rudely into full wakefulness in a hard, rocking rain.

"Listen—well—you—hind—end—of—an—ugly—mule," Jelenna panted,

snarling at him between the blows she was dealing, "The—master—orders—you—up—to—fight!"

Abruptly he was cold again, the blanket whipped away to leave him blinking at her in his leather breeches. The lamp flickered mockingly as he stared up at the furious kitchen lass, scratched himself a little dazedly, and growled, "All right, lass, I—"

There was a heavy crash in Holdyn's room, next door. Roldrick peered at her as if she was a swordsorn over him, and not a gasping and still-angry woman whose shawl had deserted her for the floor, and snapped, "What's that, yon?"

"Mistress Margathe," Jelenna replied, "rousing Holdyn. Shall I bring her in here?"

Roldrick scrambled. "Gods, no! Where's the battle?"

"Out there," she said in a voice of doom, extending one shapely arm to point at the door. Snatching up his scabbarded sword, Roldrick found himself trotting unsteadily to fumble open the latch, the echoes of her slaps still ringing around his ears.

Boots, he thought, as he got the door open. *I've forgotten my boots. . . .*

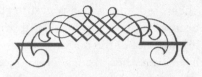

18

Noτ in Ͼꝺy Inn

The gods were smiling this night on Weldrin Hathenbruck.

The man stumbling into the corridor had his head down, hair tousled and sleepy face slack. He was hairy and much-scarred, wore leather breeches that trailed half-undone laces, and held a scabbarded sword in his hand. He was turning to face Weldrin and lifting his head as the running reaver skidded a little—and kicked the man as hard as he'd ever kicked anyone before, with all the fury of his rage and racing haste behind his boot.

The man's eyes bulged in amazed pain as his body lofted helplessly into the air, arms flailing and sword spinning away—and Weldrin crashed into the passage wall, regained his balance, and was past, feminine screams rising behind him like the shrieks of an anguished gull from the doorway whence the man had appeared.

Those shrieks followed him through the crash of the man's landing and the lesser crashings of Weldrin's own boots mounting the dark and narrow back stairs.

At the top was another sleepy man—the floor-guard, eyes still heavy-lidded as he drifted into wakefulness on his stool, driven from sleep by the screams from below. Weldrin snatched at the nearest leg of that stool and pulled, hard.

The stool came away from under the guard with surprising ease. The startled man hadn't even finished bouncing on his tailbone on the floor and opening his mouth for a roar of pain when Weldrin brought the stool down on his head, swinging with vicious force.

A few panting breaths later, the reaver was stopped outside a particular door. On the other side of it were two travelers, delivered into his hands by chance—or perhaps by the Three. They were men he knew—and the Lady Embra would know them, too, though he was sure she hadn't seen them yet, or there'd have been a battle raging on this upper floor of the Flagon long before he'd led his men out of the booth.

Vandur and Kethgan were their names. Not so long ago, they'd been hired agents of the Baron Silvertree, professional "capturers" who kidnapped and brought back to him folk of his choosing from all over the Vale. Mages, rich merchants, even the stewards of rival barons . . . Capturers who never failed, their swords and their stealth triumphing time and time again.

Wherefore he'd have to be very careful right now. Weldrin stepped carefully to one side of the door before reaching out with the pommel of his dagger and knocking—slowly and deliberately. "Vandur," he called. "Kethgan. I am a man alone, who has pressing need of hiring you, here and now."

Silence. He waited, and then hurried to the wall on the other side of the door. "Vandur?" he called flatly. "Kethgan?"

He heard the latch click, and the door of the room swung slowly open—revealing nothing but darkness. Weldrin stared into it, and asked as calmly as he could, "Are you accepting commissions?"

A gloved hand unhooded a heavily shaded lamp far across the room, descended into the small pool of light it cast, and beckoned Weldrin.

He swallowed, trying to keep his face impassive, and stepped forward. He was in midstride when the door closed behind him and the lamp was abruptly hooded once more, leaving him in darkness.

Fighting down sudden, icy fear, Weldrin came to a stop. It was some time—time he spent in tense silence, straining to hear breathing or a footfall or *something* nearby—before the reaver's eyes became accustomed to the gloom. When they did, he became aware of two drawn swords pointing at his eyeballs. They were held by masked and gloved figures that he could barely see amid a dark forest of hangings—rugs or garments hung in strips from the ceiling. "Terms?" he asked the darkness.

"Tell us the task first," came the calm reply from right beside his left ear.

It took all of Weldrin's control to refrain from either flinching or whirling to strike out at the sound of that so-near voice, but he prevailed—and in so doing, saved his own life.

At least for a little while.

Embra felt strangely happy—and judging by the deep humming sound coming from low in his throat, Hawkril did too. Despite the grim mingling of hatred and fear on the faces of the bladesmen who were trying to kill them, there was something almost carefree again in having foes one could see, and grapple with, and strike down.

Safe a good two steps above and behind Hawkril, Embra heard the smallest of sounds from behind her.

She whirled around, her hands coming up like claws, to find herself gazing into the admiring, excited face of Raulin. He was holding something out to her: Sarasper's belt, bulging with little pouches. "Your gewgaws," he announced.

The Lady of Jewels took it from him. "Raulin, this thing'll fall right down around my ankles!"

"Sling it over your shoulder and under the other arm," the boy hissed, "and take this!"

He was holding what looked like an ornately carved table leg out to her. Embra wrinkled her brow at it. "That's a—?"

"Necessary weapon," Raulin told her firmly, closing her fingers tightly around it with his own. "A dainty little table back down the passage won't be needing it any longer. Use it to bat away swords!"

He was already leaping back up the stairs. "I've got to get back to Sarasper," he called. "Fair fortune, Lady Em!"

The woman who wore only boots winced. " 'Em'?" she asked the world, in pained tones. " 'Em'?"

There was a fresh thunder of boots from below. Embra whirled around in time to see another two bladesmen charging up the stairs to join the two who'd been retreating before Hawkril's blade. She frowned, went to her knees, and opened the first pouch.

"Hurry!" Tapmaster Nortreen was more angry than they'd ever seen him. "Haste, before they set the place afire around us!"

The tapmaster usually waddled from place to place, wheezing whenever he wasn't roaring out laughter or orders, and lurching from side to side with every step. Right now he was lumbering down the passage with surprising speed, the boards thundering under his weight. The two guards he'd aroused wiped sleep from their eyes and shrugged their hastily donned armor into place as they hurried after him. The unmistakable clangor of swordplay was coming from the main stairwell; they both drew blades as they went.

"Sarghing claws of the Dark One!" Nortreen swore, as he burst out into the stairwell—and came to a dead stop.

It was almost literally a dead stop, as the guard right behind him brought his swordblade up to avoid spitting the tapmaster only just in time. He swung himself past Nortreen's bulk and skidded to his own halt, staring up at the stair.

Four men in motley armor were hacking and thrusting like men possessed, up at a half-naked giant of a man, all rippling muscles and hair, who was fending them off with a huge cleaver of a sword. At his side stood a woman with long, flowing black hair, who wore only—

"Gods above!" the second guard gasped delightedly.

—boots and a smile. She was striking aside sword-thrusts with a table leg, ducking and bobbing, and slashing back at the faces of the bladesmen with a sword or jet of flame that seemed to be growing from the empty palm of her other hand.

"Sorcery!" Nortreen and the first guard snarled, together, at about the same time as one of the bladesmen threw a knife at the giant, and his almost casual parry sent it spinning past the tapmaster to sing and ring its way down the wall.

The sorceress ducked to let a blade stab past one shapely bare shoulder and asked merrily, "How well do you like your eyeballs cooked?" as she thrust her flame up into the face of the bladesman who'd launched that thrust. He screamed, threw his head back, and flung himself a few steps back down the stairs out of her reach, shaking his head frantically from side to side.

"I've seen enough," the tapmaster growled, swinging his sword at the gong on the wall beside him. It rang protestingly—but alone: the rings that should have echoed it, all over the Flagon, did not sound.

Nortreen gaped at it, and then his face went white with fear and fury. "Someone's cut the cords!" he bellowed. *"We're under attack!"*

"What do we do?" one of the guards demanded.

The tapmaster turned on him. "What you're *paid* to do, dolt!" he snarled, peering right and left. "Where are the night guards, curse them!?! Are they deaf?"

"Are they dead?" the other guard muttered grimly. Nortreen turned slowly to stare at the man, sudden fear rising in his eyes.

"May the Three bear witness—it's *cold*!" Kether hissed, watching his breath curl away in the moonlight.

Borthor's answer was a wordless grunt, as he turned and tramped away along the fenceline. On their left was the dark wall of the forest, branches reaching out at them like claws. They could always feel unseen eyes watching them from its depths. Kether felt them now.

To their right, across the muddy yard, sprawled the unlovely bulk of the rear of the Flagon—all ladders and gutter-pipes and shuttered windows.

Kether trotted to catch up with his friend and resume their endless laconic converse about great riches and grand lives far from here, beautiful women to share it with, and warm beds one could snore in, from one end of every last Three-blessed night to another—and not spend the dark hours shivering along boundary rounds as a night guard.

They never talked about it, but Kether knew Borthor thought about waiting death just as often as he did. Prowling forest-cats and bears and brigands, he was sure, watched the Flagon from the dark forest depths on many a night—and it would only take one of them, once, to reach out at the right moment with claw or arrow or swordblade, to make the inn defenses permanently one night guard shorter.

Walking well away from the trees protected against a reaching attack, but made one a moonlit target for archers and those who liked to hurl daggers. And even the heaviest armor wouldn't stop a dagger through a visor-slit, or—

There was a faint crashing sound, and shouts, from deep inside the Flagon. Borthor's head turned, and he stopped to listen. More shouts, and a few clangs like swords meeting.

The two guards exchanged glances. More confused noise from within, but the alarm gong they were standing under remained silent. Out of habit they looked up at it—and then at the next one along the fence, about a hundred paces away—but the reign of silence continued.

The muffled tumult continued, as well. Borthor shook his head. "Wild time in the old inn this night," he observed in level tones, eyes roaming vainly in search of wisps of rising smoke or open shutters that might show more.

They stood listening for a time, looking at the silent gong once or twice, and then shook their heads in unison and resumed their patrol. "Some folk have a lot more life to them than I would, at this hour, for carousing," Borthor grunted.

"Our luck runs true," Kether replied with a rueful grin. "We always miss out on the fun."

"Invading armies, I'd not welcome," Borthor announced to the watchful night, "but I'd not mind a chance, just once, to join in a little lesser excitement. Even on this night, O watching gods, if it's not too much trouble, hmm?"

"We never have that sort of luck." Kether grinned, shaking his head.

. . .

Steel shrieked along steel as Hawkril strained against the largest guard, Embra reaching past him with flame to hold back the bladesman's fellows.

"Thought we'd be . . . easy prey, did you?" the armaragor snarled, as the guards of their blades locked together and he used his strength to carry them both sideways, to crash into the rail.

His foe, sweat streaming down his face beneath tangled hair, was panting too hard to reply. The other bladesmen tried to scramble around his flank, to strike at Hawkril—but were met by Embra's flame and table leg barring their way—and some tentative sword-thrusts at their backsides, as the inn guards advanced cautiously up the stairs with calls of, "Hoy! Down blades, now! Let this be ended!"

One of the bladesmen whirled around to hack a guard across the face. Blood spurted, a dozen men in the stairwell shouted at once, and the guard toppled back down the stair, fetching up in a loose heap against Nortreen's furious bulk.

"A rescue! A rescue!" the tapmaster bawled, waving his sword wildly. "To me, men of the Flagon!"

Abruptly steel clashed once more between Hawkril and the most weary of the bladesmen—and this time their striving blades bit together into the stair-rail. Hawkril followed it with a knee, catching the man in the chest.

The bladesman staggered, turned by the impact but reluctant to let go of his deep-sunken sword—and the thud of his armored body against the rail was followed by a splintering crash as the riven rail gave way, spilling him off the stair amid a cloud of tumbling splinters.

Sleepy guards were boiling into the stairwell from all directions, looking up at the battle on the stair and raising their swords. One of them was smashed flat under the falling bladesman—and his fellows pounced, slitting the man's throat before he could rise.

"Somehow," Embra shouted, slashing fire across another grimacing face and following it with a crack of the table leg across a nose, "I don't think this venture's going quite as these reavers had planned! Any chance of keeping one of them alive for me to use a little prying magic on as to who sent them, and why?"

"A swift question, lass," Hawkril growled, wincing back from a sword-cut that left a ribbon of crimson across his breast, "but it may take us a little time to win an answer."

A bladesman drove his sword into the upturned face of a guard trying to clamber up the outside of the stair-rail, and the man's shriek turned into a bubbling fall down into the gathering crowd below.

"I'll get to work on it," the armaragor added gravely, driving his fist into a bladesman's face and then slashing the man's gauntlet right off his sword-hand while the man reeled. "In the meantime, may I tell you what an idiot you are for charging into a fray dressed—ah—as you are?"

"No," Embra replied sweetly, catching hold of the stair-rail and swinging herself out of the way of a vicious swordcut.

"Ah," Hawkril rumbled, kicking Embra's attacker in the chest, "I see. Well enough, then. I'll say no more on this trifling matter."

Doors banged open up and down the upper passage, lamps flickering in hands and bleary-eyed people fumbling with clothes and weapons. Feet pounded, blades flashed as men shouted at each other, and the Flagon seemed to be full of milling, frightened folk.

"Stand back, you!"

"What's going on?"

"Take that, outlaw! Taste my steel!"

"Ahhh! A rescue! A res—urrghkhh!"

"Have a care, you! Back, I say! I'm a friend to Baron Brostos!"

"Really? Yet I see him not! *Die,* reaving bastard!"

Swords rang here and there in the gloom and confusion, and running, shouting folk tripped over more than one sprawled body in the darkness. More doors banged open.

"What's going on?" someone shouted, peering into the tumult. "Is there a fire?"

"Fire!" someone else bellowed, mishearing the bellowed query. "Fire!"

Others took up the cry, and more guests who'd kept behind their barred doors snatched up lamps and weapons and pounded out into the passages. "Fire! Get out! Get *out*?"

Everyone seemed to be running now, wild battles erupting here and there as men with drawn swords jostled or collided—and started hacking.

"Out of my *way*, murderous dog! Out of my—uhh—way!"

A body slumped heavily to the floor, and the man who'd sent it there clattered thankfully down the stairs. He had to get out before the smoke started, and get his precious Lighthooves out of the stables! He had to—

Someone opened a door and he crashed hard into it, clawed at the air blindly, blade spinning away, and slid down it, everything dimming into slumber. Six men or more trampled the body before it stopped moving.

"Stop!" a guard bellowed. "All of you—halt! I comm—"

As the guard sprinted down the passage to get to where three men were frantically hacking apart a window, a small woman shuffled out of her room in her shift. She saw his sword sweep up, glittering in the light of someone's lamp, and swung her only weapon, hard.

The chamberpot broke across the running guardsman's face, shattering into a thousand shards. He took another three staggering steps before falling on his face, and his senseless form slid on—taking the bowed legs out from under a sleepily squinting merchant in a nightshirt. Together the guard and the merchant bumped and crashed noisily down the back stairs.

The woman screamed. An older, far more deaf woman stuck her wrinkled face out the door of the next room and inquired of the world, "Is it always like this in backland inns? Or is there a revel going on?"

Even the candle-lanterns hanging from the ceiling were swinging crazily now, as the stairwell erupted into a veritable flood of shouting, sword-waving men. From every passage, above and below, sleepy folk were converging—and not least among them was the mistress of the Flagon.

Margathe glared around the room, got one look at the sorceress on the stair stabbing at men with fire and wearing nothing but boots, and bellowed as loudly as any warrior, "*What* is the meaning of this *strumpery*? This is *not* a pleasure-house, and we'll be having no flashing of charms around here! Gods, no wonder all the men are up and shouting! Oh, no! Not in MY inn!"

Seething, Margathe drove the sword she was carrying into the floorboards beside her, where it quivered as she flung the poker in her other hand at Embra Silvertree. The poker cracked off the railing and struck down a hapless merchant below the stair, but the sound brought Embra's head around to see who her attacker had been—in time to receive a veritable flood of hurlings from the furious mistress of the Flagon. A flower-jug burst on the rail and sent its shards and water all over an already-reeling bladesman, a ewer of wash-water spun over the rail and drenched Embra with its icy contents as it literally spun across her breasts, and the next missile—a dirty boot left outside a door for cleaning—caught the Lady of Jewels full in the face.

As she staggered, dropping her table leg with a clatter, the other boot slammed into the side of Embra's head.

Bruised and furious, Embra went to her knees, snatched at Sarasper's belt with a hand that still trailed flame, and snarled harsh, thick words that rang back off the ceiling.

The surge of power that burst forth from her an instant later took the stair-rail and most of the stairs with it, hurling them against the wall of the stairwell with splintering force, and tumbling a sobbing Margathe the length of the passage she'd come in by. The roar of the magic was like a clap of thunder inside the inn; in its ringing wake, everyone in the stairwell came to a numbed and peering halt, all eyes turning to regard the furious woman on the stairs.

Embra Silvertree's hair was standing straight out from her head in all directions, and wisps of smoke were curling up from her hands and between her parted lips. She was looking just as dazed as the folk staring at her.

"Oh, dear," she said unsteadily, looking at the gape-mouthed corpses of two guards, transfixed to the wall by shards of the stair-rail. "I—it's never done that before."

In the sudden silence, her hands went to the empty pouches on her belt, fumbling there and finding nothing—and with a sucking sound and a wet plop, someone's severed hand unpeeled itself from where her blast had sent it, driven against the ceiling amid much sticky gore, and plunged to the floor far below.

Borthor's head jerked up. "What," he asked, in the tones of a man who'd rather be cursing, "was *that*?"

"We'd best get in there," Kether said in awed tones, as they peered at the inn and heard the shouting and crashing sounds slowly begin again. The Flagon had literally been shaking—right out to the stable-mud under their boots.

The two night guards exchanged grim looks. "You know we're fools, don't you?" Borthor growled, as they drew their swords and ran to the east door.

"I was trying not to think about that," Kether replied, as the door banged open and they shouldered through it, not slowing.

The door banged shut, leaving the innyard empty of all but moonlight.

For all of about three seconds.

"I thought they'd never leave," a tree by the fence—or rather, a dark shadow detaching itself from the forest giant's trunk—muttered.

"Umm," the other moving form replied, as they stepped together over the fence and into the innyard. The moonlight showed them to be two men who might have been naked, or might have been clothed—but whatever they were or weren't wearing, it was rippling and flowing as they came . . . and their heads offered the world only smooth pink surfaces where their faces should have been.

The Koglaur seemed almost to melt through the door, in uncanny silence. It closed behind them scant moments before a panting man rushed around the corner of the Flagon, ducked down behind some barrels where he could see the east door, and allowed himself a smile.

If the gods were still smiling, Weldrin Hathenbruck would need only to wait here to have his fortune delivered right into his hands.

The flood of folk surging down the stairs had come to an abrupt halt in the ringing aftermath of the spell hurled by the sorceress. The popularity of the stair as the way to escape the fire had suddenly waned—and the frightened guests of the Flagon were still staring at each other in fearful indecision when the two men stalked through them like dark and silent shadows.

One merchant made the mistake of extending a hand to clutch at a dark-clad, passing shoulder. "Hoy," he began, "that's my bed-bl—"

The blade that took his life was no thicker than a knitting needle; it burst in and out of his eye like lightning. After the merchant's body crashed onto its face and spilled a ribbon of blood across the boards, no one else moved in the passage as the two men in dark leathers passed among them.

Vandur and Kethgan did not smile at the quivering statues they stepped around; the capturers had long ago set aside thrills and enjoyments while working. Coldly alert, they moved forward with all thought bent on a single purpose. They had a contract to fulfill.

Abruptly men were shouting and striking at each other with their swords again, down below. Steel rang again and men moved, the tapmaster striding forward with angry gestures to send his guards against the blades-men and frantic merchants entangled at the bottom of the stair. Margathe came staggering grimly back out of the passage, her face marked, battered, and covered with someone else's blood.

The armaragor in breeches still stood on the stair, holding it with the sweeping point of his great warsword—and behind him, the sorceress in boots was visibly wavering in her thoughts.

Without figurines and other gewgaws, she had no magic left—yet she dared not leave Hawkril to fight alone! On the other hand, what good could she be to him?

Embra almost growled aloud as she mounted the steps swiftly. If she could get back to their rooms quickly, and retur—

"You!" The howl from below was as loud and furious as before, though the bruised and swelling face of its owner looked more toadlike than earlier. Margathe was pointing up at her as if Embra was some evil affront to the gods, and—

She had no warning of the bed-blanket descending over her head at all, only a sudden whirling nightmare of hard-booted darkness and enthusiastic bodies taking her bruisingly down onto the worn wooden steps.

Embra struggled to roll over and rise, hearing Margathe's shouts of approval through the reeking cloth—but what felt like a fist came out of nowhere to put an end to all struggles, and she was falling into darkness, cruel applause and all fading behind her. . . .

The removal of the sorceress swept away the fears and misgivings of many angry men, and the stairwell was suddenly a furious battlefield once more, with guards slashing down roused guests, women screaming, and the air full of hurled oddments. Yelling, sword-waving men in various states of undress streamed into the central chamber from all directions, and swept like a tide over the bladesmen and the armaragor on the lower steps of the stair.

The screams rose in deafening unison when something huge and serpentine burst through the archway from the taproom, carrying benches and curtains before it. Scales shone as it reared up, flat golden eyes glaring from a dozen heads, and let as many fanged jaws yawn open almost lazily.

Men staggered back in fear—and as the serpent-thing glided forward and crashed down, heads darting here and there to bite and slay, the passages emptied in screaming terror. Men there were, however, who did not die in the mage-slayer's first strike, as it quested around the room that still thrummed with magic—and they raced forward to stab and hack frantically, plying their blades with such fervor that no less than five heads hung limp and bloody when the shimmer-scaled serpent reared up again.

White to the lips, Tapmaster Nortreen stood his ground, paunch quivering. He'd not quite believed the bards who claimed the upland Vale still held horrors such as this . . . but he believed now, and he had an inn to defend.

Golden eyes glared down at him. Nortreen swallowed, hearing Margathe's low moan of fear from behind him, and bellowed desperately, "The sorceress has sent this to hunt us down! We must slay it now, or be hunted down, one after another, and—"

The roar of rage that drowned out his last words carried the howling guards and guests forward in a hacking, stabbing wave that closed over the serpent in a red fury.

Arching necks rose desperately out of the slaughter, and more than one man screamed as he was broken in tightening jaws, or flung high and far to a sobbing landing . . . but when the tumult died wearily away, long breaths later, the floor of the Flagon was awash in thick purple gore, and a shimmering bulk lay sprawled and dead amid too many motionless men.

Tapmaster Nortreen stared around the room, on the verge of tears. All the ruin, and yet he lived, and they'd slain the beast, and . . . the battle went on. There was shouting and swordplay down one passage, and three of his guards looked at their reeling master and then trotted away to that fray together.

Nortreen Jhalanvyluk sat heavily down on a bench that creaked alarmingly under his weight, and sobbed as if his heart was broken.

The two men in dark leathers bundled their burden swiftly down the serving-stairs and along the back passage, passing kitchen doorways where frightened lasses huddled in wide-eyed fear over pots where the early stews were being born. Some of them screamed at the sight of what could only be a corpse wrapped in the bed-blanket, and others toppled silently to the floor.

The capturers paid the cooks no attention. Their pay was waiting beyond the east door of the Flagon, just ahead. When a certain crazed sorceress was delivered to a lout who happened to have coins to spend, their work would be done—and it would be back to bed, all the richer, to rise late in the bright day and smile at the strange whims of the Three.

Weldrin rose from behind the barrels, smiling anxiously. "You've got her?"

Vandur quelled a momentary urge to snap that no, they'd brought him the mistress of the Flagon instead, and merely nodded and whipped the bed-blanket away, leaving Embra Silvertree's white, openmouthed face to stare sightlessly up at the moon.

The warrior gave her bared body a long look and let out a deep breath, almost slumping in relief. Then he looked up at the two dark and silent figures and said gratefully, "Glory to you! I have your fee ready here, and—"

The door banged open, and someone large and loud stormed out, double chins quivering. "You dare!" Margathe bellowed, furiously raining slaps and cuffs on the heads and shoulders of all three men. "You dare to—to come in here, craven and corrupt panderers all, to peddle your *naked* pleasure-sluts around a respectable inn?"

The astonished capturers staggered under their beating, whirling to confront its source, and received another torrent of words spat into their faces: "And you plunge into this, this *bare*faced *outrage* without the slightest shred of a proper business arrangement with the proprietors!"

Vandur and Kethgan exchanged disgusted looks, and their daggers swept up in moon-glittering unison to gut this raging pudding of a woman.

The capturers' daggers were swift—but the arms that swept out of the darkness to sweep each man off his feet, dragging him back from the mistress of the Flagon and breaking his neck in one brutal movement, were even swifter.

Margathe Jhalanvyluk stared up into faces that were not faces, looked from one smooth mask of flesh to the other . . . and with only the briefest and faintest of peeping sounds, fainted.

Faceless heads turned together. Weldrin was backing away from them, his face white to the lips. A childhood nightmare had come to life before his eyes, and—

His screams started even before they laid their hands on him, and had become an endless, sobbing wail by the time they'd marched him around the inn to the window they thought was his, and hurled him bodily up into the air, as if their arms were as strong as catapults, to crash through its opening and vanish from view, leaving shutters banging crazily in his wake. Weldrin Hathenbruck was about to learn that the gods only smile for so long.

Raulin spun around above the old healer as something that howled blotted out the moonlight, and two borrowed daggers were ready in both trembling hands as he sprang to meet whatever it was, screaming his own terror aloud as he struck, and struck, and struck again—ere they crashed to the floor together.

The hurtling man was dead, his throat slit open and a dagger hilt-deep in his heart, almost before his face struck the floorboards.

"Where is she?" Hawkril Anharu roared, stalking along a passage. "What have you done with her?"

A guard looked him up and down contemptuously. "Lost your whore, warrior?"

The armaragor roared out his rage and struck, smashing aside the man's sword, breastplate, and all in a furious swordcut that sent the guard gasping to the floor, clutching at his bleeding chest and gasping in pain.

"Where is she?" Hawkril snarled into his face.

"We've better things to do, man," another guard snapped, as they advanced on him in careful unison, swordpoints lifting like the tails of serpents coiling to strike, "than keep track of bed-wenches, whether or not they know sorcery!"

Hawkril growled and strode to meet them, lifting his warsword almost eagerly.

One of the guards eyed it and flung up a hand to stop his fellows. "Who was she?" he snapped at the advancing armaragor.

"The Lady of Jewels," Hawkril replied grimly. "The Baroness Silvertree."

The guards fell back in shocked silence as he added bitingly, "I hope you'll have something creative ready when you try to excuse yourselves to the king."

"Warrior!" another voice snapped, from behind the guards. It was the tapmaster, and he lifted an arm to point through the archway that led into the taproom. "Let there be no more bloodletting! There's the one you seek."

Hawkril kept his warsword ready in front of him as he came around the corner.

The table the Four had shared earlier had been cleared—by the simple means of sweeping everything on it onto the floor. Embra Silvertree lay on it, asleep or senseless on her back with the bed-blanket spread over her . . . and no one else that he could see in the taproom.

Hawkril moved to stand over her, glaring all around. "How came she here?"

Tapmaster Nortreen waved at his men to keep back, and came into the room. His face was white and set as the armaragor looked up at him.

"Two men just came in," he said, swallowing, "by the front portal, and laid her as you see her."

Hawkril's blazing eyes narrowed. "You saw their faces?"

The tapmaster swallowed again. "They had no faces."

The armaragor merely nodded slowly, making no show of surprise.

Nortreen moved forward a little uncertainly, keeping his hands behind him. "Now, warrior, there has been quite enough blood spilled in my inn this night. I demand that you lay down your sword and go to your room."

Hawkril lifted one eyebrow, saying nothing.

"In my time," Nortreen Jhalanvyluk said in the deepest voice he could manage, "I was regarded as a great warrior. Men feared me up the Vale and down—and it has not been all that long since I retired here. If you expect to live longer, warrior, heed me. Lay down your sword."

Hawkril set his warsword on the table beside Embra, and said wearily, "I've no quarrel with you, tapmaster."

Nortreen stepped forward. "That is good. Is your lady wounded?"

The tapmaster laid a hand on the bed-blanket to lift it back—and the warsword flashed out like a striking serpent, cutting like fire across the knuckles of Nortreen's other hand.

The dagger the tapmaster had been bringing up to stab the sorceress clattered out of his sliced and dangling fingers . . . and Nortreen swayed above the body of the woman who'd caused so much trouble in his beloved Flagon.

Darkness was suddenly rushing up to claim him. . . .

With the hand that wasn't holding his warsword again, Hawkril reached out and spun the body of the fainting tapmaster, to keep him from dealing the death with his falling weight that he'd failed to give with his fang.

As Nortreen crashed to the floor, something stirred in the darkest shadows of the taproom. A bat that had hung calmly watching the night's proceedings suddenly took to the air and flitted silently away.

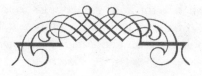

19

Perchance to Scheme

Disturbed by the noise, bats fluttered up from their accustomed rocks and flapped and swooped away. It was cold in the cave, despite the pulsing flames rising from the ring of braziers. Those flames fed the edges of a huge, slowly turning disc of flame, a waist-high floating circle of inch-thick fire that blazed away merrily in the smoky darkness.

Robed and cowled figures moved barefoot around the ring, and more than one cowl was thrown back to reveal a fanged and scaled snake-head. More than one robe, too, bulged at the back, as if a nascent tail was struggling to grow. The priests chanted as they walked, an eerie, low-pitched rising and falling recitation that slowly quickened in pace until it became strident, insistent, rising—to a moment of silence, when all the Faithful of the Serpent spread their hands in unison . . . and the flames receded to the very edges of the disc, revealing a scene upon the rest of it.

That bright, floating image was of a little valley in the upland Vale mountains not far from the cave, an overgrown draw that narrowed swiftly as it climbed, to end at a little pool and the crumbling shell of a riven, abandoned stone tower.

A man was riding alone up to that keep, bareheaded and yet full-armored, his face as blank as the cloudless sky above him and his movements slow and stiff.

"*Try* to stay in your saddle, my Lord Lackwit," one of the Serpent-priests murmured mockingly. "It's only a little farther now."

The man on the horse lurched alarmingly once or twice as the horse picked its way between loose stones and up the last, steep slope.

"So now to meet this most mysterious of mages," the priest gloated to the priestess kneeling beside him, clad only in leisurely writhing snakes, "and enlist him in the growing Army of the Serpent—or destroy him, as he chooses."

"Oh, dear," the priestess said, standing up abruptly. "I was afraid that was your intent."

The priest whirled around to face her, face darkening into a scowl—and she thrust a hand forward and touched him.

His head burst in a scarlet shower that filled the air with thousands of droplets. A moment later, all of the other Serpent-clergy around the ring suffered the same fate.

The blood-drenched priestess waded unconcernedly through the sticky wake of the dull, wet explosions, murmured an incantation, and waved a hand. One of the headless corpses rose from its bloody tangle to hang rigid in midair, hands at its sides.

The priestess gestured, and the body moved in response, until it was positioned just so. Then the priestess smiled, nodded, and moved to the next corpse.

Obediently each body in turn rose into the air and turned shoulders downmost, to hang at an angle just clear of the disc, but positioned so as to drain their lifeblood into one of the braziers that fed the disc.

The upended body of the upperpriest, straight and with its arms at its sides, floated to the center of the ring of flames, and descended to touch the scene—which vanished in spreading whorls of blood.

Then the body of the priestess grew, straightened in a sickening shifting of bulging and reshaping flesh, and became Ingryl Ambelter.

"More than one hand reaching for Aglirta's crown can be brutal in its doings," he murmured, looking around at the slaughter. "Let this meeting proceed, children of the Serpent, *without* your scrutiny or control."

He smiled at the floating corpses, gave them a mocking salute, and then turned away from the ring of fire and stepped into nothingness, fading away in midstride and leaving the cavern to the dead of his making.

Dismounting a few steps from the empty archway that led into Kaerath's Keep, a hold so long ruined that no one now remembered who Kaerath had been, or when or what he'd ruled, the Lord Baron Berias Loushoond suddenly stopped, shivered, shook his head violently several times, and then staggered back and looked around, seeming to see and know his surroundings for the first time.

After a moment, breathing heavily, the Lord of Loushoond strode forward into the ruined keep, his hand on the hilt of his sword. The floor of the entry hall was heaped with fallen stone, and most of the back wall of the great chamber beyond was gone, daylight spilling into the place where trees grew up from the floor and collapsed balconies spilled statuary onto the far-snaking roots.

"Wizard?" the baron asked the empty, waiting darkness. "Wizard, I am come. Where wait you?"

The Wizard of Stars, so the bards sang, was the mightiest mage Aglirta had ever known. He'd ruled the land centuries ago, invading the minds of the boldest baron and most innocent child alike, often and tracelessly, so that all were his unwitting slaves, and served him in small things and large.

No one quite remembered when he'd vanished, and no one had seen his body or heard reliably of his death, so there were many who thought that he'd never died, and lurked somewhere still, keeping silent for his own reasons. "Until the Wizard walks" was still a saying heard in the upland Vale, and there were some who believed that the Reign of the Wizard was more glorious than that of any king, rightful or no . . . so when the baron received a speaking-sending one night from the Wizard of Stars, the Priests of the Serpent had grown excited, and ached to close their hands on this most potent of weapons to use against a Risen King. Perhaps he'd even prove powerful enough that they need not act openly, and could work through him.

Yes, let the meeting befall, and the wizard who sought to ensnare a baron to his servitude be himself ensnared, to the greater glory of the Serpent. . . .

And now it was as if a warm and scaly mist had been lifted from the baron's thoughts, and he stood alone and a little bewildered in this cleft nigh the mountains, blinking at a ruined keep that stood on another baron's land, and wondering just who would truly be awaiting him.

Abruptly, someone was—a ghostly figure fading into dark solidity on a nearby stone seat, reclining at its ease and looking at Baron Loushoond with a slight smile quirking the corners of its lips. Well, it looked human enough—and it looked, if a brief glimpse and his own long memory served him well enough, like the mightiest of the Dark Three wizards who'd served Baron Faerod Silvertree, Ingryl Ambelter. . . .

"Greetings, Spellmaster," he said quietly, and was rewarded with a look of pleased surprise. "Are you the cause of my freedom?"

The sorcerer on the seat nodded his head. "I am—and also the means by which our converse here shall be shielded from Serpent-loving eyes and ears. Be warned that your continued survival lies in pretending to still be under the sway of the Serpent in the days ahead . . . and that the Scaly Ones will come to truly control you again if I don't place several deep spells in your mind."

"Deep—?"

A tendril of mage-light thrust forward like a needle from the seated wizard's forefinger to one of the baron's nostrils.

Loushoond stiffened, grabbed at his sword-hilt, stiffened again—and then sighed heavily and relaxed. His eyes were still flickering when a brighter radiance swam from the wizard's hands, and the baron stiffened again, his face acquiring a faint grimace of pain this time.

"Tell me, if you will," he said slowly, his eyes drifting back from distant places to meet those of the Spellmaster, "just in what way being ridden by your spells is less slavery than being under the lash of the Serpents."

Ingryl Ambelter shrugged. "Everyone is beholden to someone," he replied. "You, now, to me. Unlike the Snake-lovers, however, I have a distaste for making men into automatons jerking to my will—and I view such servants as clumsy things at best."

He spread his hands. "Serpent-priests like to sneer at the rest of us, for being fools—and in so doing, blind themselves to their own foolishness, which far outstrips ours. Their way is that of the bludgeon; mine the swift, sharp, and sure sword. They use magics to compel you; I will not. They command your every word and deed; I leave you to find your own fortune—and hope to convince you, here and now, that our strivings should be together for a time, to the same ends. If I was a Serpent-priest, I'd not trouble myself to try to convince you—I'd compel you, not caring what screaming went on behind your face so long as you did what I wanted."

The Lord of Loushoond nodded slowly. "So, then," he said softly, "here I stand, my wits free once more. Convince me."

The man who'd once been the Spellmaster of Silvertree regarded the baron thoughtfully for a moment, and then leaned forward in his seat and said in an eager rush, "Let there be a scheme hatched between us. It is a thing made possible because I recognize some of the magics that protect the Risen King, and know how to control those fields to compel the king to move and—in a crude, limited way, much as the Serpents were controlling you—act as I bid."

The baron frowned again, and took a grim step forward in the rubble. "And how is this something I would want to be part of, wizard?"

Ambelter spread his hands. "Bear in mind that this is a power best used *very* sparingly. It's my intent to use it only twice."

He rose from the seat and strolled across the chamber, his feet disturbing no rubble—and making no sound. Berias Loushoond watched him with narrowed eyes.

"Firstly," the sorcerer said, "I'd compel the king to blunder into a 'secret' Serpent ritual. When he appears, he'll doubtless be attacked by the attending clergy—whereupon agents urged on by my spells will lead a charge of well-armed courtiers to rescue their king."

"And—?" the baron growled, stroking his chin thoughtfully.

"And a lot of Serpent-priests will be slaughtered," the Spellmaster continued with a smile, "the king will end up beholden to his rescuers, and as we both—through my magics—watch everything from a safe and concealed distance, our agents will have the chance to scour the bodies and the area for Serpent-magic."

"Perhaps even the Dwaer-Stone the priests are rumored to command," the baron murmured, giving the wizard a sidelong glance.

Ingryl Ambelter smiled, shrugged, and added, "Then follows my second compulsion of the king: I bring His Risen Majesty into a private meeting with ourselves, whereat you portray yourself as the only baron truly loyal to the River Throne, who has at great personal risk defied the spells of the Serpent-clergy to make alliance with an outlander wizard—who shall be myself, wearing a different face and name—to defend the rightful Risen King from the great evil of the Serpent. In other words, I use my compulsions only to win us the royal attention that you, at least, deserve . . . and have earned, many times over, were every man in Aglirta to have his just due."

Berias Loushoond nodded, a light kindling in his eyes, and said, "So we stand face-to-face with the Lord of all Aglirta, with our fortune left riding on our tongues. And what words shall we use then?"

"We tell the king that if he grants us titles—giving me some court standing, and making you a baron above the other barons—we'll whelm the army he so desperately needs and make war on the Serpent."

"And if he refuses?"

"I *could* compel him," Ingryl said slowly, "but I'd far rather the king acted freely, out of his own judgements and desires. I need to trust *his* trust."

"And so?"

"And so, if he refuses, we meet again and plan otherwise than we do here and now. Yet I do not think he will refuse."

He'll not refuse because you will *compel him,* the baron thought grimly, staring into the wizard's eyes. *And if your spells let you hear my thoughts now—well enough: you know what I'm thinking.* "And if he accepts?" he asked, rubbing his gauntleted hands slowly together.

"We whelm the force we've promised, using sellswords I have more than enough coin to call to our banner, in Sirlptar, in the Southerlands—and on the Isles, where there are many men who'd love to slaughter Aglirtan warriors and at the same time buy a promise of peace betwixt their watery realm and the River Throne. We take them into battle against barons—your own rivals first, of course—and in one of those affrays, the outlander wizard will demonstrate his supreme loyalty to the king by sacrificing himself."

"You'll step out of that shape," the Lord of Loushoond murmured. "Whom will you find to fill it, before the swords strike?"

"The most loyal and competent close retainer of the king we can find," the wizard said with a smirk, "because having removed him, I'll have to step into his boots . . . and so come to stand that much closer to the royal ear." He would have been surprised to know that the noble frowning consideringly at him had read his next thoughts almost as precisely as if he'd spoken them aloud: *And having gained such a rank, 'twill be a matter of swift ease to have a certain Baron Loushoond slain in tumult soon to come.*

"You seem in some haste to unfold your plan," the baron growled, "leading me to think this shielding spell of yours will die soon. That raises an all-too-pointed question: what happens to me, and to these secrets of yours, the first time a Serpent-priest delves into my mind again, or tries to compel me or simply drive me down?"

Ingryl Ambelter spun around, soundlessly, and for a moment the Lord of Loushoond could have sworn his boots were hovering inches *above* the floor-rubble. "Ah!" he cried, almost as if delighted. "If any Serpent-priest tries to break your mind, and so disturbs my deep spells, I'll know it—and will come to you in speed, to hurl my own Serpent-slaying magics!"

The baron made the slightest of elegant court bows in his direction. "I'm greatly reassured to hear that," he said, in a voice so dry that Ingryl Ambelter's face darkened, and he half-lifted a hand to hurl magic.

"Wherefore," the Lord of Loushoond added, as he turned to stride back out through the ruined arch to his waiting horse, "I believe we understand each other well enough to have a deal, wizard." He knew as he said it that that he was speaking flat, cold truth—and that Ingryl Ambelter, who had been Spellmaster to Faerod Silvertree, knew it too.

The Silverflow is never far from view no matter where one stands in Aglirta, and the barges that carry the richest, most exalted, and mightiest Aglirtans are usually aflap with proud banners that none can mistake—but in times of trouble, travelers of rank and power often go mage-cloaked, and cross the Vale rather less grandly but more swiftly.

So it was with little surprise that the steward of Tathcaladorn, the private castle and hill-forest hunting lodge of the Baron of Cardassa, answered the gate-gong on the night of the same day as Baron Loushoond enjoyed an outing to ruined Kaerath's Keep, to find a small company of masked and cloaked men on splendid mounts craving entry in requests that, for all their cultured pleasantry, stood a bare shade away from being commands.

Attentively, expressionlessly, and without delay he yielded to them the forecourt, tapping the gong that would alert the archers on the battlements that ringed it to make ready their shafts, and passed into the inner ward, where he sent lancemasters to the guardhall and to the House Wizard before striding on across the central garden to rap upon the guarded doors that led into the private dining hall of the Great Lord of Cardassa.

Ithclammert Cardassa looked up from his goblet of wine, his ever-present sheaf of contracts and treaties and letters of commerce awaiting amendment or signature, his clariontar of many candles, and the remains of what looked like a very fine brace of pheasant poached in leek and river-turtle soup, and asked expressionlessly, "Visitors, Taurym?"

The steward was too senior to show surprise, even if he'd felt it; he merely bowed his head and said, "Fourteen riders, Great Lord, all armed. More than one, I'd judge, is used to command—and the six largest riders, at least, sit in their saddles armored for war. They're in the forecourt now, with our archers alerted. I've roused the guard and the House Wizard."

The Baron of Cardassa's response was a hand signal that brought a lancemaster to his side, to whom he murmured, "Bring me my sword, and have these dishes cleared away. I shall either call for a proper feast later or—more likely—give such ardent suitors no more than wine and words."

As the man turned away, the baron raised his eyes and said, "My thanks, Taurym. Have all within the walls roused, dressed for travel and ready to carry what they most value, and—but for the guards and kitchen staff—in the stables, ready to ride away on everything that can be mounted. Those who cannot stay in a saddle are to lead away the mules, or just set free and drive off every last beast . . . *if* I fall or give the order to fly."

The steward turned to go, and his master lifted a very steady hand that had a goblet in it, and added, "One more thing, Taurym. Once you've invited our guests to make their own way hence from the forecourt, see to it that the House Wizard is fully aware of the possible danger—and that, whatever his orders and wishes, his apprentices are awake and ready to fight *and* to flee."

Taurym had served the man some called the Crow of Cardassa—always well out of earshot of both the baron and his sword-sworn servants—for a long time, so he dared to tarry now and ask, "Lord, did you know these visitors were coming?"

The baron's smile was so thin that a man less familiar with him might have missed it entirely. "No, nor do I know who they are. Yet, let us say, I have my suspicions . . . and wonderments, too, one of them being why it has taken them this long to darken our doors."

Taurym regarded him in silence for the space of a long breath before murmuring, "Great Lord, it is a honor to serve you," and turning smoothly away.

Ithclammert Cardassa watched him go without moving a muscle—but the goblet that he put to his lips once his steward was gone trembled visibly ere he drained it.

20

Barons Bolder

No knock fell upon the doors facing the Baron of Cardassa before they opened, without warning but also without violence, leaving him looking up from his papers at a silent line of masked and cloaked men.

"Welcome to Tathcaladorn," he said calmly, "travelers. Wine awaits you yonder, stands for your cloaks over there. May I have the pleasure of knowing who is enjoying the hospitality of Cardassa this night?"

The largest and most heavily armored men stepped forward into the room first, looking swiftly to the right, left, and upwards, marking where all the doors were. These would be the bodyguards, and they were eight in number.

Cardassa, who sat alone with his sword now scabbarded at his side, did not let a smile come to his lips. Well, if silent menace was the game, he could at least parry. He sat back to calmly study his next paper as the plate-armored bodyguards stalked forward, exchanged wary glances, and finally—having seen that the room was empty of all men but the one seated before them—nodded back over their shoulders at the others. They, in turn, stepped forward, drawing the doors closed behind them, swung down the ornamented latch-bars that would keep all but the strongest of men out, and turned to face the baron again.

Then they all doffed their masks in unison, revealing some faces with which Cardassa was not unfamiliar, and identified themselves tersely in turn: "Adeln." "Ornentar." "Tarlagar." "Mauveiron." "Caladash." "Talasorn."

Ithclammert Cardassa gave them a smile, and waved again at the wine.

"I mark also the warrior Narvim, once of Blackgult and more recently seen, I believe, in Castle Adeln. And beside him would be Marthith of Ornentar Castle." He looked along the line of warriors, received only silence and steady stares in return, and then turned to look directly at the oldest of his foes. "So your bodyguards lack tongues?"

"No," Baron Esculph Adeln replied smoothly, "but neither do they lack discipline—or discretion."

The Lord of Cardassa raised his eyebrows. "Really? Then I must needs conclude that their masters are sorely lacking in those traits. Is any matter of state so weighty that it can draw together two barons of the realm, another man who would be, and three wizards of name to take horse together in the night . . . and yet so dark of aspect that they must needs go to a man's hunting-house in the dark, and not call at his castle in the full light of day?"

The Tersept of Tarlagar and two of the mages flushed visibly, and something that wasn't quite allowed to become a smile passed over the face of one of the silent armored statues that the bodyguards had become.

"I did not ride all this way," the Baron of Adeln replied crisply, "to fence with you, Ithclammert. We are gathered here to invite you to join us in what will very soon become a direct and open action regarding the throne of Aglirta."

"A conspiracy against the man who calls himself the Risen King?" the Baron of Cardassa asked, calmly writing something on the parchment before him.

"Not to put too fine a point on it," the mage Caladash snapped in his nasal, sneering voice, "yes."

The baron regarded him calmly from behind the table. "And is this all of you? Or, if I throw my lot in with you, am I joining also with others I do not now see?"

"No," Baron Eldagh Ornentar began, the flesh around his eyes and mouth strangely blue, "th—"

Adeln stepped in front of him, and asked loudly, "What do you mean?" As if attached to him by strings, several of the bodyguards leaned forward too, staring in hard-eyed unison at the Lord of Cardassa.

"I mean," Ithclammert Cardassa explained calmly, spreading his hands, "that I expected to see here with you the man who has led many of your more private moots: Bodemmon Sarr."

Several of the mages stiffened, and Caladash started to snap something that Adeln quelled with a direct glare before turning back to the master of Tathcaladorn and saying shortly, "Bodemmon Sarr has, it seems, vanished from Aglirta—or at least from where in the realm he has customarily been found. I know not how it is that you presume to know anything of private moots or who attended them, but it is true that he has been part of our councils, yes . . . and in sentiments stands firmly with us."

There was more than a little derision in Cardassa's smile as he inclined his head politely and replied, "Indeed."

"You seem more than idly hostile," the Tersept of Tarlagar snapped, stepping forward and crossing his arms across his breast. "Tell us plainly, Cardassa: what is *your* position?"

The Baron of Cardassa looked up at him, still writing, and asked softly, "And how is it, Ilisker Baerund, that you think to claim a barony and so abuse the courtesies and traditions of Aglirta? I am host here, you one of many self-invited guests, and yet you cannot wait to demand things of me until I am finished replying to the weighty inquiry of our Lord of Adeln?"

The tersept's face darkened, and he snarled, "You seemed done—or to have had time enough and more to be done, if you desired so. Bodemmon Sarr is not here, aye: so much all who have eyes know—so what part of your answer remains unspoken?"

"My reluctance to side with anyone in Aglirta, however fair their aims and faces, who consort with the Serpent," the Lord of Cardassa said flatly.

"What?" the tersept and the wizard Mauveiron both snapped.

"What talk's this?" the mage Talasorn asked, on their heels.

The baron behind the table gestured up at his two fellow barons and replied, "See you how silent Adeln stands? He knows, as I do, why our Lord of Ornentar wears a face so blue. The venom of the Serpent rages in him, and he must do the bidding of the Cowled Priests or die when they refuse him the drinks that keep the poison from doing its slow and burning work. So anyone who stands with Ornentar stands with the Serpent—and my dealings with the Fanged Faithful thus far have led me to the conclusion that they love no baron, no wizard . . . and no realm called Aglirta."

"What tale is this?" Caladash sneered, not looking to where Ornentar swayed, silent but with eyes blazing in fury. "You think we'll believe such a clumsy attempt to split our ranks?"

Cardassa shrugged. "If poison seems so far-fetched, why is it that none of you partakes of my wine?"

"Enough of this," Esculph Adeln snapped. "I've no time for clever-tongue fencing this night, Ithclammert. It seems increasingly clear that you stand against us; is this so?"

The Great Lord of Cardassa looked down at his writing as if considering his reply, and then looked back up at them all and said, "I was as astonished as all of you when the Sleeping King—a safely distant legend, the stuff of bards and wide-eyed children—became the Risen King, a real and disconcertingly capable and demanding man, who expects our loyalty when we've had generations to swagger our own ways and nurse our feuds, one with the other, up and down the Vale. Astonished, and . . . irritated."

He set down his pen and added, "I don't expect Snowsar's reign to last, I don't think he understands our Aglirta of today, and I don't hold with some of his decrees and much of what I've heard of his thinking, as said before his court. Yet even if he were a puling idiot, he would be what I doubt not he is: the rightful king."

"Bah! 'Rightful'!" Caladash made a mockery of the word.

The man behind the table looked up at him and shrugged. "Well, then, if men are free to call a king no king if they please, what then is any baron? If we are but brawling bravos in this land, where will it find peace but in the iron grip of the last tyrant left standing?"

He shrugged again, and resumed writing. "Yet we have a king on Flowfoam, and he is at least a change from too many years of baron knifing baron and festering grudges and senseless slaughter . . . and the sort of sneaking-in-the-night conspiracy I seem to be hosting in my own hunting-halls this night. So, all of you, hear me clearly: no, Cardassa turns not against the king."

"And that's your final stand, Baron?" Caladash snapped, raising hands that flickered with little white fires.

Ithclammert Cardassa's smile held no mirth as he said quietly, "Not as final a stand as you obviously intend it to be, Caladash. If you're foolish enough to threaten me, you'll never win power enough to be a threat to Bodemmon Sarr."

"Enough boasting, fool," Caladash sneered. *"Die!"*

Flames crackled from his hands like white lightning an instant before the flaring green bolts that burst from the hands of Mauveiron and Talasorn, and so reached Cardassa first.

Reached, and rebounded, cracking back and forth across the chamber like a coachman's whip, first the white fire and then the green. Wizards staggered, toppled, and were smoking meat upon the floor before their or the other bodyguards could even reach for ready swords.

When steel did sing out from ten scabbards to glitter across the table, the Lord of Cardassa looked up into the array of hungrily hovering swordpoints unconcernedly and said, "A wizard who attacks a man in his own castle and expects no shield is too great a fool to be allowed any chance at the throne of this or any other realm."

"Like you, we've little love or trust for mages . . . but I suppose you have little tests waiting for all of the rest of us, too?" Esculph Adeln snapped.

Cardassa looked up at him with eyes that were as cold as Adeln's were blazing, and said softly, "I had nothing waiting this night but a little wine and a wench-warmed bed—for myself. *I* was not riding through the night planning new kings for Aglirta."

"Bah!" the Tersept of Tarlagar snarled. "Let's see if clever Cardassan barons wear spell-shields against more than several good Aglirtan sword-blades at once! *Hah!*"

Swords drew back and thrust forward again in lightning unison—to strike and ring off something unseen that was as hard and immobile as stone. Cardassa gave them no more than a lifted eyebrow as he turned away from them, behind his magical shield, to strike a gong on the wall behind him in a certain rhythm, with a scepter that had been lying on a small table beneath it.

As it rang forth the signal for his folk to fly from Tathcaladorn, he rose unhurriedly, the scepter still in his hand, and went to a door not far from the gong.

"As my great-grandsire said many years ago," Ithclammert Cardassa told his guests icily, "traitors are not welcome in Tathcaladorn. I take my leave of you now—to ready myself for a journey to Flowfoam, to warn the king of one more misguided treachery riding across Aglirta."

And he closed the door on their ragings.

The slight tremor in his hands was gone. As he strode to the last set of heavy doors, the ones that opened into his private vaults, Ithclammert Cardassa found himself pleased at that.

He knew he was going to die here this night, without even a chance to hold Amanthala or Nreene or one of the Laranta girls again, bid them proper farewell with coins and thanks—and give them his fervent command to get well out of Cardassa and into hiding, to keep his unborn children safe until at least one could grow old enough to claim their heritage and rule in Cardassa again. At least he'd left instructions with Baerethos and Ubunter to watch over and aid his ladies . . . but the two old wizards were not exactly towers of strength or competence. Nor would they work together, even if all

Aglirta and their own hides hung in the balance—to say nothing of a babe fathered by the man they'd served at first out of duty to his father, and then with increasing fear and hatred: the Crow of Cardassa.

Taurym would take his warning to Flowfoam, unbidden, if the good steward survived the bows of Adeln and the swords of Ornentar. He would have to. The Great Lord of Cardassa would never leave Tathcaladorn alive—yet if he bought his own death dearly enough, few of his slayers would survive, either, and another conspiracy would falter and fail before its fingers quite closed on the River Throne. The Risen King might have a time longer to force Aglirta into being a realm once more, and not a clutch of warring baronies and brigand-roamed wilderlands.

The most crucial men standing against him were Adeln and Ornentar. Adeln was the stronger, the true blade and backbone of the conspiracy—but because of the Serpents, Ornentar was the one who absolutely had to fall this night. If he could buy only one death with his own, Eldagh Ornentar, once the Face of Stone, had to be it.

Bodemmon Sarr, wherever he was, was the truly deadly threat to the Throne—as dangerous in his own way as the Priests of the Serpent—but like them, he'd draw back from this conspiracy, dropping it like a broken sword, and try another.

That could not be the concern of Ithclammert Cardassa. He was only Great Lord of one barony; he could only hope to bring down one conspiracy. "Remember me for this, Snowsar," he murmured, as he drew on some gauntlets he'd not used for decades, and watched the gems set into their knuckles wink into life. "And let it be with honor."

He flexed the armored gloves that could make him fly, and then reached down a helm whose enchantments were even stronger. As he settled it on his head and looked around at all the other enchanted weaponry he and his forefathers had gathered here, he hoped that when his foes washed his blood off them, they wouldn't use them a day later in an attack on the king.

"Remember me," he added, surprising himself with his own calmness, "because I could have joined against you and kept my hide if not my pride—and did not. I could have run . . . and did not."

He drew on a belt as wide as both his hands set together, buckled it up tight, and told the mirror that stood against the wall, hidden here and cracked across since his grandsire had been young, "I stood and fought, because there are still some men in Aglirta—some crazed few—who think this land, or the dream of it being a land once more, is worth fighting for."

He took a mace that glowed when he touched it into his left hand, and hefted it as he settled its wrist-chain around his forearm, humming a half-remembered song that his father had sung on the way to war.

Its tune was drowned out by the sudden thunder that fell upon the doors, and Cardassa stepped swiftly aside from them and caught up his sword again—before they burst into the room in a deafening spray of shards and boiling flame and spell-smokes.

"Surrender to us, Cardassa!" Adeln shouted, from somewhere behind a raging wall of flames. "Surrender to us this little arsenal, too—now that you've led us to it! The Spear of the Falcon, rightfully mine, lies here, does it not? And the Horned Helm of Tarlagar?"

"As my father took the Spear from your grandfather," Ithclammert Cardassa called back, "so come and take the Spear from me, Adeln—if you can."

He strode swiftly away from where he'd spoken from—and so the lightnings that crashed out of the flames to snarl and snap across the floor of his vault, touching sacks of gold coins into angry glows, struck paces behind him.

"So we shall," boomed the voice of Tarlagar, as the flames rolled back and revealed the conspirators in ready-armored array in the mouth of the vaults, "for we offer you now some surprises of our own."

Ithclammert Cardassa saw his own House Wizard standing beside the Tersept of Tarlagar, with spell-lightnings leaping from their hands and triumphant smiles on both of their faces, and knew with cold certainty that his own doom was going to come down on him far more swiftly and painfully than he'd hoped. He lost no time in striking a certain gong with his mace—an act that caused the mage who'd betrayed him to throw back his head and laugh aloud.

"Calling others to die with you, Old Crow?" Darlassitur of Sirlptar called. "How selfless!"

He'd hired that blond-bearded, green-eyed rogue from the ranks of the lesser and more desperate charm-casters of Sirlptar, given him his own mansion and servants and much gold . . . and all the while, Darlassitur had been a serpent, waiting patiently by his bosom to strike. Ah, well, he wasn't the first baron to learn that wizards can never be trusted.

With visors lowered, the bodyguards strode forward as the last flames rolled away, advancing into the vault like a warily clanking wall.

Cardassa stood impassively watching them come until they were only a few paces away. Then he moved his boot onto a certain stone, which descended a trifle—and three massive portcullises slammed down from the darkness overhead, their ranks of biting points spaced to impale a man who hurled himself too slowly forwards or back.

Five menacing armored figures it harvested, one lightly enough that he was able to twist free, leaving most of a foot behind, and limp back out of the vault, hissing in pain.

His masters ignored him—and paid the twisting, transfixed figures under the points even less heed. They merely snapped, "Attack!" to the three warriors standing untouched in the vault, who strode forward as their impaled fellows slowly gasped out last agonies and fell limp and silent in their spreading blood.

As the three grim knights drew close, Cardassa clenched the knuckles of his gauntlets and muttered a word he barely remembered.

Knuckle-gems flashed, and shields melted out of the air around him—tall, upright metal ovals attached to no man, that orbited him slowly as he awaited the onslaught.

When the nearest man was three paces away, the Lord of Cardassa called on the other power of the gauntlets, springing into the air to pass over the knight—and striking down sharply at the man's head in midflight. Steel bit before it rang off the helm, and the knight staggered back, shaking his head dazedly as threads of blood laced down bright armor.

As his fellows turned to face Cardassa's landing and then turned again as their lone foe sprang aloft again, incantations were being snarled from beyond the stout bars of the fallen portcullises. The tersept who'd hidden his sorcery from the world until now and the false wizard beside him pointed and glared—and where they bent their will, weapons sprang from the walls of Cardassa's own vault, glowing fitfully and tugging free of hooks and straps, until the air was full of floating death.

The Crow knew his fate, and sank hastily back down to the floor where the three warriors were waiting for him, plunging deliberately into their midst, circling shields and all, to provoke a furious exchange of spark-striking blows and cuts and parries, lumbering men swinging with all their might in the tangle of steel.

The two mages waited with increasing impatience for their warriors to stand clear . . . and when no lull came in the hacking and gasping and skirling of steel on steel, they shrugged, gestured, and sent glittering death rushing in from all sides with no care for whom they felled.

Men screamed or grunted, and threw up gauntleted hands or stiffened, as Cardassan lances and spears and glaives struck home, spitting them like boars felled in the forest. So passed three knights of the conspiracy, sword-swingers deemed expendable by their masters.

The two wizards and the two barons glared into the vault. In the heart of that maelstrom of metal their lone foe still stood, staggering and groaning, pierced a dozen times and more. Yet the Lord of Cardassa managed to keep his feet and to hiss words that made certain blades draw back from him, or even whirl to dart through the portcullises. Some became entangled there, and a few even lanced right through, forcing hasty spell-casting to bring them to quivering halts or rend them into bright shards and dust.

A hidden door split a wall among the weapon-racks, and men in the armor of Cardassa rushed forth, doorguards summoned by the gong—men swiftly transfixed and struck down by a hail of flying, darting weapons, as the two mages laughed maniacally.

Baron Cardassa spat out a word and some blood together as the last of his men fell—impaled on spears that raced their arched and convulsing bodies to the walls, and struck deep there, pinning grisly trophies to the sides of the vault. In response to his command, the doors of the vault grew blades of their own, thrusting forth so abruptly as to cause Adeln to curse and clutch at a sliced elbow, and Ornentar to scream as a blade thrust deep into his side.

The wizards stepped swiftly back from between the cursing barons, darting wary glances to rear and to either side to ensure they yet stood in safety. Finding it so, they bent their glares upon the Baron of Cardassa, and raised their hands in cruel unison.

"Die, faithless worm," the tersept said softly, as if, rather than repudiating the conspirators, Ithclammert Cardassa had promised aid and loyalty and then gone back on his word. The Great Lord of Cardassa floated helplessly up into the air, thrashing and fighting with his gauntlets against the grip of a greater magic, and floated there as swords and spears and long horse-lances darted in at him from all sides . . . and slid wetly home.

Then Darlassitur of Sirlptar almost mockingly cast a spell of healing, and let its blue-white beam reach the twisted face of the Baron Cardassa, holding him alive in his dying agony.

"Speak, Old Crow," he purred, as he and the tersept moved their hands in a deft dance that made weapons glistening with blood withdraw a little and twist, torturing their trapped and gasping foe into fresh sobs of pain. "Tell us what else you have hidden here, and how we may use it on a king."

"N-Never," Ithclammert Cardassa snarled, and then wept and thrashed as barbed spears were dragged through him in two directions at once, and great gouts of blood and innards poured forth from his rent body.

"Tell us, and know peace," Ilisker Baerund snapped, "or defy us, and live what will seem a very long time to you, in the agony we shall visit upon you."

He gestured viciously with one hand, and the floating baron screamed.

"What else of magic have you hidden," the tersept demanded, "and where?"

"Aye," the Baron of Adeln snarled, clutching an elbow from which blood dripped, despite a binding cut from a very expensive hanging. "What else have you, Cardassa?"

The baron's reply was a thick, wet gurgling. Blood spewed forth from his mouth to spatter on the floor, and he rolled desperate, helpless eyes at them as the red torrent went on. Almost disgustedly the wizard Darlassitur spent another healing magic, and the red rain ended, leaving their floating foe coughing weakly.

"Yes, tell us, Cardassa," the Baron Ornentar growled, from where he sat hunched over, fingers pressed to his own leaking side. "Tell us all!"

"I—much magic," Cardassa gasped, blood weeping from his eyes. "Where you'll *never* find it . . . unworthy, disloyal dogs . . . traitors to the rr*rurrrkhh!*"

The wizards pulled on unseen spell-strings, and in response blades forged slow, burrowing journeys through the arching, bucking body of the Crow of Cardassa. "I—uhh! I—uhhh!" he panted in pain, struggling to say more, but even before one of the swords burst forth in a fresh gout of blood, like a shark cleaving harbor waters, Ithclammert Cardassa's head flopped, and his body went limp, arms dangling.

In the wet noise of his dying, no one noticed the armored warrior who'd been injured by the portcullis earlier rise suddenly from his wounded sprawl—and put his blade through the neck of the wizard Darlassitur from behind.

The false House Wizard of Cardassa coughed, stared round-eyed at the dead, floating baron he'd betrayed—and then toppled to the floor, lowered on the slick sword of a man who knelt swiftly back to the floor, and feigned collapse once more.

It was the turn of the tersept to snarl and curse, but even the light of Darlassitur's last healing spell playing about the bloody, floating body could not make those staring eyes see again, or the blood dripping from dangling fingertips cease its slow, dark flow.

"Revive him!" Adeln snapped, advancing on Baerund of Tarlagar furiously. "Get me those answers!"

The tersept turned a face dark with anger to Esculph Adeln, and raised one hand in a silent warning of spells waiting to be used on other barons. Even as Adeln recoiled, going white to the lips with rage, the man who wanted to be a baron told him grimly, "It's no use. Neither Darlassitur nor I can bring men back from death, without a Dwaer or a hand-count or more wizards to aid us . . . at least two of whom must be mages who know far more than we do about just which enchantments have to be cast when. Magic shocks the body, you see, and life fades swiftly. He is lost to us."

"Then this has all been for nothing," Adeln said bitterly.

"Not so!" the tersept said firmly. "We've these weapons here—and Cardassa is ours, its castles and coin and warriors ours to spend in our charge to sweep clean the River Throne. Narvim lives, and can ascend to the barony as we planned." He waved his hand at the warrior lying in pain, clutching a foot from which blood still leaked—and then waved it a second time, causing blue-white radiance to speed forth healing to the stricken man. Then he saw the wizard lying sprawled in his blood, and stiffened to glare suspiciously at the warrior he'd just healed.

Inside his concealing helm, the man who was really Craer broke into a sweat, and reached for the bloody blade he'd set down behind himself. If he hoped to shatter a spell, his throw would have to be hard, accurate, and very, very swift. . . .

Adeln nodded sourly. "This is so, and yet we could have had so much more, if Cardassa could have been made to ta—"

"Even more," Ornentar snarled, still savage from the pain of his wounding, "if he'd thrown his lot in with us, Adeln. More still if the Risen King had come to us and begged us to take the throne from him. 'If only' is a phrase that prefaces empty dreams that but waste breath in the telling of them. Cardassa is dead and his vault lies before us—you truly need a guide to help you in plundering and pillaging?"

Adeln sighed and glared again through the bars of the fallen portcullises at the man hanging in the air like a dripping sack. "We could have had so much more," he muttered, clenching his fists as if by sheer will he could wring something out of the air within them.

After a moment he turned away and snapped at the tersept, "Spend another spell to float that carrion out to the gate we rode in at. We'll spit him on a spear there, as a warning to anyone feeling great loyalty to the Cardassas of the fate awaiting traitors to the new baron."

"I've a spell that should melt those bars," the tersept said slowly, nodding, "but I'd best see to my Lord of Ornentar first."

Adeln nodded and turned away—and so it was that no one was looking directly into the vault a moment later, when the slack-jawed corpse of a Cardassan doorguard impaled on the vault wall smiled, lifted a hand that had a round stone in it, and sent bright beams of force across the vault.

Those beams struck two other rounded stones set on high ledges in the vault walls, and as the conspirators turned with shouts of surprise and alarm, the three Dwaer pulsed as one—and beams of ravening force lashed out through portcullis bars that vanished like smoke before them, to stab through barons and a tersept as if they, too, had been smoke.

The warrior was already on his feet, sword whirling from his hand—but the tersept's fall made it spin harmlessly through empty air, to bite and clang down ranked halberds on a distant wall.

Ornentar spun, sobbing, as life erupted from him—but out of nowhere a green, glistening radiance burst into being, raging up and down him as if he stood cloaked in many hissing, writhing snakes . . . and the baron stood whole and amazed again even as he and the snake-headed magic began to fade together, the fell hand of distant Serpent-priests snatching him elsewhere.

The guard impaled on the wall waved a hand, and bright bolts of force flashed anew through the flickering space where the baron had been—but seared no blood or flesh. Ornentar was gone elsewhere, spared from death one more time.

The last of the conspirators stood alone, blinking at the guard impaled on the vault wall, until that imperious armored hand waved again, and a voice said, "Fare well, Craer. You made a good Narvim, if a bit overcautious. Perhaps I should make your tasks clearer in future." Dwaer-shimmering had claimed the lone armored warrior before the last words had been spoken; the man on the wall doubted Craer had heard the last sentence.

With a sigh, the guard who was no guard floated down from his impalement and beckoned his Stones to him. Weapons drew forth from many bloody resting places to wheel around him in slow, stately array, enchantments winking and glimmering down many of them, and the man at their center smiled again and let his face become once more that of Inderos Stormharp.

"Fools," he murmured, shaking his head . . . and slowly faded away.

A moment later, in silence and without ceremony, the floating weapons winked out in twos and threes, following him into otherwhere, until the vault was completely empty.

It stayed that way for perhaps the space of three breaths before the poundings of many booted feet erupted in the passages—and many hard-eyed men in the armor of Adeln and Ornentar burst into the chamber, drawn swords in their hands, to stare in disbelief at one more empty room in this deserted hold.

So swift was their haste to find their masters and do as they were bid, in this night in which all Cardassa was to be taken, that none of them noticed the papers their passing had whirled into the air, in a dining room where candles were now guttering out, and no cheer was left but casks and bottles of untouched wine.

Parchments flapped and fluttered perilously close to the dying flames, ere they found the floor, and most of them bore the neat, flourish-adorned hand of the Baron Ithclammert Cardassa. One of those was in fresh ink, and consisted of a list of names and a description of some demands of those conspirators—in hopes that it might prove useful as a warning to, or evidence in the hand of, a Risen King.

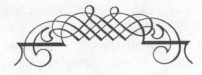

21

Valestorm Building

The Band of Four stood in the dappled shade of the laneway, sunken here and overhung by old and many-branched trees, and looked up the sunlit hillside ahead, past the crumbling wall and the leaning markers and tombs it enclosed, to where a familiar sprawling stone mansion rose out of the trees and clinging vines to stare endlessly down at the river.

The Silent House looked very much as they'd left it, the entry hall collapsed into rubble that held and hid many buried Silvertree warriors. Thankfully they'd not have to dig through that fall; the mansion walls were studded with many other doors—and a few of them even led into the dark and dusty halls, if one knew just how to proceed, without offering their users to the jaws of deadly traps.

A few.

"Well," Raulin observed with an impish smile, "at least it's not another inn."

His companions gave him sour looks, and Embra muttered to the old man who stood at her elbow, "I hope you know a safe way in. My memory seems to hold none . . . this side, that is, of Adeln."

Sarasper smiled thinly. "Lady, I do recall one. The way lies through yonder tomb." He nodded his head at one of the cottage-sized stone crypts that studded the overgrown hillside, and started forward. "We'd best make good time. Raulin's little rumor preceded us to that last tavern, and I'd like to be settled in again before whelmed warbands start dropping swords-first into our laps looking for Dwaer."

Embra nodded. True enough; their own trap was baited but not built.

Folk of the Vale, ever anxious for gossip a little darker and more local than the latest word of barons whelming armies and Serpent-priests holding sinister rituals in the mountains, had with Raulin's sly assistance (after Sarasper and Embra had told him what to say and *not* to say) wagged their tongues eagerly about the four adventurers who knew the king—and, some said, called him from slumber to rule the realm once more—who were even now in the depths of the Silent House, Doom of the Silvertrees, using a fabled Dwaer-Stone to find and summon to them the legendary Swords of the Lost—to make Aglirta invincible against all foes.

The Doom had already twisted the Lady Embra Silvertree into a horrible, slithering monster, that farmer in the last tavern had told his friend across the table—and half the taproom besides—in a hoarse whisper, and she'd eaten one of her three companions already, leaving the other two hiding from her in terror in the deepest dungeons of the House!

A peddler had turned from the bar then to insist that *he'd* heard—from a minstrel who'd dared to sleep in the ruins, and barely escaped with his life from ghosts that had risen straight up out of the ground like glowing pillars of death—that the Four had succeeded in summoning at least two of the Swords, which were now floating in the Silent House, slaying all who dared touch them (two of the Four, thus far). Their summoning had alerted no less a wizard than Bodemmon Sarr, who'd magically transported himself to the ruined mansion and there forced Embra Silvertree out of monster-shape so that he could mate with her, and had done, and that she was even now bearing a babe in her womb who'd hurl spells like none ever seen before in Darsar, and be able to turn into a monster at will, or to be man one night and a woman the next—a child who would seize Aglirta's throne not long after it tore itself free of her womb, or ate its way out, or from within her used its nascent mastery of magic to send the Swords of the Lost forth to slay wizards and barons and Risen Kings alike. . . .

"Gods," Raulin had hissed, around the knuckle he was gnawing on to stifle his mirth, "but it gets steadily better!"

"*That,* lad," Hawkril had growled from beside him, "is how all bards' ballads and tales build . . . into something their own mothers wouldn't recognize."

As they took their first strides towards the overgrown ancestral home of the Silvertrees, a shimmering occurred in the air before them—and Hawkril snarled and flung wide his arms, knocking Raulin flat in the road and sending Sarasper staggering to one side.

The shimmering became a wash of light that spat forth a staggering man stumbling amid the loose, clanging plates of splendid armor that was much too large for him. He took two unsteady strides and toppled, metal bouncing and rolling in the dirt all around.

"Craer!" the armaragor roared, racing forward to pluck the coughing procurer to his feet. "You're alive!"

His old friend looked down at his nakedness and the fresh weals made by the armor that had now fallen entirely away, rotting underpadding and all, and said a little wearily, "I suppose so. I've been killing barons and wizards. Thirsty work. I don't suppose anyone has—?"

"Here, sir," Raulin chirped eagerly, holding out a flask into which he'd poured some wine too fiery to finish at the last inn. Craer squinted hard at the lad.

"And who," he asked in somewhat amused tones, between quaffs, "are you?"

The lad drew himself up and said, "Raulin Tilbar Castlecloaks, sir. Son of the bard Helgrym."

Craer lifted an eyebrow. "Oh? You look a little too old for Em to be your mother—though perhaps I misjudge her. She may have been far more preco—"

"Craer," Embra said crisply, as Raulin's face went bloodred, "that'll do. Give Raulin what little you've left of his wine back—nicely. He's saved my life and Sarasper's while you were off gallivanting, rendered us much gallant aid, held his tongue far more than you know how to do—and I've just been puzzling over how to politely part ways with him, before we step into yonder deathtrap and half the reavers in Aglirta come down on our heads."

Raulin spun around. "*No*, Lady!" he protested. "You can't! Not now! Not when—"

"The adventure's just getting to the good part?" Craer said mockingly. "That'd be the shining moment where some sword or other spills your guts into your lap, and you begin to spend a long, long afternoon with the flies, dying . . . but not quite fast enough that you won't still feel it when darkness comes, and the wolves find you."

Raulin's eyes blazed. "You wouldn't! Why—"

Naked but uncaring, Craer strode grandly to the youth's side, put an arm around his shoulders, and said reassuringly, "No, lad, of *course* I wouldn't." Then he smirked and added brightly, "I'd use a dagger, never a sword."

Raulin tore himself free, glared at the little man, and snarled, "Y-You, you—"

Almost lovingly Craer's fist sank into the boy's gut, leaving him winded and gasping. Then his other fist took the boy under the chin, snapping his head back and laying him out on his shoulders in the dust of the road. Raulin bounced once, staring sightlessly up at the sun, and then lay still, slack-jawed.

"Craer!" Embra snapped. "You didn't have to—"

"Oh, but I did," the procurer replied, looking down at the young man sprawled on the road at his feet, "or he'd've come creeping along behind us, sure as the Silverflow finds the sea, and some armaragor would've cut his throat for him." He looked up at his companions and grinned suddenly.

"Besides," he added, "he's almost my size."

Sarasper and Embra rolled their eyes; Hawkril merely chuckled.

"Welcome back, Longfingers," Embra said with a sigh.

Craer put his hands on his bare hips and said with mock hauteur, "That's *Sir* Longfingers to you."

Embra shook her head and turned away. "But of course. How remiss of me. You must remember not to dare to punish me later."

"Ah, she's learning at last," Craer announced, as he bent to tug at Raulin's clothing.

"Unfortunately," Sarasper said, crouching to help, "I don't think she's the one of us with the most learning to do."

Craer gave the old healer a sharp look, but Sarasper added nothing more except the comment, "Roll the lad your way, hey? This is caught, here. . . ."

They'd carried Raulin a good way back down the road and into a thicket, and Embra was now two figurines lighter as a result of leaving the still-senseless lad a knife, and furnishing Craer with an identical weapon.

Mindful of Raulin's rumors, they had been more cautious on their return to the Silent House. As the Four climbed the overgrown hill in the bright sun, it seemed their care had been well advised. Some folk in the Vale listened as well as talked: six tombs away or so, a helmed head bobbed briefly into view to peer at them, and swiftly descended into concealment once more. Hawkril and Craer exchanged glances, and then made their own burrowings into the brush.

Sarasper sighed. "Couldn't we just get *inside*? Why all this love of blood and battle?"

"They're young yet," the Lady of Jewels told him soothingly. "It's just play to them."

"Embra," the old healer growled, squinting at her, "I'm reluctant to dismiss any fray where men bleed and are maimed and die as 'play'—if you take my meaning."

The sorceress gave him a thin smile. "Regarding it this way makes the heart a lot lighter, but if you *like* worrying and trudging about in gloom . . ."

Sarasper's reply was an exasperated growl, as he ducked through an open doorway into a spiderweb-shrouded burial chamber. Crouching in the gloom behind its central casket, he reached his hand down into a hollow under one end of the stone bier. Flinging forth the fox skeleton he'd left there, he thrust his fingers farther, to find and pull on a cold stone lever.

There was a faint clink of dropping stone. Sarasper nodded, straightened up with a grunt, and snapped, "Where *are* those two bloodthirsty idiots?"

Embra shrugged, smiled, and spread her hands—and from somewhere over her left shoulder came a sudden skirl of steel upon steel, a choked-off cry, and then a thrashing of brambles and branches.

A few breaths later Craer came into view, grinning, with a leather bottle held triumphantly in one hand, and a shouldersack that bristled with dagger-belts and scabbarded swords in the other. "Food—and toys!" he exclaimed brightly.

"Did getting them cost you Hawkril?" the old healer asked darkly. "Or were you too excited to notice?"

"No, no," the procurer said airily, thrusting the bottle into Sarasper's hands. "He's yonder, dealing with another band of greedy fools. Encamped and with a feast-fire, no less."

" 'Another'?" Embra asked, amused, as she watched Sarasper sniff the bottle suspiciously and then trickle a drop or two of its contents onto his fingertips, to feel and sniff and—touch with his tongue. "As opposed to us?"

The old healer evidently found the drink to his liking. He threw back his head and swigged enough to make him sigh loudly when he was done, and blink happily up at her. Embra shook her head.

"You don't seem approving," Craer said almost mockingly to the sorceress, adopting the effete tones and gracefully exaggerated hand flourishes of a foppish courtier.

"I'm not looking forward to bearing that child who's supposed to eat his way out of me," she replied darkly, and then turned, hands on hips, to glare into the underbrush in the general direction of where she believed Hawkril to be. "You don't suppose our mountain of an armaragor will think to delay slaying his playfriends until after they finish cooking a proper mornmeal, do you?"

Her flat and shapely stomach promptly growled loudly, causing Craer to chuckle, look at the sky, and announce, "Ah, the true Doom of the Silvertrees: gluttony!"

"If you're finished being the jester for a breath or two," Sarasper told him, firmly stoppering the bottle and slinging it about his own shoulders with its strap, "do you suppose you can help me shift this casket?"

Craer's eyebrows went up. "Seeking more exotic meals?" he asked. "Tomb-bone soup, perhaps?"

"Just push here," the healer replied sourly. The procurer shrugged and did as he was bid . . . and after a moment of immobility, long-frozen stone grated into motion, turning on an unseen stone peg. The casket turned perhaps half the height of a man, revealing a dark opening beneath it.

Bushes rustled, and the two men turned quickly to flank Embra—but the dark bulk that rose suddenly from behind the dancing leaves, with a smile on its face, was Hawkril Anharu. He was holding a still-warm skillet of enormous size—and in it were alternating strips of riverfin and what looked like rabbit, bubbling in the dying aftermath of sizzling.

"Gods," he said, "have you ever seen such a pan? 'Tis near as big as a shield!"

"Big enough, I'll grant, for some," Sarasper said, jostling Craer meaningfully.

The procurer eyed the skillet's contents. "Well, 'tis a safe wager that this won't stretch to fill more than one particular belly, to name no names—but Hawk *did* find it, and we've eaten already, so . . . the food's yours, Tall Post."

"Mmm—hey!" Embra burst out, reaching involuntarily for the food as her innards rumbled again. Craer and Sarasper chuckled as Hawkril wordlessly held out the pan.

The Lady of Jewels wrinkled her nose, cast the men by the casket an imploring glance that yielded her no aid, and then sighed and reached gingerly into the greasy pan.

Her eyes fluttered shut for a moment as she bit down, moaned in pleasure, and wolfed a strip of riverfin. She was still licking her fingers and wiping at her shiny chin when Hawkril returned with an emptied and grass-scoured pan in his hand, and a brisk, "I suppose you've found a way in—and that it's some sort of dark, too-cramped-for-me tunnel, too, eh?"

"Of course," Sarasper said with a shrug. "The builders had to hide ways out from a succession of Barons Silvertree, didn't they?"

"And just what does *that* mean?" Embra asked in mock anger, as she was helped down into the earthy darkness. A moment later, as light flared up in front of her from some sort of small stone lamp Craer seemed to have been carrying hidden in his clothing, she looked up and back at Hawkril, and asked, "Do we leave it open behind us, or—?"

"There's a handle by Hawk's head," Craer called back softly, "but I want him to get his lamp lit, too, before—"

"Let me past, youngling," Sarasper muttered, "and keep back. Oh—and take care of this bottle for me *without* emptying it, hey?"

"What're—oh," Craer replied, accepting item after item of clothing as the old man disrobed and stalked forward, becoming a longfangs by his third or fourth step.

"The burial ground is alive with hopeful adventurers and treasure-seekers," Hawkril growled as the palm-sized oil lamp he'd bought back at the Flagon flared up. "More than one band of them may have found their ways in already. . . ."

"I begin to think this is no more sensible a way to gain Dwaer than blundering around the countryside was," Embra said with a sigh.

"Going from inn to inn?" the procurer teased. "Your display was deeply appreciated at one such establishment, or so I've just been told!"

"Craer," Embra replied with a snort, "I think I killed rather fewer folk than Hawk did, we saw no trace of the Dwaerindim, and I've no love for anyone bold enough to burst into our rooms with swords drawn in the dark hours!"

"Ah, but someone did just that," the procurer replied smugly. "Behold: our lure at work! Why, I heard men talking in the stables—when we arrived, *before* all the fun—about what they'd do to fix broken Aglirta, if *they* somehow had a Dwaer fall into their hands!"

A furred forelimb tipped with a cruel, rending claw came out of the darkness ahead of Craer then to deal him a sharp slap on the shoulders, and he turned to Hawkril and Embra and hissed, "Silence! Sass wants quiet!"

They fell silent, moving forward with slow, tentative caution for what seemed like a long time, ere Sarasper came back to them, shuffling his feet on the cold stone, and growled, "Hand me a cloak—'tis *cold*!"

"Your being naked might have something to do with that," Craer said helpfully. "Perhaps if we got someone younger to go about bare-skinned . . . Embra, say . . ."

The Lady of Jewels calmly cuffed one of the procurer's ears, and asked, "What news?"

"Six dead in fall-traps, that I've found so far," the healer growled, "and at least four alive and wandering. There were two more, but they fell afoul of a longfangs."

"Dangerous beasts," Hawkril agreed expressionlessly. "Do you want Craer and me to go play?"

Sarasper shook his head, stamping his boots back onto his feet. "They'll

run into each other a few rooms hence—and then we'll just have the survivors to see to. There's—"

He suddenly threw up an urgent hand for silence, and pressed his head
against a panel. Then he beckoned Hawkril forward with a whirling of his
hand, and mimed the thrusting of a warsword through the wall.

When the armaragor joined him with a frown, Sarasper guided Hawk's
lamp to a certain place, pointed at it, collected the armaragor's nod, and
then blew the lamp out. Craer hooded his with his cloak, and the healer
nodded and pulled at something on the wall.

Stone moved, and Hawk struck, twisting his blade as he drew it back
into the passage to shake free the body he'd thrust it into. As the healer slid
the panel back into place, Craer turned around and let the light of his lamp
spill forth—and they saw that Hawkril's blade was red with bright blood for
almost two feet back from its point.

"Dangerous place, the Silent House," Sarasper murmured grimly, as he
beckoned them on down the dank passage.

"Dangerous indeed, yes. That's why you're being paid so much! I'll see to it
that word reaches my masters that the Four are in the Silent House," the
soft-faced merchant said coldly. "Now go in, as you've taken coin to do!
Enough delay! Or shall I mention a coward's tarrying in my report, too?"

The man with the scar down his cheek and a sword in his hand
answered with a wordless snarl that held more fear than anger—and ducked
into a dark opening in a leaning wall of one wing of Silvertree House. The
merchant stood back thoughtfully, listening for a scream from within. He
seemed almost disappointed when it didn't come.

He'd turned away and taken three steps before an arrow hummed out
from behind a nearby tree and snatched him off his feet, to spill him dead in
the grass with a look of amazement on his face and his throat sprouting a
goosefeather shaft.

The man who first knelt over the body to make sure of death murmured, "Adeln's man?"

Another man crouching beside him shrugged. "One of the downriver
barons. Every last one of them has a pet conspiracy—and half of them don't
even know they're doing the work of the Serpents. Our masters at least—
uhulurrkkhh!"

A good strangler needs only a waxed cord and enough purchase to use
it, but the man flailing useless hands and going purple was still struggling
feebly when a needle-slim blade burst through the breast of the masked man

holding the cord and sent both slayer and victim thudding onto the merchant's body.

That same blade descended smoothly into the face of the man who'd asked about Adeln at about the same time as its wielder remarked, "Getting a mite crowded around here!"

"Well," a new voice said softly and menacingly, as yet another strangling-cord found the bladesman's throat, "it's not every day that legends come to life, and Dwaer-Stones roll out of bards' fireside tales into hands eager to use them."

Another messenger moved hastily away from the burial ground, heading to report another conspiracy, as the last group left standing exchanged grim glances and slipped into the opening that led into the Silent House, leaving the bodies sprawled in the grass.

Overhead, vultures were already circling. A bat eyed them thoughtfully for a moment before it took wing from a nearby branch and flitted away—only to intercept a flash of silver in midair, and crash to earth curled lifeless around the hurled dagger that had spitted it.

"Wizards are becoming creatures driven by persistence," murmured the owner of the gloved hand that twisted the dagger free. "Now, that's a disquieting development."

Like a silent, grimly smiling shadow, the man called Velvetfoot skulked to the opening in the wall and vanished into the Silent House. A kingslaying was just one more fee, but Dwaerindim, now . . .

The coins of the Delcampers bought much in Ragalar. Streets, the shops that lined them, ships to bring their contents and to take craftwork to far docks, the loyalty of men to do all this work—and the best healings all the gathered Ragalan priests of the Three could work.

Wherefore Flaeros Delcamper yet clung to life, albeit as a much-bandaged bag of splintered bones sprawled helpless for yet another day, in a heavily guarded bed that had felt his scant weight for many such days now.

The tale of his daring escape from the daggers of the Serpent—a score of hired swords and even his own tutor, an old Ragalan minstrel named Baergin who'd paid for his treachery with his life, hacked down by the Serpent's warriors in the shouting wake of the fray—had become old news in Ragalar, and more. It was part of city lore now, one of the tales that told Ragalar's long and oft-lawless history . . . and it was a tale all the better because it was, with all its improbable leaping from one balcony to another, its warriors racing about with swords drawn to do butchery in the broad light of day, and its sinister blasts of Serpent-magic smashing away balcony and fleeing Delcamper into a bone-shattering fall into a dung-cart, and the spell-battle that followed as outraged mages staying at the Lion traded spells with a cowled Serpent-priest until the Scaled One was torn bloodily apart, true. Every word of it.

Old men seized on that with a kind of fierce joy over their tankards. Here was a story that needed no betterment in the telling, not one embellishment, to stir listeners at every retelling, even to the balding Delcamper uncles who'd sneered at a young kinsman wanting to prance about with a harp hurling down their coins in a dozen shops and grand offices, and racing red-faced through the streets with their swords drawn to hew down veteran warriors for daring to blood one of their own.

Ah, but even the mightiest rallied to defend their cubs—and Astalen the dung-carter, who'd thrown himself over the fallen lad in the waist-deep dung (or, some said, merely stumbled over Flaeros in his rage at the breaking of his cart) and snarled fist-shaking fury up at the Scaled One hurling down fell magics at him from so high above, was a rich man now. The Delcampers paid their debts, and Astalen's days with the dung-buckets were over; he commanded a dozen carts now, and was a firm friend to all Delcampers.

And if Flaeros Delcamper was suddenly a hero in Ragalar, he was measured differently by his own kin, too—for what other family had a mere youngling who yet was important enough to be chased by Serpent-priests, and hounded by a score of expensive sellswords?

One or more of the eldest Delcampers wondered privately about what the lad must have seen, or done, to make him thus marked . . . wherefore the four or five Delcampers too old and aching to spend their days striding about making the clan richer divided a new duty among themselves: that of sitting by the young lad's bedside, as he slowly—for the priests had done what they could, and no wizard could be trusted to essay more—drifted back to health.

It was on the same bright morning that saw the Band of Four go back into the Silent House that a Sirl bard of middling name came to the gates of the Delcampers craving audience with Flaeros, and submitted to suspicious searches there, and then purging spells cast on him by the few bonfire-wizards retained by the Delcampers, and hard questions by Delcamper matrons, to at last win admittance, under guard, to the inner house where Flaeros lay.

"Why have you come?" was the blunt question put to him by the uncle on watch there.

The bard—one Kaulistur Peldratha by name, a handsome man of almost womanly singing voice and a calm, patient manner—swallowed and replied, "O-Out of respect, Lord. Flaeros Delcamper has stood in the court of the Risen King, and spoken with King Snowsar personally. It is only right that—as one of us struck him down—one of us should aid him as bards do, to tell him the news of Aglirta."

The uncle had regarded the young bard in steady silence for an uncomfortably long time, and then simply nodded and beckoned, turning away.

"Respect," Kaulistur had heard him murmur, in tones of satisfaction, as they mounted a grand stair and passed the crossed blades of guard after guard, to reach at last a room where another aged Delcamper uncle sat watchfully at a bedside, wearing a frown that deepened at their arrival, but gave way at last with the quiet command, "Speak freely, as if we were not here, one bard to another."

Hesitantly—for Kaulistur had been one of those who'd sneered at Flaeros, long ago in the Sighing Gargoyle, at his first stammered queries about how one joined the Moot—the visitor greeted the pale man in the bed. He was, however, received with eager welcome, and warmed to his task, speaking candidly and colorfully—as bards do, never noticing how often two old faces not far behind him smiled or raised their brows or frowned—of doings in Aglirta.

Kaulistur spoke of the whelmed might of treachery in barony after barony, and the latest news of the Band of Four and the fabled Dwaerindim, until Flaeros, in wild and mounting excitement, cursed his injuries for keeping him abed at this time.

With a sudden sob of pain and effort, the pale, thin man in the bed struggled out of the bed-blankets, and set one thin and hairy foot upon the floor.

"I must be there!" he half-snarled, half-howled, clutching at the astonished Kaulistur for support. "I must—"

And then those large and dark eyes rolled up in the sweating Delcamper face, and Flaeros Delcamper fell, dragging his visitor over and down with him.

"My Lords!" Kaulistur cried frantically, as old men and guards with drawn swords closed in around him like vultures. "I did nothing to him! I meant no harm! I—"

"Ease yourself, youngling," a Delcamper uncle snapped. "We know that! 'Tis the pain of a fool trying to walk on unhealed bones that struck him down."

As they hustled Kaulistur Peldratha to where a gleaming forest of decanters awaited him, and the same uncle gruffly bid him slake his thirst after all that talk, he looked back over his shoulder past hard-eyed and vigilant guards.

Kaulistur saw the other Delcamper uncle, amid a welter of priests and attentive guards, lifting Flaeros back into bed with infinite care and gentleness.

As that uncle joined them at the decanters, taking a large one by the neck with a contemptuous disregard for proffered goblets, he told the world gruffly, "A true bard, not a wayward pose on the lad's part. The Delcampers have a songster at last."

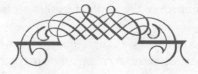

22

When Magic Fades Away

A man walked the corridors of Flowfoam under that same bright sun, and was not happy. He strode unopposed and oft-saluted, for he was the man called in Aglirta "the Risen King."

He loved the Vale, every tree and sward and bend of the Silverflow of it, and yet held no love for what the men who led Aglirta had become. In the time of his long Slumber the land had fallen into a ruin of warring baronies, ruled by barons hard or decadent, but every last one of them deceitful.

Nor was that ruination banished. After restless miles of polished tiles and pillars and echoing vaulting ceilings and servants turning discreetly away, Kelgrael Snowsar leaned at last upon the sill of a high window built by one of the most cruel barons of all, looked out on the endless silver sparkling of the wide river, and sighed.

The realm now was very much as it had been at his Rising, his writ extending only as far as his own eye and hand—but the days ahead held far worse for Aglirta than the days since his Awakening. His fair Vale was going to be torn apart in war while he sat helpless to defend it.

That meant death not so much for barons and those rich enough to take ship away from Sirlptar, but for the farmers and carters and shopkeepers, the honest faces of the Vale be they merry or grumbling, who carried the realm on their backs. They *were* Aglirta, and all Kelgrael did—no matter what grand enchantments had been worked long ago to anoint him and confirm him and enable him to make magic swords and the like do more than they could in the hands of others—was for them, and was as nothing if it did not aid or defend or better them.

Kelgrael sighed, and told the passing breeze that he was heartily sick of barons and those so eager to become barons—or kings—that they'd slay their own mothers and climb over the cooling bodies to better reach the prize they sought.

Around him the court was well nigh deserted, for everyone knew what was coming. Some barons were even openly ordering war-banners in the shops of Sirlptar. Most of the fawning courtiers were fled out of Aglirta, or to defend their own holdings, or to join conspiracies in time to be seen as staunch allies on the day when certain victory came.

Kelgrael smiled grimly. It almost seemed a pity that such a triumph would only come to one cabal . . . and if he somehow lived to see it, 'twould be a matter of interest and dark amusement to see how long it took that victorious cabal to savage itself, until only one traitor to the realm was left standing to make himself its next king.

And behind them all, every mighty wizard or ambitious tersept or arrogant baron, staying silent just now but showing itself more and more, was the darker, slithering shadow of the Serpent.

A Serpent Rising because the king was Risen.

There came the smallest of sounds. Kelgrael Snowsar turned from the window with his lips set in a grim line, and drew his sword even before the figure melted out of the tapestries to attack.

The courtiers who'd remained on Flowfoam seemed to politely take their turns attacking him; the royal blade had spilled the blood of six yestereve. If they ever attacked all at once . . .

It did not bear thinking about. Not while a man in full plate armor, richly chased with flourishes in the manner of Urngallond, but bearing no device—a man anonymous behind his closed visor—was striding confidently forward with blade in one hand and a long knife in the other, on regicide bent.

"This is not," Kelgrael Snowsar announced almost pleasantly, as he hefted his sword and drifted to the right, moving with a smoothness and a grace seen more in dancers than in ruling kings, "why I Rose. All too many seem to want me dead."

Unlike the others, this attacker made no reply. His sword swept forward with dizzying speed, seeking to reach over the royal blade and pierce Snowsar's right side—and the king's parry left his pelvis undefended against the knife, stabbing in low and viciously.

Its point struck unseen armor, and drove aside, amid sparks. Kelgrael gave his attacker an unlovely smile and ducked suddenly down and forward, taking the man's knife-wrist in his hand and twisting as they fell together.

The move put the weight of Kelgrael's falling body behind the driven knife as it plunged up and under his attacker's tassets, between the high hip-plates and the armored skirt above—and bit deep into the groin, shearing leather as if it had been silk. A thin scream escaped from the visor even before the hot flood of blood gushed forth. The king rolled away, found his feet, and without pause drove the point of his sword between gorget and the bottom of his would-be slayer's helm.

More blood, and the armored form went limp. There was a thunder now, approaching down the long corridors of Flowfoam, as the pounding boots of many guards raced nearer. The king paid them no heed, bending instead to tear away the visor of his attacker.

There was no face within the helm, but neither was he gazing at one of the fabled Faceless. Rather, eyeballs stared crazily up out of a skull shrouded in flesh that seemed to have melted like candle wax.

Guards gasped and cursed at the sight, and one man was sick, but King Snowsar said nothing to them. Frowning down at the sight, he turned away and left them with the carrion, taking secret ways across sprawling Flow-foam, to reach at last the hidden chamber where he'd once met with his four loyal Awakeners.

There he drew a small cylinder of gold from where it rode behind the broad and flaring buckle of his belt, twisted off its unicorn-head top, and with the stick of sparkling clay thus revealed drew certain symbols across the seams where doors and ornate panels and shutters could be made to open in the walls. Those symbols glowed, a radiance that faded only slowly as the king paid special attention in his drawings to the panel that could become a window. Lastly he drew signs upon the floor and—standing on a chair—on the ceiling.

When he judged the room secure, Kelgrael Snowsar made a gesture in the air that would have surprised many wizards, and then did off his sword-belt, and the filigreed bracers he wore upon his wrists, and a pendant from around his neck.

Each item, as he released it, floated slowly up to hang in the air at about the level he'd made the gesture, chest-high for a tall man.

There were very few folk in the Aglirta of today who had even an inkling of what Kelgrael Snowsar truly was. A tall warrior hero with a crown on his head was all most courtiers saw, loyal and noble and a bit of a naive dolt . . . of course.

Kelgrael gave the room around him a bitter smile at that thought, and went right on unbuckling and unclasping and plucking forth. He was not disrobing, but rather divesting himself of all of his many small items of magic, from the enspelled daggers in his boots to the ring that could call up an unseen shield against blades and his Garter of Slow Healing, identical to those worn by all folk of the court in the Aglirta of long ago.

He'd unclasped it from high around his right thigh, feeling the air cold upon his bare shanks, and was reaching for his breeches to draw them on again when he remembered the last item, worn for so long that he often forgot it now. It was a leather luck-thong, worn around his hips like a belt, its ends beaded to prevent fraying and its length studded with many intricate knots. He drew it off carefully, remembering long-dead hands that had made those knots, and murmured advice given long, long ago.

He did not want to do this thing. He did not want to have Aglirta taken from him again, swept away into the long and drifting darkness that might never relinquish him once more. Would it not be better to go down fighting, to at least strive for the land he loved? Fight, rather than run and hide? Even if he failed and died, does not Darsar end for each man at his death? Why should he care, after he was gone, if flames rose and walls fell and blood flowed and the beasts came down to gnaw on the fallen?

No. He would know. He'd know what he'd done to Aglirta, purely for his own pride. The gods would see to that. Moreover, there'd be no Slumber, no chance—however slim—to awake again to a greener land. He must do this.

He would do this.

When he was dressed again and lighter—even to the glow-gems gone from the hollow heels of his boots—Kelgrael began undoing the knots in the thong. Each unbinding brought its own small and whirling cloud of lights, motes of magic that faded away to leave behind the long-stored enchanted item they had brought from otherwhere: coffers and decanters, figurines and bracelets, scepters and goblets, bowls and lamps, all of them small and beautiful of making. These, too, joined the floating array now almost filling one end of the chamber.

Last of all the Risen King drew a tiny dagger from one bootheel—the only blade he possessed that did not bear magic—and made a small cut in one of his palms. As the blood welled out, he took the thong so that its beads were pressed together, closed his palms upon them so as to touch them with his blood, and murmured three words.

It unfolded silently, and did not take long.

As the thong melted away, a book melted into visibility above Kelgrael's opened hands: a small tome, bound in plates of polished dragontooth clasped with truesilver, its pages sheets of thin metal of a bluish sheen, chased and stamped with characters that set forth six puissant spells. Just now, he needed only one of them.

The Last Snowsar drew in a deep breath, opened his hands wide in a flourish that made his spellbook turn its pages to a certain spread, and there halt—and spoke the well-remembered words that began the ritual that would send him back into Slumber.

"*Lorth aladroes,*" he told the ceiling. "*Ammanath kuleera.*" The tongue had been old before Aglirta had ever been thought of, the spells crafted in a land long fallen, Davalaun of the wizards, but the words shaped magic into other magic, and would bend the world to his will. He would send himself back into the long sleep, but take the Serpent away too, binding them both once more in otherwhere, to leave Aglirta free of kings and Serpents both. Thank the Three that the Fanged One woke but slowly from its torpor, or he might never be able to manage this.

It would be hard even now. The Deeping Ritual or Calling to Slumber drank magic—other magic, and lots of it. If used on someone unwilling, it needed castlefuls of enchantments to succeed. When he'd first cast it on himself, more than a dozen mages of power had cast spells for it to drink in . . . but he knew not a single mage he could trust now, save perhaps one, and he'd sent her off to roam the realm and be his shield and a distraction to his gathering foes while she and her companions found their own dooms . . . or succeeded in an almost impossible task. The Dwaerindim were the only other way he knew of, given the paltry magic men commanded in Darsar today, of driving down the Serpent.

And the Lady Embra *was* a Silvertree. Perhaps, if she'd been standing here in this spell-locked chamber with him and so much magic, she might try to slay him and seize the throne herself. Would he yield it willingly, Kelgrael wondered, if she asked for it rather than trying to take? It would mean his life, that giving, but . . . would he?

Never to see the Silverflow again, never to hear the winds rustling through the trees of the Vale . . .

Then Kelgrael reached the place where he had to read aloud from the spellbook, and put such thoughts out of his mind. "*Ammador,*" he said crisply—and a decanter floating a few feet from his nose sighed softly away into smoke, and was no more.

"*Thalpurtim,*" he added, and watched a coronet collapse into dust and winking nothingness.

"*Haladreeos,*" he read next, and a bowl died. Not for the first time, the king wondered if he had enough magic gathered here to complete the ritual. Soon now, the Serpent would feel and know what he was doing, and be able to manifest here, in the place of his Calling. . . .

The first scaly shadows came six words later, as one of his favorite daggers melted away, its scabbard falling into glittering sparks, but Kelgrael kept his voice and pace steady, not able to break off the ritual without ruining it—and he'd have to do just that to work spells enough to drive the Serpent from this place, or even move the floating items so as to deny it space within these walls in which to manifest.

"Marindra," he said next, knowing he was saying the name of a sorceress who'd given her life, untold ages ago, to the forging of this ritual, as mages he would never know had struggled to make a magic that would snatch their bodies otherwhere, to take them and an entity of their choosing, bound to them, from dangerous times and places into a sleep that would only end when someone else freed them. Kelgrael's sword blazed with sudden fire, and the flames became drifting smoke, and the ashes of the scabbard fell away from emptiness, into emptiness . . .

The room was growing darker, the corners farthest from him—farthest from the sealed-off window—filling up with Serpent. It was a vast beast, far too large for even its head to materialize in this chamber . . . but all it needed to place here, to deal death to him and shatter the magic, was the venomed tip of its forked tongue—a pale pink ribbon of soft but sword-edged flesh that would be, he remembered, as wide as he stood tall, and swifter in its curling and darting than he'd ever been in his most frenzied sprinting.

He could only go on. *"Hamdaereth,"* he said calmly, a moment before the first muffled crash came from somewhere behind the wall on his left.

"Tessyre," he read flatly, the name of a sorceress of flame-red hair and a temper to match, if bards long dust could be believed—and who might yet live, in a Slumber of her own, if one believed those ballads strongly enough—as another crash heralded a succession of heavy blows, as if someone was using an axe on something that was about to . . . give way, with another crash of rending wood.

Almost immediately there came another, much louder splintering crash, and one of the panels in the darkest corner thrust some splinters into the room.

"Halan darammareth sooloun trae crommadar," the king read on, not bothering to glance up at the bright point of the axe as it widened that hole. Besides, there were other thumps and crashes from several points about the walls now, shaking the room, and he still had more than a page to go.

That first panel flew into the room in shards, propelled by the mailed fist of a man in half-armor whose open helm showed the world another face drooping like wax. The Melted tore vainly at the wood around the panel with his fists, and then drew back and brought down his axe on the paneling that remained in his way.

Elsewhere, another panel split with a crack as deafening as thunder, and a third fell forward into the room, revealing another of the Melted behind it.

Panels all around the room were groaning under attacks from behind them as Kelgrael grimly read on, glancing up not at the armored torsos now leaning into the chamber, or at swimming ruins of faces, but looking instead at his steadily dwindling collection of floating enchanted items. A small coffer winked out of being, and then a handharp. There weren't going to be enough. . . .

A door burst open, and then two panels fell together, and men with melted faces were in the room, drawn swords in their hands. There were only five floating magics left—no, four now—and the Risen King spoke more swiftly for the first time, keeping his voice flat and his eyes on the page to avoid errors, hoping the hopeless, trying to get to the end of—

Another door burst open, so close beside Kelgrael that the wind of its moving cooled his ear. Before he could taste despair, someone was racing past him, ducking under floating enchantments with slim blades in both hands, and there was another someone behind the first. Those blades bit into the breast and belly of a Melted, who reeled, dropping or feebly hurling his sword, and fell. Kelgrael read on.

The new arrivals were flooding into the room now, in a steady, silent stream as the foremost crossed swords with the Melted, and scaly shadows raged around them recoiling from where one man unhooded a hand-lamp and dragged a sash through its flame. That man had no face, and no melted flesh, either, but only blankness that glanced alertly at Snowsar without eyes.

As the sash flared up, the shadowy outlines of the Serpent's tongue grew darker and less distinct, shrinking back from it—and then from another corner a ball of fire burst across the room, spattering everything, and a Faceless was staggering back in maimed and broken agony from where the Melted he'd been fighting had exploded, and Kelgrael Snowsar set his jaw grimly and read the word that made the last magic item wink away . . .

Someone Faceless turned to him, in the confused brawl of shadowy scales and hacking, stabbing men that the chamber had suddenly become, and thrust a glowing handful of items into the air—two heavy candlesticks, and what looked like a bull-goad, and a small box whose lid was one huge rose-hued gem, and some sort of dangle-adorned length of fine chain that had probably been someone's anklet. Snowsar read on without stopping to gasp his relief, and kept reading as another Melted exploded wetly across the room—and then another.

Everything was covered with wet, sticky blood. The Melted and the Koglaur were surging around him now, slipping and stabbing and hacking in a brutal frenzy, and from belts and the breasts of robes and boots of the

Faceless, magic was plucked forth, to whirl up into the air—and promptly be reduced to spreading sparks.

The blue thunder he'd felt once before was rising beneath Kelgrael Snowsar's boots even before he read the last word and saw the last enchanted item extinguished in a whirl of tiny sparks, banishing all despair. Kelgrael laughed aloud.

The forked tongue of the Serpent was still a thing of crumbling smoke in a dark and yawning gullet that was but shadow filling the end of the room where men reeled and fenced and thrust and fell, as the blue light rose around the king, growing deeper and darker until it seemed like the night sky studded with stars.

He was floating himself now, sinking into the silence that held no Serpents or melt-faced men or helpful Koglaur, but only the long sleep.

Farewell again, Aglirta, until next—the Three willing—I see thee.

And quietly, without further fuss, King Kelgrael Snowsar went Fading Away.

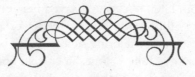

23

Lies, Death, and Other Certainties

The lady sighed as they strapped her into the armor.

"Worried about the Silvertree Curse, Em?" Craer asked gently, buckling and shifting and holding, her ribs like silken rungs under his thumbs.

Very blue eyes met his coolly. "A little," Embra replied, "but more that we're wasting our time here, putting ourselves in danger facing the blades of outlaw after hiresword after guard eager to win his fortune, while anyone who really has a Dwaer stands safely outside, sending the rats in at us!"

Sarasper shrugged—as much as a longfangs can shrug—and Hawkril growled, "It's the risk we have to take . . . at least until one of us can come up with a better plan."

The sorceress winced as a buckle not made for her dug into one shapely hip, and the armaragor's fingers froze on the gorget he was settling into place. "All right, Em?"

"I will be," the sorceress replied, "if Craer would learn to keep his hands on the buckles!"

Hawk gave his friend a pointed look. The procurer grinned, spread his hands in a gesture of innocence, and asked the room, "Is it my fault that none of this fits? Silvertrees didn't expect their daughters to put on armor— and they all had big, meaty sons, it seems."

"Don't just happen to look at me when you say that," Hawkril growled. "I've no choice about my size, either. At least these new plates fit me well enough."

The Band of Four had fought at least six intruders in the dark and dusty rooms of the Silent House, and slain five. The sixth had fled too far and fast to easily hunt down—and they'd heard others creeping about in distant chambers. A thrown knife had laid open Embra's right forearm from wrist to elbow. A room later, after she'd saved her throat from a desperate swordslash by offering that blade bosom to carve, instead, Hawkril had grimly bustled her down a bewildering succession of back passages—in one, clambering over a massive fallen stone block that sported a dark pool of blood spreading from beneath it, and a smell—to an armory of sorts that Sarasper knew of, to encase her in armor before worse befell her.

"We aren't fighting sleepy, drunken chuckleskulls in inns now," the armaragor had growled, positioning Embra by her hips as if she'd been some nursery doll. "Anyone coming at us here will be good, or desperate . . . or both."

"You make it sound quite inviting," Craer had said, calmly stealing Silvertree dagger after Silvertree dagger and sliding their crumbling leather sheaths here, there, and everywhere about his person.

When Embra had snapped at him to leave her a *little* of her ancestral property, he'd smiled sweetly from his high perch atop a wardrobe, and begun removing small items from hiding places here and there on his body, dropping them with casual plinks into the open top of the breastplate Hawkril had already laced up around her. They were more magical statuettes and trays and salt-knights for the table and decanter-stoppers that glowed and the like—and they all dropped bruisingly onto her breasts before rattling down to various uncomfortable lodgings between her and the unfamiliar armor.

Embra's angry sputters had almost, but not quite, drowned out the snorts and oh-so-innocent hums of mirth from Hawk and Sarasper—the product, it seemed, of seeing her face during Craer's lazy barrage. The armor was heavy and hot, despite her snarled insistence on not wearing half the padding that Hawk claimed was essential. He'd warned her darkly of metal edges cutting into her as she twisted or the armor took blows—but most of the leather underarmor had crumbled into ruin despite its enchantments, and what was left was little more than scraps, so Embra was now encased in a too-large, echoing casing of armor that might, or might not, keep her from being slain before her fellows even knew they were under attack. Dwaer-hunters seemed to love throwing knives.

Hawkril had gained some new and better armor, too, and seemed as happy as a young boy with new toys. Embra sighed; that was probably *just* what he was.

"What if I have to cast spells in a hurry?" she asked. "This is all going to get in the way, and—"

Craer gave her a look. "Sarasper warned me about that," he said, waving at the furry and menacing bulk of the longfangs. "Don't. Just don't. Fire and lightning will backlash around the armor and hurt you as well as whoever you're hurling it at. The rest . . . only if you *really* have to."

Embra sighed again. "This is not . . . as wise as it seemed. Some King's Heroes we are."

"He did not," Hawkril growled, turning to look at them suddenly, "seem to me to have many loyal Aglirtans from which to choose. But we said yes . . . and we're standing in much better boots now, Craer and I, than when we were wavering on the banks of the Silverflow, eyeing the cold current, and wondering how we were going to manage to steal one of your gowns."

Embra smiled at him. "You won me my freedom that night, and kept me alive after, through all that my father's Dark Three could hurl at us." She drew on the open-faced helm he'd insisted she wear and took a few experimental steps, looking to left and right . . . before turning, hands on hips, to stare back at them.

"When this is all done," she said softly, "the two of you can have every last one of those gowns."

"And you'll go naked?" Craer asked hopefully, knowing he was safely out of reach of an armored slap.

"Gentlesirs," the Lady of Jewels asked the armaragor and the longfangs sweetly, "is the survival of a certain small and overly sly sneak thief from among our number absolutely imperative? Or, if so, is it permitted that he suffer some, ah, light battle damage?"

"Yes to the latter!" an unfamiliar voice snarled from the darkness at the end of the passage—as a crossbow clacked.

A moment later, its quarrel cracked off a wall and shivered into fragments on its way to the floor. Craer was already there, rolling forward from table to table with the merry words, "Well, I don't know what sort of a fashion figure I'd quite present, sporting light battle damage and wearing an endless succession of gowns made for a shapely lady near twice my height. Black silks, now . . ."

" 'Ware, Longfingers!" Hawkril snapped, as he clapped a helm over his head and lumbered forward, warsword grating out. "There're more of them!"

"Not any . . . more," Embra said slowly, wincing, as the longfangs clinging to the ceiling wrenched a last head from its shoulders, a crossbow firing wildly back down the passage outside the armory, and their attackers were reduced to a bloody heap of sprawled arms and legs and staring heads.

Hawkril came to a stop and waved his blade at the longfangs. "Swiftly done," he grunted, before he knelt by the bodies and peered at faces and gear. "Adelnans," he added a moment later, opening the front of a tunic. "A warband. Chosen by a baron's own hand, I'd say."

Craer's last roll brought him to a halt on his knees beside the armaragor. He nodded. "And I'd say you'd be right." He peered into the darkness down the passage out of habit, and seeing no further foe, added, "Dwaer seem to be very popular in the Vale just now."

"Gods," Embra said, joining them, "how do armaragors *wear* all of this? I'm drenched!"

Hawk and Craer looked up at her, and the procurer murmured, "And so the brave heroes advanced to glory, slaying all who came up against them in their clever trap in the House that had been the palace of the Silvertrees in ages past, and yea, all the most dastardly of Aglirta went up against them in battle, and much blood was spilled—and all this time the Lady Embra, let it be cried from the battlements, was *hot*! Nay, *sweaty*!"

Embra put her gauntleted hands around the procurer's neck and asked, "Did I say 'light' battle damage? I fear I was mistaken. . . ."

A red-furred leg slapped her shoulder hard enough to send her staggering back to a crashing sit-down on the stone floor. Hawk brought his blade up in front of his face as he rolled one way, and Craer dove face-first into the corpses—so the shimmering spray of bone shards clawed only the longfangs, as it scuttled forward along the ceiling with claws extended and head ducked low.

Roaring in pain, it launched itself at the source of the ravening bone magic.

The Serpent-priest standing in the darkness below made the fatal mistake of thinking something so large and heavy couldn't possibly spring far enough to reach him. He was still hissing his next spell when a furry forelimb tore his jaw off and dashed his body to the floor—where the rest of the longfangs crashed down on top of him, crushing him like a ripe fruit.

The priest had not ventured into the Silent House alone. An underpriestess, or his lover, or both, was stumbling back in her robes, white-faced and retching in fear, and a handcount of hard-faced hired warriors were backing away uncertainly, guessing they'd get paid no more and wondering whether it would be best to run . . . or back out fighting, against a longfangs that could run up the walls at any time to get above them—and do what it had just done to their employer.

"We're not butchers," Embra said bitterly, as Hawkril sprinted forward and the longfangs uncurled from its kill like lightning and swarmed up the nearest wall. "Do they all have to die?"

Craer looked back at her and said gently, "Yes. That's what setting a trap means. Will it help if you think of it as cleansing Aglirta of as many trouble-bringers as we can reach—when we can only reach those who choose to come in here and try to slay us?"

Embra looked at him, her face as white as that of the underpriestess, and said slowly, "Y-Yes. Yes, it does."

Craer stared into her eyes for what seemed like a long time, as warriors screamed and died down the passage, and said slowly, "Welcome, Lady Baron, to the work of a King's Hero. Or, for that matter, of being the king. It's not much different than gardening, really. You nurture where you can, and prune what you have to."

He rose from among the corpses, cast a quick glance down the passage at the battle and saw that it was already ended, and then looked back at the sorceress. "It's not a lot different from what your father did, either—but we're doing it for very different reasons . . . and unlike him, thank the Three, you're not enjoying it."

Embra Silvertree looked back at the procurer and whispered, "All this because you came to steal one of my gowns so you could eat?"

Craer shrugged. "I was a warrior of Blackgult before that night, Lady. Just like a Vale farmer or a tapmaster or a young lady trapped into becoming a 'Living Castle,' I was doing what I had to do."

Embra nodded as they went forward together to join Hawkril and the longfangs. "And when you faltered, or sickened or tired of it?" she asked, waving back at where she'd been sitting on her bruised behind in the armory. "What kept you going then?"

Craer waved at the hulking armored shoulders ahead of them and said, "I had Hawkril. He had me."

She stared at him thoughtfully, and made no reply.

"New dark-work," Hawkril growled to them as they joined him, and moved a bloodied sleeve with his sword. The underpriestess looked very young and very surprised as she lay on her back in the passage, sprawled and dead—and one of her slender arms ended in a scaly, serpentine body, with a fanged serpent-head where her hand should have been. It had been hacked and almost severed at its neck, and its own blood, spilling forth, was purple where hers was red.

"I had to kill it twice," Hawkril grunted, his face dark with anger. "I struck it through—so—and it dangled and couldn't bite me, but sargh if it didn't start to heal, right there in front of me. I chopped it again, and again the wound sank away and the blood stopped. I tried severing it from her, here, but no, still it healed. It wouldn't die until I struck her down. The snake was *feeding* off her!"

Embra drew in a deep, shuddering breath, and suddenly turned her face away. Craer and Hawkril watched armored shoulders shudder for a bit before the procurer jerked his head at the armaragor to go and comfort their sorceress, and then turned to look up at the longfangs and asked, "Are you all right, Sass? I saw that bone-spell tear into you."

The longfangs shrugged eloquently. Then it moved along the ceiling a little way and pointed with a forelimb. Craer nodded.

"This way, Heroes," he said, stepping through a doorway. "Sass says we've more bold guests coming."

The man called Velvetfoot smiled a cold gray smile as he passed the ninth body. This one was dangling by its shoulders from a falling-block trap, in a window that had allowed the warrior to peer from his high passage into a room below—until the block had fallen and crushed his head.

Weeding out the dangerous. Hmm . . . if only barons would come personally into such traps, and offer themselves up to the perils.

The ithraba sap was wearing off Velvetfoot's gloves and soles; soon he'd be in danger of falling from the ceiling—but he was almost in place. The only rooms that the Band of Four could rest in both safely and comfortably were in the south end of the Silent House, and the only safe way to reach them was through the room that held the much-hacked, gem-studded Throne of Silvertree. If he had time to prepare, it would shortly become their collective tomb. If not, he'd fade and wait; there would be other times. . . .

The throne looked very much as it had the last time he'd seen it. There were fewer tapestries around the walls than he remembered, though, and those that were left were little better that dust-cloaked rags. Time gnaws at all, it does. The pillars were the features of most importance to him, anyway; they'd hide his preparations.

The man called Velvetfoot worked swiftly, stringing a cord here and a hook there, using liberal handfuls of ithraba sap from his belt-sack. When he was done, he stood where he'd planned to, in the lee of the largest pillar, and carefully coated the points of his five flingstars with sleepsar. The venom was as swift-drying as it was expensive, and harmless when it got that way, but he knew he'd not have long to wait.

Time to draw only two breaths, as it turned out. The Four came through the expected doorway quickly, moving with more speed than care along a familiar route, Craer in the lead and Hawkril a pace behind. Velvetfoot waited; Embra Silvertree had to fall first.

There. Her face pale in the gloom, scarcely touched by the small lamp glimmering in the armaragor's hand. Velvetfoot measured his distance carefully, wrung out his arm one last time, took up a flingstar with practiced care, and threw.

He dipped and scooped up the next flingstar without waiting for the result. The old man could be ignored, his spells too slow to do harm, but the arm—

Gods, but they were fast! Hawkril was charging already; they must have seen his arm swinging! Velvetfoot pulled on the cord that hung beside him, and threw his second star as hard as he could—not at the sprinting armaragor, but at the small man in leathers darting to one side.

The net came down in a dark and silent cloud, its weights keeping it from drifting, but the warrior's sword was held high, and he was coming fast indeed; he might even be able to burst through . . .

The second flingstar missed the procurer. Velvetfoot caught up two more and backed away from the pillar in case Craer dodged to come up behind it. Embra was reeling, her cheek sliced open by the star. She'd torn it away, but was—falling. So where was the old man?

The net enfolded the armaragor and his sword, but he kept coming, roaring curses and hacking. The sap would keep it around him, in a clinging shroud, so as long as a certain Velvetfoot kept clear—

Craer came leaping at him out of the darkness, but Velvetfoot had time for two clear throws. The first was struck aside with a deft dagger—but that left the procurer open for the second, and he was staggering face-first to the floor by the time he reached where Velvetfoot had been.

By then Velvetfoot was dodging forward, past the raging armaragor, to scoop up the last flingstar. 'Twould be hard to stab the heavily armored warrior with it, so—

Something slapped him hard across his face, something large and strong and possessed of fur that wrapped around his head, smelling faintly spicy. The most expensive "deadly shadow" for hire in all Sirlptar had just time to wonder what it might be before the longfangs almost lazily wrenched his head around . . . and off.

The lithe, headless body in leathers hopped forward like a grotesque frog, limbs spasming, and blundered into the end of the net, falling on it and providing enough of a drag on it that Hawkril's raging strength and sharp blade managed to cut a way free. For the next few frantic breaths the armaragor cursed and sawed and thrashed until at last he was free, and staring wildly around in the gloom that was not quite utter darkness, but not enough for him to see anything useful.

The longfangs found the spilled lamp and struck sparks over it with a flingstar that their foe wouldn't be needing again; when the oil flared, the wolf-spider caught up one end of the net and fed it into the flames to make a brief bonfire.

Hawkril stared around in the light of the leaping flames at Craer and

Embra, both sprawled on their faces, and said in a voice that quavered only a little, "Sarasper? I think I need you more than the beast, just now!"

The longfangs stared at him for what seemed a long time, its eyes expressionless and dark, before it seemed to shrug, and then shudder, and then suddenly dwindle . . . into a grizzled, naked old man whose face was pinched in pain, and who dripped blood from gashes on one forearm, and hobbled on a foot that left smudges of blood where it trod.

"I suppose," Sarasper wheezed, glaring around at the battlefield, "you'd be right about that, sword-swinger. Sargh it all."

He went to Embra, turned her over as gently as his grunting weakness would allow—Hawkril hastened to assist—and muttered, "If your rock-headed flirtation with encasing the lass in armor is quite over, armaragor, suppose we have this whang-iron off her."

Hawkril's brows drew down into a frown. "Why?" he asked bluntly.

Sarasper gave him a look. "I need to be getting at all the trinkets Craer dropped down inside it, to have any means of healing either of them—or these old bones of mine—or you, for that matter. I see blood here and there, for all your boldness. Now, help me with these buckles!"

Hawkril's answer was a curt nod and a swift and skillful assault on the straps and fastenings of Embra's breastplate. They were half-done when a flash of amber radiance made both men whirl around, still on their knees. That sort of light could only mean magic.

A cloud of spreading, winking balls of spell-glow was fading towards the floor, and at its heart was its source: a pale blue gemstone set on a ring of thrice normal size, on the finger of a staggering, blinking man in rich robes.

Hawkril lifted his warsword back over his should to throw, if need be, as both he and Sarasper stared hard at the newcomer.

He did not look like a man ready to attack anything. He was fat, his flesh quivering with his exertions and glistening with sweat. He had wild black hair, wilder brown eyes, and a fringe of a beard, straggling over jowls as heavy-folded as those of a mastiff. Those eyes roved the room wildly in the dying firelight, until they fixed on the two kneeling men, and in them was a little leaping hope—and much dark despair.

The man wore brown velvets and silks, much stained with food and crammed into tall and magnificent shining black leather boots. A breastplate had been hastily buckled over the robes, and it displayed to the world a black dragon and flanking gauntlets, on a bronzen field. Brostos. This must be—gods, yes it was: Baron Thanglar Brostos!

Gone to fat and fallen into desperation, by the looks of him. "Be you—?" he gasped, waving his arms like a man seeking balance. "Be you men of the Band of Four?"

"Aye," Hawkril said firmly. "Are you Baron Brostos?"

"Yes," the man almost sobbed, "and I need your aid! An army ravages Brostos, raging at my gates even now! I need the Dwaer! Come with me, I beg of you, or Brostos falls!"

"And if we refuse to give you a Stone?" the armaragor growled, rising slowly to his feet like a menacing mountain.

Brostos fixed him with anguished eyes. "No, no—come with me to wield it, and whatever else of all the fabled Silvertree magics you have! My people die! Brostos *will fall!*"

His hands were outstretched, pleading claws as he stepped forward, weeping openly now; Hawkril motioned Sarasper back and lifted his warsword warningly.

Brostos seemed not to see it. "King's Heroes," he howled, "aid, for the love of Aglirta! I've no one else to turn to! I've—aarrrrrrraawggh!"

He struggled as if being plucked away by a gale, clawing at the air as he shouted that despairing cry. Hawkril gaped at the sight as the fat baron started to fade away, the pillars of the room becoming visible through him.

"No! No!" Brostos shouted faintly, as if from far away. Despair darkened his eyes, and he shook his head slightly, as if in disbelief, as he cried, "Their wizards strike! Spellsnatchinooooaaahhh!"

And then the chamber was empty of shouting barons, and in the sudden silence Hawkril and Sarasper found themselves blinking at each other.

"Three above," the armaragor whispered, and grounded the tip of his warsword on the floor. It grated, and Sarasper saw that the large warrior's hands were trembling. Hawkril's next whisper was so quiet that he almost didn't catch it.

" 'King's Heroes,' he called us," the armaragor said to the floor, "and we did nothing for him."

"Hawkril," the healer said gravely, "there's worse. Craer's gone again."

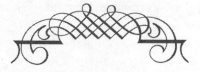

24

A Bold Harvest of Barons

*L*ight burst forth in darkness, spreading in magical motes that were winking and dying even as they hurtled silently outward. The closet made no comment, for it was both a patient closet and an empty one.

Empty, that is, but for the man who'd arrived in the light's pulsing heart. A man whom any minstrel, had there been a selection of such standing in the closet, would have recognized at once as the great bard Inderos Stormharp.

They would not, however, have expected the bard to be clad in dark leather-and-plate armor, with a gleaming array of magical rings upon his gloved hands, or to carry a glowing, obviously enchanted longsword in the manner of one who knows well how to use such things.

But then, the world is full of surprises for bards.

The man in dark leathers cocked his head, listened to faint shouting and the pounding of running feet, and gave the darkness around him a smile. Then he opened the door and went out into the light.

By the sounds of it, the army of Glarond and Maerlin (barons whom the man in leathers knew well, professionally, and had some—small—measure of respect for) was more than at the gates of Brostos: the attacking warriors were inside the castle.

This would make the bold stroke he was about to try even more dangerous . . . but then, he'd never been a stranger to peril, nor afraid of it. Stormharp smiled again as he slipped out of the top-turret apartments that had lain unused since the death of the Dowager-Baroness Maegla Brostos, mother of the present baron, and hastened down a stair to the passage that led to the other turret. As he went, he took a piece of cloth about the size of a man's chest from a belt-pouch, and held it ready in his free hand. It looked to be made of . . . shadow, and that was apt once one knew it was the Shroud of Sleepness.

For years Inderos Stormharp had made a career of gathering magic, by fair means or foul, both for the fascination inherent in such works (representing, as most did, the skill in spellcraft of one mage and the death of another) and against the day when he might need them—or might need someone else *not* to have them. A ruthless baron, for instance. It was well known by a long history of their deeds that barons, with their hatred and fear of wizards and of each other, were the chief collectors of enchanted things in Aglirta.

Inderos was, he hoped, engaged in gathering magic right now. Ahead lay the private apartments of Thanglar Brostos, a coldly efficient merchant trader and taker of taxes who'd no doubt gone to pieces when war had come for him with sharp swords drawn. The baron would probably be there, frantically snatching things out of hiding and strapping them to himself or into this pouch and that carrysack right now. With too few warriors and no one to lead them against the whelmed might of two baronies, Brostos was doomed. Twice Inderos had risked his own hide on forays into Brostos to watch keep after village after town fall almost without a sword being drawn, as folk too wealthy and busy becoming wealthier to defend themselves stared openmouthed at hard-riding lancers and hard-faced mages, leading a sea of bright-helmed warriors.

Those journeys had been more dangerous than they might have been because of the eagerness with which men making war in the Vale these days let loose with loaded and ready crossbows . . . and because Inderos had left the three Dwaer behind.

He'd kept the Stones hidden in the floor drain of a dark monk's cell in the dank depths of Orlordaern, the eldest temple of the Old One in all the Vale, safe from spell-prying within its wards of singing magic. Inderos wore a different face in Orlordaern, where the faithful of Holy Hoaradrim knew him as Seeker Aldus, come back from decades of wandering the wilds of the Vale. Only Inderos knew that Aldus would never return anywhere again, for in his own wanderings he had found the dying priest high in the Wildrocks, and buried Aldus alone after Forefather Oak had claimed him.

He'd moved the Stones only last night, to the only other place in the Vale he knew of that bore so many magics, like overlapping veils, that even the shrewdest prying-spell wouldn't find them. Until he knew who held the last Dwaer, Inderos didn't quite dare to use them when he didn't truly have to—and his other magics were surprisingly many for a man who'd never called himself a wizard, or worked magic openly. As he rounded a corner, two startled guards flanking a closed door snapped to alert watchfulness, and drew their swords.

"Pleasant day," the man in dark leathers greeted them easily, letting his swordpoint dip to the floor. "Thanglar called for me, and here I am." He flourished a shadowy scent-cloth airily, striking a pose.

Guards stared hard at him, their faces anxious and angry with fear. They'd been listening to the shouts, cries, and clang of steel from below for some time now, and were beginning to understand that death—painful death—was likely to claim them well before dark. "Who are you?" one snapped.

"I am the bard Inderos Stormharp," the man who should not have been standing before them told them grandly. "Thanglar requested my presence here . . . and I trust you'll not want to disappoint him any more than I do. The magics in my mind might just allow us all to escape the swords you hear coming for us now."

"I—" one guard said uncertainly; the other gave his fellow a hard look, fitted something that did not look like a key into an opening that did not look like a keyhole, and swung the door wide with a gesture.

Inderos thanked him with a nod, a smile, and the words, "Please stand guard here until we call for you—it shouldn't be long," and passed within. One of the guards started to sketch a Brostar salute, but let his hand fall uncertainly as the man in dark leathers strode by as calmly and arrogantly as any baron.

Those steps took Inderos into a robing room larger than many grand chambers, a tribute in silk and velvet and fur to the good taste, wealth, careful thrift, and steadily increasing girth of the Baron Brostos. No baronial garment, it seemed, had ever been thrown away, but merely hung here as the baron outgrew it or wore it beyond flourishing appearance. Racks upon wardrobes upon wooden baron-shoulder stands crowded on all sides; without pause or comment Inderos threaded his way through them, slowing only when he approached a far door, which stood open. His boots were silent on a succession of deep floor furs, and the room was lit only by a few low lanterns; the baron was not, it appeared, expecting to change his clothes at the moment.

Inderos cast a look behind him to be sure that neither the guards nor anyone else was creeping up behind him and therefore needed to be introduced to enspelled slumber, found no such person, and drifted to a halt behind a set of feasting robes that hung to their full and florid length upon a wooden shoulder stand. Unless someone in the room ahead happened to be peering through the doorway right at him, his arrival should pass unnoticed.

It did. One of the three men in the room wasn't looking at anything, and the other two weren't looking at anything but each other.

A wild-eyed man in brown velvets and silks who could only be Thanglar Brostos gone to fat—and into a total collapse of terror—was on his knees, weeping openly as he stared up into the coldly smiling face of . . . the wizard Huldaerus.

Hmm. Death, it seemed, did not easily claim the Master of Bats. Behind him was a blank-faced, tottering man who was lurching very slowly past the wizard, heading for the baron with hands outstretched to strangle. They were bloodless, dead hands; Huldaerus had made a dead man walk.

"I've lifted my spell of silence, Brostos," the wizard said pleasantly, "but if you scream or shout again, the Baron Silvertree here will throttle you."

Thanglar Brostos uttered something that could only be called a squeak of disbelief as the dead man bore down on him. The wizard's smile widened. "Oh, yes, this is Faerod Silvertree, though the body until recently belonged to someone else—one of your stable-guards, I believe. Its joints will begin to fail soon, but by then we won't need it."

Huldaerus rubbed his hands together gloatingly as the dead man took Baron Brostos by the throat and shook him. Thanglar whimpered, clawing tentatively at the dead fingers as he looked pleadingly at the wizard.

The Master of Bats gave him an even wider smile. "Not too tight to breathe? No? Good, good. That will last, Brostos, just as long as you answer my questions." He paced a few idle steps, and looked around at the opulent bedchamber. Drenched in silks and velvets and gilded hanging lamps, it looked more like a Sirl pleasure-house than the room where a baron slept. Huldaerus shook his head a little, sneering at it.

"It's fortunate I was able to drag you back from your little spell-jaunt without hurting you," he remarked. "The Silent House is *such* a dangerous place . . . and you left it empty-handed, didn't you?"

The wizard turned to regard some things floating in midair behind him. The movement just left Inderos clear passage to peer at the tiny whirling spell-cloud and its contents: a dainty, spiral-gilded scepter, and a huge finger-ring set with a pale blue gemstone that would just be as long as the hidden bard's longest finger. "The reason I'm here, Thanglar, rather than somewhere else getting Faerod a body stronger and more handsome than yours, and one men waving swords won't so quickly recognize as baronial, is all the magic you've collected over the years. I know this isn't all of it—and I also know that you're going to tell me where everything else is. Every last little thing. Or I'll have the good baron here break all of your fingers, one by one."

"Uh-uh-uh—" the Baron Brostos gabbled desperately, through the cold dead hands wrapped firmly around his throat. The Master of Bats grinned down at him.

"Start with just one thing," he suggested, his voice a mockery of kind concern. "Another ring, perhaps."

The wizard lifted his gaze idly from the sweating face before him, letting it rove to a nearby dark doorway—and found himself looking right into the eyes of Inderos Stormharp.

Lightning cracked from his hand bare moments later, setting feasting robes aflame and sending wooden stands tumbling. The body that should have fallen among them, stiff and smoking, however, ducked and dodged and raced forward, spell-glows winking on gloved hands. The charging man bore a sword whose edges shone with their own racing glows, and his face—his smiling face—seemed somehow familiar.

Huldaerus reared back in alarm. "Faerod!" he snarled, as if dead ears could hear, as he frantically goaded the walking corpse into action. Brostos was flung aside as the shambling body wheeled around, almost toppling, and reached—

Far too late, and far too slowly. A gloved fist crashed into a wizardly stomach, and as Huldaerus staggered back and fell with a most undignified sound gurgling from his lips, he thrust lightnings—the only spell he could muster and hurl fast enough—from his fingertips right into the eyes of his attacker, mere inches away.

Lightnings that never reached their target, though a ring exploded in bright waves of rending magic, causing the swordsman in dark leathers to cry out in pain as he lost a finger. The wound could not slow the blade already sweeping down, however—and Huldaerus the Master of Bats had only a brief feeling of intense cold in his throat and a crazily whirling glimpse of the luridly painted ceiling before the darkness claimed him.

As the wizard died again, Inderos found himself hacking repeatedly at a cloud of flapping, forming bats. He sliced viciously, snarling curses as his steel bit small and squalling bodies . . . but inevitably some escaped, storming out of the bedchamber through doors and windows.

"How long," he wondered aloud, shaking his mangled hand, "does it take that mage to make himself a new body again? Hey?"

And then he felt a hand clawing at his shoulder, and whirled around, springing away in case the desperate Baron Brostos had found a dagger somewhere.

He found himself staring into madness.

The corpse held the formerly floating scepter in one of its hands as it toppled stiffly to the floor, still staring blankly at nothing, in the wake of the flailing, sweating Baron of Brostos.

Thanglar Brostos, with his quivering jowls, untidy fringe of beard and tousled hair, and swimming eyes, had seemed less than in command of his wits from the first moment Inderos had laid eyes on him—but now he was barking and jerking his arms in sudden, convulsive movements, his hands closing around unseen things and his lips trying to shape words that never emerged.

Inderos kept his distance, deftly snaring the floating ring on his swordtip and taking it well clear of fat and sweaty fingers that seemed to be reaching for it one moment, and flailing aimlessly the next.

He didn't bother to tell the ruin of Thanglar Brostos to keep back—the man was clearly beyond hearing anything as he struggled inside himself. The man in dark leathers backed quickly away, looking for things that might bear an enchantment.

Shrieking and sobbing and snarling nonsense half-words, the drooling Baron of Brostos followed, step by staggering step.

Inderos Stormharp cursed softly as the clash and clang of swords crossing other swords came through the robing room, from where he'd passed the guards. He hadn't much time left. Hurriedly drawing off one of his rings and slipping it into a belt-pouch, he put on the heavy bluestone monstrosity from the end of his sword and smiled wryly as it slowly showed him, as was the way of many rings, what it could do. The Silent House indeed. That would be useful—very useful, and very soon.

"You're not going to be able to tell me anything, are you?" he asked the staggering husk of the baron aloud. Someone screamed at the other end of the robing room. Sargh and bebolt, it was time to go. A warding-ring gone, and this one of fartravel gained; not much of a magic-gathering success.

And then the Baron of Brostos pulled on a gilded cord and sprang back with a look of lucid triumph in eyes that were suddenly darker than their former brown hue.

The bed was huge, and it came thundering down from the ceiling as it always did, a way for fat and perfumed Thanglar Brostos to impress the young ladies paid to visit his private bedchamber. Inderos Stormharp leaped for his life—and almost got clear.

One massive lionclaw-carved corner struck his shoulder and side, smashing that arm into uselessness. As he bounced—gods, the pain!—and rolled over, his sword clanging away, he saw his foe leaping at him.

"I know," the fat man howled, in a raw voice far deeper than that of Thanglar Brostos, "who you are!"

A hand closed cruelly on Stormharp's throat, and hauled hard. The bard tucked his chin against his chest, knowing what was coming. His head was going to be struck repeatedly against the floor . . .

"You're Blackgult," the fat man spat into the bard's face, not dashing his head against anything, but instead dragging him along the floor around the many-pillared, ornately canopied bed that now filled the center of the room, "and your body will do me much better than this fool's!"

The man who was sometimes Stormharp and sometimes Blackgult hissed something desperate then, and felt whatever ring he was touching with fingers thrust desperately into his belt-pouch sigh into nothingness. The shimmering began.

Faerod Silvertree stopped and smiled down fiercely into the face of his old enemy. "More than that," he snarled, "I know how to use the scepter properly now. You'll *be* Thanglar Brostos, enough to feel everything they do to his body when they get in here! You're going to *die,* Blackgult! I know what that feels like now—the wizard raised me, he said, from spatters of blood on the bats he built himself from! Oh, you're going to feel agony like you've never fel–"

And then his face changed again, as behind him a bewildered, wounded Craer Delnbone appeared out of shimmerings, heard a voice he'd hoped never to hear again, and stabbed with his dagger, as hard as bright, burning pain would let him.

As Faerod's borrowed body grunted in astonished pain and Craer's second thrust turned into a whimpering collapse onto the floor, Ezendor Blackgult twisted desperately in Silvertree's quivering grasp, and smashed the fat body that was dragging him across the face, with all the strength he could manage.

Silvertree dropped him. The man in dark leathers rolled away, moaning in pain. At least he'd get his sword back before he left. The warriors who rushed in here could butcher Silvertree for him. There was no time now to do anything more than just get his own skin to safety–

"*No,* you don't!" Silvertree roared, his voice a horrible, sliding fluting of two speakers wrestling for supremacy, as he flung himself down on Blackgult again.

The man in leathers screamed as his shattered shoulder was ground into the floor. As tears of pain blinded him, he clawed blindly with his maimed sword-hand at the fat body atop his.

Silvertree punched him, bouncing Blackgult's head off the floor. Sobbing, the man in leathers punched back. Knuckles crashed into knuckles in midair, and they both fell onto their sides and raked at each other.

Rolling and punching and clawing each other, the two old foes flailed about on the floor. Silvertree barked and hooted and flopped like a fish from time to time as his wits struggled against the insane remnants of those that had been Thanglar Brostos, still sharing the same skull, and in those moments he stopped fighting. The baron who had hidden in the shape of a bard was too badly wounded, however, to do more than crawl away whenever he could, weeping and gasping, with never time enough to call on the magic of the one ring he wore that could heal him.

In his moments of control, Silvertree was dragging them both around the bed to where the sprawled corpse of a guard held the scepter he needed, and Ezendor Blackgult was writhing in the cruel, tightening grip of more pain than he'd felt in years.

He clenched his teeth as Silvertree threw back his head, howled wildly, and hauled him—hard—into the last corner of the bed. The barking, drooling, flailing husk of his foe was short and fat and should have been little trouble to him, but by the Three, such *agony*!

Silvertree tugged at him again, twisting at the foot he had hold of, and Blackgult found himself flipped onto his face, skidding along on bunched-up furs, and—

And a cloth that looked like a small cloud of shadows. Ezendor Blackgult dug his fingers into it and twisted around desperately, kicking out.

From pain-wracked somewhere, Craer Delnbone saw a booted foot in front of his nose. He snatched at it, and Faerod Silvertree tripped, lost his grip, and went for a brief stagger. Snarling, he strode back and bent to close his hands around a throat again . . . whereupon Blackgult thrust the Shroud of Sleepness into the snarling face of his foe, and gathered the tatters of his will to make it work.

And Faerod Silvertree, or Thanglar Brostos, or whoever he was at the moment, slumped over onto his face and lay still. His body didn't even shudder when a bloody hand reached up from the floor to drive a dagger home hilt-deep. "Die," Craer Delnbone husked fiercely, to ears that could not hear. "Die, Silvertree!"

Then the procurer fell back on the carpet, and bled.

Beside him, the bard who'd been a baron let his tears flow as the pain raged through him. He didn't need to be able to see, to call on the healing ring.

Thank the Three. Ahhh, but it felt good. . . .

The red mists that had been threatening to drag him down into darkness slowly faded, and Ezendor Blackgult was able to roll over, find his knees and then his feet, and scoop up the scepter—gods, but it lay close by!—before loping around the bed, feeling better with each stride, to find his sword.

He bent and touched the healing ring to the limp body of the procurer, smiled down at Craer's slack, empty face, and murmured, "Nary a hesitation or complaint, Delnbone. You've served me better than many a warrior—

and all of my other procurers put together. Now, stop your bleeding and get you back to the Silent House, where your fellows have, I doubt not, great need of you."

Craer's eyelids flickered—and the man in dark leathers gave him a tight smile and wove the spell that would take him away, just as the procurer moaned and lifted his dagger.

Its shimmering had died away again by the time the Baron Blackgult straightened up from the body of Brostos, so recently used by his old foe Silvertree—and warriors with blood on their swords and the blazons of Glarond and Maerlin on their breastplates burst into the bedchamber.

Ezendor Blackgult gave them a brittle smile as they shouted at him. A bejeweled silver coffer that had been lying on the bed-pillows was in the crook of his arm, the humming of one of his rings telling him it held strong magic, he had his sword back, and blue mists were rising around him as the fartravel ring began its work.

Let them rend the body of Thanglar Brostos, no more than just asleep. To be sure that Faerod Silvertree was dead at last, he'd wrung its neck, doused it in lamp oil, and set its rich silks aflame with the nearest lit lamp.

They could stare at him all they wanted. He was fading away.

Blackgult waved at the charging guards cheerfully. He was going . . . going . . . snatched away by the magic to where he'd moved and hidden the Dwaerindim. He was going to the Silent House.

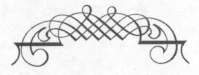

25

A Shortage of Kings

Two men whose rich robes were only outshone by their hauteur strode across a polished marble floor that seemed to stretch forever. As they passed pair after pair of flanking pillars worked into the likenesses of alert sentinels and welcoming women, they never so much as glanced at each other.

Stone-faced guards threw open the first huge, high doors of the Royal High Court at their approach, and the courtiers strutted on, looking neither to left nor to right—and never at each other. Bootheels clicking, they passed along a darker hall hung with many huge, rich tapestries. These were illuminated by drifting spell-motes that made their scenes of hunts in the high wilderlands and deep forests of the long-ago Vale seem alive, but the courtiers spared them not a glance.

The two came at last to the huge, high doors of the Inner Court. More stone-faced guards in gilded armor drew these open with gentle grace, to allow admittance to the throne chamber itself.

The courtiers strode straight down the center of its vast expanse of gleaming tiles, their swords jingling at their hips in the gentle chimings of gilded loops of chain and dangle-ornaments and even tiny bells, and drew nigh the steps that ascended to the River Throne, also called the Flame Throne, seat of the ruler of all Aglirta. The court seemed unusually quiet around them, but they looked neither to left nor to right, for their business was with none other than the king.

They bowed at the foot of those steps, made the bent-knee gesture that passes for kneeling among men who feel themselves too important to truly kneel before anyone but their wives, in private, and waited for the royal greeting, eyes carefully downcast. Neither wanted to be the one to slight royal favor by the tiniest misstep, so that the Risen King acknowledged the other first—for their quarrel was with each other, and they were come from near the mouth of the Vale upriver to see to the settling of it.

Silence stretched, until they could contain their tension no longer—and both peered up under their brows, more or less at once, at the River Throne.

And found it empty.

After a long, dreadful, disbelieving moment, they reluctantly dragged their heads around to regard each other, shared a look of amazement, stared again at the vacant throne—and then whirled around to stare in all directions.

The throne chamber was empty of all life. Not a steward, servant, courtier, or gawking commoner could be seen. Their eyes met again, in utter bewilderment. Where was the king? Where was all his court?

A sudden thought struck one courtier, and he strode to the door that flanked the throne to the left. Unlike its counterpart on the right, it stood slightly ajar.

Not to be left behind, the second courtier hastened after him. They jostled elbows as they tried to push open the door and pass through it together—and came to a halt again, blinking. The grand passage beyond was also empty, of all but its usual pillars, tapestries, and potted trees.

As one the courtiers burst into motion again, striding as swiftly as they could now without actually breaking stride into a trot, their polished boots striking the polished tiles in perfect—and frantic—unison. The passage was long, and opened into a stairwell which gave, on the same level, through several archways to as many rooms beyond. The courtiers reluctantly exchanged glances again, slowing as they neared a point at which they'd have to choose just one destination. Perhaps . . . A magnificently embroidered pantaloon leg swept to one side and its boot pivoted smoothly, veering right—

Through the leftmost archway came a faint, distant crashing, and the echoes of what might be clashing metal. Then there was a fading snatch of what could only be a scream of pain.

Swallowing oaths more or less in unison, the courtiers abandoned all ceremony and dashed through the leftmost archway together, running now along passages and up short flights of steps into chambers they'd not seen before, adorned with cascades of tinted-glass—and unlit—lanterns hanging from lofty ceilings on long chains . . . and then down more steps again, hurrying to the sounds of battle.

Gods, but it sounded like an invading army! Steel rang on much steel, and there were spellbursts, or blasts of another sort, and even—among many screams and cries—the hollow ringing sounds of falling timbers bouncing. Two elegantly moustachioed faces paled, two hands drew swords that their wielders suddenly wished were a lot less ceremonial and a lot heavier, and two men raced ahead once more.

They pelted around corners and into thickening smoke, heading for the steadily rising din of battle. The blasts were more frequent now, axes thudded into splintering wood, and there was even the high singing sound that often accompanies strong magic. Then they could see rushing figures and swords glittering, a rising blue radiance of magic somewhere beyond. The courtiers charged, hacking aside the few who turned to offer them sword-points—and cursed in fear as they found themselves fighting men whose flesh sagged, twisted, and contorted like wax running from candles.

When they broke free, wincing as some of the melt-faced men burst apart in the blasts they'd been hearing, covering everything with wet spatterings, the courtiers saw the Risen King floating in the blue light, a smile upon his face, with armed men surrounding him in a ring.

Gods, they could see right *through* the king!

"Stop it!" one of them cried. "What mage tries to steal away the king? Stop it, I say!" He raised his blade to hack, but found no wizard to strike at, only the backs of the unbroken ring of men around the fading blue light that seemed to be taking Kelgrael Snowsar away. So he tried to push his way between them—and was hurled back with sudden force by the men as they whirled around in unison . . . and both courtiers found themselves staring into the faces of men who had no faces, but only smooth flesh where eyes and noses and ears and mouths should have been.

Beyond the Faceless men, across the dwindling blue radiance and beyond the far side of the Faceless ring, other men still fought, striving to bear forward against other Faceless ones—and these attackers had faces that dripped flesh in grotesque swirls and melting blobs, laying bare bone here and leaving eyes unsupported there.

Both courtiers screamed before they ran.

"One of these days you won't come back," Hawkril grunted, as he wrapped his arms around Craer in an embrace that made the procurer wince. "Just stop these little jaunts, hear?"

Craer looked down at the bloody dagger clenched in his hand and hissed, "Easily said, Tall Post . . . but I don't even know who's doing it! A man who took Embra's Dwaer, yes—and how can I stand against magic like that?"

"First," Hawkril growled, setting Craer gently down again, "we cut the

Stones out of his hands. Then we hand them to Embra, and let her think of something to do to him."

Craer wrinkled his nose. "And what'll he be doing, while she's thinking?"

"Making little cracking noises under my boots," the armaragor rumbled, "as I jump up and down on all of his bones."

The procurer winced before he started to chuckle.

Ingryl Ambelter, who had been Spellmaster in Silvertree and would be again—that, and more—backed his head out of the enchanted mask and turned away with a smile quirking his lips.

"Fools," he told the close darkness around him. Fancy Priests of the Serpent being so arrogant as to choose a ruined temple of Hoaradrim for their plotting. Had they no fear of lurking magics, or the anger of the gods?

That particular temple stood on a hill overgrown with trees, hard by Flowfoam on the Silvertree shore. Handy to the Risen King's court, it afforded conspirators cover and a vantage-view down on anyone else approaching . . . and like all older temples, was liberally adorned with carved stone faces of Forefather Oak. Were the Serpents so stupid as not to know of the Mask of Eyes spell, familiar to nearly every wizard of more than the most fumbling accomplishments? If they thought mages might fear to cast such a spell on a holy carving . . . well, they were wrong.

All he'd had to do, as a Spellmaster hiding behind a Changeface spell as he idly sipped wine and enjoyed the pleasant fall of evening, was watch out his window as the Serpents stole up the hill so furtively as to draw every eye from here to the horizon, go to his mask and say the right word, fit his face into its cold contours—and he'd seen and heard all at the moot as if he'd been part of it.

Two of the plotters had been local Snake-lovers, excited at the thought of many important superiors attending and scared at the thought of offending by any misstep they might make; two had been more senior, visiting clergy eager that the Faithful of the Serpent were possibly preparing for a bold strike at the Throne itself; and the highest-ranking priest, a hissing monstrosity carefully shrouded in a too-large hooded cloak, had been agitated by some greater news that he kept to himself, but that drove him to make this a ritual attended by many. Whatever that news was, it did not seem entirely good for Serpents.

The ritual would begin at the ruins as the moon rose over Harrowhelm Hill—not long hence, but time enough. While senior Serpent priests were making their slow and slithering ways from wherever they customarily laired—for the longest-serving and most devout Faithful of the Serpent, over ritual after ritual of submitting to spells and drinking venom, slowly grew tails and lost their legs, becoming in the end manserpents with venom of their own—Ingryl Ambelter would be compelling the king and a small clutch of courtiers into a journey of sudden whim, straight to a certain ruined temple, where . . .

The Spellmaster chuckled and poured himself another flagon of Sirl Starfall. It sparkled on the tongue and slid down with its usual cool tang that spread slowly into deep warmth . . . ahhh, delicious. When *he* ruled from Flowfoam, he'd—

Ah, but let's not make that mistake. Faerod Silvertree was the one who counted the coins before the coffer was his, not his oh-so-faithful Spellmaster.

Faithful. Indeed. Sniggering at that thought, Ingryl turned to the table overhung by a glowstone, where he worked his most exacting enchantments.

First, the Stealing Touch spell, to delicately find and create a link with one of the three magics always awake and surrounding the Risen King. The Touch was subtle by nature, but the compelling, later, would have to be a matter of oh-so-carefully feeding images and feelings into Snowsar's mind—or its manacles would become obvious to the king, and Ingryl a known foe.

That, in turn, might just become necessary, but open brutality was not Ingryl's way. Any baron had sword-swingers aplenty for that.

Now, to work . . . Ingryl crafted the spell with swift skill and sent it forth, questing after the now-familiar fields of magic that meant Kelgrael Snowsar since his Rising. Questing, and . . . Gods, but 'twas taking long. Was the king far afield?

He must be, for time passed and the three candles that were part of the spell burned lower and lower . . . and still the Touch found the king not.

Ingryl frowned and spun a swift amendment, to seek traces of the one royal magic that died but slowly, in case Snowsar had dropped his enchantments for some reason—or died, dragging the linked enchantments into their own slow, shared demise. The amendment settled upon his original Touch in a bright net, locked to it with tendrils of delicate force, merged . . . and still found nothing.

Ingryl frowned. A shielding? A spellscrying ward, raised after the king's enchantments had been ended. But—why? And . . . how? The age-old binding between Snowsar and the Serpent would prevent a normal Hide-From-All enchantment from working, and anything stronger and more specialized would stand out like a blazing beacon—as the temples did, and the Silent House—to his questing Touch.

He could find no trace of the Risen King in Aglirta . . . or in all of Darsar. Kelgrael Snowsar was simply . . . gone!

Mind awhirl, Ingryl Ambelter spun another amendment to his Touch, making it seek the known firewarding magics on the Flame Throne. In a moment he was "there," seeing the empty high seat as if hovering over it. Murmuring another incantation while he held that image of the throne steady in his mind with an iron discipline very few in Aglirta could match, he willed himself along the link.

There was a moment of whirling blue fire amid slowly rotating darkness— and the polished marble tiles of the throne chamber were under his boots. A guard shouted, and Ingryl Ambelter turned slowly from where he stood beside the throne like a disinterested shadow. "Yes?"

"I–ah, pardon, Lord, I thought you were . . . Who *are* you?"

"One who is *very* concerned as to the king's whereabouts," Ingryl answered crisply, stepping down from the dais. "Do you know where he is?"

"Ah, no. There're some as has been saying he, uh, 'faded away,' in some sort of a battle back in the private chambers of the palace."

Ingryl's puzzled frown wasn't as much of an act as he'd meant it to be. " 'Some as has been saying'? Who–and how do *they* know?"

"Saerlor for one, Lord. He says they saw it themselves."

"Who is Saerlor, and who's 'they'?"

"Saerlor and Phlundrivval. The royal factors in Sirlptar, Lord, but they were here, to report to the king–and both saw it. The tale's all over the palace! I saw Phlundrivval depart to the docks after the evening feast, but Saerlor was up in Strongstone Hall, in the west wing, not long ago. He–"

"Take me to him," Ingryl snapped, every inch a ruling lord.

The guard blinked, and said, "Yes, and who'll be guar–"

"An empty throne, man? Take me to him *now*."

The guard blinked again, and then gave Ingryl a hand-salute and set off through the palace, heading west.

"What's that?" Embra hissed, trying to roll up onto one elbow.

"No, you don't," Sarasper muttered, pulling her back down. She gasped in pain and tried to twist out of his grasp. "Not until I'm finished healing you. *Then* you can try to get yourself slain all over again."

The Lady of Jewels quivered under his fingers as another Silvertree gewgaw faded into dust and darkness, banishing the last of her pain.

"My thanks, Sarasper," she murmured, stretching slowly. She'd been clenched against pain forever, it seemed. . . .

This time, when she rolled up, he hauled her back down even more swiftly.

"Old man," she snarled, "what're y—"

The crossbow bolt shivered as it cracked off the stone wall nearby, and some of its splinters tumbled onto Embra's legs.

"Keeping you alive long enough to admire my handiwork," Sarasper muttered. "We're not alone in here anymore, Lady. Try crawling for a bit, not standing up and waving your arms around, hey?"

"A new tactic that'll confuse our foes, hmm?" Embra murmured back, as she rolled over onto her stomach and started to crawl towards the archway he was pointing to.

From out of that archway Craer bounded over her with a shrill scream, hurling his dagger with one hand and a piece of stone he'd snatched up somewhere with the other, at an unseen foe beyond.

"Something like that," Sarasper agreed in dry tones, joining the sorceress in the archway as someone else screamed, Craer laughed, and there was a crash and clatter from where he landed. "I think we've more than fulfilled our turn at being confused already."

"Oh, yes," Embra agreed with a heartfelt sigh.

"Oh, yes," Saerlor Dyndrie said grandly, squaring his chest and flicking one up-pointed end of his magnificently waxed moustache with an idle finger. "I personally witnessed the Fading of the king."

"You did? Good, good," Ingryl said eagerly, resisting a sudden impulse to rub his hands together in satisfaction. He turned to the guard. "You may leave us."

"But—" the guard began, and found himself measured by the Spellmaster's level stare. The wizard's eyes promised slow and certain death, its bestowal befalling soon . . . if he was worth bothering about at all, and not merely ignored. He took a step back, uncertainly.

"I will," Ingryl said softly, "inform the king about your diligence and loyalty . . . or lack of it. Believe me, I will."

The guard gulped visibly, and then saluted, whirled around, and stammered, "Returning to throneguard, lord!" as he set off at a swift march. He looked back just once, whereupon Ingryl gave him an encouraging smile.

"And just who, sirrah, are you?" Saerlor Dyndrie demanded. "A wizard, so much I can guess, but by what right do y—"

Ingryl Ambelter knelt humbly before the courtier to hide his spreading smile, the one word he had to whisper, and the pouring of a certain powder from one of his palms into the other. A swift tingling in his palms told him the enchantment was at work; he did not have to wait long.

Saerlor made a small, whimpering sound. Surging upright, the Spellmaster clamped his hands over the courtier's mouth and grinned into the man's suddenly despairing eyes. They stared at each other in silence as Ingryl's magical worm wriggled slowly into Saerlor's mind, peering this way and that at memories. The courtier squirmed, tried to call out . . . and then, as the wizard released him, simply swayed on his feet, staring at nothing and making a sort of growling moan, deep in his throat. For where the worm went, it gnawed and tunneled, destroying the mind it was ransacking. Ingryl needed only particular, recent memories . . . and they poured out readily enough, vivid and almost eager to flow forth.

It had been the ritual of the Fading Away, yes, and as far as he could tell, undertaken voluntarily by the Risen King, although it was possible the Faceless had forced him into it, and not merely guarded him. The Serpent had manifested, no doubt to try to slay Snowsar and thus break the binding. It had failed, and therefore, still bound, must now be Driven Down. No wonder the Hissing One at the moot on the hill had been so upset.

The scenes Saerlor remembered left the Spellmaster a little wary. For all his haughty ways and preoccupation with looks, trappings, and wealth, the courtier was (or had been; he was little better than a drooling statue now) a good witness. Ingryl hadn't known there *were* that many Faceless . . . and where were they all now? Was every second palace maid or cook a Koglaur? Was he being watched right now?

Well, set a wolf to hunt a wolf. Who better to make miserable the lives of the lurking Faceless than the Snake-lovers?

Turning away from the swaying, moaning courtier without a backward glance, the Spellmaster hastened to the nearest hidden door—a panel between two pillars carved into likenesses of Dathgath and Elroumrae, ancient rulers of Aglirta. Cobwebs hung like furry webs between Elroumrae's beseeching stone hands; the staff were certainly behind on their dusting.

It opened under his sure touch, into dusty darkness. The king, it seemed, hadn't known about, or cared to use, this secret passage. There were almost three dozen such that Ingryl could recall; perhaps Snowsar had simply never got around to this one.

Like a vengeful wind Ingryl ran to the nearest stair and whirled down it, surefooted in the dank darkness, counting the turns. When the total was high enough he turned on a landing to where there would be a door, outlined it with cautious fingers, and pressed on the right frame-stone to make it open.

Faint light greeted the Spellmaster as he stepped into the passage beyond. Though the lower levels of the sprawling castle were disused, some rooms had windows; here and there sunlight stabbed past dusty curtains.

Hastening to his own most secret place in all the palace, the Spellmaster stopped at a certain closed stone door that looked no different from many others he'd passed. Kissing it in a certain place, Ingryl murmured a word of opening and then, more loudly, a word that was nonsense, and laid his hand upon another spot on the door—and the stone melted away under his hand. In the brief moments before it became solid again, the Spellmaster ducked through the empty doorway into the slime-worm curtains beyond. He hated their cold sucking mouths and the smell of their slime, but only he could pass it and live. Drawing in a deep breath of revulsion, he stepped forward, into his hanging curtain of guardians.

And stiffened in agony, clutching at the hanging net of little slitherers. The blade that was sliding wetly out of his chest had come without warning— as had the hand that now slapped across his nose and mouth and jerked his head around, breaking his neck.

Red agony lashed like lightning through a hungrily spreading mouth of darkness rushing up to claim him. Elsewhere, numbness was racing through him. The Spellmaster tried to speak, but couldn't. He consoled himself with watching, with fading eyes, the glistening ropes of slime-worms adhering to the back of his slayer's hand—and knowing that whoever the man was, he was doomed.

Struggling to move limbs that felt like heavy stones, Ingryl Ambelter drove one elbow viciously back, and then the other. When his killer's grip broke a few moments later, and the Spellmaster felt the wrenching ache of the sword being dragged out of him by the man's fall, he turned his own collapsing body around, shuddering in pain as he drove his own fingers—the ones bearing magic rings—into the bubbling wound the sword had made and held them there, arms trembling.

Gods, but it hurt! He reeled . . . and fell headlong atop the man who'd killed him.

More agony as he bounced bone-shatteringly, trying—through a strangling froth of blood—to scream. As the last of the vitality left the body he'd crafted, and everything went dark, Ingryl saw one last thing: his slayer had no face.

A long while later, Ingryl Ambelter became aware again. The cold, humming fire of magic was coursing through him, and had been for a long, long time. Its work was almost done now, the rings that had yielded up their age-old enchantments crumbling to dust and ash; their stream of magical power was beginning to pulse as it faded. Soon the flow would die away altogether.

No matter; its work was done. He was unspun from the body he'd crafted earlier, and yet lived. From the body of the Koglaur who'd dared to strike him down, he'd build a new one. It mattered not if Koglaur weren't entirely human; in this haven he had more than enough magic to twist and reshape and make things match his own carefully stored hair and flesh and shards of fingernails. Oh, no; Darsar would not so easily be rid of Ingryl Ambelter.

The man who'd been a Spellmaster gathered his will and set about the slow, grim work of becoming a man again.

Up, he thought fiercely. *Up!*

Thrice he whelmed his will, feeling magic swirl and surge in response, and taking pride in that. Though it might take him many tries to move things with only the magic storming within him, few men in all Darsar could weave with magic as he did. Most of the rare few who had the power to work magic, and knew they did, could do so only by painstakingly following the spells and notes set down by others who'd gone before them, like novice cooks blindly following a feast recipe. Ingryl Ambelter was far more than a recipe-reader; he could make magic dance for him. "Dance!" he tried to say, and was aware of splitting skin and spitting blood. "Dance!"

Filled with sudden exultation, he willed himself to rise with more fierceness than ever—and something gave way around and beneath him, something wet and sighing. Ingryl tugged, and surged . . . and came free.

The Spellmaster would have scoffed at the idea that his carefully nurtured slime-worms could think, and see well enough to recognize him or any particular creature. They were mindless, gnawing things whose slime, thanks to a careful many-spells procedure, happened to be only distasteful to him—but fatal to others.

Nevertheless, their many tiny heads turned in unison to watch as a blood-drenched skull burst up out of the bloody sprawl that had been Ingryl Ambelter, trailing a backbone like a grotesque tail, and flew through the air at them.

Ingryl did notice what happened next, and was astonished: as he approached the curtain of worms, it silently parted.

He ignored everything in the small stone chamber beyond the curtain except the coffin on its table. Its protective lightnings would help and not harm him in the state he was in now, but he had to hook or smash the coffin lid open without losing much of himself in the process . . . and the enchantments on the coffin made it much harder than bone.

Within lay the skeleton of his former master, Gadaster Mulkyn, still holding fire enough, if he could but touch it and hiss out a word, to charge him with so much magic that he could shape a body with ease. Gadaster would crumble a little more, of course . . . but then, that was what enspelled skeletons—of masters one has treacherously slain—were for.

Swooping carefully to just the right place, Ingryl hooked his jaw onto a coffin handle, and flew upwards. The coffin opened as easily as if its lid had been made of silk. He let the lid fall open to crash and bounce against the table amid much dust, and then lowered himself thankfully within, hissing the word that would awaken Gadaster's cold fire.

Once his body was rebuilt, he'd hide here for a time, spying on Koglaur with his spells, and betimes, when they slept, sending forth "godly visions" into the minds of some senior Serpent clergy, of specific Koglaur and the guises they took—if he could discover such. In the Snake-lovers' dreams he would hiss commands to destroy these "our darkest foe," speaking as if he was the Serpent himself.

For Ingryl Ambelter was the Spellmaster, and he would dare to do such things.

And more than that. When he was strong enough, Ingryl would shape his new body into the likeness of the Risen King, and take the River Throne as the ruler of Aglirta.

Who would say he was not? A mind-blasted man, or a courtier now back in Sirlptar, or the Faceless of legend, whom Aglirtans would hate and fear on sight?

His first imperial act would be to summon the Lord Baron Berias Loushoond to attend him at court. He'd mindspeak Loushoond first, to make sure the dolt brought a goodly whelming of armaragors with him, in case Flowfoam needed defending. With the Serpent and the king both gone, this was back to a battle of warriors and spells. So long as he sat on the throne, hunger for it should bring all his foes to him.

A bloody worm of bone lying in an open coffin, Ingryl laughed aloud as he thought of all the traps he could contruct in the former Castle Silvertree, using magics he'd hidden long ago in various secret places, like this one, all over the castle.

As for the Lady Embra and her three bumpkins of lovers—well, Velvetfoot was worth his fees. He should have taken care of those irritating adventurers by now. . . .

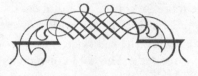

26

Deaτh, Old Spells, and Old Enemies

The Lady of Jewels shook her head in disbelief. "It's a good thing my ancestors believed in magical junk," she said, thrusting tankard after figurine after knickknack into the pouches of the slinger's belt Hawkril had given her. He'd taken it as battle booty, long ago, and had never found useless trifles enough to fill all of the pouches that had been meant for sling-stones. "I can't believe there are still roomfuls of such trifles for us to plunder!"

"Just be glad we have them," Hawkril growled from behind her. "I've no love for spellhurling, but healing you took five of the ugliest little statues I'd ever seen."

Embra shook her head ruefully as she turned to smile at him. "I don't doubt it."

Across the room, Sarasper was stuffing his own row of enchanted oddities into pouches and satchels and boot-tops—and Embra suspected that Craer was carrying a dozen more or so hidden within his clothing, that he wasn't admitting to.

They were standing in a huge, high chamber at the heart of a huge round tower at the southern end of the Silent House. Overhead was a magnificent vaulted ceiling, held up by several massive stone pillars. The walls were girt in dark and once-splendid wood paneling, but long years of water seeping from above had damaged panels and several once-splendid tall cabinets of the many that stood around the walls, their display shelves empty of all but dust and cobwebs. Wherever the water had touched, it had left wood mold-splotched, blistered, and sagging.

After two more vicious little fights in the darkness, Sarasper had healed his companions enough that they could all stagger, and led the way hence. On that painful journey, he'd walled the Four away behind no fewer than six locked and barred doors.

Since arriving here, they'd slept and eaten and been healed and slept again, and had heard at least two of those doors forced open: crashing falls (and muffled groans and curses) caused by the collapses of the upturned tableful of broken furniture Sarasper had balanced behind one door, and the furniture he'd piled against the other.

Intruders were roaming all over the Silent House: warrior bands, mages with their bodyguards, and more. Whenever they met each other, battles broke out. Until someone with a crossbow had objected forcefully, their ranks had included a band of hunters using trained, prowling night-cats—and someone else had animated a corpse to stagger along stiffly clubbing down foes until it had been hacked apart. Dying screams and angry shouts rang out often, and the Band of Four sat in their sanctum and shook their heads in disgust.

Had all Aglirtans become grasping outlaws? The abandoned palace of the Silvertrees was another Indraevyn right now—and even Embra was now determined to cleanse the realm of the greedy Dwaer-seekers wandering its dark halls.

Striding across the room, she firmly tossed away the helm Hawkril had put back on her head and told him with a glare, "I'm *not* wearing that."

He opened his mouth to reply as it crashed to the floor and rang and rattled its way to silent stillness, but she held up a hand to halt his words and reminded her companions, "None of this has found us a Dwaer-Stone. . . . All it's brought us is armies of fellow Dwaer-hunters."

Three grim and silent nods answered her—a moment before the door of the room burst open, trailing splinters, and armored men charged in, yelling.

"Why, visitors!" Craer cried joyfully, kicking the barrel whose removal would cause a flood of furniture to crash down onto the intruders. "Welcome! This *is* a pleasure!"

"Ours," Hawkril added with a growl, as he threw the rotting remnants of a once-heavy table overhand at the warrior leading the charge.

The wood smashed the man over backwards as it flew apart—and a moment later his arched body was swept away by the roaring tide of falling furniture that had already claimed his fellows. The groaning, tumbling chaos of heavy wood fetched up against the far wall with a deafening crash—and then, amid the curling dust, silence fell.

The Band of Four waited, weapons at the ready, but there was only one groaning, feebly moving body to deal with. Craer did that, and they settled themselves down in the wreckage to play victims and wait for the next band of Dwaer-hunters.

They did not have to wait long. A grand voice could soon be heard rolling down the passage outside . . . and drawing steadily nearer.

"While Tanthus is our most capable skulker, Sargin here also has his share of daring blunderings and bold butcherings, which I'm sure he'll be happy to share with you at a more appropriate time. Just now, we near a place of possible peril, so Shamurl and I will stride to the fore and do what we do best: storm the foe!"

Embra and Craer, who were sprawled where they could see each other, had just time enough to exchange incredulous looks before armored figures sprang through the open door and struck heroic poses, drawn swords glittering.

Their full armor shone with a spell-glowing plating of silver, and amid its cold fire could be seen two helmless heads: a grim and scar-faced woman, and a fat-cheeked man who sported a ferocious black spade of a beard. "Ready for battle," the latter declaimed in that rolling richness of a voice, "we hold the front whilst our companions advance!"

Two men in black leathers and black silk masks glided forward, holding splayed trios of throwing knives ready in their hands. Behind them shuffled four minstrels with handharps and pipes—and it could be seen that the bearded man was addressing them.

"Before us lies the bloody wrack of battle," he declared, gesturing with his blade. "We must be nigh some fearsome beast, to lay low such capable and valiant blades—or perhaps the fell Sorceress Silvertree wields her Dwaer to deadly effect, whirling the very furniture into flight to smite her foes at her bidding! I know no fear, for I, Amarandus the Lion, have never yet tasted defeat. Whatever dark danger might await us, we the Bright Blade and Hope of Aglirta shall not fail, but win our way on to glory! Watch now, as forth we fare, into—"

"Blessed silence," Craer snarled, rearing up to hurl a dagger with heartfelt force.

Amarandus the Lion was fast. The glittering blade in his hand swept up and struck the dagger aside with a bell-like clang.

Unfortunately, Craer had thrown a second blade, only a little behind the first. A bearded throat stopped it with a gurgle, and Amarandus the Lion spun slowly around in arch-backed agony, dramatic to the last—and toppled over on his face with a crash.

The procurers of the Bright Blade had their own knives, and flung them at Craer both hard and fast—but Hawkril rose out of the sea of furniture like an armored mountain, and most of the daggers rattled off his armor plates as he waded forward, sweeping his longsword in low, vicious cuts that kept the leather-armored men ducking or leaping away. As the other armored warrior, Shamurl, waded into the wrack of shattered wood and sprawled bodies to reach Hawkril, the bards gasped and peered like commoners around a dueling ring.

"They'll be taking bets next," Sarasper growled, glaring at them—and then ducking hastily away from a pair of hurled knives. Embra pursed her lips and loosed some blades of her own, needles of magical force that sang through the air, fast and arrow-straight. Tanthus was fast enough to dive headlong out of the way of the one sent to doom him; Sargin wasn't.

"Have they no wizard?" Embra muttered to Sarasper, as they crouched together behind the leaning ruin of a massive and once-magnificent cabinet. "Was this Liontongue that much of an arrogant fool?"

"Perhaps so," Sarasper replied, watching the warrior-woman with narrowed eyes as she closed with Hawkril. "And yet . . ."

Shamurl raised her sword when she was just beyond the reach of Hawkril's blade, gave him a brittle smile, and carefully cut open her own palm. Turning her hand to cup the welling blood, she dropped some flakes of rust and metal shards into her own gore, and whispered a word over it.

"Hawk, get back!" Embra shouted. "That's a flowmetal spell!"

A blade whirred at her head as Tanthus saw a chance to fell the Lady of Jewels—but even as she stared at it and jerked back, knowing the move had been anticipated and she was moving in the wrong direction and too late, another dagger whirled out of nowhere to strike aside the fang spinning to claim her with a musical clang. A moment later, Tanthus doubled over with a cough, clutching at a hilt standing out of his throat. Craer liked to throw his blades in pairs.

The warrior Shamurl was wading forward in clanking triumph now, as metal fell away from her like tinkling shards of glass—and Hawkril's own armor, as he staggered back in a hasty retreat, almost falling amid the tangle of splintered table legs and broken stools, grew a sudden webwork of cracks.

Frantically the armaragor hurled away his warsword, flinging it back behind him to crash down in a far corner. As he turned and fled in earnest after it, metal slid off the bulging muscles of his shoulders, showing the world sweat-stained underarmor.

Shamurl's own leathers bristled with sheaths, and she drew thorns as long as her forearms from two of them as she pursued Hawkril. Embra gasped at their size. They must have come from vines in the hot forests of the far south, and were big enough to serve as stabbing daggers, and then some!

The moment he was free of fallen furniture, Hawkril spun around and crouched to await his foe. "Does the magic move with her?" he growled over his shoulder.

Embra and Sarasper both shook their heads before they realized the armaragor wasn't looking at them. "No," they called together.

" 'Tis done," the healer added. "It never spreads far."

"Right," Hawkril said grimly—even as buckles crumbled, belts and baldrics fell away with a sudden crash, and he was reduced to his boots, breeches, and padding. Undaunted, he strode forward. "Surrender, woman!" he growled.

"Die!" Shamurl snarled back, charging. Hawkril shrugged and stood his ground.

"Hawk!" Embra snapped warningly, but as the bards gawked and shifted about to get a better view, the armaragor and the warrior-woman crashed together. As they grappled, Shamurl stabbed viciously.

Hawkril struck aside one blade with a twist of his body and a slap at her forearm; when the other blade came curving in, he caught it just below her own grip, wrenched it until it pointed away from him, and then—as she brought up her knee hard and bit at his face—he swung his free hand across them both in a blow to the side of Shamurl's head that spun the warrior-woman around like a doll, thorns flying, and laid her out across the furniture with a crash.

She convulsed in pain, clawing at the air . . . and then slowly went limp and lay still.

Across the chamber, several bards cheered. Hawkril gave them a dark look.

"You were right," he told Embra curtly, as he joined them. "This was a stoneheaded idea. First Brostos and now this; some King's Heroes we are. I *liked* that armor."

"There's more back at the armory," Sarasper told him.

"We have to get there first," Craer put in.

Hawkril craned his neck to see over the smaller man, and the procurer ducked to let him do so better and murmured, "What befalls thy brains now, Tall Post?"

"Did my warsword survive?"

Embra patted his chest reassuringly. "If it didn't shatter when it landed—and I didn't hear that sort of sound—it'll be fine."

The armaragor pushed through them, heading for the corner where his blade had clattered down. "If you don't mind . . ." he growled.

Back at the door, a bard screamed as someone thrust a sword through him from behind. As he gasped and coughed bloodily forward to the floor, aided by a cruel boot shoving at his backside, his fellow songweavers clawed their ways hastily up the walls and atop cabinets, gibbering in fear as cold laughter arose in their wake.

"Leave them, Kordul," someone snapped, as Craer and Embra crouched low behind the tangled barricade of furniture and peered at this new foe. Behind them, Sarasper wasted no time in looking; he let fall his belts and carrysacks without pause, draped his robes over them, and started to grow both spidery legs and fur. Hawkril came stalking back to join them with his warsword in his hand—in time to witness the next grand arrival.

Three tall and capable-looking armaragors pushed into the room to join the three already there, and in their midst strode two tall, grandly robed wizards wearing tall boots and sneers of cold command. One of those mages carried a staff as tall as himself. As he hefted it, spell-glows winked and raced up and down its dark length. The Four measured them: eight men who looked very ready for battle.

"Band of Four!" one of them called, glaring at Hawkril and the heads peering back from behind the wrack of broken woods and bodies. "I call on you to surrender, for the good of the realm, your Dwaer-Stones to us!"

"Leave this to me," Craer muttered quickly, raising a quelling hand to Embra. "I know yon mage, by his deeds and talk about him rather than direct dealings." Raising his voice, he called back, "And how would giving such powerful magic into the hands of a hire-for-coins warband out of Sirlptar be good for Aglirta?"

"We have power enough to drive the barons now on the march back to their own towers, put down the dark work of those who serve the Serpent, and restore peace to the land. With the Dwaer, we could do this in days— and more than that: we could keep wizards and the barons they serve from working against us."

"We serve the Risen King," Craer called. "Whom do you serve?"

"We all serve the rightful king of Aglirta," the mage replied sternly. "Let no one question the loyalty of the Swords of Sirlptar!"

"Horse dung," Hawkril growled. "Sirl mages serve none but themselves."

"Think you so, warrior?" replied the mage who'd been silent until now. He stepped forward, a plume of flame making a slow spiral around one end of his magical staff. Embra's eyes narrowed as she got a good look at it; unlike any such she'd ever seen before, this one looked to be made of some dark metal, and to have a long, thick central shaft adorned with hooks and barbed fingers, which slimmed at either end into thin cylinders resembling the ends of many a wooden staff. If it did as much as what mages liked to call "a true staff," it could be made to unleash two magics at once.

Its wielder gave her a cold smile of scorn, and added to Hawkril, "Your dealings, warrior, must have been with low, dishonest men. Sirlptar is home to rich and starving, the mighty and those of no account, men and less than men, from scores of ports in as many lands. We trade with them all, and live with them all—which makes us far more suited to leading Aglirta than backcountry barons, with their bonfire-wizards and their crude plots."

"Ah," Craer responded almost merrily, "so now we have it. *You* are the suitable leaders of Aglirta. I daresay all eight of you will find the throne a trifle crowded."

"That was not our meaning," the first mage snapped, "and not what we said, either, Delnbone. We've little interest in posturings and wasted banter, either, so we'll ask once more for the yielding of what we have more than enough power to take: will you surrender your Dwaer to us, or not?"

Embra laid firm hands on the arms of both Craer and Hawkril, bidding their silence, and stepped forward to the splintered edge of a table. "Before any magic leaves my hands—either as a gift or as a spell sent to slay," she said pleasantly, "I would know rather better who I'm dealing with. I see a warband of six veteran armaragors, led by two mages, and am given to understand you hail from Sirl town. Capable swords, so much I can see; obedient to you, so much I've heard. So who, sirs, are you? Or am I going to have to ask these bards to introduce you?"

The silently staring bards suddenly cowered as the mage with the staff snapped his head in their direction to glare warningly; the other wizard smiled a soft and catlike smile and said, "Ah, but where have my manners been? Lady Silvertree, may I present Nlorvold 'Balestaff,' so named for the thing of wondrous magic he bears? He and I met far away from here, some years back, while on the same hunt. We sought a land that yet holds dragons, and the rare ladies who have the magic to tame them."

"And did you find such a place, Sir Nameless?"

"Ah, forgive me, Lady. No, we did not. As of yet. I did forget to unfold to you my name. Know that I am Ressheven, of Two Moons."

Craer made a small sound in his throat that might have been a "harrumph" had it been louder. He looked sidelong up at Embra and whispered, "He is who he says he is."

Embra did not look impressed. Two Moons was a name known to all who hoisted tankards in taverns up and down the Vale: a notorious, now fallen, "cursed" mage-school whose students had been trained to make war with magic.

Ressheven favored the procurer with that catlike smile. "I see the name of my former home is not unknown to you."

Embra shrugged. "So now we know each other, sir, yet find that this familiarity brings us—"

She broke off as two of the armaragors whirled around, blades flashing, to face the door they'd come in by, and a small commotion ensued. "We come to bear witness!" was said loudly, more than once.

"More bards?" Hawkril growled in disbelief, as a dozen men or more, one at least bearing a lute, and two more carrying a third man on a litter, shuffled hesitantly in through the door.

"Your chroniclers?" Embra asked the Swords wizards. "Or admirers who trail everywhere avidly behind you?"

"Enough!" Nlorvold "Balestaff" spat disgustedly to his fellow Swords. "They'll never yield a Dwaer! They just want to unburden themselves of a lot of clever preening talk before bards!"

He raised his staff as he spoke, and fire spat from it. Hawkril dove head-long for the floor. The wizard turned his staff to follow the armaragor, and its arc of flames caught alight much shattered furniture.

"He sounds like me grumbling about wizards!" Hawkril said with a grin, hefting his warsword.

Embra smiled crookedly and released a spell that had been whirling ready in her cupped hand, behind her back. It caused the floor tiles around the staff-wielding wizard to rise up in a small, snarling whirlwind that plucked Nlorvold off his feet and slammed him into two of the warriors behind him, driving them together heavily to the ground.

"Really?" the Lady of Jewels replied to the armaragor as Hawkril scrambled to his feet. "He *looks* a lot like you grumbling about wizards, too!"

Ressheven had intoned his own spell by then—and the air was suddenly full of dozens of darting, swooping daggers that flew on black crow-wings. In a dark flock of stabbing death they fell on the Four and bards alike, as the Swords warriors crouched low around their wizard and watched the carnage.

Craer fell and rolled, wincing and clutching at his shoulder. Hawkril swore as two lines of blood were laced across his side and back in as many seconds, and batted blades away as they swerved and then banked hungrily down at him.

Two bards toppled from their high perches, clutching at their throats. Another sprouted a flying fang in one eye, and toppled over in silence.

As each dagger drew blood, the Lady of Jewels saw, it faded slowly away, but its damage remained behind. She shrieked as one came right at her eyes—and struck it aside with a desperate slap that made her palm burn.

As it tumbled away, it faded . . . and she did not have to look down to know that her hand was running wet with blood.

"Embra!" Hawk snarled, his face contorting in agony as he stopped a dagger through the palm of his hand. "Do something!"

27

Gods Serve Up Surprises

The Lady of Jewels stared at Hawkril and the swarming daggers around them, swallowed, and thought hard. A "Many Lightnings"? She had nothing that could ensnare and drag down these knives, and her Banishment could destroy only one flying blade, not the whole spell. If she could slay or strike senseless the mage who'd cast it, now . . .

But it was Sarasper who acted first. Unseen by bard or any man of the Swords, he'd climbed the heap of fallen furniture and lurked just behind its crest. Now he sprang high into the air and forward, like a gigantic, shaggy spider jumping into the air, and crashed down with all of his legs bent forward to shove together at the heap—causing another slide of old and heavy wood that smashed into the wizard Ressheven like a galloping horse, burying the startled mage before he could do more than start to yell.

All over the room, dark-winged daggers abruptly winked out of existence.

Sarasper rode that avalanche of tumbling furniture down into the midst of the Swords of Sirlptar, watching armaragors leap or sprint out of the way—or run out of room or time to flee, and get bowled over as if they were flung toys. Well before the furniture came to rest, the longfangs sprang from it to crash into the chest of Nlorvold the Balestaff, who'd just found his feet again, to stand leaning on his staff and breathing heavily.

The wizard went down, wolflike jaws tore out a throat, and claws tore off the head that had sported that throat and tossed it into the lap of a horrified bard, all in a whirl of motion that was begun and ended before the warriors of the Swords could do more than gape and yell.

Furry limbs snatched at a bouncing staff, missed, and then caught hold. A terrified Swords armaragor flung himself forward and hacked desperately at the wolf-spider's limbs, right at the spot where they curved around the staff.

A flood of blue sparks and flame flared in the wake of that swordblow, even as Sarasper roared in pain and shrank back, trailing a spray of blood. Emboldened, the Swords warrior struck again, and one of his fellows joined him in the hacking. Twice, thrice—brutal chopping blows that rained down before a shouting Hawkril, smashing and bounding his way through knee-deep wrack, could get to the fray.

And the Balestaff exploded.

The force of the blast flung the longfangs the length of the chamber, plucked Hawkril off his feet and dashed him against the base of a pillar halfway down the room, and sent a shower of Swords warriors' legs and arms tumbling and spattering bards and tall cabinets and riven furniture alike. On his litter, Flaeros Delcamper winced and curled his half-healed arms over his head, huddling down desperately as the world around him tore itself apart with a roar. The force of the blast spun the litter around end for end and slammed it back into the doorway with a splintering crash. Moments later, the head of another Swords armaragor sailed over it, almost catching Flaeros in the face, to thump and bounce wetly to a stop well down the passage.

And then, almost unbelievably to the numbed and near-deafened survivors, a stillness fell upon the room at the heart of the tower. Flaeros peered into the vast chamber from the ruin of his litter and saw four or five of his fellow bards doing the same thing, while another handful moaned and twisted in pain.

Right in front of him, two armaragors of the Swords of Sirlptar were staggering unsteadily forward to where someone was moving in the rubble. In the distance, Flaeros could see the procurer and the Lady of Jewels doing their own staggering.

Then, with a snarl of rage from between clenched teeth and some helpful tugs by the armaragors, Ressheven of Two Moons reared upright with blood on his face and fury in his eyes.

Raising his trembling hands like claws, he fought for control over them, shaped a spell the moment he gained it, and then whirled around and pointed down the room at the Lady Embra Silvertree.

"*Die,* whore of the king!" he spat—and something rushed from his hands that was neither fire nor lightning, but blazed red and white as it howled forth, in a beam like the shaft of a thrusting spear, swift and straight down the room to where Embra flung herself desperately through the air, frantic to get out of the way.

The ravening magic thrust past Embra and Craer and tore on—to smash straight into the base of one of the massive pillars, like a wave breaking on the rocks of a savage shore.

And with a flash that blinded the eyes and a crash that shrieked in already-ringing ears, stone shattered and was flung away—and for a brief, jaw-dropping moment, there was only rushing, tortured air for about the height of a man between the floor and the rest of the pillar.

Then, with a groan that shook all the Silent House and flung everyone in the room off their feet, the pillar broke free of its vaulting, trailing huge slabs of ceiling, and toppled like a great stone tree, as wide as all the world and thundering a room-shaking song of doom, towards Flaeros.

Somehow he remembered to scream.

Lying in an open coffin, Ingryl Ambelter shuddered as a sudden surge of magic crackled up from Gadaster's bones, their glow becoming briefly blinding. "Three above," the onetime Spellmaster hissed at the ceiling. "Who's using that much magic—and for *what?*"

For a moment he was almost frantic to get himself a body and get up into the palace to find out . . . and a moment later, he was very glad that he was lying down in its lowest levels, in the chill, deserted darkness in a room no one still alive knew about, where he would have to remain for some time to come. That just might help him to survive.

The room shuddered and then leaped from end to tile-clattering end as the mighty pillar crashed down, obliterating two running bards in an instant. A third minstrel, sobbing in his fear, raced towards Flaeros screaming, "Out of the way! Out of the way! Out! Out! *Out!*"

Flaeros struggled to rise or roll away—but the terrified man launched himself over the litter in a dive that took him headlong out into the passage. The two injured bards had to clamber over the splintered ruin of the litter, so they took the time to snatch Flaeros up and stagger a few paces along the passage with him. When they set him down, gasping, he told them to leave him—and, with thankful glances and without another word, they ran off down the passage in the wake of their vanished fellow.

Flaeros Delcamper dragged himself up into a sitting position against the wall, weeping with pain. His leg felt like it was broken again. Biting his lips, he bent his will to ignoring the pain and staring back into the room over his litter. It was so firmly jammed in the doorway that it seemed now to belong there.

It seemed to Embra that she had been crawling for a very long time—that she had always been crawling. Coughing in the thick dust, she dragged herself on over sharp points of rock, one leg useless. She was hurt somewhere inside, too, low on her right side, though only a few small tumbling stones had struck her.

Hawkril, over by his own pillar, had already staggered upright, but Sarasper had made no movement save the slow shrinkings of spidery limbs fading back into the bloody and broken limbs of an old man. "Three preserve us," she gasped, spitting blood with each word.

"No, no, that's my task!" Craer said merrily, from somewhere nearby. A breath or so later lightning cracked through the dust, stabbing blindly at where the procurer's voice had come from. The wizard Ressheven was very much alive, it seemed—and anxious that others in the room not be.

The spell emptied the air of dust in an eye-blink. Embra twisted her head to look back at the Sirl mage, wondering if she could hurl any spell back at him in time—and then, sliding down the far side of a slope of rubble onto a few bare floor tiles, was glad she wouldn't have to.

Craer was scrambling around in the wrack, hurling furniture legs, bloody armaragor limbs, fragments of tabletops, and shattered swords at Ressheven, peppering the snarling wizard with a storm of things that bruised and bounced and clanged. Crashes from behind her made Embra roll over—aahh! Gods, the pain!—to look in the other direction, where she saw a grim and blood-streaked Hawkril, bared to the waist and beyond now, lurching slowly toward the mage, holding the remains of a massive table up in front of him as a shield.

Sarasper's eyes were open, and he was groaning slightly as she reached him. Lightning crackled again behind Embra, but it was followed by Craer's derisive laughter, so she didn't bother to look back.

"Lass," the old healer growled, as she propped herself unsteadily on one arm above him, "give me some Silvertree gewgaws! Gods, but I hurt!"

"I believe it's a common complaint," the Lady of Jewels told him, drooling blood as she spoke—and tremblingly conveyed a scratched statuette into his fingers.

Sarasper gave her a lopsided smile. "You didn't take very good care of it, did you?"

His eyes flickered closed before she could give him a rude answer, and the statuette flared with spell-light. Embra devoted herself to retrieving another.

It took six Silvertree knickknacks, with lightnings lashing the room behind them and Craer hurling weak gibe after lame jest at the wizard, before Sarasper said, "That's better. I'll live now." He lifted bloody fingers that glowed slightly and put them to her mouth; Embra kissed them, fresh tears suddenly flooding forth from her, as the tingling that brought relief flowed slowly through her.

"Hmmph. You didn't take good care of yourself, either," Sarasper muttered. His hands moved down her body, pushing and probing—and when they came to another pouch, he tore it open and plucked out whatever Silvertree enchantment lay within.

Embra gasped and shuddered as the healing went on, purging pain in cooling waves of relief. Sarasper smiled as she writhed atop him. "Not long now, lass," he growled, straining to reach his fingertips down to her shattered leg. "Not long."

Atop him, Embra suddenly stiffened and arched herself almost upright. Sarasper clutched at her shoulders to keep her from falling into a flailing that might do her worse damage, and snapped, "*What,* lass?"

Embra fell back into his embrace, shivering. "The Dwaer are here!" she hissed, staring into his eyes with hope and fear warring in her own. "More than one of them, very close!"

"You're sure?" the healer asked hoarsely.

"Certain." Embra nodded, shivering again. "I can feel them; it's unmistakable."

Then she put her arms around Sarasper and flung herself sideways, rolling both of them down into a hollow in the rubble.

"What the *sargh!*" the old healer snarled. "Lass, are you crazed! Th—"

"That's a Stream-of-Stones," Embra told him tersely, as they lay nose-to-nose amid still-rolling rubble. She jerked her head back towards a distant Ressheven, who was chanting a swift but curiously flat-toned incantation. "I just hope he misses."

The words ended, there was a moment of tense silence—and then flagstones tore themselves up from the floor somewhere in the room and roared through the air, thudding and rattling hard on something. A moment later, Hawkril and his table cartwheeled helplessly past in the heart of a pelting cloud of rocks—stones that struck like deafening thunder against the pillar Hawkril had been flung into, earlier, as the tumbling cloud howled on past.

Embra heaved herself up again for a pain-wracked moment before her arm gave way beneath her and brought her crashing down atop a wincing

Sarasper—but it was time enough to see Hawkril strike the end wall of the chamber, one arm outflung to grasp at nothing, amid enough stones to build a wall. The crash shook the room, and in its wake something happened to the pillar that the stones had grazed: it grew the outlines of a hitherto-hidden door that shuddered a few inches open.

The sorceress had no time to see more, and she wallowed frantically atop the old healer, trying to turn herself as she rose again so as to get a quick glimpse of the pillar once more—in case something was bursting out through that door—as she spun around to see what Ressheven was up to.

The leader of the Swords of Sirlptar was gesturing his way grandly through the final moments of a Salanger's Thrust. Embra groaned aloud and clenched her teeth in anticipation of the bone-shattering agony to come, as—

The incantation abruptly ended, incomplete, with a wet *glub* sound. Craer's hurled dagger sprouted in Ressheven's mouth, and the wizard's eyes just had time to widen in surprise before a second dagger plunged home to the hilt in his right eye.

Craer always liked to throw his daggers in pairs.

No Thrust to suffer through, then, and unless a bard was stupid enough to return, no possible foes left to harm the beleaguered Band of Four.

Which was a good thing, Embra thought, as she shouted her thanks to Craer—and fell silent as she saw the procurer looking back past her with alarm on his face.

She kept on turning, almost wearily, to see what new danger was coming down on her, as Sarasper groaned and cursed weakly under her.

"Gods, woman, if this is how you treat your lovers . . ." he growled, clamping one hand firmly around her injured leg to stop her from moving about.

Embra shrieked and flopped down on her face, shuddering in pain—and Sarasper got himself out from under her with several heaves and wheezes, until he could snatch another figurine from one of her pouches and finish healing a shapely Silvertree leg.

"Sass!" Craer shouted. "'Ware! Look up! Look *up*!"

Frowning, the old healer looked up—and his mouth dropped open. Drifting silently towards him, close enough now to be looming up over him, was a ghostly, faintly glowing cloud that had two dark holes that might be eyes, a larger hole that was probably a gaping mouth, and two outstretched arms that definitely ended in hands. The wraith looked almost comical, but it was as large as a dozen men . . . and it did not look friendly.

"Embra, we need a Banishment!" Sarasper growled, as he felt the figurine melt away in his grasp and healing magic surging through and out of him, into the sorceress. "Embra!"

The heir of the Silvertrees groaned under his hands, and Sarasper Codelmer realized that whatever spells Embra might be able to weave, she didn't have time to do anything. With frantic hands he hauled her up into a sitting position, ignoring her moans and gasps of protest, and tried to drag her to one side, out of the hollow, out from beneath the wraith now right above them, and beginning to descend.

"Gods above!" Embra gasped, staring up at it. "What in the name of the Holy Horned Huntress is *that*?"

The cloud was filling the air above the hollow now, stretching for a goodly way to either side; there was no escape from it.

Sarasper looked wildly around the room, but saw no aid to be found. Distant disturbances marked Hawkril's slow and painful attempts to dig himself out from under the stones that had battered him, and another ridge of heaped rubble separated them from Craer. The little man in leathers was struggling over shifting stones towards them, but he was going to be some time getting to them. Some too much time.

With a sigh, the old man stopped trying to manhandle Embra up out of the hollow, and tried instead to claw as many enchanted gewgaws as he could out of her pouches. Perhaps he could heal them both as the ghostly could settled over them, and so save the Lady and a certain old healer from the worst of whatever harm it did.

"Look!" Craer shouted, from somewhere close behind them. "The door!"

Sarasper dragged his gaze down from the ghostly face drifting down to envelop them with its endless, silent scream to look at the door in the pillar from whence the ghostly apparition had come. Beyond the pillar, Hawkril was slowly hobbling and stumbling towards them all, his face a mask of pain and weariness.

Slowly, very slowly, something was blotting out Sarasper's view of the struggling armaragor. That door was swinging open, propelled by the weight of something that was leaning on it. That something was . . . a human corpse.

It leaned farther, coming into better view: a shriveled, immobile body standing stiffly upright in mold-dappled cobwebs that must have once been robes. The mummified man—if it was a man—was clutching a coffer to his chest. He toppled stiffly and slowly, almost majestically, at first . . . a fall that ended in a sudden rush to the floor.

There was an explosion of rolling dust as that rigid form shattered, bounced . . . and was gone. In the instant of its vanishing, the wraithlike cloud seeping down into the hollow whirled up into a gale that blew to nowhere—and with a despairing wail, the ghostly guardian wraith overhead, if that was what it had been, vanished.

Sarasper and Embra blinked at each other in astonishment, and then stared again at the pillar. The door stood open, revealing a now-empty niche, but the coffer was lying in front of it, where the mummy had fallen. Even as Craer came clambering down over the last of the rubble into the hollow, the old healer scrambled up out of it, to get to the coffer first.

It was a small thing, no broader than the length of his hand and twice that long, but it was very heavy. As thick as two of his hands, of metal, and both old and dirty. It had once borne an intricate chased design of curlicues that seemed to illustrate nothing and bear no writing, but much of the design had been worn or battered away, and one corner of the coffer had been smashed in by a long-ago blow. The lid was latched but not locked.

Sarasper lifted his head to make sure Embra and Craer were watching— and then, without hesitation, opened the coffer.

It held only one thing: a sheet or plate of shining silvery metal, its surface etched here and stamped there with writing. Sarasper peered at it, caring nothing for magical curses or suchlike that bards so liked to babble about.

The script had more swirls and flourishes than many a bridal gown, but he could read it. His face acquired a slow frown as he puzzled out line after line, stopping only when Embra's head, bending over him, blotted out the light.

"What is it?" she asked, more eager than apprehensive.

"Magic, of course," Sarasper told her. "A ritual and instructions for . . ."

"For?"

The old healer smiled up at her. Gods, but at moments like this she was like a child who knows that she's going to be given a new toy, and can barely contain herself.

"A way of mentally 'entering' a Stone and altering it," he announced, as Craer and a limping Hawkril joined them. "Binding oneself to the Dwaer and it to the caster, that is, so the caster will survive, down the years, as long as the Stone does . . . and only he will be able to awaken and wield that Dwaer-Stone's powers."

He lifted his head from the writing—and looked into three grim stares.

"If you ever try to accomplish that," Embra whispered, "I will try to kill you. Not with any pleasure . . . but for Aglirta, and for all Darsar. One Serpent is enough."

"More than enough," Hawkril rumbled.

Sarasper looked up at them and nodded slowly. "I'm not opposed to that view." He clapped the coffer shut and asked wearily, "So what should I do with this? Destroy it?"

"No," a new voice broke in, broad and deep and impressive. "Give it here!"

As the Four turned their heads, three Dwaer-Stones flashed as one, eerie stars in the gloom of the chamber.

Lines of magical radiance streaked from that pulse of light, to surround the coffer with a glowing sphere of force—and Sarasper, kneeling with the coffer in his hand, with another sphere whose glow was less bright.

The Band of Four stared in shared astonishment as the three Dwaer flew, as if they were small hovering hummingbirds and not fist-sized stones, around behind another pillar.

When they came out the other side, they were describing lazy orbits around a slowly striding man none of them had ever thought to see again: the Baron Blackgult.

"You go to all the trouble of awakening a king . . . and he just fades away," he observed sardonically, a little smile on his lips as he gazed back at their astonished stares. "I almost think it's time Aglirta had a new king."

One Dwaer flashed forth some spell-motes, and Ezendor Blackgult was suddenly wearing a crown and holding a scepter of eerie light.

They flashed into splendor and then faded away, as his smile broadened. "Fair greeting, Band of Four. I believe two of you are still in my service."

Embra Silvertree's eyes blazed like an autumn fire. "You!"

She glared at the traditional enemy of all Silvertrees, trembling with rage as the fire of her own rising magic blazed up around her fists, and snapped, "Did you kill my father?"

"No," Blackgult told her with a weary smile. "That's one thing not in my power, Embra. You see, I *am* your father."

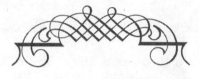

28

No Barons Without Battles

The Smiling Wolf of Sart wasn't smiling his famous smile just now. The wind was whipping his hair into his face as he galloped along, the groaning Tersept of Gilth bouncing like a rag doll in the saddle of the mount beside his. A few factors and local merchants had been brave enough to come along, too, and were eating the mud of pounding hooves behind him right now. The best armaragors Sart's coin could buy were all around them, bent low in their saddles as they all thundered along the river road together, just as fast as their horses could be goaded into moving.

It wasn't going to be fast enough. All Aglirta was on its way to the Silent House, and armies were on the march. Glarsimber Belklarravus had seen the glittering spears of baronial hireswords sweep past Sart as if the fields had grown a sudden crop of war-metal, more than ten times the men he could afford to buy the services of—and there were other armies, he'd heard, all of them hastening to the Silent House.

The ruined home of the Silvertrees. Somehow, when darknesses fell upon Aglirta, the Silvertrees were always lurking in the thick of things. . . .

More than one horse was breathing raggedly, and it wouldn't be long, Sart knew, before the first faltered and fell—and a man going down from a horse at this speed, with the hooves of the others behind to crash down on him, rarely lived to rise up in their wake. Just a little farther, now . . .

They swept around a bend in the road, saw the hillside that stretched up to the ruin before them—and groaned aloud at what they saw.

Two bands of heavily armored warriors were there before them, scrambling out of their saddles and drawing blades in ringing haste. Men who wore the best armor, scores of them, lumbering forward to butcher each other on the overgrown hillside, amid the leaning tombs.

Steel clashed, men shouted and thrust and reeled—and then the armored figures were staggering back.

The Wolf of Sart hauled hard on his reins, trying to slow his racing mount smoothly and hoping no idiot behind him would crash into his mount's hindquarters. Horses reared and complained all around him as he peered up the hill, trying to see just what was happening. He'd hoped to seize whatever magic the Band of Four had gathered, or failing that, fight beside whatever baron carried the day—or, if there was a strong royal force, under the king's banner, in hopes that Sart would become a barony, and . . .

All that was done now, swept away by barons who'd mustered more ready swords and ridden harder. And by something else . . .

There was a flash and a flicker amid the armored figures. Spells were hurling the armaragors back! Spells, with not a mage to be seen, and . . .

Out of the tombs came hooded figures, some of them moving in a slow and slithering manner. The spells were coming from their hands—scaled hands.

"The Serpents!" Belklarravus spat, as he wrestled his lathered mount to a halt. "Gods curse them!"

Spells were hurling warriors back now, clearing a way to the gates of the Silent House, and cowled figures were beckoning to the men who wore the most gleaming armor, and rode the most splendid horses.

Barons of Aglirta swung down from their saddles and strode forward, clanking rank and power with every stride. Their visors were down and their drawn swords hung in the crooks of their elbows, and the Wolf of Sart saw the arms of Glarond and Maerlin on the broad bright backs of two of those gleaming figures. Hooded figures hurried along beside them, ushering them in through the gates. Scaled hands stabbed at the sky, blue fire rose to shape a portal in a hitherto blank stone wall, and the mighty of Aglirta passed into the Silent House.

Tersept Glarsimber Belklarravus was too cold with anger and despair to want to look at the Tersept of Gilth, but he heard the soft voice that could only belong to one man say, from near at hand, "Well . . . perhaps *next* time."

The Smiling Wolf of Sart shook his head silently. He knew that neither of them, even if no spell or blade ever touched them, would live long enough to ever see a "next time." The bright chance to snatch a crown had passed through their fingers.

Snatched away by slow horses . . . and the Serpent.

.   .   .

In the gloom of a shattered room in the Silent House, Embra uncurled one fist with a flick of her fingers that freed Sarasper and sent the coffer skipping away across the rubble.

The Baron Blackgult watched it go with a little smile, and made only a small gesture when it came to a halt, far away across the stones. A single Dwaer flared obediently—and a small whirlwind of stones rose from the nearby rubble and gently entombed the coffer.

Hawkril looked at his longtime master and growled, "You, Lord—as king?"

Before Blackgult could reply, Sarasper snapped, "Never!" His body sank into a sudden whirl of ruddy fur and fangs. Embra raised her other hand, her eyes very dark in her pale, trembling face as she gazed fixedly at the baron, but he never moved.

"You, my father? I don't believe you," she whispered at last. As Blackgult turned his head to reply to her, still wearing that gentle smile, the long-fangs that Sarasper had become leaped forward, springing at the baron.

"It's a tale," the baron told her simply, ignoring the wolf-spider. "One of those about love, and two barons who were idiots—but it's yours. One day I hope you'll want to hear it."

Two of the Dwaer flashed as he spoke, orbiting each other in a gentle dance—and Sarasper Codelmer was suddenly himself again, a near-naked, frail old man, all bones and brown spots, frozen in midleap with his eyes aglare and his hands spread into reaching claws.

There was a commotion in the doorway as a shattered litter was roughly hurled aside, and barons of Aglirta, magnificent in their best battle armor, burst into the room. Blackgult included them in the bright and merry smile he gave to the Four then, as he added, "In answer to your question, Hawkril, I was actually thinking of ruling as regent until the king feels ready to walk among us again."

"Blasphemy!" a baron shouted—and all over the chamber, swords rang as they were drawn.

As the barons advanced, armaragors and Serpent-priests, tense tersepts and courtiers, and even bards white-faced with fear crowded through the doorway into the room behind them. High up on the walls, amid clashings, dusty and boarded-over doors were forced open. Other men strode out of them onto landings that gave onto stairs that descended only a few treads before ending in long-crumbled ruin. Nevertheless, they stayed on these unreliable perches like so many vultures, staring down eagerly as many hands tensed on sword-hilts.

The Baron Blackgult looked around at them all and said, "As Aglirta seems to be gathering in earnest for the first time in my memory, let us have more room." The three Dwaer flashed in unison and rose up around him in sinuous arcs—and rubble left the floor of the room everywhere, broken bodies and splintered wood and all, to fly into a far corner and there settle into a huge and untidy heap.

Into the awed silence, the Baron Maerlin spat, "You as regent? Blackgult, your villainy is the reason we *need* a regent! What makes you better than me? Why not Maerlin as regent?"

"Maerlin! Maerlin!" Some of the armaragors standing behind him took up the cry.

"Silence!" another baron roared. "I see no need for the great hurry in naming a regent that you, Blackgult the Skulker, seem to feel—or you, Maerlin the Grasping! Let there—"

Someone threw a dagger, high over the heads of the crowd—and it flashed past a baronial ear and sliced open the chin of the armaragor behind him.

In an instant, the room erupted into wild, shouting battle. Swords clanged like a smith's hammerblows on his forge, fast and ragged and furious, and men punched and shoved and flailed and died.

Craer and Hawkril stepped protectively in front of Embra as the air filled with hurled daggers, swords, and even stones. Their eyes stayed mostly on the cowled Serpent-priests—who'd moved to the outer edges of the room and were using only defensive shielding spells. If there were any mages present, they were being just as circumspect in their spellhurlings.

Embra turned to Blackgult, threw one hand up to point at Sarasper, and said fiercely, "Father or not, put him down! I'll fight you and *die* fighting you, if you don't *put him down!*"

The Baron Blackgult did not smile at her or mock her, but merely nodded and said gently, " 'Tis done, Embra. Guard yourself from others, not from me." As he spoke, the Dwaer flashed and Sarasper Codelmer descended gently to earth.

"Sargh and bebolt!" the healer cursed, throwing his hands protectively across his crotch as he blinked and then gaped at the room full of surging, hacking men. "What *now*?"

A factor died from a sword thrust up through his mouth into his brain, and fell back against a wall, squalling, to slide bloodily down it to the floor. He almost crushed a cursing bard who whimpered from time to time in pain, but kept on his painful way, crawling along the wall.

Flaeros Delcamper was a bard of Aglirta, and wasn't going to miss any of this unless the gods themselves dragged him away. The factor's bloody fall gave him an idea. Struggling to a sitting position beside the dead man, Flaeros feigned a lapse into senselessness and called on the Vodal. The battered ring that never left his finger awakened into life, and through half-closed eyes he watched men die and shout and charge and hack—looking for those who were other than they outwardly seemed.

It did not take him long to find one. Baron Maerlin was not a brawny man in gleaming battle-plate, but a Priest of the Serpent with a scaled head, an air-licking forked tongue, and the beginnings of a tail! Moreover, he was murmuring something and pointing a scepter tipped with serpent-fangs at . . . the Baron Blackgult! A green shimmering was pulsing at one end of the scepter, and beginning to creep slowly along it. . . .

Before he thought about what he was doing, Flaeros Delcamper had drawn the slender sword his uncles had given him and surged upright, his shoulders scraping along the wall. Licking his lips, Flaeros steeled himself against the agony to come. He'd only have one chance to do this . . . and for all Aglirta's sake, it must be a chance not wasted.

Drawing in a deep, shuddering breath, Flaeros Delcamper took two agonized, staggering steps, his teeth clenched against the pain—and only let a roar of anguish escape his lips as he hacked down the Serpent-priest from behind, chopping the man's neck furiously until the hissing, scaled man fell. In agony, fresh fire flaring in his legs, Flaeros fell atop him, and wrestled the wand out of the priest's hand.

He was pounding it on the floor, trying to break it, when men came rushing at him out of the fray from all sides, blades extended to stab. Serpent-worshippers!

"Uncles," Flaeros snarled, "I died well. I died for Aglirta!"

But before those slim, dark blades could reach him, other men were pouncing on the warriors, driving them aside or running them through, and as Flaeros twisted desperately away from the priest he'd felled, he called on the Vodal to see who his rescuers were—and saw that they had no faces. He swallowed and kept on rolling.

Hands were still reaching for the scepter, though—but half a room away, Ezendor Blackgult saw, and smiled. A Dwaer flashed, and the scepter in the bard's hand caught fire, blazing up blinding white as Flaeros screamed and dropped it.

As the scion of the Delcampers crawled away in trampled agony, the scepter remained behind on the stones, too hot for any man to touch, let alone take up and wield.

The Baron of Blackgult waved a hand that trailed Dwaer-fire, and Flaeros Delcamper was suddenly blinking and trembling on his knees at the baron's feet. The man who stood in a ring of spiraling Dwaer said to Sarasper, "Heal him. Please."

The old man looked back at him for a silent moment and then turned and plucked a gewgaw from one of Embra's pouches, and bent to his work.

Embra stared at Blackgult, and then at the battle surging ever closer to them. Bards were hastening along the walls now, biting their lips, their faces white with fear, and some of them had drawn daggers in their hands. Their eyes were seeking Flaeros.

And then there was something new to see. More warriors were pushing through the door—men whose flesh dripped from their jawbones, frozen in grotesquerie. The Melted were come to war.

Among them strode a burly mage whose hair was like dirty straw, and whose eyes were gray ice, snapping incantations and orders venomously as he came. Corloun, Court Mage of Maerlin, gave Embra one triumphant smile as his eyes met hers—and ordered his Melted straight at her.

Like a fearless armored wedge they came, hacking and thrusting—and where determined men stood against them, a Melted would burst into grume and flying bone, taking that foe with him into oblivion.

As if Corloun's magic had been a signal, the room was suddenly alive with magic, Serpent-priests and hitherto-hidden mages chanting and stammering incantations furiously.

Flamespells severed stairs and sent them crashing down into the fray, men tumbling helplessly onto the heads of bards and Serpent-priests alike. But the shimmering spell-serpents that ate away flesh with each bite were almost all sent at the Melted or at the mage in their midst, and Corloun's wedge became a small, embattled ring—even before armaragors wearing the badge of Adeln began to stream in through the door behind them, and carve their own bloody path into the fray.

The floor was red and wet with gore and strewn with the fallen now, and still screaming warriors were spitted on blades, wizards shrieked spells but were chopped down with axes nonetheless, and terrified bards and factors dodged this way and that among the thrusting blades.

The Melted had been beaten to one side, and were grappling with many cowled, hissing Serpent-priests—and the armaragors of Adeln, like a great and gleaming arrowhead, striding forward with an armored giant in the lead, were heading straight for Baron Blackgult . . . and straight for the Band of Four.

"Gods," Craer gasped, as the giant of a man deftly struck aside the procurer's third hurled dagger. "Look at him!"

"Mine," Hawkril growled promptly, and strode forward, his face set.

Embra sent a quick burst of lightning past the nearly naked armaragor, but when it struck the armor of the Adelnan giant, it flared into a nimbus of cracklings—and then flashed back at her. Lady preserve, a defensive enchantment!

When the searing bolt struck and clawed at her, the Lady of Jewels threw back her head and screamed. As she reeled, limbs trembling, tiny lightnings spat raggedly from her mouth, nose, and even eyes, but Blackgult looked at her, Dwaer flashed—and she was healed before Sarasper could even lift a hand.

Embra moaned and swayed on her feet. Before bending her attention back on the battle, she stole a quick, sidelong glance at the man who claimed to be her father. Their eyes met, and she quickly looked away. After a moment, as if of its own accord, her hand lifted in a gesture of thanks. Blackgult smiled thinly when he saw it.

The leader of the Adelnan charge was larger than Hawkril, and the long spike-headed axe in his hand was longer and heavier than Anharu's warsword—but the King's Hero sprang to meet him almost eagerly. Scorning any wary circling or menacing posturing, the two men crashed together like angry bulls, shoving shoulder-to-shoulder and growling before their shared whirlwind of hacking and punching began.

Warriors of Adeln crowded forward on both sides of the battling men, blades held low and wide to stab and hamstring Hawkril, but Embra grimly sent them fire—and they fell back with shrieks as Blackgult waved a hand and the flames became a purple ring around the two hulking armaragors, flames that roared man-high and steadily widened their ring until it was pushing men back towards the walls. There it stopped, becoming almost transparent—but so hot as to melt slung stones and daggers hurled through it. Men soon stopped trying, and a stillness of sorts fell upon the room as everyone watched the two big men battle.

Sword strained against axe, locked together with the weight and strength of their wielders behind them, and there came a shriek of tortured steel as the weapons sawed slowly back and forth, a contest of brute force that stretched on until the arms of both men were trembling.

Then, suddenly, one of the barbs on the Adelnan axe broke, Hawkril's sword slipped, and the two men staggered apart.

A roar went up from the Adelnans peering through the flames—for where the arms of their champion were encased in blue-sheen battle armor, the arms of his foe were covered only in hair, sweat, and now a line of crimson. An axe-barb had opened a long, serpentine swordcut along one of Hawkril's forearms.

The champion of Adeln stalked forward, menacing now, with rising triumph written in his cold smile and a cruel light in his eyes. He meant to slay swiftly and stride on to seize the Dwaer, encased in armor that—he'd been told—was proof against all magics.

All he had to do was fell one near-naked man. A big man, to be sure, but only one . . . one who couldn't possibly know about his little treasure.

The champion of Adeln kicked a bootheel against the floor, and then took two running steps and kicked out hard with that foot. He liked to drive men up into the air with their guts impaled on the toe-blade his kick had just unleashed—but all he had to do was gash them somewhere, if they were fast enough to slip away, for his little treasure was smeared thickly with poison. This would be good, this would be—

Both men moved too fast for the watchers to see clearly, the one kicking upwards, and the other bounding high and hurling himself in desperation.

Hawkril launched himself face-first at the Adelnan, whose kick struck only empty air, an armored calf striking Hawkril's boots. By then, one solid Anharu fist had slammed home on an Adelnan gorget, crumpling it and leaving the man behind it wheezing and strangling for air, toppling over backwards.

It was unfortunate for the champion of Adeln that Hawkril had once visited the back-street shop in Sirlptar that sold boots with spring-forth toe-blades, fancied a pair himself, and knew very well what they looked like.

It was fortunate for Hawkril that he was sufficiently wary of a last, desperate kick to bound free and fling himself hard to the right, to roll and come up to his feet far from his foe—for somewhere in the crowd behind the flames stood a Sirl wizard who'd helped enchant the champion's armor, and was even then working a desperate spell. If the armaragor fell, all of the mages here could surely overwhelm the Silvertree lass . . . and what would be left of the vaunted Four then? An old man and a thief? *Hah*! Die, *warrior!*

The winking Dwaer now hovering behind Blackgult's shoulder was guarding Hawkril against spells, and so did nothing to stop the Sirl mage's spell. Its magic landed like a bright net, winked once—and the armor of the champion of Adeln exploded with a roar, shredding its wearer and hurling shards of battle-steel in all directions.

Craer leaped in front of Embra—too slowly, of course. Men howled as shrapnel skidded through the flames and bit into flesh here, there, and everywhere. Hawkril threw up his hands to protect his eyes—what, after all, were a few more gashes now?—there were high-pitched clangs and singings of metal wherever shrapnel glanced off plate or blade . . . and the Lady of Jewels cried out sharply as flying metal tore through her shoulder.

Reeling, she fell before Craer, Sarasper, or Blackgult could reach her.

The ring of flames, born of her magic, promptly faded—and with a hungry roar, the warriors of Adeln charged.

Baron Blackgult strode to meet them. As he went, he plucked one Stone from the air and thrust it into his codpiece for safekeeping, snatching the other two Dwaer into his hands a pace farther.

Before he'd finished his next step, blades of glowing light had sprouted from both Stones, shimmering in the air as if the baron was holding two drawn longswords. He wove lines of spell-light in the air as he met the onrushing warriors—and where charging man or slashing blade met those radiances, they were hurled back.

Hawkril raced in to stand beside the baron, and Craer sprang to his feet on Blackgult's other flank and began hurling daggers and leaping about like a madman, trying to keep the men of Adeln at bay.

Men were shouting and shoving again, all over the chamber. Priests of the Serpent were skulking forward along the walls, watched only by grim bards with drawn daggers in their hands—but out in the main fray, something seemed to be driving the men of Adeln on, striking at them from the rear. . . .

Craer peered, leaped high as he kicked a man in the face, and peered again on the way down. Yes! The Melted were hacking down Adelnan armaragors!

Blades rose and fell like threshing flails, close-packed men screamed and convulsed and died, some of them pinned so close together that it was minutes after they'd died before their bodies could topple, and the Adelnan ranks grew thinner and thinner . . . and more and more frantic.

Such was the fury of the warriors hacking at Hawkril—always at least three, no matter how many he sent to the floor dead or dying—that there came a time at last when five blades struck against his own at once.

There was a soft groan of metal, almost like the sound Embra made when sorely hurt, and the warsword that had served Hawkril so well for so long broke in three places, bright shards tumbling, and left him wielding a broken stump of a blade.

In an instant steel had scored thrice in or across the corded muscles of his midriff. With a roar of pain and fury, Hawkril punched aside the last blade to plunge into him and rushed in behind its bloody arc to grab its wielder around the middle. Lifting the kicking and twisting Adelnan warrior on high, the snarling armaragor hurled the man to the floor. The shivering crack of an Adelnan back breaking fell loudly into a momentary lull in the battle din, and then there came a roar from the men hearing it—a roar that broke off into stunned silence a moment later by an apparition.

In the air above Hawkril, a figure of glowing white light appeared, as if standing on an unseen podium. It was the ghostly image of the Risen King.

A Serpent hissed and his fingers writhed in Banishing magic, but the image ignored him. There were murmurs at that, and men started to push forward—but silence and stillness fell again when the voice of the king resounded in every head: "Blackgult, open your mind to me!"

The Baron Blackgult went to his knees. "Of course, Majesty," he said simply. Men stared, and saw him grow pale.

Silence stretched.

There was suddenly a sheen of sweat on Blackgult's calm face. It gathered into beads, and then became a dripping torrent.

Stillness deepened. The kneeling baron began to tremble, and his face worked in uncontrolled spasms.

"I—" he whispered, in the tense silence. "I am loyal."

Ezendor Blackgult's eyes closed, and he swayed. Men murmured, anticipating his fall.

Then the voice of the Risen King echoed through the chamber: "He speaks truth! Arise, Blackgult, as Regent of Aglirta!"

There came a gathering rumble of wordless discontent, awe, and fear from the men crowded into that room—and the Risen King's voice rose over all to quell it, rolling through heads until men winced and cowered under its thunder.

"Let there be no more strife among my barons and the warriors of Aglirta! Drive out the Serpent-spawn! Let the realm be scoured of all who'll not kneel to Regent Blackgult! Let them be cast out, part of Aglirta no more! *I have spoken!*"

By the time those last words rang back from the vaulting overhead like a thunderclap, everyone was on their knees, wincing or huddled to the floor with their hands clutching at their heads.

It was a long, numbed, warily-looking-around-and-blinking time before men rose and fumbled for their swords again—and as they did, three Dwaer spinning around a wolfishly smiling baron's head spat dark bolts of fell magic with whipcracks that made men wince and clutch at their ears again.

Dazed, the men in the chamber saw that the image of the king was gone—and where those three black bolts had stabbed, pillars of flame roared up to lick at the ceiling. Trapped men danced in dying agony in the heart of each: the mage Corloun, Baron Glarond, and the Tersept of Tarlagar. The tersept's body changed as he clawed vainly at the air and died—and men staring at it, contorted as it was, recognized the face of the mighty mage Tharlorn of the Thunders.

The pillars of flame suddenly collapsed and died away, the burning men within them falling away to ash—and amid a roar from scores of throats, the chamber erupted in bloodshed once more.

Bards stabbed at hissing Serpent-priests, who bit at some unarmored faces and thrust long knives into others. Men sought specific foes, seeking to settle old scores before the regent could restore order. Freed of Corloun's control, the Melted began to wander like dazed men, responding to no one but blundering everywhere, until one by one the disgusted and fearful cut them down.

It was only to be expected that, with no ghostly image of King Snowsar thundering overhead, men loyal to their barons would follow the hastily snapped orders of their masters—and try to slay the new regent before he could speak a single edict.

A hail of arrows, darts, hurled spears and blades descended on Blackgult, and warriors in plenty tried to charge in or hack from a distance . . . but the three Dwaer whirled around the head of the gently smiling baron, and nothing could penetrate the web they wove.

Sarasper dared to kneel down and put his hands on Hawkril and Embra, to heal—and Craer felt around for a fallen sword and put it into the bleeding armaragor's hand. Their eyes never left the battle.

Soon enough they saw what they'd feared: Serpent-priests and wizards stepping forward in ragged unison, spell-glows spinning in their cupped hands. Without a word of plotting or agreement, they were trying together what none of them could hope to do alone: breach the barrier of the Dwaer, so that someone could fell the Baron Blackgult.

As the glow of a dwindling statuette faded under his fingers and Embra made a faint, sleepy sound of relief under his other hand, Sarasper caught at Hawkril's arm and gestured. The armaragor in turn alerted Craer—and together they half-lifted, half-dragged the limp Lady of Jewels forward, to almost touch Blackgult's boots.

The baron looked down, saw what they were about, and stepped smoothly back a pace, so that the still-bleeding Embra lay in front of him, and the three men of the Four were clustered around his feet.

And that was when the endless flash and shudder of spells shattering against the woven magic of the three whirling Dwaer and being sucked away to nothingness ended in a searing rift of purple and white radiance—the work of a certain triumphant Sirl mage who'd seen his last attempt to shatter the Four fail—and a thrown sword whipped through that fleeting breach to bite deep into a baronial shoulder.

Ezendor Blackgult reeled and then sagged back, the Dwaer dimming and drawing close around him as they descended.

With another roar—exulting, this time—the remaining warriors surged forward. The men of the Four stood ready to meet them, above the sprawled bodies of the baron and his daughter.

As the first blades crossed, Craer traded quick glances with the old man on the other side of Hawkril and shouted, "No fangshape, Sass?"

"No time!" the reply came back, a moment before they both took nicks from the swords of foes who didn't quite dare to lean close enough to slay— and so be slain. Procurer and healer grunted and shuddered in unison, before Sarasper laughed suddenly.

"Happy?" Craer called to Sarasper in disbelief.

The old man laughed again.

"The realm hanging in the balance, hundreds of knights trying to hack me into bloody beef, and with good friends fighting at my side?" Sarasper called back. "There's no place I'd rather be!"

29

No Small Strife Unseen

The Risen King smiled a little frostily as the gleamingly armored knights of Loushoond crowded into the throne chamber. Their Lord strode at their head, and the handful of courtiers in attendance fell back to give them passage to the River Throne.

"Be welcome," the king said smoothly, as the Lord Baron Berias Loushoond ascended the dais with slow, deliberate steps, his face impassive. "I called you here today, my Lord of Loushoond, because of great peril to the realm, and—"

The baron had probably never moved so swiftly in his life before. His sword sang out and swung down in one smooth motion—to ring and shatter amid bright sparks against something unseen, a fingerwidth from an astonished royal face.

The Risen King fell back onto his throne. "Loushoond!" he snarled furiously. "It's me!" His face changed, eyes first, as the armored baron drew both of his daggers and rained down blows with them on the shield of magic that cloaked the king.

"It's me, Ingryl!" the man on the throne snarled, and it was: Ingryl Ambelter sat in the royal armor. "Stop this!" he hissed. "You fool, can't you—"

Berias Loushoond redoubled his efforts, his daggers ringing like bells in a whirlwind of stabs and cuts that harmed only enchanted air, as his eyes burned into the Spellmaster's own, and he growled through clenched teeth, "I know . . . quite well . . . who you are!"

There came a brighter flash as tortured magic failed—and a dagger, plunging home at last, bit into the wizard's cheek as Ingryl twisted desperately away.

The wizard flung up a hand to shield his face—and from it poured forth fire, in a raging storm that swallowed the armored baron, and went on and on, as Ingryl Ambelter slowly stood, his face white with fury. Still the fire streamed, until melting armor plates fell clanging to the floor, and the flesh beneath them bubbled away from blackening bones . . . and the Lord Baron Berias Loushoond was no more.

Ingryl Ambelter straightened slowly, and let smoking hands drop to his sides. He glared down with glittering eyes at the armaragors of Loushoond standing silent before him, and snarled, "Anyone *else?*"

His answer was a stirring of steel as every last knight silently drew his sword . . . and then they were charging up the steps as one, blades sweeping up to hack.

"Back!" the wizard roared, sending forth little spinning balls of flame as light flared around his limbs. He struggled to rebuild his shield—courtiers shouting and shrieking in the distance—as the blades came for him, striking like a wall of spiked steel.

In an instant he was cut thrice, and more, and as swordpoints he could not hope to avoid slid at him like striking snakes, Ingryl Ambelter shouted a desperate word—and snatched his new body elsewhere, leaving blades and an empty crown to crash down on the throne he'd risen from, moments before.

Blades struck against blades and faltered. Cursing, the warriors of Loushoond let their swords fall. One of them took up the fallen crown, looked at it wonderingly, and was about to toss it down onto the River Throne when the warrior beside it plucked it out of his hands.

An armored hand settled the crown over a helm, and its wearer turned grandly and announced, "Hearken! I, Riovryn, am now King of all Aglirta! Let—"

His next word was lost in a wet groan, as the sword that had plunged through the gap in Riovryn's mail, under his arm, slid back out again.

"There'll be no more of that," his slayer growled, catching up the crown on a bloody swordtip as the body toppled, and setting it, alone, on the seat of the empty throne.

"Let it sit there and await a rightful ruler."

From the warriors around came a low, nodding rumble of assent.

"I doubt Embra Silvertree will be all that happy a lass, by nightfall," the Tersept of Gilth remarked to the Tersept of Sart, as they stared together at the ragged opening in the southernmost sweep of the west wall of the Silent House.

A mage had made it, not all that long ago, with a spell whose deadly shearing force had made the more restive of the warriors waiting tensely outside the ruined palace fall grim and silent for a time. No one wanted to be obliberated in an instant—or, as that same smiling wizard had done to one armaragor who menaced him a trifle too crudely, lose an arm and a leg on the same side of one's body, sheared off and cauterized in the same horrifying instant by a spell called up with a casual wave of one wizardly hand.

Hot in their armor, the fighting men had traded hard stares with each other and flicked away swarming flies and waited . . . and waited. Now at long last it seemed that something had happened inside the Silent House—something that had shaken the ground briefly, made a terrible echoing din inside, and caused at least one spell to fail: the unseen barrier that the wizard who'd blasted the new entrance had raised, after he'd stepped within, to seal it off from the small armies waiting impatiently outside.

The Tersept of Sart turned his head sharply to stare at a warrior who was gingerly stepping forward into the hole. Long moments later, the man reappeared, and beckoned his fellows—whereupon someone let go with a sling and felled the warrior, and swords flashed out all over the hillside.

"Defend yourselves," the Smiling Wolf roared to his men, "but stand together! No fighting off in this direction or that—stand as one!"

The Tersept of Gilth gave him a cool look. "I did not hear you confer with me before uttering that order," he said thinly.

"No, and you're not going to, either!" Glarsimber Belklarravus snarled, thrusting his face close to that of his ally. "This is war, and I'm not dying or seeing my men cut up around me because of anyone's pride, see? When it's time to talk and deal, I'll defer to you. Out here, with swords and men dying and such unpleasantness, *you* defer to *me*."

Battle had erupted in earnest around the breach in the wall. The Wolf of Sart watched warriors hack and struggle for a few moments more, and then stood up in his stirrups and shouted, "To yonder way! *Charge!*"

The Tersept of Gilth was still sputtering in indignation and fear when the hired armaragors rose up around him and swept up the hill, galloping with enthusiasm and swinging their long blades at anything that got in the way.

They struck the knots of struggling warriors like a giant's fist, hurling men aside and trampling those who couldn't or wouldn't give way swiftly enough. In the space of a few swift breaths the two tersepts were swinging down from their saddles, as abandoned mounts reared and ran in confusion all around them, and horses briefly commanded the breach in the wall of the Silent House. And then they were inside, in sudden gloom, slipping in blood and stepping over sprawled bodies, their blades ready.

Ahead, there was shouting, and men running with swords, and confused hackings and stabbings. Men sobbed as they crashed into walls, metal armor shrieking, and grunted or screamed as they took wounds—or died.

Sart slipped in sticky blood, chopped with brisk efficiency at a snarling warrior who appeared out of nowhere to sword him, and then burst out into a wider way—a passage crowded with the dead and dying, where a few of their hired armaragors were wading uncertainly towards a door.

"Here?" the Wolf of Sart snapped.

"Whence they came, Lord," one of the hireswords replied calmly, "and where they fled back again through."

Sart nodded and waved one heavy-gauntleted hand. "Lead on then!" He looked back once, more to make sure Gilth wasn't gathering himself to sink a sword into the back of a certain Wolf than for any other reason, and then plunged through the door into a cross-passage, over more bodies, and into another passage strewn with more battle dead and the splintered remnants of a litter. There was an open doorway across that passage, and the shout and clang of battle was coming out of it.

Glarsimber Belklarravus looked at his hireswords and waved his hand imperiously at the doorway. Faces impassive, the armaragors looked back, and stayed where they were.

The Wolf shook his head in disgust and strode through the door, not bothering to look back and see if anyone followed.

He was looking into a huge, high-vaulted chamber, choked with rubble and sprawled bodies. A pillar had cracked and fallen—recently, by the looks of things—and stairs had broken away from balconies here and there, some of which still sprouted a crop of watching men.

They were looking at a battle going on at the heart of the chamber—where an old man was grimly holding a Dwaer in his shaking hands, flanked by a hulking armaragor and a slim, snake-swift procurer, and using its mage-fires to hold back armaragors of several baronies, while other Dwaer-Stones circled above them. Along the walls of the chamber, amid many dead and groaning dying, what looked to be minstrels grappled with and stabbed Serpent-priests, who fought back viciously.

The Smiling Wolf of Sart strode nearer, his sword ready, and saw a wounded man struggling up from his knees. Baron Blackgult, by the Three!

More than that—the Lady of Jewels was lying bleeding at his feet, and so the rogues around him must be the Band of Four.

Even as Belklarravus of Sart peered, a Serpent-priest snarled something desperate. Glows of magic promptly appeared around a close-helmed, armored warrior who'd been standing slumped against one wall of the chamber. The magic ran like fire along burly limbs, and the warrior stiffened, tottered forward—and screamed.

Heads turned in time to see, and gasp, and swear. With frantic hands the shuddering warrior tore away his helm and gorget. He seemed almost to pulse, and grow with each flicker of magic, and ragged cries of pain came from his throat.

He *was* growing taller, and broader, too, as armor bulged and snapped and sang its way from his thickening limbs, springing away from blood-soaked underpadding and leathers that themselves were groaning under the strain. Through the twisting that pain brought to the warrior's revealed face, Sart recognized those features.

It was Ornentar, the baron widely rumored to be captive to the Serpent's venom. Looking at foam now coming from between—were those fangs?—lips in a mouth that was wider than it should have been, in a purpling face, with the skin below that gone blue with veins throbbing all over it, Sart could well believe the tales of poisonings and dark Serpent magic.

Wailing, his eyes wide with horror, Baron Ornentar was growing into some sort of monster before their eyes. Wavering upwards like an erect snake, his arms dwindling to boneless streamers, scales racing all over his mottled and thickening body now, as the last of his armor and garments fell away in shards around legs that had become the restless coils of a giant snake.

Serpent-priests were chanting something triumphant all over the chamber, something hissing and in unison, as the last humanity slipped away from Eldagh Ornentar's face and it lengthened into a serpent's snout . . . and his last, despairing cry of "NnnnoodooooOOOO!" became a wet, burbling hiss.

"Divine creature!" the Serpent-priest who'd cast the spell shouted. "Heed me!" Even before the strange, hissing words that followed had finished streaming forth, Sart—like many other men in the chamber—had hurled a dagger at the priest. The man went down under a hail of biting steel, clawing at the air as if it would shield him, but the monstrous serpent no longer seemed to need him.

Rearing up almost to the cracked and sundered ceiling, it swooped at the struggling fray in front of the pillar—and opened its jaws, fangs gaping wide as men cowered away, as that terrible head came down.

Biting air, not men, and snapping up—the Dwaer!

The old man holding the third Stone staggered and fell, still holding on to it, as the great serpent reared up again, tall and dark and terrible, with two of the Dwaerindim in its gullet.

"Gods above, it's doom for us all now!" a young voice gasped nearby, and Belklarravus of Sart could not find fault with that judgement.

The serpent looked down at them all, with triumph glittering in its eyes—and opened its jaws almost in a yawn, fangs as tall as men gleaming, as it turned to survey the chamber, as if deciding whom to devour first.

And then, as if night had come early, the very air in the room dimmed, and the look on the face of the serpent somehow changed.

Two lazily circling stones suddenly kindled like twin lamps, as if the serpent around them were transparent—and then blazed up into blinding brightness.

And the serpent exploded with a roar.

Hot black-and-green gore drenched the chamber, spattering down walls and sobbing men, and the headless serpent body writhed and then cracked like a whip, smashing men to pulp against the walls as it thrashed.

Sart turned to run, boots slipping in the gore—but where to run to? The dark, nightmare coils swept everywhere, thrashing and thundering against the walls with bone-shattering force, and men and the torn remnants of what had been men were hurled through the air like clods of dirt flung by a vigorous shovel.

Then, slowly, the scales became smoke, and the great body dwindled, and frantic gore-soaked men were grimly dragging down the last few fleeing Serpent-priests . . . and Belklarravus of Sart could breathe again.

Enough to utter a startled shout, as bare hands snatched his sword out of his grasp and hurled it, bright and spinning, across the room. The young man who'd gasped about doom moments ago ran after it, half-naked and slender, and the Wolf of Sart charged after him, too astonished to be angry.

The boy had flung the sword to strike down a warrior attacking the Band of Four. Even as Sart peered again at that fray, a snarling Craer slipped, and four warriors charged in over him, heedless of their own safety, to put their steel through Hawkril.

The armaragor's sword swept through the throat of one, and struck the blade out of the numbed hand of a second, but the fury of their onslaught bore him off his feet, and other warriors surged forward. A young boy snatched bare-handed at them from behind, spinning at least one off his feet. Belklarravus of Sart smashed into another, even as a backhand slash sent Raulin Castlecloaks reeling. He sat down hard on Embra Silvertree.

"They'll kill Hawk!" she gasped, spitting blood weakly, trying feebly to claw her way to her feet.

Above her, a deep voice laughed. "Oh, no, they won't!" Baron Black-gult said merrily, as Dwaer-fire lashed down to heal him and raced up again to the circling stone orbs above—and the third Dwaer sprang up out of Sarasper's hand to rejoin them.

"Hah!" the baron cried. The Stones suddenly blazed up in a quickening whirl overhead—and the air was suddenly shining around Hawkril, a shield of shimmering nothingness that moved with him, forcing swordtips away.

Another shield appeared around Blackgult himself, like a cylinder of hard air, and then others sprang into being around Embra, Raulin, Sarasper, and Craer—hurling Belklarravus of Sart back.

The Silvertree sorceress gasped as her wounds began to close. She closed her eyes briefly and gave in to her need to shudder, as grunts around her told her Hawkril and Craer were feeling the same relief. And then, heavily, silence fell.

Embra opened her eyes, to find the man who claimed to be her father standing beside her. He was smiling, his hands on his hips, as he looked at the warriors who'd been trying to slay him—now drawn back from him uncertainly, staring in grim silence.

"I've waited a long time for this," Blackgult announced to the silent room. "A long, long time." He raised his hands suddenly above his head, like a wizard about to strike, and his eyes were dark and terrible.

The men who'd not yet found their deaths in that chamber cowered back, awaiting their doom. The Dwaer circled, bright and menacing, above the baron.

And then, within the shimmering that shielded him, the body of the Baron Blackgult changed, flowing and slumping and shifting eerily, as men gasped in amazement . . . and even the Four fell back.

They were no longer looking at Ezendor Blackgult, the Golden Griffon. They were staring, dumbfounded, at old and smiling Inderos Stormharp, perhaps the greatest of living bards. His long fingers moved in gestures that said "spellcasting" to every mage who watched, and there was suddenly a harp in them.

"Three above," the Wolf of Sart gasped hoarsely, and his was not the only throat to give the room an oath in that moment.

Stormharp smiled at them all, turning his head to look briefly into the wondering eyes of Embra Silvertree, and then—in the voice they'd all heard last coming from the lips of the Baron Blackgult—announced calmly, "This calls for a ballad to resound down the years. Down steel, all, and hearken, then. . . ."

.   .   .

In this dell high above the river, a little oval of shrubs and stormgrass high above the Vale, boulders as old as the baronies stood like teeth out of the rough sward. Birds called and whirred, butterflies beat and swooped—and of a sudden there came a shimmering in the air by one rock. The shimmering grew larger and darker, seeming to slow, spin, and then slow again, shot through with silver—before suddenly it was gone, and a man stood blinking and swaying in its space.

Ingryl Ambelter looked all around, smiled a little, and then lifted his head into the breeze, looked to the mountainside rising behind him, and took a few slow steps, leaving bloody bootprints in his wake. Gods, the pain! Oh, by the Serpent that sleeps not, when he was himself again . . .

Yes, now the desolation looked more familiar! What he sought would be right—here.

He plunged his hand into a tangle of stones, turned it so as to reach in under the protruding edge of a boulder as large as a cottage, and found what he sought. The Spellmaster drew it carefully forth: a tarnished handle attached to a mold-spotted metal coffer. It was latched with a slide that could be made to work even when brown with rust, and he demonstrated this, sighing with relief as the healing magics were revealed.

After the third muttered incantation, he felt much better . . . but the world still insisted on whirling, so he laid himself down on the ground, or fell.

The light had changed when he blinked up at the sky and knew where he was again. He must have been lying here for hours. Still, thank the Three, the pain was all gone. Now to—

Grass rustled, and Ingryl raised himself hastily on one elbow and felt for the wand at his belt. A man shouldered past leaves, shuffling clumsily—and at the first sight of his drooping, disfigured face the wizard relaxed.

Ingryl smiled as the first Melted stepped into the hollow, followed by another . . . and another, to stand blank-faced before him.

His smile broadened. "So it worked." He pointed. "Pick up yonder log." The Melted turned as one to obey, and the wizard chuckled.

"Now, where did Tharlorn hide the way into his lair, I wonder?" he asked the air aloud. There were more rustlings, and he turned to watch a dozen more Melted trudging into his dell.

"Ah, well," he told the uncaring sky, "I've certainly victims enough, now, to find all his traps. . . ."

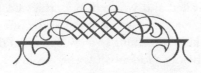

30

Thrones and Overdukes and More

*C*rowded now with all the mighty of the realm, the throne chamber looked a different place. Even the echoes were different. Armaragors and Flowfoam guards and bards stood shoulder-to-shoulder along the walls, and folk of rank crowded the benches—the surviving barons and tersepts stone-faced and full-armored in the front rows.

All save one. The Baron Blackgult, gleaming in the black plate armor that too many of those in the front row had seen on bloody fields of battle in years past, stood facing them all at the foot of the throne dais, with his arms folded across his chest and three fabled Dwaer-Stones circling almost lazily about his shoulders. His drawn sword was in his hands, and the faintest of smiles was lurking at one corner of his mouth.

From his armored boots a carpet of blue edged with silver stretched back to the doors of the chamber, flanked at the end of each bench with tall candlestands. Talk in the chamber had begun as murmurings, and slowly died away, until now all that remained was tense, watchful silence.

All eyes were on that dark figure, standing below the empty River Throne, yet very few of them saw the faint nod he gave the guards down the swordblade of the empty central aisle. They obeyed, shutting the doors with a boom, and trumpeters beside the doors blew a fanfare as the doorguards went down the aisle, blowing candles to dim the lofty chamber, until only the flickering clusters of candles on the dais remained alight.

The fanfare quavered to a last note that held and then faded—and in the moment of its dying, the Risen King quietly appeared on his throne.

There was a momentary gasp, and then heavier silence. King Kelgrael had faded into view from otherwhere, a ghostly, translucent figure of flickering magics; every eye could see the River Throne through him. Yet he looked back at them, turning his head to regard this courtier and that baron, as if he was truly present—and when he spoke, his voice was as deep and as firm as ever.

"Aglirtans all, bear witness to this my recoronation. I, Kelgrael Snowsar, being Master of the River and Its Vale, do now require of my barons and tersepts their sworn allegiance. Let each one I name and summon approach, and lay his sword upon the lowest step, there to kneel by it and swear his loyalty to me for all to hear."

There was a moment of tight silence, and then the wraith of the Risen King said abruptly, "Adeln."

No one stood forth, and after a moment Blackgult said over his shoulder, "I slew him, Majesty."

Another moment of murmuring, swiftly hushed. Impassively the king named the next baron. "Blackgult."

Ezendor Blackgult turned and set down his sword, kneeling beside it and saying, "Lord of Aglirta, I am here."

"Do you swear upon your sword and life to obey my royal commands absolutely, faithfully, and before all other desires and compulsions?"

"Kelgrael Snowsar, I do, as Ezendor is my name and Blackgult my barony." The words were as old as Aglirta, but all but one in the room—if he *was* truly in the room—had only heard bards say them before.

"Will you also so serve any regent or officer who bears my writ and speaks in my name?"

"Lord of Aglirta, I will."

"Will you uphold my laws as your own, and defend, keep, and cherish Aglirta as I would?"

"Majesty, I will."

"Then I accept your loyalty and name you my Baron of Blackgult. Rise, Ezendor, and take up your sword."

The Golden Griffon bowed his head to the dais, kissed its topmost step, and took up his sword, rising and returning smoothly to his former stance.

"Brightpennant," the king said next. There was a moment of silence, and then the royal lips said calmly, "Glarsimber Belklarravus of Sart but of Sart no more, stand forth!"

Blinking with astonishment, the Smiling Wolf of Sart rose from his seat on the second row of benches, clearing his throat nervously.

"Will you be my Baron of Brightpennant?"

"I—uh—ahem, Majesty, I will," the Wolf of Sart stammered, not quite knowing how it was that he'd been even noticed at Flowfoam.

"Then stand forth here to the steps, and bring your sword!"

There was a murmur of mirth at those words, a ripple that held a note of excitement. New men would be named here today! And so it was, as the Risen King summoned all of the barons to him, one by one, reserving some now-empty titles and naming tersepts to others. No baron refused to swear, or offered violence or disrespect . . . but then, many silences stood to show them the fates of those who had. Two bewildered tersepts rose as the new Barons of Phelinndar and Tarlagar, amid much murmuring and muttering from the assembled, before Snowsar began the long list of tersepts.

One barony was not named, as the hours passed: Silvertree. But all men there knew that Silvertree had claimed Flowfoam Isle, and ruled from this very castle . . . and all men there had feared and hated Faerod Silvertree. Wherefore it came as a surprise, when the last tersept returned to his seat, for the king to say firmly, "Silvertree."

Silence fell. No one moved or spoke. The king cast his gaze down the aisle, but no one came forward for Silvertree.

Kelgrael Snowsar shifted on his throne and murmured, "Lady Embra, to me."

A large but gentle hand nudged Embra Silvertree's armored hip, where the Band of Four stood together in the shadows at the back of the hall, and its owner growled, "Go, lass."

She gave Hawkril a look, bit her lip for a moment, and then, reluctantly, the Lady of Jewels—clad in armor, and with a long, slender sword at her hip—slipped out from among the doorguards, strode silently down the aisle as heads turned to stare all over the room, knelt, and laid her sword at the feet of the Risen King.

"Rise, Embra Silvertree," the king said, "and approach the throne."

Hesitantly the slender sorceress did so. When she stood near the flickering figure, Kelgrael Snowsar turned his face up to her and asked, "If I asked you, most brave of ladies, for your hand in marriage, to rule Aglirta at my side . . . what would you say to me?"

There came a gasp—in some cases almost a shriek—from a hundred throats, and every eye stared at the Lady Silvertree, standing tall and alone. Not a few of those eyes were filled with dismay or even horror. Among those who looked less stricken was Raulin Castlecloaks, standing in his accustomed spot along the wall . . . white-faced and trembling with excitement.

At least one other person in that chamber was white-faced and trembling too. She was obviously astonished, and Embra Silvertree swallowed several times before she managed to whisper, "F-Forgive me, Majesty, but I would be forced to refuse you. I—"

Her head turned for a moment towards Hawkril Anharu, standing like a patient giant back by the doors, his face anxious and yet as sternly expressionless as he could make it, and she added, "I have already chosen."

Though she whispered, her every word could be heard clearly to the very back of that still, silent chamber. The king bowed his head to her calmly, smiled, and said, "And I would honor you for your choice. I suspected as much. Stand down, Lady, and be rightful Lady Baron over Silvertree still."

Embra bowed her head and backed from the dais, eyes downcast. *Gods above, what have I done?*

A black-armored arm reached out to her, and drew her smoothly around. "Take up your sword and stand with me," Baron Blackgult, the man who claimed to be her father, murmured out of the side of his mouth. Numbly, trying not to tremble with fear for the realm and for herself, Embra did so. As she took her stance beside Blackgult at the head of the aisle, their drawn swords in their hands, the Dwaer drifted out in smooth arcs to circle around them both.

"Hear then my will, loyal subjects of Aglirta," the Risen King intoned, as calmly as if nothing had happened that morn beyond his rising and sipping of something pleasant. "I shall not now return to Aglirta, and instead keep bound the darksome Serpent for time to come. Blackgult shall rule as regent in my stead, and as Lord Marshal of the Realm. He alone is allowed to assemble in arms more than a baronial bodyguard of sixty warriors. His shall be the tongue and hand that guide fair Aglirta, and all barons shall bow to his will. He can make barons and tersepts—and unmake them. Four persons only shall be free of his commands, so long as they keep the laws of the realm—four Overdukes of Aglirta, whom I hereby confirm in their powers: to judge and apply royal law as the regent does, to command warriors with authority equal to his own, and to demand funds, shelter, food, and aid as he does. These four are Hawkril Anharu, Craer Delnbone, Sarasper Codelmer, and Embra Silvertree. They stand here among us; mark them well—and obey them as you would me."

The wraithlike figure on the throne began to fade. "Fare you well, folk of Aglirta. Make this land strong and proud once more, sparing hatreds for outlanders, outlaws, and those who consort with serpents. Live in peace with Sirlptar, and stretch forth no hand to seize it nor islands elsewhere nor any other territory; instead, turn your hands to making what we have ever more splendid. Forget not these my words, lest red war and dark magic return."

And at the end of those words, the Risen King simply—vanished.

There was a long moment of astonished silence, and then one excited murmur broke forth, and—as if it had been a dam, holding back a river-flood—voices were raised excitedly, all over the chamber.

Blackgult turned his head and hissed urgent words to Embra, and together they worked magic—a swift spell so strong that the three Dwaerindim dimmed momentarily.

Then the new Regent of Aglirta smiled, ascended the dais until he stood beside the throne, and called, "Barons of the realm, to me!"

Looking down from beside the River Throne, Blackgult saw struggles here and there in the crowd, and fists flying. He smiled a little sadly, and added, "I see some of you have already discovered that blades drawn here will draw no blood, but pass through flesh as if it is smoke, doing no harm. This is not a time for deaths and settling scores; we all begin anew here this day. Barons, to me! Overdukes too, if you'd be so good as to humor me with one small act of obedience?"

As the few armored figures approached and ascended the steps, the Dwaer above the regent's head began to shine more brightly, until they were like golden stars. Blackgult glanced up at them, puzzlement clear on his face, and then looked around the huddle of anxious baronial faces, saw both anger and fear in them, and muttered, "I've no desire to become a tyrant. All of you, go home and set your baronies in order. Offer no violence to my heralds when they come; they report to me, aye, but they'd rather hear your frank complaints and requests than a lot of sugared nothing-words. If you plot and conspire against each other, or trade with the Serpents, I'll simply close your borders to the rest of Aglirta until your own people tear you apart. Tell me as fast as you can send word of strange magic or stranger mages, and Serpent-worship, and aid shall be sent. Overdukes, will you be my heralds?"

"If you can find us," Craer said carelessly. "We prefer adventuring."

One of the barons gasped at this rudeness, but Blackgult merely smiled and shook his head in appreciative envy. "Go then," he chuckled. "You've earned that, and more."

The regent looked around the faces of the barons again, and added, "One last thing. Watch around you always for faceless men—the Koglaur who can change their features as swiftly as a lady dons a new gown. Offer them no violence, for they seem to guard Aglirta as dearly as our king, but try to know of their presence, lest you need warn them of something—or warn us of them."

Then he grinned suddenly and asked, "Heard enough, Flaeros?"

The flower of the Delcampers had been standing silent and goggle-eyed, part of the ring, having wormed his way into the group with a deftness more worthy of a procurer than a bard. He now blushed deeply, and started to stammer a reply, but the baron next to him reached out angrily and took him by the throat.

Hawkril Anharu took that baronial wrist in a grip of iron and said softly to its owner, "Good rulers keep a minimum of secrets from their subjects. Think: your people will draw comfort from truly knowing what words passed here, out of their hearing."

There were slow and reluctant murmurs of agreement from around the ring—before all the barons looked to the regent for his reaction. Blackgult smiled slowly, and said to the armaragor who towered over them all, "My thanks, good Hawk. You're right, and I was not."

Embra deliberately reached up then, her eyes on his, and took her Dwaer out of the air. She knew it was the one she'd borne without even looking at it.

Blackgult's eyes narrowed, his brows drew together darkly—and then he shrugged and waved at her to keep it. "Go, now," he told the Four, "and rule. We've a kingdom to rebuild."

Together the Band of Four strode down the long carpet, and the guards threw open the doors before them. As one, they turned for a last look back at the River Throne, and the black-armored man standing beside it.

As the Golden Griffon raised his hand to give the new Overdukes of Aglirta a salute, the face of a doorguard slid into smooth flesh for a brief moment, faceless except for a wry grin. The Koglaur were watching—as they always did.

Epilogue

oonlight was bright white and silver as it fell upon the River Throne—an empty chair now, standing still and silent in the room that held only three kneeling, scrubbing maids, several splendidly armored guards . . . and one dark-eyed young man.

As Raulin Castlecloaks gazed at the place where the Risen King had sat and the tall, dark Baron Blackgult had stood, unshed tears glimmered in his eyes. He barely saw the squat armored bulk moving to stand before him.

"Lad, 'twas wondrous to see, aye," the guard growled, "but it's time and past time for you to go. We'll be barring the doors now. Go and get some sleep. Aglirta will need strong younglings like you, in the years ahead. There's much to be done yet, regents and overdukes or none."

"Yes," Raulin replied quietly, turning to follow the guard's pointing arm and go out by the doors. "They said the same to me, too."

" 'They,' lad?"

"Hawk and Craer, and the Lady Embra. And sad old Sarasper. The—the overdukes. They said I'd be needed . . . all too soon."

"Sure they did, lad," the guard said, gentle disbelief clear in his tone. "Sure they did. You've been looking a little too long at the moonlight, you have, dreaming of being a hero."

Raulin turned back, outside the doors, and drew himself up, slender and tall. "I know," he replied with dignity, "but that's what bards do."

He turned on his heel and walked away, down the Inner Court. The guard shook his head, smiled, and reached for the door.

Ilibar Quelver was getting old, but not slow, and he was almost too swift in closing the portal to see it: from out of nothingness, in the darkest part of the hall, ghostly light shimmered . . . and became the Risen King, raising his hand in salute.

The boy went to his knees on the tiles—and as the guard gaped, King Kelgrael shook his head, smiled, and faded away. The boy rose with as much dignity as if he'd been knighted, and strode on.

That end of the Inner Court was dark, but moonlight from nowhere shone about the lad's head and shoulders, and old Quelver stood with his hand on the door and a cold prickling running through him, and did his best to remember and whisper aloud every last prayer to the Three that he'd ever heard.

Moonlight was bright white and silver as it fell on the Wildrocks—and, in a particular high hollow above what was now Brightpennant again, upon four bare bodies.

The Band of Four lay beside their dying fire, and felt no chill from the night breezes, thanks to the Dwaer.

It floated, as ugly and nondescript as ever, in the air above Embra's breast, flickering as it wove protective wards around them, driven by her will. With one fingertip the sorceress beneath it was wonderingly tracing the angry red half-healed line that snaked along Hawkril's forearm, as they lay together on one side of the fire, with Craer and Sarasper on the other.

Suddenly Embra sat up. The three men stiffened, reaching hastily for the swords that were never far from their hands. "What is it?" Craer hissed.

"The Dwaer shone like stars, too bright to look at, as Bla—as my father summoned us all to gather!" the Lady of Jewels murmured almost fiercely. "Remember?"

"Aye," Hawkril rumbled, as the others nodded. "We all saw it. . . . What of it?"

"They can only do that," Embra told them in a voice barely more than a whisper, "when all four Dwaerindim are very close together—little more than a few paces apart."

None of her companions was slow-witted. "So the fourth Stone is held by someone now among the Barons of the realm . . . and held in secret," Sarasper said into the sudden darkness, as a swift-scudding cloud covered the moon.

"But who?" Craer asked the night.

Somehow, they could all hear Hawkril shrug before he spoke. "Whoever he is, our royal mission remains unfinished. We start looking for him in the morning."

Craer and Sarasper heard Embra's disgusted groan and the playful slap she gave the armaragor at her side, but Hawkril could act in uncanny silence when he needed to; they heard nothing of his reaction until the Lady of Jewels gave a low, delighted gasp that became a chuckle, and then sank back into being a gasp again.

"So, healer," Craer remarked conversationally to the glittering stars, "did I ever tell you about the time I unintentionally stole someone's left boot in Sirlptar? He's probably got mine, and may still be tracing me by it, for all I know . . ."

"No, Most Exalted Overduke Delnbone," Sarasper replied with bright heartiness, as the moon came out again, and they heard a growl and a stifled laugh from the other side of the fire, "I don't believe you did . . ."

Dramatis Personae

ADELN, ESCULPH: Baron (Lord) of Adeln, a handsome, ruthless and unprincipled ruler of a wealthy barony that boasts a large army; an enthusiastic conspirator against the Risen King.

AMARANDUS the Lion: the dramatic and talkative leader of the Bright Blade and Hope of Aglirta adventuring band; a warrior possessed of a rich, mellifluous voice and a striking black spade beard.

AMBELTER, INGRYL: Spellmaster of Silvertree and strongest wizard of the Three (the Dark Three), the unscrupulous, evil mages who served Baron Faerod Silvertree; ambitious, shrewd in the ways of life and politics in the Vale, he's a creative and very powerful spellweaver; though slain in *The Kingless Land,* he seems to have found a way to live on, beyond death.

ANDALUS of Sirl: "the Fang," an infamous slayer-for-hire killed by his rival "Velvetfoot" Luthtuth; known for wearing a grinning "battle ghost" feast-mask while working (battle ghosts are the vengeful spirits of jovial warriors slain on the battlefield with tasks left undone; they haunt and goad the living in many plays of Darsar, always with dark humor).

ANHARU, HAWKRIL: "the Boar of Blackgult," an armaragor (unranked battle knight) in the service of the Baron Blackgult, whom he was once personal bodyguard to; a man of unusually large build and strength; member of the Band of Four and longtime friend and sword-companion of Craer Delnbone, who often calls him "Tall Post."

BAERETHOS, YAULN: an old, incompetent wizard of Cardassa, sage (advisor) to the Baron; a sharp-tongued, fussy old man, and a bitter rival of Ubunter.

BAERGIN: The Delcamper House Minstrel, sometime harp tutor of Flaeros Delcamper–and Serpent agent.

BAERUND, ILISKER: Tersept (non-noble ruler) of the fallen barony of Tarlagar, now much recovered in importance and prosperity; a ruthless, bold man who few know is an accomplished wizard, and who has no hesitation in conspiring against the Risen King; note that the last appearance of "the Tersept of Tarlagar" in *The Vacant Throne* is a magical disguise assumed by the wizard Tharlorn of the Thunders.

Band of Four, the: our heroes, the King's Heroes, the Awakeners of the Risen King; an independent band of four adventurers thrown together in *The Kingless Land* (see Anharu, Hawkril; Codelmer, Sarasper; Delnbone, Craer; and Silvertree, Embra), whose adventures bid fair to change the face of Aglirta.

BELKLARRAVUS, GLARSIMBER: Tersept (non-noble ruler) of Sart (an independent town formerly in the barony of Brightpennant); a stout, brawny warrior going to fat, but still infamous from his days as a mercenary war captain, "the Smiling Wolf of Sart"; longtime rival of Daragus of Gilth.

BLACKGULT, EZENDOR: Baron (Lord) of Blackgult, known as the Golden Griffon for his heraldic badge, rival to Faerod Silvertree for rule of Aglirta and leader of a disastrous attack on (planned conquering of) the Isles of Ieirembor just prior to *The Kingless Land,* which resulted in the seizure of his lands by Silvertree, and his warriors (including Craer and Hawkril of the Four) all being declared outlaw; a sophisticated, intelligent warrior and aesthete, Blackgult dabbled in spellcraft and collected many enchanted items, using their powers to wear another shape, wherein, as the seldom-seen bard Inderos Stormharp, Master Bard of Darsar, he's become famous as the greatest living bard of Asmarand, if not all Darsar.

BOWDRAGON, CATHALEIRA: sorceress and lover of Tharlorn of the Thunders (who called her "Cathlass"), the eldest, most skilled, and only female of his three young, eager, utterly loyal apprentices; ambitious, deeply in love with Tharlorn, and accomplished in magecraft, of a family (the Bowdragons of Arlund) known for its sorcery.

BRITHRA: cook to, and sometime lover of, the wizard Bodemmon Sarr; a dark, quiet, calm, loyal, and capable woman purchased by him as a slave, and later freed into his service after his spells determined her loyalty.

BROSTOS, MAEGLA: Dowager-Baroness of Brostos, the recently deceased mother of Thanglar Brostos; an iron-willed, unlovely, deep-voiced, and prominently jowled woman (once unkindly described as "a barking dog that walks") who was the architect of most of the treaties, contracts, and agreements that have enriched Brostos (after the death of her husband, the Baron Thorlyn Brostos).

BROSTOS, THANGLAR: Baron (Lord) of Brostos, a coward when endangered, but otherwise a coldly efficient merchant trader and tax collector, ruler of one of the most prosperous baronies of all; a man with unruly black hair, a luxurious and fashionable wardrobe, and piercing brown eyes; gone to fat and increasingly fearful as Aglirta drifts towards war.

CALADASH, BRYLDAR: a haughty, quick-tempered, ambitious wizard of Sirlptar, allied with the Baron Adeln in conspiracy against the Risen King purely for personal gain; handsome but rude, with a nasal, sneering voice and an imperious manner; once accurately described by the mage Ingryl Ambelter as "fully half the wizard he thinks he is."

CARDASSA, ITHCLAMMERT: Baron (Great Lord) of Cardassa, severe in both manner and dress, and a miser (hence his nickname, "the Crow of Cardassa" or, less politely, "the Old Crow"), but a cultured, principled man who believes in laws and adhering to them.

CARTHEL, JOLYNTH: Factor (trade agent) of Sirlptar; slim, sarcastic, and swift-tempered; a perfumed, haughty dandy; the agent of Sirl merchants and moneylenders.

CASTLECLOAKS, HELGRYM: one of the most famous and well-regarded of bards in the Vale; a bearded, cautiously polite, wise and impressive man slain in *The Kingless Land*.

CASTLECLOAKS, RAULIN TILBAR: young would-be bard and son of the respected bard Helgrym Castlecloaks; briefly a companion to three of the Band of Four.

CODELMER, SARASPER: a healer and former courtier long in hiding in one of three beast shapes he can take: bat, ground snake, or (his most favored) the man-eating "wolf-spider" or longfangs; old, gruff, and homely; member of the Band of Four and friend to Craer when the latter first entered the service of the Baron Blackgult.

CORLOUN: Court Mage of Maerlin, arrogant and ambitious; creator of the Melted.

DARAGUS, INTHER: Factor (trade agent) of Gilth (an independent town formerly in the Barony of Brightpennant); an intelligent, vigorous man and longtime rival of Belklarravus of Sart.

Dark Three, the: a trio of evil, powerful, and treacherous wizards who served the Baron Faerod Silvertree; they all perished in *The Kingless Land,* and in descending order of rank, power, and age, were: Spellmaster Ingryl Ambelter, Klamantle Beirldoun, and Markoun Yarynd.

DARLASSITUR, OEN: House Wizard of Cardassa; a blond-bearded, green-eyed rogue and traitor, hired by the baron when a rising but still untried wizard ("charm-caster") of Sirlptar.

DATHGATH, KORSTYN: King of Aglirta, an ancient ruler now remembered only as a great warrior who rode a winged horse into battle, and loved his wine; statues and carvings of him show a hugely muscled, bare-armed, and helmless warrior.

DELCAMPER, FLAEROS: young bard, of the wealthy Delcamper merchant family of Ragalar, equipped when traveling with the Vodal, an enchanted ring that's an heirloom of the Delcampers and allows (among other things) its wearer to see through magical disguises and illusions.

DELDROUN, YISKER: an elderly former warrior in the service of Silvertree, where he was swordsorn (military officer equivalent to a sergeant) over Roldrick; stern, cold-eyed, and the owner of a bristling white moustache, a sharp tongue, and a very alert eye.

DELNBONE, CRAER: procurer (scout and thief) in the service of the Baron Blackgult; small, agile, clever-tongued member of the Band of Four and longtime friend and sword-companion of Hawkril Anharu, who often calls him "Longfingers."

DUTHJACK, SENDRITH "BLOODBLADE": charismatic warrior in the service of the Baron Blackgult who becomes the leader of an outlaw fighting band ("Bloodblade's Band"), whom he leads in a foray to slay the Risen King and put himself on the throne.

DYNDRIE, SAERLOR: royal factor (trade agent) in Sirlptar, one of two financial representatives of the Risen King stationed in the Glittering City (Theth Phlundrivval is the other); a pompous, handsome courtier of white-haired years whose importance is only outstripped by his ego and eyes for all passing ladies.

ELROUMRAE: Queen of Aglirta, who ruled in her own right in ancient times, and is now remembered only as very beautiful, a graceful dancer, and a patron of bards who could outdrink all of her court without losing her serene dignity—but her other names, and why she came to the throne, are now lost to bardic histories and sagecraft.

FAULKRON, RUSTAL: Court Wizard of Glarond, an old sharp-witted man called by some "Old Man Rat" for his looks and furtive manner.

GLAROND, AUDEMAN: Baron (Lord) of Glarond, a lover of poetry and conspirator against the Risen King.

HALIDYNOR, ONTHALUS: claimant to the fallen upriver barony of Phelinndar; a large, fat, selfish, and spoiled man, now head of a long-successful merchant family largely based in Sirlptar, where Halidynor oars, sweeps, and barges have long seen everyday use.

HOLDYN: a former warrior in the service of Silvertree, now a duty guard at the Flagon and the Gauntlet inn in rural Phelinndar.

HULDAERUS, ARKLE: "the Master of Bats," sometime Lord Wizard of Ornentar, an ambitious, cruel, grasping mage known for using bat-related magic, commanding bats, and taking bat-shape; the minstrel Vilcabras once said at a moot that "Aglirta's worst nightmare would be Huldaerus and Silvertree, working together—a terror for Silverflow Vale one year, and all Darsar the next," and Huldaerus soon killed him for that utterance.

JHALANVYLUK, MARGATHE: Mistress of the Flagon, wife to Nortreen, and matron (mistress) and part owner of the prosperous The

Flagon and the Gauntlet inn, Margathe is a large, loud mountain of a woman once described as "pure viper venom. Always sour, doesn't miss a thing, rules her kitchens like a cruel swordsorn" (a swordsorn is a military officer, equivalent to sergeant); and in truth she rules Nortreen and the entire inn the same way.

JHALANVYLUK, NORTREEN: the prosperous tapmaster and proud part owner of the Flagon and the Gauntlet inn in rural Phelinndar for the better part of the two decades, and its tapmaster and second flagonman for another two before that; a large, jovial, bustling, fussy man now going to fat, who was in his day a feared brawler and accomplished warrior.

KALARTH: a formidable warrior, famous for his adventures both before and after his time in the service of the Baron Blackgult, who refuses to join Bloodblade's Band.

KESSRA: matron of the Old Lion inn in Ragalar, known to Ragalans for the prodigious and never-ending washing she hangs out from every rail and pillar and balcony of the Lion.

KETHER: a former warrior in the service of Silvertree, now a duty guard at the Flagon and the Gauntlet inn in rural Phelinndar.

KETHGAN: slayer-for-hire and professional "capturer" (hired kidnapper), formerly in the service of Baron Faerod Silvertree; a capable warrior and stealthy killer, who now works and travels with his partner, Vandur.

Koglaur, the: the "Faceless" or "Faceless Ones," legendary lurking human-like shapeshifting beings who watch over Aglirta and meddle in its affairs for mysterious reasons of their own.

KORDUL: outland armaragor, long a member of the Swords of Sirlptar band.

LOUSHOOND, BERIAS: Lord Baron of Loushoond, a principled yet often cowardly man who reluctantly conspires against the Risen King; naive in the ways of the world and overly reliant on his factors, he's sometimes called "Baron Lackwit" (or "Lord Lackwit") behind his back.

LULTUS: a warrior in the service of the Baron Blackgult, who becomes one of Bloodblade's Band.

LUTHTUTH, EEIMGUR "VELVETFOOT": an accomplished, clever, and urbane lastalan (thief for hire or military scavenger and scout, sometimes also called a "procurer") and slayer-for-hire.

MAERBOTHAM, BELGUR: "Bel," a kindly, rather cowardly warrior and brigand who works with Weldrin, his onetime commander in (Silvertree) military service.

MAERLIN, URWYTHE: Baron (Lord) of Maerlin, an urbane conspirator against the Risen King.

MARINDRA: long-ago sorceress who gave her life to craft and perfect the great magic by which the King of Aglirta can be made to sleep, the Deeping Ritual or Calling to Slumber.

MARTHITH, CALARD: an accomplished, disciplined professional warrior and bodyguard, in the personal service of Baron Ornentar; seneschal of Ornentar Castle.

MAUVEIRON, AMMANTAS: a soft-spoken, urbane, and powerful outland wizard allied to the Baron Adeln, in conspiracy against the Risen King.

Melted, the: men burned by a special firespell of the mage Corloun; their flesh droops and disfigures, and they become conduits of his magic (he can cast spells from afar, through their touch, or cause them to explode in flames).

MULKYN, GADASTER: first and most infamous Spellmaster of Silvertree; an aging, ruthless, evil archwizard who was tutor to Ingryl Ambelter—and whom Ingryl slew by a succession of life- and magic-stealing spells that forced Gadaster into a strange unlife.

MURGIN: an easygoing warrior and brigand who works with Weldrin, his onetime commander in (Silvertree) military service.

NAERIMDON, AUGRATH: Tersept (non-noble ruler) of Rithrym, a grasping, brutish tyrant ruling through his cortahars (sworn-to-him warriors).

NAOR: personal bodyblade (bodyguard) to Sendrith "Bloodblade" Duthjack who becomes a staunch member of Bloodblade's Band.

NARVIM, USTER: an accomplished, disciplined professional warrior and bodyguard, in the service of Blackgult but taken in by the Baron of Adeln after the disappearance of the Baron Blackgult and the collapse of that barony.

NIMMOR: a callous, ruthless Serpent-priest active in rural Phelinndar.

NLORVOLD the Balestaff: an experienced battle-mage who bears the Balestaff, an enchanted staff of fearsome properties beyond his complete control or understanding; one of the co-leaders of the Swords of Sirlptar (the other is its other wizard, Ressheven).

OBLARRAM, GURKYN: a cook and warrior in the service of the Baron Blackgult, who becomes one of Bloodblade's Band.

ORNENTAR, ELDAGH: Baron (Lord of Ornentar, venom-poisoned by the Serpents in *The Kingless Land,* and thus controlled by them (he must follow their orders to receive antidotes); thinks himself subtle but isn't; pudgy, sweating, and often blue-skinned due to the venom raging within him, and known for wearing many rings, formerly famous as "the Face of Stone" for his ability to control his features and emotions; a desperate conspirator, as the ruler of a barony weakened by the loss of its wizards soon after the rise of Baron Silvertree.

PELARD, YONTH: Tersept (non-noble ruler) of Yarsimbra; aging, short, stout, and grasping.

PELDRATHA, KAULISTUR: a young bard of Aglirta, a handsome man possessed of an almost womanly singing voice and a calm, patient manner.

PELDRUS: a warrior in the service of the Baron Blackgult, who becomes one of Bloodblade's Band.

PHALAGH of Ornentar: wizard slain in the ruins of Indraevyn in *The Kingless Land,* but animated into undeath by the lingering magic of the Stone of Life.

PHELODIIR, MONTHER: Master Factor (highest-ranking trade agent) of Sirlptar, a haughty and greedy man.

PHLUNDRIVVAL, THETH: royal factor (trade agent) in Sirlptar, one of two financial representatives of the Risen King stationed in the Glittering

City (Saerlor Dyndrie is the other); a young, darkly handsome, carefully diplomatic courtier who seeks to impress with his utmost loyalty and honesty—and to make for the king coins enough to assemble an army that can sweep any baron to the nearest bonepit, and make a united Aglirta truly great again . . . with, of course, a certain Theth Phlundrivval as Master of the Vaults.

Priest of the Serpent: oldest in service and most powerful worshipper of the Serpent, an anonymous and very clever man who among many other fell deeds slew a Koglaur and tricked Baron Ornentar into Serpent-servitude.

Priestess of the Serpent: the first woman seduced into love of the Serpent by the Priest of the Serpent, this anonymous woman meets with Baron Loushoond early on in *The Vacant Throne*.

QUELVER, ILIBAR: a gruff, gentle old warrior, once of Silvertree and now doorguard of the throne chamber of Flowfoam Castle.

QUOLDO, RESZVAR: Tersept (non-noble ruler) of Gilth, a soft-spoken, slender, and small man possessed of a sharp mind, a sharper temper, and an even sharper tongue; the bane of his factor's career (see Daragus Inther); a poor horseman who's afraid of battle with swords, but not with coins or contracts.

RANTHALUS, PELDER: First Steward of Flowfoam, Master of the Court of the Risen King; a tall, slender, haughty, severe, and magnificently bearded man who orders all royal protocol, speaks first in all debates and at all feasts, and is a dabbler in magic who pretends to far more magecraft than he's truly mastered.

RESSHEVEN of Two Moons: a ruthless, confident, and capable battle-mage, one of the leaders of the Swords of Sirlptar (the other is its only other wizard, Nlorvold).

RIOVRYN, STELGAR: ambitious warrior of Loushoond, who briefly crowns himself King of Aglirta.

ROLDRICK: a former warrior in the service of Silvertree, now a duty guard at the Flagon and the Gauntlet inn in rural Phelinndar.

SARGIN: junior thief of the Bright Blade and Hope of Aglirta adventuring band; openly dresses in black leathers and a black silk mask.

SARR, BODEMMON: one of the two mightiest independent wizards of the Vale (his rival Tharlorn of the Thunders is the other).

Serpent, the: "the Serpent in the Shadows," "the Sacred Serpent," "the Great Serpent," "the Fanged One," a great evil being, formerly a human wizard (name now forgotten; it's thought he worked to purge records of it) who helped enchant the Dwaerindim, but went mad or was mad, and murdered several rival mages to strengthen the Dwaer enchantments; when confronted by the other mages of the Shaping, he fled into serpent-form to fight his way free of their spells—and was imprisoned by them in serpent-shape; now a gigantic serpent bound into Slumber by a mighty magic worked by the King of Aglirta (fated to sleep when he does); worshipped by humans who revere him as divine—and to whom he grants spells.

Serpents, the: worshippers of the Serpent (humans who often become snakelike; they refer formally to themselves as "the Faithful of the Serpent," but others call them "the Cowled Priests," "the Fanged Faithful," "the Scaly Ones," "the Serpent-spawn" and worse; those with snakelike heads and forked tongues are known (not to their faces) as "Hissing Ones."

SHAMURL: warrior and sorceress of the Bright Blade and Hope of Aglirta adventuring band; a grim, scar-faced woman, taller, more burly, and stronger than many men.

SILVERTREE, EMBRA: the Lady of Jewels (so called for her opulent, gem-studded gowns), Lady Baron (Baroness) of Silvertree; a young, beautiful sorceress; member of the Band of Four and daughter of the cruel Faerod Silvertree, who intended her to become a captive "Living Castle."

SILVERTREE, FAEROD: cruel and grasping Baron of Silvertree, who came very close to ruling all Aglirta in *The Kingless Land*, and survived longer than most Aglirtans thought, ruling for a time as Lord (equivalent to mayor) of the village of Tarlarnastar.

SILVERTREE, THAALEN: long-ago Baron of Silvertree, a wealthy and very paranoid man who hired many wizards to craft Thaalen's Nightguard, an inner stronghold within Silvertree House to which he retreated every night to sleep "properly guarded."

SILVERTREE, TLARINDA: Baroness of Silvertree, mother to Embra and wife of Faerod, one of the most beautiful women in Aglirta; tortured and slain by Faerod for suspected infidelity, whispered to have been the lover of Baron Blackgult.

SKULDUS: a warrior in the service of the Baron Blackgult who becomes one of Bloodblade's Band.

SNOWSAR, KELGRAEL: the Risen King, the Lost King, the Sleeping King, the Sleeper of Legend, the Last Snowsar; King of Aglirta, the Lion of Aglirta, the Crown of Aglirta, Lord of all Aglirta, Master of the River and Its Vale; rightful crowned ruler of Aglirta, a wise and perceptive warrior and wizard who for too long (centuries) slept in a spell-hidden "otherwhere," while warring barons tore his realm apart.

Swords of Sirlptar, the: famous hiresword (mercenary) fighting band based in the Glittering City; six veteran armaragors led by two mages (see Kordul, Nlorvold, and Ressheven).

Swords of the Castle, the: the standing army of the Risen King and garrison of Flowfoam Castle; in the latter reign of Kelgrael Snowsar, a splendidly armored shadow of its former strength.

TALASORN, RAEVUR: a courteous, diplomatic wizard of Sirlptar, allied with the Baron Adeln in conspiracy against the Risen King because he seeks a strong, united Aglirta wherein increased trade and wealth will mean more patrons seeking to hire wizards (for Raevur has four daughters whose spellcraft already outstrips his, too clever and beautiful to be "brutalized by some warrior-baron" and denied any chance to use their magic; Raevur's wife, Iyrinda, is dead, and he dotes on his lasses).

TANTHUS: senior thief of the Bright Blade and Hope of Aglirta adventuring band; haughty and clever; openly dresses in black leathers and a black silk mask.

TATHTORN: a warrior in the service of the Baron Blackgult, who becomes one of Bloodblade's Band.

TAURYM, IMBRETH: the steward of Tathcaladorn, the private castle and hill-forest hunting lodge of the Baron of Cardassa; an attentive, diplomatic, and perceptive senior servant.

TELABRAS, DIRL: Factor (trade agent) of Sirlptar; tall, handsome, and close-mouthed; the agent of Sirl ship captains and shipping lines.

TESSYRE: a long-ago sorceress of flame-red hair and a temper to match, according to bardic ballads, who when sorely wounded took herself into magical Slumber, in the ritual later used by the King of Aglirta, to lie hidden awaiting succor from someone now forgotten.

THARLORN of the Thunders: "Lord of Thunders," "Master of the Thunders"; one of the two mightiest independent wizards of the Vale (Bodemmon Sarr, his bitter rival, is the other); see also Baerund, Ilisker.

TLALASH: a junior Koglaur, habitually female, who unlike most others of her kind is vulnerable to snake venom and other poisons.

TURSTRIN, MAELOCH: an impetuous warrior and brigand who works with Weldrin, his onetime commander in (Silvertree) military service.

UBUNTER, VELMOS: an old, incompetent wizard of Cardassa, sage (advisor) to the baron; a sharp-tongued, fussy old man, and a bitter rival of Baerethos.

ULGUND, INTHRIS: Tersept (non-noble ruler) of Helvand; young, and known for his boldness and swift temper.

UMMERTYDE, GLOUN: a warrior in the service of the Baron Blackgult and boyhood acquaintance of Sendrith Duthjack, the "Bloodblade," who becomes one of Bloodblade's Band.

VANDUR: slayer-for-hire and professional "capturer" (hired kidnapper), formerly in the service of Baron Faerod Silvertree; a capable warrior and stealthy killer, who now works and travels with his partner, Kethgan.

VILCABRAS, INTHYL: bard of Aglirta; wise, flashily handsome, and best known for the ballad *Five Feasts of Tears;* slain by the wizard Huldaerus.

WELDRIN, SORTH: a cruel, clever, ambitious brigand leader and accomplished warrior who was once a swordsorn (officer equivalent to sergeant) in the service of Silvertree, commander of the "Sixth Sword" of twenty warriors.

Wizard of Stars, the: according to bards, the mightiest mage Aglirta has ever known; its ruler centuries ago, in a Reign of the Wizard thought by many to be the height of Aglirtan glory; vanished rather than being confirmed dead, so some believe he'll return, hence the upland Vale saying "Until the Wizard Walks"; though few besides sages and wizards know it, the Wizard of Stars habitually and tracelessly invaded the minds of all his subjects, rendering them his unwitting slaves.

XAVALANDRO, FORL: the "Champion of Adeln," a hulking giant of an armaragor, equaled in size and strength only by Hawkril Anharu of the Four, but possessed of far more cruelty and bloodlust than the Boar of Blackgult.